Since You've Been Gone

Emma Heatherington

POOLBEG

992,040/AF1

This novel is entirely a work of fiction. The names, characters and incidents portrayed in it are the work of the author's imagination. Any resemblance to actual persons, living or dead, events or localities is entirely coincidental.

Published 2010
by Poolbeg Press Ltd.
123 Grange Hill, Baldoyle,
Dublin 13, Ireland
Email: poolbeg@poolbeg.com

© Emma Heatherington 2010

The moral right of the author has been asserted.

Copyright for typesetting, layout, design
© Poolbeg Press Ltd.

13 5 7 9 10 8 6 4 2

A catalogue record for this book is available from the British Library.

ISBN 978-1-84223-409-9

Typeset by Patricia Hope in Sabon 10.6/14.5

Printed by
CPI Cox & Wyman, UK

www.poolbeg.com

MEET THE CAST

Darryl Smith

Fifty-year-old artistic director of Millfield Players Theatre Group. Eccentric, lively, loves flirting with ladies of any age and wears Hush Puppy shoes and corduroy trousers (all the time). Owner of The Stage Bar and if the people of Millfield were to elect a Mayor, Darryl would be the man – or so he tells everyone.

Krystal Smith

Darryl's other half who loves attention from younger men. Bit of a tart, really. Think mutton and lamb and you're not too far off the mark. Think Whitney dressed as Britney. Loves her son, hates his choice of woman.

Taylor Smith

A thirty-year-old "occasional" TV actor who was right next to Brad Pitt when good looks were given out. Sporty, athletic, cool and talented, he's the type of guy other men want to *be*, and the type women want to be *with*. Fact.

John Smith

Taylor's younger brother who was a bit further back in the beautiful queue – he was somewhere *near* the back, actually. A cynical barman who has never

In loving memory of my aunt
Deirdre (Diddles)
Kizzy is for you xxx

after *you*!). Thank you most of all for all the happy memories and sayings you have left us with and the laughs we can still share in your memory. Rest in peace, Diddles, and keep singing in heaven – because, as you used to say, it's all right singing when you're winning!

privileged to share this amazing journey with. Go on, the Northern Girls! Thanks to all the libraries we have visited for your warm welcome and promotion and to everyone who came along to listen to our stories of our path to publication and our writing lives – plus a lot of waffle about Simon Cowell and our various random obsessions!

To Gaye Shortland – once again, you made the editing process a pleasure and I'm so glad you love Little Hollywood as much as I do.

I am delighted to have such a fantastic agent in Ger Nichol who really keeps my chin up when the chips are down and cheers me on with praise and encouragement. Thanks, Ger.

Thanks to all my Facebook friends for help with character names and everything "va va voom". I hope you enjoy the end result.

To everyone who reads and enjoys my books – thank you for your continued support.

And to my family as always – thank you for your patience and understanding as I burned the midnight oil in the early part of 2010 to make this book happen. I couldn't do it without you.

I am dedicating *Since You've Been Gone* to the memory of my Aunt Deirdre who sadly left us on Valentine's Day this year after a brave battle with cancer. You were a huge part of our lives, Diddles, and the world is a much quieter and much lonelier place without you. Thank you for all you have done for me down the years – for friendship, support, giggles, holidays, baby-sitting, Christmas presents, birthday presents and "running the roads" (mind you, it was mostly *me* running

Acknowledgements

Don't make a drama out of a crisis, they say, but sure where's the fun in that? There's nothing like a bit of drama to get tongues wagging in a small village and I had great fun creating all the characters in 'Little Hollywood' which is loosely (and I mean loosely!) based on my own little village of Donaghmore – so be afraid, be very afraid! Donaghmore is bursting with talent which centres on the Bardic Theatre Group so thanks, first of all, to all those involved in amateur dramatics which essentially inspired this story.

Thanks also to the Greensword family – Ian, Charlene and Kitty Rose for giving me the term "Little Hollywood". Being a Yorkshireman who is fortunate enough to have married into our extended family, Ian was blown away when he realised that for a tiny place like Donaghmore, there really was a "Who's Who" list that is quite enviable. Come on, Greenswords – come and live here! Come to Little Hollywood!

Thanks to everyone at Poolbeg – Paula, thanks for your patience with the name change. It came to me eventually.

Thanks as always to my wonderful Poolbeg writing colleagues, Claire Allan and Fiona Cassidy, who I am

Also by Emma Heatherington

Playing the Field

Note on the Author

Emma Heatherington lives in the village of Donaghmore, Co Tyrone, with her husband Dalglish and three children; Jordyn (14), Jade (9) and Adam (8). She works full-time as a writer/arts consultant.

www.emmaheatherington.com

followed the family acting trait, he is stuck in the belief that the whole "drama thing" is a pile of shite. In fact, everything is pile of shite to John, really. Apart from *Gavin and Stacey*. He loves *Gavin and Stacey*.

Agnes O'Brien

Former Miss Northern Ireland and founder member of the Millfield Players, this multi-talented sixty-something is also the village agony aunt. If you fancy a cup of tea and a chance to cry your eyes out, Agnes is your girl – and she always has a cupboard full to the brim of Jaffa Cakes and Mr Kiplings so don't go there if you're on a diet.

Geri O'Brien

Agnes's glamorous daughter who was once backing singer for a band who made it onto *Top of the Pops* in the seventies – she's been a bit stuck in a time warp since. She now runs the village hairdressing salon at the back of her house which still has Farrah Fawcett posters on the wall, just in case you need some inspiration for your new "do".

Erin O'Brien

Agnes's granddaughter and Taylor's girlfriend who is TV presenter of popular magazine show *It's Your Friday*. She is the darling of the Millfield community but has lately developed a secret fondness for red wine, which is causing the odd problem with her day job – and her love life. Everybody wants to be Erin, except Erin herself.

Sorcha Daly

Erin's arch-enemy and Taylor's bit on the side (though only in her dreams and in his worst nightmares). Journalist on the local rag with a tongue like a viper and a face like a hatchet . . . but lovely girl, apart from all that.

Eugene Daly

Sorcha's long-suffering twin brother who is secretly in love with Erin. A tortured soul who is a writer by night and a bin-man by day. And he's not gay. He's not! Even if he does drive a yellow convertible VW Beetle . . .

Kizzy Parks

Erin's best friend and mother to twin girls. Kizzy has always lived in Erin's shadow and is known as a bit of a "square". But Kizzy has a secret talent that is ready to shine – and it doesn't go well with her "pure as driven snow, butter wouldn't melt in her mouth" reputation. Tut tut, Kizzy. Tut tut.

Olivier Laurent

Handsome newcomer whose devilish humour and wicked ways are set to rock the pants off all the women of Little Hollywood – and put a few men back in their place too! But can this Patrick Swayze-a-like fill the gap left by Taylor Smith? Nah! Never. Well . . . maybe . . . he just might . . .

PREFACE

They call it "Little Hollywood", but to a passer-by like you or me, the village of Millfield is nothing more than a "blink and you'll miss it" one-street no-man's-land nestled somewhere in the north of Ireland.

To the naked eye it's nothing special, but if you lift the ivy back from the sign at the village entrance, you'll see the name of Millfield stamped in black capital letters with its Gaelic translation underneath and then the slogan "Taylor Smith is a big ride" scrawled in red marker.

The people of Millfield are immensely proud of their reputation for producing fine talent and with a resident list of Who's Who, if you haven't heard of it by now, you soon will.

Because Taylor Smith is indeed a big ride (think Colin Farrell meets Johnny Depp with a splash of Jude Law in for good measure) and the good folk of Millfield have always been in awe not only of his beauty, but also his

1

charm and his talent – and they all love him more than life itself.

In a little village like Millfield, where writers, actors, artists and a list of wannabes are two a penny, you can always be guaranteed a lot of drama, tantrums, tears and love affairs of all sorts. From whispers in the cosy corners and low lighting of The Stage Bar, gossip behind magazines at The Hairdresser's, catching up on news at The Supermarkets and fighting over the last sausage at The Butcher's (yes, everything just begins with "The"), this is as entertaining a village as you'll ever come across.

Enjoy your visit and welcome to life in Little Hollywood . . .

ACT ONE

Before the Big Time

SCENE ONE

The end title music of *It's Your Friday* jingled in Erin's ear and she thanked the Lord for small mercies. She swivelled round on the navy-blue sofa, flicked back her glossy hair and said with a smile into Camera One:

"And don't forget to join me again next week when I'll be chatting to award-winning novelist and ultimate scrummy mummy, Jenny Bree, on what men *really* want for Christmas, plus all the latest fashion, food and who's hot and who's not. It's Your Friday, It's Your Weekend and I'm Erin O'Brien. Have a good one! I know *I* will!"

With the credits still rolling, Erin pulled a hair bobble from her back pocket and tied her dark hair into a loose bun, then swept past the camera crew without as much as a word and slipped into her tiny dressing room. She plonked down on the orange armchair and sprayed her face with mist, then laid her head back and closed her eyes.

"Please, Mr Hangover, I'm begging you. Please, not today!" she chanted. "You are getting worse. You are supposed to get better as the day goes on. I cannot fight with you any more with your bang-bang-banging in my head and the way you burn my insides. You win. I lose. Game over."

Her mouth felt like sandpaper and her blotchy skin had needed an extra layer of foundation in the make-up room that morning, plus her eyes were like piss-holes in snow and her breath had enough alcoholic fumes to pollute a small country. Erin O'Brien – media darling and beauty queen by day, little old wine-drinker by night. It had to stop. It just had to.

"A word," said Ryan The Producer, peeping his bespectacled face around the door. "Now!"

Erin jumped to her feet and followed Ryan down the narrow corridor that led to his office. She tried to keep up with his sprint-like strides, which baffled her because he was really quite a short-arse (think a grown-up Milky Bar Kid), and she sucked in her breath when she walked past him as he held the door open for her. Not that he could possibly smell anything over the stench in here, she thought when she went inside his poky office. It always stank of chips and vinegar.

Ryan The Producer had wall-planners pasted all over the place and a dying plant sat withered and sad, mirroring Erin's mood, in a dark corner. He slammed the door behind them and folded his arms, waiting for her to speak.

"I – I'm just going through a bit of a shitty –"

"Crap!" said Ryan The Producer. "Crap, crap, crap, crap, *crap*! You said *Christmas*, Erin. *Christmas*!"

"Christmas? Oh God. Did I? Gosh!"

"Yes! '*Gosh!*' You did," he squealed in bad temper.

"We were talking about Valentine's Day and you fucking said *Christmas*! The phones are hopping now with confused viewers who said they are still trying to get over the last festive season and don't even want to think of the 'C' word! It's fucking February!"

Erin peeped out through the Venetian blinds that overlooked the television station's administration centre and sure enough, all of the receptionists were flat out on the phones, shaking their heads in apology to the *It's Your Friday* fan club all of whose weekends were evidently ruined.

"Yikes. So shoot me," said Erin with a shrug. "It's hardly going to spark a Christmasgate Scandal and make national media, is it? Though that wouldn't do the ratings any harm. You know what they say . . . all publicity is good pub –"

"Wake up, Erin! Wake up and smell the roses!" yelled Ryan The Producer. "Do you know how many women out there would kill for your job? Hundreds! *Thousands* even and you don't have to look too far to find them. Aimee Kennedy is sniffing at your heels for one! You have the world at your feet, Erin O'Brien, and you choose to piss it up against a wall! That's what you're doing right now! Pissing your whole career and pissing *It's Your Friday* right up against a wall!"

Erin noticed that Ryan The Producer's glasses were steamed up and his little short arms flew around like a baby bird's wings as he spoke. He really was in a terrible fluster.

"For a start, I could never piss *anything* against a wall," said Erin, hoping to raise a smirk from her boss. "I mean it's not physically possible for me to do so. Only *men* can piss against a wall. You know . . ."

She wiggled her finger and urged Ryan The Producer to laugh, but oh no. Not a hope. Not a pup's chance. He was in a rip. He was bouncing, hopping, doing a short-arsed man's jig.

"Don't mess with me, Erin! You know *exactly* what I mean. I was *this* close. *This* close to pulling you off the air today." He pinched his fingers into her face and his grey complexion told Erin that he really was deadly serious. "You are on your last chance, girl. Your *very* last chance. Now get the hell home, get some sleep, stay off the booze and I want to see you in here Monday morning looking fresh as paint and ready to greet our viewers with the respect they deserve!"

Wake up and smell the roses, fresh as paint, piss it up against the wall. Young Ryan The Producer was on a roll this evening but Erin couldn't move. She thought she was going to be sick. No, she *knew* she was going to be sick. It had been working on her all day, even when she was on air she was swallowing and gulping back the urge to vomit but now Mr Hangover really meant business. He was giving her no more warning signs. Nuh-uh. Her stomach burned and she could feel a tsunami of saliva build up in her mouth, so much she thought she might drown in it. Her head was spinning, her stomach heaved. She swallowed. It heaved. She swallowed again. She gulped. Oh no. Oh shit. Oh mummy. She covered her mouth with her hand.

"The bin! Where's the –"

She grabbed a metal wastepaper bin and lashed out rich red vomit as Ryan The Producer looked away in disgust.

"Oh God! Oh God, I'm so sorry," she said, wiping her mouth on a stringy tissue she found up her sleeve.

"Oh my God, I'm mortified. I'm so sorry, Ryan, the –"

She looked at him but he was staring at the floor. No, he was staring at his shoes. It looked like someone had sprayed blood all over Ryan The Producer's shoes and now his face was a matching scarlet colour to her red-wine vomit.

"I'll get a cloth. I'll clean it up. I'm so –"

"Get out! Get out of here! Get out of here now!"

"Well, at least his office will smell of something different than chips and vinegar," said Kizzy as she dabbed baby puke from her top with a wipe.

Erin sipped an energy drink that had gone flat at the island in Kizzy's kitchen as Kizzy's adorable twin baby daughters played tennis with their baked beans across the room, much to their mother's oblivion. Charlotte, the tiny twin, was eyeballing Erin as if she sensed that Erin had done something very wrong indeed.

"I puked over my boss, Charlotte," said Erin to the one-year-old who looked genuinely disgusted. "I know. Horrible. I could get the sack."

"Oh, he'll get over it," said Kizzy. "It's not as if you stabbed him or anything and you can always buy him a new pair of shoes as a peace offering. I hear there's a sale on in Peacock's."

Erin sipped her drink again and winced at its warm, salty taste.

"It's not just Ryan The Producer, Kizzy," she said in a serious tone. Her head throbbed and she could still smell puke from her hands no matter how many times she washed them. "It's everything. It's me. I'm drinking far too much and I can't stop."

"What's far too much?" said Kizzy with her hand on her hip. "You glamorous ladies who lunch all drink too much. I'm lucky if I as much as sniff a West Coast Cooler for fear of the shakes the next day."

"Two bottles of wine," said Erin.

"A week?"

"A *night* . . . ish."

Kizzy rolled her eyes into the heavens and continued rubbing the stain off her top.

"It's well for you who can afford it. Some of us couldn't even buy one bottle a week, never mind two a night. What does Taylor say about all this?"

"He doesn't really know. I kind of . . . well, I've been hiding it from him."

Kizzy looked horrified. To hide something from your other half was like committing adultery in the rules of marriage/relationships according to Kizzy Parks. She told her Dermot everything and would feel so guilty if she didn't. She'd even told him about the five Creme Eggs she ate yesterday while watching *Loose Women*. Five in an hour. And poor Dermot, being as nice as he was, never even said a word and just continued to eat up his mince and spuds.

"Everything is shite at the minute, Kizzy. I just feel like I can't admit to feeling this way and I have to put up this smiley, false face of how wonderful my life is because that's what everyone expects. I meet people in the supermarket and they swoon over what I was wearing on telly, or my necklace or my make-up and they tell me how lucky I am to have interviewed some flash-in-the-pan wannabe from *Big Brother* who I couldn't give a toss about, when all I want to do is scream. Everyone seems to think I have it all, so why don't I see it that way? Why am I threatening to ruin my whole life like this? Why am I so bloody miserable?"

Kizzy poured out two cups of coffee, avoiding a trip over Igglepiggle on her way to the kettle.

"You're only human, Erin, and you have a right to be miserable like the rest of us. We all have down days. It's known as 'being called Superwoman and feeling like Grotbags'. Don't beat yourself up about it."

Erin looked surprised. "Oh. Oh, I do? Thanks, Kizzy. At least you understand. I knew you would."

"Of course I do. Think about it. You have a thriving TV career," said Kizzy, "a hot-shit boyfriend who is also on the telly and who makes most women faint at the very sight of him, you have no money worries, you have no ties, a super-fast car, a wardrobe to die for and – oh, did I mention a fantastic house which you happen to share with said hot-shit boyfriend who makes most women faint at the very sight of him?" Kizzy paused. "Sorry, but no. I don't feel sorry for you at all, sister. No way. Sympathy levels in this camp? Nadda! You just need to give yourself a good reality shake."

Erin took the cup of coffee from her so-called best friend and made a face at her. So much for Kizzy being on her side. This was serious! She could lose her job if she didn't get her head together.

"I know, I know," she mumbled. "And when you rhyme everything off like that, I can see how it looks from the outside to be me, but believe me, it's not all fun and games being me. It sucks sometimes."

"Ha! Not all fun and games? I'll tell you what," said Kizzy, settling her pudgy derriere onto a stool at the island. "I'll swap lives with you for just one day."

11

"Huh?"

"Just one day! You can come here and drown in ironing and washing and nappies and constant worry about what you've fed your children since breakfast and if you're really fit to be a mother, then look at the bills and check the bank balance and practically faint because the two don't match, then watch your husband come home from work deflated because the construction industry is on its arse and then switch on the TV to see your best friend looking stunning and relaxed as she chats to the latest soap-star hunk and see how you feel then! It's ficking wonderful!"

Cue burst of silence as little Charlotte and her twin sister Emily had a field day squirting bubbles of washing-up liquid on to the floor but neither of the friends noticed. Instead they both stared at each other, contemplating their existence and each wondering what to say next.

Erin went first. "You chose this life."

"And you chose yours!"

"There are women who would love to have children but can't!"

"There are women who would love to be *you* but can't!"

"So we're even, then! Look, I better get going," Erin lifted her phone and keys and her handbag and jumped down from her stool.

"But you didn't finish your coffee!"

"Sorry, but I've just remembered we have rehearsals this evening for a new play down at the community centre and Taylor wants to take me out for dinner first but I still feel sick. Shit!"

"Oh, what a dilemma. Life really *is* shit. Boo fucking hoo."

"Whatever. I'll see you later on Facebook for a catch-up?"

"You will. Later."

Erin quickly kissed each of the twins goodbye and stepped around patches of slippery floor and across to the back door of Kizzy's semi-detached house, avoiding a range of obstacles on her way.

"Oh, and Erin?" said Kizzy. "Can I ask you something before you go?"

"Yes?"

Erin fixed her handbag strap on her shoulder and waited for Kizzy's next "be grateful for what you have and stop being a moaning bitch" comment.

"Could this be something to do with Taylor and the *'you know what'* in *'you know where'* opportunity of a lifetime?"

Erin fidgeted. Was it? Could it be?

"I . . . maybe. But, sure it might never happen. He's even said so himself."

"Ah. Suppose. Yeah," said Kizzy. "It might never happen. Bye."

Kizzy bent down, scooped her two little daughters off the floor and carried them into a safer environment so she could clean up the mess, hoping that for the lovely Taylor's sake that it would happen but for Erin's sake that it wouldn't.

Scene Two

Taylor was home already when Erin reached their house on the outskirts of Millfield in the new River View complex, which did exactly what it said on the tin, as the Old Mill River babbled and flowed below the range of detached luxurious homes.

The spanking new housing development was very popular with young couples and super-successful singletons and, with its easy access to the motorway, it was a hit with commuters who wanted to keep a city day job but enjoy the perks of easygoing countryside in their lifestyle. Yet, though Erin's house was decorated with the most impeccable taste, she still couldn't call it home.

"So, how was your day, gorgeous?" asked Taylor Smith when his girlfriend arrived into the kitchen, looking dishevelled and stressed. He walked around the kitchen with a white towel wrapped around his waist and his tanned upper body glistened with droplets of water in a look that women would auction their lives away for just one real-life

14

glimpse of. Oh yes, their entire family circle would be sacrificed for one live view of this hunk of burning love.

"Great," said Erin, not even noticing his sculpted body and fine manly figure. "Did you catch the show this evening?"

She crossed her fingers as she walked past him, hoping and praying he would say no and dodging contact with him when he leaned forward for a kiss. She needed a shower and a mini-makeover, not to mention a major mouthwash before she would let him anywhere near her. Mr Hangover had overstayed his welcome and she needed to get rid of him fast.

"Sorry, babe, but I didn't get to see it," said Taylor. "I really am sorry."

"No, no, it's fine."

"No, it's not fine at all but I *will* make it up to you. You see, I popped in to see Al on the way through the city and we got talking about that audition I went for a few weeks ago."

Erin paused at the doorway. The audition. The two words that struck fear into her heart more than "put your hands up" or "don't talk or I'll shoot" ever would.

"*The* audition?" Her eyes widened and she turned to face him. Oh no.

"Yip. *The* audition." His gorgeous face was beaming. "Now go and get ready as quickly as you can. I've booked us a cab for seven and I'll tell you everything over dinner. Then we'd better get down to the Community Centre to break the news to my parents."

Darryl Smith fixed his cravat in the mirror and smoothed down his silver-grey hair in the bathrooms at

Millfield Community Centre. He liked to keep his hair slightly long at the back, in salute to his thespian days in different cities across Ireland, and in his brown corduroy trousers and loafer shoes, he cut a striking dash – in his own mind, of course. To you or me, the resemblance might be more Kenneth Williams than Kenneth Branagh.

He wondered if all of his team of dramatists would turn up for the cast announcement and the all-important first rehearsal tonight. He loved cast announcement. It made him feel like a small-town Simon Cowell when he watched the anticipation on the group's faces, waiting in awe to see if they'd land a lead role, and then debating with him over hot toddies at The Stage Bar afterwards as to whether or not he made the right decision.

Of course he had favourites – didn't everyone? It was healthy to have an opinion and he couldn't switch off to true talent, but he hated to be accused of choosing the same people for the lead roles all the time. Tonight, he would shock them all though. Tonight he would announce his cast for his brand-new production and no-one could possibly argue with his choice. This was going to be an amazing showcase of Millfield's finest talent and would be a breathtaking marker for The Players' thirtieth anniversary.

"Anyone here yet?" he asked his wife when he returned from the bathroom into the hallway of the community centre.

"Nope."

He looked at his wife of thirty-two years, a question written all over his face.

"Honey, isn't that skirt a bit, er, short for this time of year?"

Krystal Smith poised her pen and looked up at her husband from her desk and chair where she sat huddled by a radiator in a low-cut top and mini-skirt that would look immodest on a teenager, never mind a woman kicking the ass of fifty.

"It's my style, Darryl. My God, you'd think you'd know me by now. And isn't your hair a little too long for your age?"

"To cut my hair would be to cut off my soul. In your own fair words, 'it's my style'."

Darryl strode across the dark-tiled floor and admired the rows of photos that were proudly displayed on the wall of the foyer. The range of black and white snaps of costumed characters, some now dead and gone, made his heart soar at the start of theatre season each year. He sniffed the air and fixed his navy jumper which was tied around his shoulders and smoothed down his white shirt over his slightly portly belly. He had a good feeling about tonight. A really good feeling.

"Can you smell that?" he asked his wife who was polishing her nails.

"What?"

"Oh, Krys, Krys, you know what it is. Close your eyes and inhale the sweet, sweet smell of success and the theatre. *Ahhhh*!"

"All I can smell in here is mothballs," said Krystal and she sprayed an extra waft of perfume on her generous bosom. "And my new nail polish."

The front door clicked open and Darryl stood to attention like a soldier while Krystal adjusted her posture to meet the first member of The Players to arrive for the casting. She adopted a baby doll, doe-eyed look and then

17

changed it to her normal expression (somewhere between sour and sourer) when she saw it was those ghastly Daly twins from down the road.

"Sorcha, Dennis!" said Darryl with open arms as if he was King of the Castle. "Welcome, welcome, welcome! Welcome to Theatreland!"

"It's . . . it's Eugene," said the boy and he shuffled his feet behind his sister. "Dennis is our dad."

"And it's a community centre, not a theatre," said his oh-so-charming sister.

"Well, in my heart it's a theatre," said Darryl. "And that's where it counts. Oh, Sorcha, you look as pretty as a picture, but then what would I expect? You never let me down."

He leaned in and gave Sorcha an air-kiss, much to her delight and to Krystal's revulsion. Sorcha was as pretty as a picture all right. A picture of bitterness and that poor, hapless brother of hers was so slow he made a snail look like The Road Runner.

"I . . . er . . . I wasn't going to bother this year, you know, taking part," said Eugene. "You know, after last year I didn't think you'd want me back but Sorcha made me come along. She didn't want to come here on her own so –"

He broke off as Darryl treated them to a verse of "All God's Critters Have a Place in the Choir."

"We get the picture," said Krystal. "Oh, here's Agnes and Geri. Would you look at the set of her? What *is* she wearing?"

Geri O'Brien linked her mother on the way into The Community Centre and gave Agnes a playful nudge when she saw old Vinegar Tits Krystal at the door, taking a roll call as if they were at school.

"Ah, Geri, I love your coat. Where did you purchase? Dunnes?" asked Krystal with right-angled pencilled eyebrows raised.

"Yes, it was Dunnes actually," said Geri, whose natural beauty and elegance knocked the socks off Krystal's over-the-top efforts every time, no matter what her chosen brand or label. "Did you forget your own coat, Mrs Smith? You're making me cold looking at you."

Krystal teetered. She hated being called Mrs Smith.

"No, *Miss* O'Brien. But at my age I barely feel the cold. Can't say the same for the rest of you," she said with a bright pink smile. "I'm hot-blooded, you see."

"Yeah, and you have lipstick on your teeth," said Geri and she breezed past Krystal and the rest of the company, leaving a trail of elegance in her wake.

Erin and Taylor sat in Taylor's car outside The Community Centre with the engine still running as they delayed going in for the rehearsal. They both took part in Darryl's infamous theatre production every year out of loyalty and courtesy – after all, neither of them needed the work experience or the credit on their CV, but they were conscious that Millfield Players was where they both learned the tricks of their trade and they always honoured this connection by getting in on the act.

"Say something, Erin," said Taylor. "My God, I really wasn't expecting this reaction from you at all. You've barely spoken a word all evening and you didn't finish dinner. You always finish your dinner."

"Are you saying I'm a greedy pig, Taylor Smith?"

"No." Taylor laughed. "But you have to admit, you do love your grub. I thought we'd be celebrating together, but you've a face on you like that witch Sorcha Daly on a wet weekend."

"Don't even mention that cow's name in my presence," said Erin. "God, but I can just imagine her smarmy, hatchet face when she hears the news. She'll glare at me with those evil-looking cat's eyes and – *eew* – I can't bear the thought of it!"

It was fantastic news. It was "name up in lights" news. It was the news that dreams are made of and Erin was delighted, she really was, but underneath her happiness she felt a weighty dread because, in her heart, she believed that Taylor's big acting break could also mean a big break-up for their relationship.

"Talk to me," said Taylor, seriously and he took Erin's hand. "You seem worried."

"I'm . . . it's just . . . well, this is going to change things so much. I'm being selfish, I know I am. I don't mean to be but –"

"No. This won't change anything, I promise! What we have is so good that I'd never let anything, not even this, come between us. You mean the world to me. It's always been you and it always will, no matter where my career takes me."

Erin smiled and squeezed Taylor's hand. His dark-brown eyes looked so sad and this was supposed to be one of the biggest moments of his life. She had to shake out of this doom and gloom for his sake but she was terrified.

"I know and you mean everything to me too. Forget my silly pettiness. I'll get over it. And believe me, Taylor, no one is more proud of you than I am right now, even though I've a funny way of showing it. I am so, so proud of you and everything that you have achieved. You never cease to amaze me. You're a fantastic actor and you'll blow them away."

Taylor leaned across and kissed Erin full on the lips. His mouth was hot and she gasped at the feeling behind his touch and she urged herself not to cry as the thought of being without him stung her heart.

"I hope I do," he said, then he kissed her again. "But always remember that my leading lady is right here in Millfield. She's right here in Little Hollywood and nothing will ever change that."

Erin pulled him close and nestled her head into his neck, inhaling his clean, manly scent. She was being ridiculous thinking that a sniff of success and a few months' absence could come between them. They were the true sweethearts of Little Hollywood and nothing would ever change that. Nothing.

The members of Millfield Players sat in a circle in the community hall and Darryl was in full swing when Taylor and Erin made their entrance. He was prancing around the inner space like the ringmaster of a circus, talking with his hands which were the size of tennis rackets and using passionate words he could only ever have dreamed of using in this centre-stage position.

"This is our ultimate year. This is the year when Millfield will be put on the map! It's an historic year! It will be the season of all seasons and one which will go down in history as we present the cream of community theatre, remember the glory of days gone by, honour the lists of people who have walked through these doors as unknown wallflowers and walked back out of them, having emerged as stars in our midst after theatre season. This is our moment. This is theatre season in Millfield! This is our time. This is our . . . oh, Taylor, Erin, how kind of you to grace us with your presence."

Taylor and Erin pulled out plastic chairs and set them behind the circle, forming a second row. Some of the younger girls nudged each other and whispered when the two local celebrities took their places while Sorcha Daly gave an exaggerated yawn.

"Well, if it isn't the poor man's Brangelina," she said and let out her trademark rusty cackle that sounded more like nails on a blackboard than a laugh.

"You are just in time for tonight's big announcement," said Darryl, rubbing his hands. He had waited for months for this moment. He had plotted and prepared his director's notes, he had cast the entire production and he'd even hired in a professional to guide the team through the trickier parts of the show.

"Excellent," said Taylor. "We wouldn't miss this for the world, Dad."

Erin gave her mum and grandmother a wave but then shifted in her seat as she noticed Krystal "Vinegar Tits" Smith glare at her like she was some sort of snotty rag. She linked Taylor's arm and then stuck out her tongue at the stuck-up old bitch. Krystal did the same back.

"Well," said Darryl, and he paused for effect. "I am delighted to announce that this year, we will not be producing a play after all . . ."

He waited and then when he was satisfied that everyone was in the appropriate shock and riddled with fear that "theatre season" in Millfield was no more, he delivered his punch line . . .

"We will be producing . . . a musical!"

"A musical?" said Hatchet Face Sorcha Daly. "But most of us can't sing worth a shite!"

The others whispered and grunted to each other but Darryl was unperturbed. He would let them have a moment for the news to sink in. He expected this. It was going to be difficult for this group of fine "am-dram" festival winners to swallow a change in direction but he truly believed this was the best idea he had ever had.

"It's our anniversary year!" he bellowed with delight and great pride. "We must mark this occasion with a bang! So, we will put together a musical production which will have audiences flocking in through those doors and we'll be the talk of the town. Now, are you ready to hear what I've chosen?"

"If it's *Les Misérables* I'll slash my wrists," said the ever-so-charming Sorcha. "My God but these faces in here look miserable enough as it is."

"Can I guess? Please?" said Eugene Daly in a light whisper.

"Go ahead, Eugene. Nice to see some enthusiasm and hopefully this will rub off on some of our longer-serving members."

Eugene's cheeks turned pink and he drew in a breath and closed his eyes. "I think . . . well, I hope . . . is it by any chance, *Dirty Dancing*?"

"*Dirty Dancing*? *Dirty flaming Dancing*? That's not a musical!"

"It is!" said Eugene. "It's on in the West End of London. I went to see it."

"You big gay!" said one of the teenagers who were huddled together on the floor now and the rest of the group sniggered. The hall was Baltic and they all

23

had their hoods up and their scarves covered their mouths.

"I'll take your word, Eugene," said Darryl. "No. I have decided that we will do a musical mixture – a medley of musicals – a musical – a musical explosion!"

The group looked at each other, each person wondering if Darryl Smith had finally gone off his rocker. He had been teetering on the edge for quite a while, but no one could have anticipated this musical explosion!

"I'm not sure where that leaves some of us older members," said Agnes O'Brien. She was in her sixty-second year and didn't fancy "musically exploding" for anyone. She loved the stage, but this sounded way out of her comfort zone.

"Now, Agnes, not to worry," said Darryl. "There's a place for everyone here, isn't that our motto? It's early days and we have three whole months to prepare but don't panic, I won't put you in the *Rocky Horror Picture Show* scenes, I promise."

"*Rocky Horror*? My ma always said you were an ould perv behind it all, Darryl," said one of the hooded scarf gang but Darryl's mellow mood did not alter.

"Respect, young man, is one of life's most basic requisites. If you don't show respect, then your place will be as a car-park attendant or a programme-seller, and that's a promise, not a threat. Now, let me tell you what treats we have in store for you, here in what is affectionately known as Little Hollywood . . ."

Darryl began to run through his cast list and his plans to stage the biggest and best production Millfield had ever seen, with a sample of songs which ranged from

Webber/Rice classics, to family favourites such as *The Sound of Music* and *Annie*, and as he gave each member of the cast their roles, his audience gradually warmed as they began to picture the end result and the prospect of being famous for a fortnight in their locality. Amateur dramatics gave the ordinary people of Millfield a sniff of fame at a very local level as they signed autographs in the foyer and after the show at The Stage Bar, but within a week of the production's demise, they were back to being plain old Jimmy the Milkman, or Brenda the Shelf Stacker at the local Tesco store. But it did wonders for the ego while it lasted.

"So, Sorcha, you will take the role of the Wicked Witch of the West and Krystal darling, you will be the Wicked Witch of the East. . ."

"But you said I was Dorothy!" snapped Krystal. She would murder her husband for this.

"Sorry, but I changed my mind. Geri, you will be Dorothy and finally, having saved the best to last, the role of Danny Zuko will be played by Taylor Smith and Sandy will be played by Erin in a scene from that timeless classic, *Grease*, and that scene will close what I promise to be a magnificent showcase of our finest talent."

The Millfield Players broke into applause, all apart from Krystal who was thoroughly pissed off at having been given the Wicked Witch role, and Taylor and Erin who were engrossed in their own conversation. Finally, Taylor realised that all eyes were on them, awaiting a response of some sort.

"Sorry, I must have missed that. I'm sorry, Dad. What did you say?"

Darryl put his palms up and the applause stopped. He looked hurt that his grand announcement had been missed, but he repeated it nonetheless in anticipation of his son's response. What young man wouldn't be thrilled to be given the role of Danny Zuko?

"But . . . but I can't, Dad," said Taylor and the room fell silent. "I . . . I won't be able to take part in this year's production."

An echo of gasps filtered round the room. Taylor Smith wouldn't be in this year's production? Taylor always was the star of the show. He was Millfield's main man. He was the reason the audiences came to see the plays. He was one of the reasons why the town was called Little Hollywood, and if he wasn't going to take part, then what about Erin? Did that mean she was out too?

Darryl looked like a slowly deflating balloon as his enthusiasm and excitement hissed out of him and up into the air.

"Taylor . . .? What do you mean?"

"He's pulling your leg, aren't you, son?" said Vinegar Tits. "You're just having a joke with your dad. Of course you'll be taking part, Taylor. *Taylor*?"

"I won't be able to take the part, Mum," said Taylor and he stood up to make his announcement.

Erin could see his hands were shaking by his sides so she reached for one and clasped in between her own two hands to show her support as he spoke.

"You see, as some of you may know, I went for a very important audition recently. A very, *very* important audition and well . . . guys . . . I got the part. You'll never guess what, everyone. I'm going to Hollywood! I'm going to Hollywood USA!!!"

SCENE THREE

John Smith flicked through the channels on the television in The Stage Bar. It was quiet for a Friday night and he leaned on the counter and craned his neck to watch a re-run of the early-afternoon horseracing at Doncaster just to remind himself that he had lost the guts of fifty quid this week so far on horses with ridiculous names.

"Same again?" he said to a regular who had drained his glass and who was staring at him as if he would shoot him if he didn't get him another drink and quick. He served the elderly customer his half pint of Guinness and a separate measure of Jameson whiskey and sighed as the old man shuffled back down to his seat.

John noticed a small tear on one of the leather seats and his mouth tightened. How the hell did these things happen so easily? It must have been that rowdy stag night from the weekend before – they'd stopped in to use the bathroom en route to Donegal and ended up staying till nearly two in the morning. John had a terrible job trying to convince them he was closing and when he discovered the bus driver was also drunk as a skunk, he knew it was a lost cause and had to let them sleep on the floor and the newly refurbished seats of The Stage. His father would chuck a mental when he saw it.

Speaking of whom, it was almost time for his arrival. They would be in soon, all of The Players, or "The Swingers" as he preferred to call them. They were an eclectic bunch all right, his own parents included, and this was the time of year when they really got on his tits.

"Did you see the play, John?" they'd ask him, at least four times a night while the show was running in the theatre. "Wasn't your Taylor great at his part, but then he's always great no matter if he's playing a poof or a priest. He's a born entertainer, is that boy."

John would bite his tongue and serve up drinks as he listened to all the mutual-appreciation-society comments and the luvvie-hugging and smooching and arse-licking that would go on.

"You were great tonight."

"No, you were great."

"But you were better!"

"No, really, you were amazing."

"Oh, okay then. Maybe I was. Tell me more . . ."

It was nauseating! It was downright vomiticious and then, just when he couldn't take any more, the inevitable question would be asked of him.

"What happened to you, John? Why don't you help out with the drama group?"

"I'd say he'd be great at it," they'd say as if he couldn't hear them.

"So would I."

"Ah, shut the fuck up!" he'd mumble and close his ears as he rang up the tills on the bar. "Act? Half of you wouldn't know where to start. You pack of wannabes and fuckin' lick-arses and after this is all over, you don't even darken the doors of this pub, nor would you speak to each other if you met each other on the street. A crowd of fakes, that's what you are. There isn't a star among you!"

Oh, he had it so bad. The black sheep would rear its ugly head at every theatre season and he couldn't control the hatred he had for the whole pile of nonsense that he believed it to be. He couldn't take away from the success of The Millfield Players, of course, but he couldn't fuckin' stand half the assholes who took part. They got up his nose and round the fuckin' corner, that's what they did.

And the praise for his brother – oh good God, but it was gut-wrenching! It was bad enough living in his shadow when he was growing up, but he thought by now it would have stopped. Taylor Smith, Grade A student, Captain of the Soccer team, All Ireland GAA medallist, First Class Honours degree in English, model good looks, gorgeous girlfriend (even if she was carrying a few extra pounds these days) and a CV of bit-part acting that could only get better and better and better . . .

Even Taylor's bloody name was different. There wasn't another Taylor within a ten-mile radius of Millfield, whereas there were two John Smiths in nearly every class of the Primary School. What chance did he ever have to make his mark when you had to go through a list of people with the same name to find him? It had to be the most common name, not only in Millfield, and it was possibly the most boring name in the whole world. John fuckin' Smith. It sucked. Big time.

It was as if God had given Darryl and Krystal Smith the most perfect child in the world first time round and left no qualities whatsoever for the next, when they were just fed the scraps. "No bright sparks available, sorry. Nah, we're all done with the lookers too. Personality, charisma and confidence? A bit late for that. And talent? You gotta be kidding! That's long gone!"

John lifted a tea towel from the drawer under the tills and began to polish some glasses, having grown tired of the horseracing. He already knew who won, after all. He already knew how much money he'd lost on the stupid nag. Loser was his middle name, isn't that what he always had reason to believe?

He heard his father's laugh in the distance and the door swung open and the team of babbling idiots spilled into the bar, laughing and cheering even more raucously than normal. Perhaps his father had thrown caution to the wind and given the lead role to someone other than Taylor – perhaps he had lost his marbles altogether and given that poor pathetic lump Eugene Daly a starring role just to shock his audience. Chance would be a fine thing!

"Drinks are on me!" called Darryl and his posse cheered and clapped like a bunch of drunken ladies on a hen night. "Come on, John. Let's get these good people served. It's not every day you learn your son hits the big time!"

John grunted and listened to the overlapping voices who spluttered their orders at him.

"A gin and tonic, love," said his mother. "And a hot port for your dad. Actually, give him a brandy. He needs it for the shock."

"I'll have a WKD Blue," said Hatchet Face Daly. "And a Smirnoff Ice for Eugene. With crushed ice."

"I'll have a white wine spritzer," said Geri O'Brien. "I just can't take this in. It's like a dream come true for all of us. John, you must be so proud of your brother."

Their voices came at him from all directions and he fired out the drinks at record speed. So, *quelle surprise*, the lead role had evidently gone to his precious big brother. What shite would he have to listen to now? Lines from a McDonagh black comedy, or a Friel classic, or perhaps a dark moving tale by Keane? He had all the names of playwrights shoved down his throat since he was knee-high and still he failed to be sucked in or indeed impressed by their obsession with all things artistic. Give him a game of darts or pool any day.

A flock of women circled Taylor at the far end of the bar and looked up at him with adoring eyes, but there was no sign of Erin who was normally wrapped around him on every occasion. Taylor didn't seem like his usual uber-cool self either. He seemed uncomfortable and was rubbing the back of his neck as he spoke – his grey woollen coat with the collar turned up was still on and he hadn't even ordered a drink. For someone who had just landed the lead role he didn't seem too happy at all.

"Taylor, what are you having?" called John. He wanted to get this big round out of the way so he could go back to the racing fixtures and mark out his bets for tomorrow's race at Leopardstown. His brother seemed relieved to be distracted from his eager-beaver fans and

31

he made his way towards the bar, then came in behind it and helped himself to a bottle of Bud.

"Did you hear my news?" he asked John, taking a drink from the bottle and looking refreshed already. "God, I needed that!"

"What is it this time, Taylor? A Nobel Peace Prize? A Humanitarian Award? It's hard to keep up with you, to be honest."

"Well, you know the way I went for this really big audition in London a few weeks ago?"

John nodded. He vaguely remembered. Taylor was always reaching for the stars.

"Well, you'll never guess what! I got the part! I got a part in the movie. Like, a *real* movie, not some crappy low-budget straight-to-DVD effort – I'm talking blockbuster here. I've got a proper speaking role and everything, man! I'm moving to Hollywood for six months."

John poured a pint of Guinness halfway full and carefully put it down to let it settle without responding to his brother. He searched for words but they wouldn't come his way. He looked at Taylor who was waiting for a reply, his eyebrows raised and a dazzling smile across his handsome face. Hollywood, huh? He's moving to Hollywood, thought John. What the fuck do you say to that?

"Erm . . . can I buy you a drink?"

"You must be so proud, darling," said Geri O'Brien to her daughter as she fixed her make-up in the bathroom at The Stage Bar. "I mean, imagine our Taylor going to be a real actor!"

"Yeah," said Erin. She had been hiding out in a cubicle ever since she arrived at The Stage Bar, trying to convince herself not to take any alcoholic drink and thinking up excuses for why she was sipping a 7Up. They would all automatically jump to the conclusion that she was pregnant. That was one of the only two times any woman refused a drink in Millfield – if they were pregnant or if they were dead. There was no such thing as a Pioneer Pin in this town, and anyone who did wear one was said to be a bluffer.

"And to think that we'll all be invited to the première!" gushed Geri. Her glamorous neat bob shone under the lights in the bathroom and she touched it up with a brush, and then shook it gently in a routine she had mastered to a tee. "I wonder who else is in the film? Does he know yet? Erin, are you all right? You're very quiet."

Erin seemed to be in a world of her own, chanting inwardly with her eyes closed and she wasn't listening to a word her mother was saying. Geri gave her a nudge.

"Oh, right, yes, come on, let's go," said Erin and she walked out into the bar like a robot ahead of her mother. "I'm fine. Of course, I'll be fine. I can say no. I really can."

By midnight, the party was in full swing and most of The Millfield Players had decided to take full advantage of Darryl Smith's generosity by totally outstaying their welcome and benefiting from his earlier "drinks are on me" statement. Krystal Smith was engrossed in a heart-to-heart in a corner by the fireplace with a terrified Eugene Daly and the more gin and tonics she downed, the louder and more flirtatious she became.

"I always knew my son was special. Ever since he was born he just . . . well, he just had that special thing that told me he was so special and that he was going to do special things with all these special gifts he had been given. He is just so –"

"Special!" said John from behind the bar.

Krystal glared at him, her glassy bloodshot eyes squinting from too much alcohol. "I think we got that loud and clear," said John. "We all get it, Mum. No need to repeat it on the hour, every hour, every minute of every day. And it's home time, remember?"

"But, he *is* special," said Krystal, her words blurring into one another. "He is very, very, vayvay, vayvay ssshpecial. Isn't he, Eugene? Look, even Eugene agrees that my Taylor is sooo sshpecial."

Eugene looked horrified to be brought into such close family affairs. He was only talking to Krystal Smith because Sorcha had left him in a corner on his own while she went in pursuit of Taylor at every given opportunity. Krystal sort of scared him on a good day and now her leg was pressing into his in a way that made him feel most uncomfortable, plus he could see down her top and it looked like his mother's cleavage and that was just so wrong!

"Tell it to someone who cares," said John and he went on about his work around the bar, wiping down surfaces that didn't need cleaning and emptying out spill-trays – he even changed a keg that still had one or two pints left in it. He would do anything right now to switch off from the We Love Taylor brigade as they gushed and smooched around him. So Taylor had hit the big time at long last and he was going to have to grin and bear it. He would try to swallow his pride and be pleased for his brother, he really would. But right now, he would try his best to ignore his mother's incessant drunken ramblings and try to convince his father to call it a night. There was a tension in the air, not just on his part, and he couldn't quite put his finger on it but he had a feeling it was something to do with Erin who was uncomfortably staring at her glass of 7Up in between her mother and her grandma who were both pleasantly pissed.

"Are you sure you don't want a wee drink?" said Geri to her daughter. "It's not like you to be such a party pooper! Or are we embarrassing you? Maybe you'd rather we left you younger folk to it?"

"No, Mum. Just ignore me. I'm having a selfish sulk which is perfectly abnormal and there is absolutely nothing I can do about it," said Erin. "I'll come round in time."

She smiled across at Taylor who was signalling at her to rescue him from a bunch of ladies who had just heard the news of his big career move. They were a clique of married women who were often seen in the bar on regular occasions and who would take over the whole place in time with their theme of "wine, women and song" even though they hadn't a note in their heads. Maybe Darryl could recruit some of them for his new exploding musical, Erin thought.

She longed for a drink. It was calling her and calling her and she was finding it more and more difficult to refuse the constant stream of offers that were coming her way. Darryl was mightily pissed off with her for being so quiet and sensible on such an "historic occasion". If he had said that once to her, he had said it forty flippin' times and she was almost going to give in just to shut him up. Krystal was throwing her dagger looks that said "If you are pregnant and ruin this all for my boy then I will pop your eyeballs out with a spoon," so for badness Erin had rubbed her midriff every time the sour old bitch caught her eye and Vinegar Tits couldn't help but look away in horror.

Hatchet Face Sorcha was doing her nut in as well. Every time she had the opportunity (i.e. when she had her own audience) she would wish Erin a Merry Christmas on her way past and laugh out loud, so much so that Erin's grandmother had noticed and had asked her what the joke was.

"Is Sorcha stuck in some sort of a time warp or am I going senile?" she asked Erin. "What's all this 'Merry Christmas' all about?"

"She's just a nasty bitch who has no life of her own so she chooses to dissect mine into tiny little pieces," said Erin. "It's nice to know she pays so much attention to detail, I suppose."

"But what has Christmas got to do with the price of fish?" asked Agnes in earnest.

"Oh, I made a boo-boo today at work," whispered Erin. "I said Christmas instead of Valentine's Day."

"Oh," said her gran. "Well, that's an easy mistake to make. They're only about ten weeks apart and . . ."

"No, it's not an easy mistake to make at all, Gran, but thanks anyway. Ryan The Producer went ape-shit and now I have to live to tell the tale and kiss his arse for a day or two to get away with it. No doubt your woman will have it splashed all over *The Herald* on Tuesday but to be honest it's the least of my worries. Look at her gloating as she quizzes Taylor on his move to Hollywood. She is more sickening than being force-fed a whole box of French Fancies in one go."

Agnes shrugged and took another sip of her gin and bitter. "I can't say I noticed. But then, she always did have it in for you since you came first in the Feis with your rendition of 'The Merry Mice' in Primary One. I'll never forget her pinched-up little face when your name was called out and she was relegated to being Highly Commended. I mean, you can hardly hang a Highly Commended on the wall, can you? Pure jealousy, that's all I can say."

Erin had just about decided she'd had enough of the festivities when Krystal Vinegar Tits wobbled across her way, stumbling past tables with her drink slapping around her glass and a mission in her eyes. Her normally coiffed hairdo was ever so slightly skewed, her eyeliner was almost at her cheekbones and her lipstick nearly met her nostrils. How on earth could such a disgusting creature create such a divine piece of humanity like Taylor? He was different to his bloodline in every way. Erin had resigned to the fact that they had ordered him in from some catalogue. There was no way he was related to this Addams Family.

She braced herself for the inevitable tongue-lashing that was to come her way . . . and by God it did.

"You thought you had it all in the bag, didn't you, Miss Tippy Toes?" Krystal hissed. "You thought you had him snared by luring him to live with you in your new house and taking him from under my roof, but my son has bigger fish to fry than you and your small-town status. He is destined for much bigger things. Much better things! Because my Taylor is –"

"Special," said John as he lifted glasses from the table.

Krystal hadn't realised he was in earshot. She hadn't meant for anyone but Erin to hear her rant and she felt like a mouse who had just been approached by a lion – a lion with a rug who had just swept it from under her little mouse-like feet.

"Get out of my face, Spitfire," said Erin. "I am not going to waste my breath, nor am I going to annoy Taylor tonight by stooping to your disgusting level. You hate me, I know that but believe me the feeling is mutual. Now get out of my face!"

Krystal backed off and Erin looked at John who seemed quite pleased with how she had just handled his mother.

"John, can you get me a drink?" she said, straightening her skirt.

"Of course," said John with a smile. A crooked smile which showed his crooked teeth, but a smile nonetheless. "What will you be having, Erin?"

Erin paused. She had been so good all night. It was past midnight. She could last the night without a proper drink, couldn't she? But then look at what she had to put up with? Girls swarming around Taylor, Taylor leaving her for "bigger fish to fry", the whole potential of Christmasgate and that silly wench Sorcha Daly breathing like a dragon down her neck, not to mention a semi-drunk – no, make that a thoroughly pissed mother and grandmother and now the Wrath of Vinegar

Tits and the potential of losing her prime-time job on Ulster's premier television magazine programme . . . oh yes, she really did need a drink.

"I'll just have a 7Up," she said meekly.

"A 7Up?" asked John.

Temptation wriggled through her bones. She wanted some red wine. She wanted it so badly she could taste it, but it was so late in the evening and she had done so well. Could she resist? Could she get through the night without it? Could she?

"Yes, a 7Up. No wait! I'll have . . . I'll have . . . oh, sod it," she said. "Give me a fuckin' red wine. No, give me two fuckin' glasses since you're about to close the bar. And it's all your bloody mother's fault that I'm doing this so make it quick, John. Make it really quick!"

SCENE FOUR

A touch of frost sparkled on the pavement as Taylor and Erin made their way home after the impromptu evening celebrations. They linked arms and staggered merrily down the main street, past The Butcher's and the church and all the familiar surroundings that made Millfield their favourite place in the whole world. It was a safe and friendly community where everyone knew each other's business, and both of them knew every inch of the place they called home. Hollywood really couldn't be any further from here.

"Penny for your thoughts," said Taylor whose permanent grin simply couldn't be wiped from his face. He had to pinch himself every now and then to help it all sink in and now that Erin seemed a little more content with the news, he could really let his imagination flow as to what life might be like in the real Hollywood.

"Nothing much, just stuff," said Erin, leaning her

head on his shoulder as they walked. The two glasses of red wine had made her relax a little and once Taylor's mother was escorted from the bar, she actually found the evening quite enjoyable.

"I'm sorry about my mother. John told me –"

"Don't be," said Erin. "If you were to apologise every time your mother insulted me then you'd constantly be saying sorry. She really doesn't bother me, I swear. It used to, but now I would be much more shocked if she actually said something nice to me. She thinks this move will split us up and I'm sure she's not the only one."

Taylor stopped in his tracks and cupped Erin's face in his cold hands.

"I don't care what anyone thinks. They can say what they want but you and I know that this will be a step forward for both of us, not a step further apart. I want to share this with you and if there's any way I could take you with me, I would, but I believe we're strong enough to survive six months apart, don't you?"

Erin snuggled into him and took a deep breath in and out. "Fuck the begrudgers!"

Her words were muffled and Taylor laughed. "Exactly. Fuck the begrudgers. We'll show them. Now let's go home and make the most of our time together because I am going to miss you so, so much."

"Yes, yes, it's just absolutely wonderful. We're thrilled. Hold on, let me just get this right . . ."

Darryl Smith covered the telephone's mouthpiece and called out to Krystal from the bottom of the stairs.

"Krystal? Krystal darling? The movie's called *Benny, Meet Frankie*, isn't that right? Krystal?"

No answer.

"Krystal! Aunt Marge is on the phone and she wants to tell her friends at the poker club? Look, I can't locate my wife at the minute," he said into the phone again. "I'm afraid we over-celebrated, if there is such a term, last night and she hasn't really spoken much this morning. She's been in the bathroom for almost an hour. Yes, maybe I should go and check. Thanks for calling. Yes, yes, I heard you the first time. If Taylor bumps into any of the cast of *Priscilla, Queen of the Desert* he is to pass on your regards. And Aunt Bridie's regards too, yes. Bye, Aunt Marge. Bye."

Darryl hung up the phone and walked up the stairwell in search of his wife who had been uncharacteristically quiet for some time now. He really should have checked on her earlier but the phone hadn't stopped all morning. He had just settled down to a boiled egg and soldiers (since no one was there to tell him he was being a big child with dunking his soldiers and he couldn't really eat it any other way) when the first call came from Krystal's sister in County Mayo and it had been non-stop since. Good news really did travel fast in and out of Millfield, that was for sure.

"Krystal? Krystal, are you okay?" Darryl knocked on the bathroom door and then opened it but Krystal wasn't there. He walked across the landing towards the bedroom with a tentative feeling inside. She had been so quiet all morning and he had assumed it was a hangover as she was terribly sloshed the night before but maybe he had been too presumptuous . . . but then he heard movement. He opened the door and relaxed when he saw her, alive and kicking (well, alive anyway) and sobbing on the bed.

"What's up, darling? Are we cringing slightly about our behaviour last night? Are we having little flashbacks of what we said and who we said it to? Are we?"

"What the hell is all this '*we*' business, you pompous git?" said Krystal. "Speak for yourself but don't ever try and predict what my problems might be."

"Well, excuse me for breathing," said Darryl. Now that he knew that Krystal hadn't vomited to death or fallen or jumped out of a window, he felt he had a license to jibe at her just as she deserved. Her behaviour the night before was right out of order as it always was when she had one too many. "I just think you might want to wallow for a while, not in self-pity, but in remorse. Your big mouth will soon get you into a lot of trouble."

Krystal reached down from the bed, grabbed a bedroom slipper and hurled it across the room at her husband. Then she found the other and just as he was finished ducking from the first missile, the second slipper hit him right across the gob.

"Bullseye!" she said. "You don't know how long I've been waiting to do that! Now, don't you have some gardening to do or a dog to walk because I'm sick looking at your smug face already and my head doesn't need any more excuses to be throbbing like it's about to explode!"

Darryl lifted the slippers from the floor, patted his sore jaw and sat the two pink lumps of fluff back by the bedside, then walked out of the bedroom. He stopped and then turned to his wife.

"You'll never break them up, you know," he said with his chin tilted.

"What on earth are you talking about?"

"Taylor and Erin. He loves her and she loves him. It's quite simple and it's very real, so you can stop rubbing your hands and quit with your scathing threats because Erin will be right here waiting for Taylor when he gets back from LA and he will be still as in love with her then as he is now."

He spun on his heels and walked down the stairs, ignoring Krystal's rants from the bedroom, marched out through the front door, then down the pathway and out towards the main street of Millfield where he hoped he might bump into someone with whom he could have a sensible conversation on this fine Saturday afternoon.

Taylor and Erin were having a luxurious lie-in and had just finished breakfast in bed, prepared by Taylor who quite fancied himself as a budding Jamie Oliver in the kitchen. His speciality, scrambled eggs and crispy bacon, had gone down a treat as always, washed down with hot milky coffee.

"So . . ." he said, tracing his fingers across Erin's bare belly. She was a curvy girl, who was shaped well in all the right places and not the skinny bag of bones most actors found appealing. "What can we do today? It's your choice. I'm all yours."

To Taylor, Erin O'Brien was everything he wanted in a woman – fun, passionate, talented and with a beauty he felt at home with.

Erin looked up at the ceiling and thought for a moment. She didn't want the day to end. She dreaded the days going by until Taylor left and, as the clock ticked by, her sense of panic heightened at the thought of not seeing him for so long. They had been together six years now (not counting a brief high-school courtship which ended when she went to university) and since he moved into her new house a few months ago, they had grown so much closer and had so much fun together. Watching him leave would be like losing a limb. It just didn't bear thinking about.

"Well, I sort of have an idea," she said, still staring upwards.

"Good, good. Ideas are a good place to start. Tell me . . ."

"Well, from tomorrow we have six days left before you leave for Hollywood on Friday. So how about we do something special on each of those days. Something that we can hold on to – an occasion for every month that you'll be away."

Taylor leaned up on his side and Erin gasped at the sight of his tanned, toned torso. She couldn't afford to take his beauty for granted any longer and would have to savour every glimpse of him that she could. He was set to be a big star and she knew it, but he would always be hers. Wouldn't he?

"Hold on a minute," said Taylor, playfully looking under the sheets and onto the floor as if he had lost something. "Who are you, Miss Imposter, and what have you done with my girlfriend? Could the real Erin O'Brien please stand up?"

"Too cheesy, eh? Fuck, I knew it," she said. "Forgive me, I don't know where it came from. One minute I was spotting cobwebs on the ceiling and the next it just came to me but the real Erin is back now. She just lost the run of herself there. Sorry."

"No, no, I love that idea! We can have a March event

tomorrow, an April on Monday, a May on Tuesday which can be your birthday party and so on. Excellent! It's a killer what you can think of from counting cobwebs. Genius!"

Maybe it *was* a good idea, thought Erin. It just might take her mind off things and maybe it would even keep her off the red wine she had become so accustomed to late at night when the world was sleeping. It had scared her how she had craved alcohol so much when most people would settle for a nice cuppa or a hot chocolate before they went to bed. What began as a harmless nightcap had spiralled into a bottle per night and lately it had progressed even further as she'd find herself cracking open a second bottle on a weeknight.

Taylor had no idea. She used every excuse in the book to get him out of her way when bedtime came – she had "notes to make for work the next day", she would "just clear out the dishwasher", or "just prepare a packed lunch for work". She had used up a list of domestic chores and if Taylor insisted on her joining him in the bedroom, she would slip back out when he was asleep and feel relief when the rich red liquid and the alcohol seeped into her veins. Then she would hide the empty bottles (in a stash out by the boiler house which she really should empty soon) and slump into a deep sleep before dragging her aching body into a shower the next morning and facing the day ahead. She couldn't remember when it started, but she knew it had to stop. Yes, this would help her get through the next few days. It would give her a purpose and might even help her get her work-life back on track if she had something fun to focus on.

"So, tomorrow, it's March so that's the beginning of spring . . . an Easter Egg hunt?" she suggested.

"Or we could have our own mini St Patrick's Day and get sozzled?" said Taylor. "We could go for Sunday lunch and wear green and drown our shamrock together and wear silly hats but we won't care how stupid we look because it'll be St Patrick's Day and we won't care?"

Alcohol. Again. Shit, there was just no getting away from it, but if she paced herself . . . if she didn't overdo it . . . she had to work the next day . . .

"Well, as long as it's a 'mini' drowning of the shamrock, then that sounds good," she said. "So Monday it's April and April means . . .?"

"Well, that can be Easter bunnies, I suppose, since we're dedicating March to St Paddy. Is Easter in March or April this year?"

"Dunno . . . but in our calendar it will have to be April," said Erin. "'Cos I can't be bothered to check and it's only a technicality anyhow."

"Okay, so bunnies, eggs, chocolate . . . ah, and another word for bunnies is . . .?"

"Er, rabbits?"

"Top of the class, Miss O'Brien! Rabbits it is! Monday is the Day of the Rabbit, from this day on. I can live with that!" Taylor nuzzled into her neck and she giggled out loud. "An early night starting with a long, relaxing bubble bath, candles, champagne . . . the works? Oh, I'm looking forward to April already."

"Well, after all that physical activity in April, looks like May might be a quiet one?" said Erin, with a smile. "How about a movie night with lots of goodies and . . ."

"No, no, no. It's your birthday in May so I will plan a surprise for you then. You choose what you want to do for June aka Wednesday. We could be pretty tired by then so go easy."

"Okay then, June is movie time – with a difference! You choose your favourite movie of all time and I'll choose mine and we'll snuggle up and watch them back to back on DVD. Then we'll do the same with our favourite songs so that we can play them while we're apart . . ."

They lay together in silence before Taylor spoke up.

"Gosh, now you're going to make me all weepy!" he said. "I can just see me now, sitting in a hotel room all by myself listening to sad music and drinking myself into oblivion just to get through the night."

Erin lifted a pillow and playfully hit him across the head and he pinned her down and tickled her until she squealed for mercy.

"Yeah and Sandra Bullock will be by your side nursing you through all your pain and agony and in a few weeks it will be, Erin who? Oh, she was *so* yesterday, Sandy."

"Sandra Bullock? I was hoping for Angelina if you don't mind . . ." He lay back on the bed and put his hands behind his head. "This is crazy, isn't it? I mean, the full cast hasn't been announced yet but there is a chance it could be an A-lister – and then little old me. I just can't believe this is happening. Is this real?"

"It's real," said Erin, leaning up on her elbow and watching him think. "And you deserve every moment that is coming your way. But first of all, buster, you have another few days to fill with me, so what are we doing in July and August, which technically is your last day here on home turf?"

48

Taylor turned to face her and he saw that her fear and sadness at letting him go was very real.

"Mmm, summertime . . . well, that means only one thing, doesn't it? The beach. And a barbecue and I don't care what the weather is, we will be wearing shorts."

"Are you for real? In this country?"

"Oh yeah. It's our last day together for a little while and so, goose-bumps and all, we will have a day to remember. In fact, we will have quite a few days to remember, beginning with today which is February, which means Valentine's Day. Now, let me show you just how much I love you . . ."

SCENE FIVE

Erin walked into the television studios on Monday morning with a heavy feeling inside. She was proud of herself in a way, having avoided any alcoholic binges over the weekend but she knew in her heart that if Taylor hadn't paid her so much attention, she would have had her usual Monday-morning hangover to deal with. Still, baby steps is what it takes, she said inwardly and she pushed the heavy glass doors and walked tall across the marble foyer.

Valentine's Day on Saturday had been so wonderful and she still swooned when she remembered how much romance was in their day together. A pub lunch (just one glass of wine!) followed by a walk in the frosty park and an evening in front of the telly and a roaring fire was simple but blissful. Yesterday (St Patrick's Day) was a hoot and she would never forget Taylor's leprechaun hat which he borrowed from the wardrobe of the theatre group, nor his efforts to find shamrock only to end up creatively working on lettuce leaves and pinning them to both of their jackets. Erin wore an emerald-green jumper dress and black tights and she thought she might have choked with laughter when Taylor made her join him for a Riverdance in her living room. They took photos and made Irish Stew and when they went to the pub for a nightcap she had one more glass of wine and, despite the temptation, she declined to crack open another bottle when they got home, instead preferring to go straight to bed and be fresh for the day ahead.

"Good morning, Erin," said the security man in his strong Belfast twang. "Lookin' lovely as always, pet. Don't listen to any of them ould Christmas jokes. They're all just jealous, so they are."

"Thanks, Bill," she replied with a smile and she could feel his eyes on her hips as she waited for the elevator to take her to the office floors. She tried to recall what was in store for this week's show and it frightened her that she could barely remember being on air a few days ago, never mind what they had loosely discussed in production meetings the day before. Could she have been so hung over all last week that she couldn't even recall her works schedule? Shit!

Still, Mondays were a good day to start anew, and here she was, just as Ryan The Producer had instructed her to be – on time, refreshed, well-slept, and she had laid off the booze. What could possibly go wrong?

Ryan The Producer drummed his fingers on his desk and looked like he'd had approximately three hours' sleep at the very most. His feathery blond tufts of hair were fluffed up and pointed north, south, east and west and his skin was a lighter shade of grey than usual. Even his shirt was crinkled and he looked like he might have slept in his suit. Erin felt a "one up" already in her immaculately pressed black pencil skirt with its high waist that showed off her curves, and her hair was neatly tied back in a bun. Red lipstick and a sweep of bronzer finished her look and a spray of Marc Jacobs perfume made her feel confident enough to defend her Christmasgate and Hangovergate episodes from Friday. This was a new beginning. She could take it.

"Okay," she said. "I have apologised for what has happened in the past and I have done what you told me to, so why are you looking at me like I have two heads?"

Ryan The Producer clasped his hands and twiddled his thumbs and breathed through his gaping nostrils. His mouth was tight and he looked like a coiled spring which was ready to bounce up from the chair and attack her.

"This is your last chance, Erin. If you only knew the grief I have taken from Head Office over your behaviour. They had a *list*, for Christ sake! A fucking *list* of faux-pas and 'whoopsies' the length of my arm –"

Not that long then, thought Erin, considering he was just a bit bigger than Dopey and Sneezy and the gang. In fact his arms were the length of those of a small boy.

"– and I am mortified at how much I have let you away with. Totally mortified."

Erin wanted to know more but then didn't want to at the same time. Saying "Christmas" in February was bad enough, and she could admit to have had cringe-worthy flashbacks of her mistake at the most inappropriate times over the weekend – could she cope with any further humiliation about what she said on days when she might just have been a bit tipsy? Looked like she had no choice . . .

"Friday 7th January – the chef was making an Italian dish. You referred to a bowl of olives as a bowl of grapes. Three times."

"Er –"

"Friday 14th January – you called one of our special guests *Jack* at least twice."

"So I got his name wrong. That's a human enough mistake."

"Not when her name was fucking Josephine! It was a woman! Need I go on?"

Shit! Erin could feel her face flush hotter and hotter. What was she playing at? It sounded like Ryan was talking about a different person – she didn't recognise this flippant, careless, distracted idiot who was being chastised by a Milky Bar Kid-alike. She had always been so career-focused, so ambitious and she had fought tooth and nail to get her name attached to this show and had always been reminded by her peers how much she deserved it. There were colleagues who would stand on her head to fill her slot and now she dreaded to think of how she had let everyone down – Ryan The Producer, her colleagues, but most of all herself.

"I can assure you, Ryan," she said in earnest, "that I will not let my personal life and my professional life blur again. Believe me, I am as humiliated as you are."

"I hope so. By God, I hope so!"

"Please! I ask your forgiveness and I promise that if you can bear to give me this second chance, I will remind you of why I was given this role in the first place. I really am ever so sorry. It's just been so . . ."

She trailed off and Ryan put his head in his hands and sniffed. He took off his glasses, rubbed his eyes and then replaced them and looked up at Erin.

"To be perfectly honest, Erin," he said, "if it were any of the others, *any* of the others who behaved the way you have been behaving, they would have been out on their ear and back to the start where they would be writing obituaries on the local free weeklies in a heartbeat. But not you, Erin. I have always held you in high regard in the belief you have the whole package to succeed in this game. You will go far if you can overcome whatever it is you are going through at the minute. That's why I am giving you a chance."

"Oh my God, thank you so much, Ryan! And I will show you that you are absolutely right to believe in me. I'm sorted now with all my personal stuff anyhow. Taylor going to Hollywood is simply not an issue any more so I have absolutely no reason to drown my sorrows whatsoever."

"What? Where?"

"Really. We have talked and I have wised up to the fact that no matter who he meets, be it Sandra Bullock or Catherine Zeta Jones or even Angelina herself, I will always be Number One. Always. So I'm back in the real world now and I'm all yours and I will never take my eye off the ball again."

"Hold on, hold on. Did you say Hollywood?" said Ryan The Producer, now sucking on the end of his pen. He leaned back on his revolving chair and it clicked back into recline. "To make a movie? Taylor? Wow! Well, lucky Taylor, eh? Lucky, lucky bastard."

Erin smiled and nodded. She really was so proud of

him now that she had overcome her strop and she loved the way people reacted when they heard the news.

"Jeez," said Ryan The Producer, shaking his head. "Makes all of us seem like little fish in here, doesn't it?"

"Suppose it does if you want to think of it that way," said Erin. "But he's very loyal to his roots. He still talks about the work experience you gave him when he was at university and how you didn't overreact when he broke the photocopier on his first day."

Ryan The Producer looked like he was in a cloudy, dreamy daze.

"Wow," he said. "Sandra Bullock."

"Oh no, I was just using her as an example. It hasn't been announced yet. It's just he has a thing for her."

"Who doesn't? Sandra fucking Bullock! I *so* would." He sat up straight again. "But don't tell my wife I said that! With the new baby her hormones are all over the place at the minute and I'd get less sleep than I'm getting at the minute! Best to let sleeping dogs lie and all that. But Sandra? *Hm, mm, mmm . . .*"

Erin pulled out a chair opposite him and sat down, crossing her legs with confidence. Ryan The Producer wasn't so bad at all, she supposed, and he really did look bedraggled and exhausted in his new role as Baby Daddy so she'd better go easy on him and try and keep him sweet.

"Now, let's talk about this week's programme," she said, wanting to get down to business. "I have an idea. I'm not sure if I can pull it off as yet, but if I can *It's Your Friday* will be the talk of the nation."

Ryan brightened up as Erin told him her ideas for the week ahead. Things would work out okay, she had a feeling. She had so much to live for and she wouldn't care if she never saw a glass of wine again. And it was Monday, which meant in her and Taylor's world it was April which meant the Day of the Rabbits and the bubble bath and a night of passion with her man with not an alcoholic drink in sight. She smiled in contentment. Even Sandra Bullock wouldn't have a prayer when she was finished with Taylor. Not even a prayer.

Taylor sat by the fire in The Stage Bar and tried to finish a crossword as he sipped a morning coffee. He could hear the hum of the traffic outside over the familiar chant of the commentator on the television's usual horseracing station and John's own version of the race from behind the bar.

It was homely and cosy and quiet – just as he liked it.

He really would miss this place and all its familiarities and beyond his excitement was an element of fear that he wasn't really cut out for the dizzy heights of fame. Sure, it was what he wanted and he would never even pause to consider his options, but lurking beneath the big, big boost to his life and a potential life-changing experience, was a babbling brook of concern that he might be the proverbial fish out of water in the bright lights of LA.

His agent Al was arranging flights and downloading the latest script right now and had booked him into accommodation with the rest of the cast, the names of whom he was yet to know. He wouldn't let his mind wander as to who he might be working with, and at the end of the day it didn't really matter. He was to play a supporting role to the lead in the movie and that was good enough for him. To be plucked from a television series in Ireland to the ultimate dream of working in Hollywood was more than fate – it was down to hard grafting and determination and Al, a fast-talking American ex-pat who had contacts to die for from his work on film sets in days gone by.

"Hey, John. Help me out here," Taylor said with his pen poised. "An 'old school' person – fourteen letters. Begins with T, I think."

John lifted his head from *The Daily Sport* and thought about it. Then shook his head and returned to his newspaper. "Sorry, bro. You're the one with the brains. Don't know why the hell you even waste your breath sometimes, asking me for answers. I wouldn't have a clue."

"It's okay I got it. 'Traditionalist'," said Taylor and he filled in the letters on the tiny grid. He liked to sit and chat with John when he could, even if they were like chalk and cheese and getting a word or two out of John on a good day was like pulling teeth.

No matter how much he tried, he and John were worlds apart and always had been. When John was kicking footballs against the gable of the house, Taylor would have been writing songs in his bedroom or hanging out at the community centre with his dad where they would discuss set-building ideas and research plays for the coming season. When Taylor was exceeding in his exams, John was down the town swigging beer from a can and smoking cigarettes and skipping classes and when they went to discos together, you'd find Taylor surrounded by giggling girls while John looked bored and out of sorts, checking his watch or wallowing in a pint of beer.

And now that Taylor was making a proper name for himself in the world of film, John looked like the picture of misery who was doing a job in the family pub just because there was nothing else out there for him.

John wasn't even a *good* barman – everyone complained about his grumpy manner and sour expression and if it weren't for the support of The Millfield Players drama group, the horseracing fanatics and the local football team who held their weekly lotto draw on the premises every Wednesday night, then The Stage would have gone down the tubes long ago.

"Why don't you do a course on something you're interested in, John?" asked Taylor as he watched his brother flick through the same paper for the second time. He didn't mean to come out of the blue with it, but he felt sorry for John sometimes. He felt guilty that John had lived in his shadow forever and that they were constantly compared to each other. There was nothing wrong with being a barman but John evidently hated it so there had to be more reason for him to get up in the morning than watching Teletext flat out for tips and ground conditions on horserace tracks.

"Why don't you go and learn your lines, Mr Cruise?" said John and he closed his newspaper. "I don't know why you stare at me with such pity. I'm fine the way I am. And do you honestly think I'd leave all this? Some of us are quite happy here in Little Hollywood. There's enough bright lights in this little town for me."

Taylor looked around the bar and wondered if John could be telling the truth. Old Jimmy McLernon the Ex-

Postman who was a trained opera singer, sat nursing a pint of Guinness in one corner, Rita the Local Councillor sat sipping a hot whiskey (her fifth that morning) on a high stool as she wrote poetry and a bunch of the local unemployed who were members of both the football team and The Millfield Players drama group threw darts in the corner.

No, John would never leave all of this, thought Taylor. Little Hollywood was John's life, but Taylor had bigger plans for his own life. Plans that would either make or break his life in Little Hollywood, but he had to take the chance.

SCENE SIX

Come Friday, Erin had set off for work with a spring in her step. She wore a blood-red tulip skirt with a black V-neck jumper and patterned black tights with patent heels and she felt as good as she looked for the first time in a long time.

The atmosphere in the studio was electric and she was over the moon that her plans for this week's show had come to fruition. It had been a lively broadcast so far, and now as she came out of the final ad break, she knew that she had saved the best for last.

She took a breath, donned her best smile and said into the camera:

"Welcome back to today's show and if you have just tuned in, you are just in time for some exciting news straight from the horse's mouth." She turned around and the camera followed her to the sofa where she took a seat, still talking as she walked. "You've read it in the papers, you've heard it on the news, now you can see for yourself just why Hollywood producers have offered Taylor Smith a role in the forthcoming 'buddy movie' – *Benny, Meet Frankie* for which filming will begin in just two weeks' time at the famous Universal Studios and on location at Malibu Beach. But before we speak to the man of the moment, let's take a look at him in a more familiar role as the wayward but handsome paediatrician Brian O'Hara in the RTÉ soap opera, *Surgeons*.

As viewers at home watched the clip of Taylor in action, she reached across for his hand and gave it a tight squeeze. He looked stunning today in his white shirt and faded blue jeans and she had choked back tears all morning, knowing that this was their last day together for a while. But to have him here with her, live on air, had given her a much-needed boost and focus to what was going to be a sad but exciting day for both of them.

"Yes, Taylor Smith who hails from the village of Millfield in Mid Ulster, may be a familiar face to some for his role in popular medical drama *Surgeons* but Taylor is set to become a household name since the news broke this week that he is Hollywood bound. Jealous yet? Well, you will be. It's Taylor Smith, everyone!"

Erin felt a giggle tickle her mouth and she urged her nerves not to get the better of her. It was always going to be surreal to interview her own boyfriend on live television and even though viewers knew of their long-term relationship, she felt it best to keep the conversation strictly professional and without bias for as long as she could. Grabbing an hour out of Taylor's schedule today had been a juggling act but he was well organised for his trip and, since it meant an extra hour in each other's company, it was an effort they both felt just had to be made – plus it had gained Erin some much-needed brownie points with her bosses. Ratings would rocket with this exclusive and the wider media loved the story of the small-town Irish boy who was plucked from bit parts in an Irish soap opera to star alongside some of the Hollywood greats.

"Taylor, it's a pleasure to have you here on *It's Your Friday* and thanks so much for taking time out of your busy day to be with us. So, tell us how this came about? It really is a dream come true. Tell us how you came across the role."

"It sure is a dream come true, Erin. Well, my agent heard that the producers of *Benny, Meet Frankie* were looking for an Irish actor to play the part of Benny's cousin and he rang me straight away. We thought it was a long shot but they liked what they saw from my profile and after a screen test in London just a few weeks ago and a few more questions they offered me the part. I'm still pinching myself. Like you say, it's a dream come true."

Erin could almost feel the heat from the beam on Ryan The Producer's face from the studio floor. Taylor had been hot news all week and apart from vox-pop snippets on regional radio and television news, no one had been granted a live interview with the latest talent to emerge from the North of Ireland.

"It's quite a big part, isn't it, and the rumours have been flying around as to who you will be sharing the screen with? Liam Neeson, for one?"

"Yes, I'm thrilled to say I'll be acting alongside one of my heroes, Liam Neeson, who plays the lead role of Benny. It's fantastic to be working with one of my fellow countrymen on my first big international role. He's always been someone I've looked up to. Ever since I first got the acting bug, Neeson has been the main man."

The interview was swimming along, with Taylor and Erin chatting openly and the chemistry between the two of them sparking. Ryan The Producer was fit to burst with delight and had tripped over at least three cables as he moved closer and closer to get a better view.

"Basically, Benny is an Irish ex-pat who works as a cop in Malibu," said Taylor when Erin asked for the movie storyline. "He randomly bumps into an old friend Dan who is on honeymoon with his wife Frankie which disrupts the happy couple's two-week break as the two men rekindle a long-lost friendship. However, this disruption is set to change Benny's whole life in more ways than one because he falls madly in love with Frankie and, to his surprise, the feeling is mutual. I play the part of Benny's playboy cousin Gerard who turns up on his doorstep just when Benny's life is already in turmoil, so it's a bit like the Irish invasion of Malibu in the funniest way you can imagine. I've heard I have lots of interesting swimwear scenes."

Taylor raised an eyebrow and gave a sexy glance into the camera and Erin was sure that Ryan The Producer was actually bouncing with glee on the sidelines. This was such a coup, such a scoop for the *It's Your Friday* show but he hadn't heard the best yet – Erin still had an ace up her sleeve.

"Well, I'm sure the ladies at home will look forward to that! Taylor Smith in swimwear is bound to raise temperatures, even if I do say so myself. But just when you thought you'd heard it all, I am delighted to

announce an exclusive right here on *It's Your Friday*."
Erin pursed her lips and spoke to the camera. "There
have been many rumours floating around about who the
leading lady will be in your new movie but it has all been
quite secretive as to who will play the part of Frankie.
The media have been playing a guessing game with all
sorts of Hollywood greats being namedropped but with
no confirmation . . . that is, until now. Yes, we are
delighted to have been given permission to announce
right here that Taylor will be working alongside, not
only Liam Neeson, but also . . . I'll hand this over to the
man of the moment. Tell us, Taylor . . ."

"I'm honoured and thrilled to be starring alongside
the one and only . . . Sandra Bullock."

"Sandra fucking Bullock!" said Ryan The Producer
way too loud from the wings. He was getting really
carried away now and he clasped his mouth, relieved
that he wasn't wearing a microphone and praying that
the viewers at home wouldn't hear him but he couldn't
help himself. "Sandra fucking Bullock!"

"Yes, you heard it here first! *Benny, Meet Frankie* will
be on our screens in eighteen months' time with Liam
Neeson, Sandra Bullock and our very own Taylor Smith,
but for now, Taylor leaves us with our warmest wishes
from the *It's Your Friday* team! Thank you for joining
us, Taylor and good luck in Hollywood."

"Thank you, Erin. Thank you very much."

Taylor and Erin left the *It's Your Friday* studios on a
high and when they got to the car there was an
excitement in the air that was almost tangible.

"That went so well. I can't thank you enough," said

Erin. She was delighted with the reaction from her colleagues and Ryan The Producer was acting like he was on speed – the drug, not the Sandra movie. "You don't know how much I needed to get back into the good books with Ryan and I swear he almost had an orgasm when you made that announcement. I think that may have been our best show ever!"

"Do you honestly think I would have let you down?" said Taylor, delighted to see Erin so happy. "It's the least I can do. We did have a great week though and this was the perfect finish."

"We did have an unbelievable week and thank you for the birthday meal and the bracelet in May. Seems so long ago, with it now being July," she laughed.

"Glad you liked it, even though the pepper sauce was lumpy, I forgot the wine and I sort of char-grilled the steaks a little too much?"

"It was amazing. I'll never forget it."

"Me neither."

They sat in silence, both smiling and Taylor clasped Erin's hand. Then he started up the engine in the car and they made their way home for their last meal together. The only way was up for Taylor Smith, and for the first time in ages, Erin felt like she was taking this amazing journey right alongside him.

Krystal Smith was in her glory when Taylor called to say his farewells.

"Mum, really there is no need for all this fuss."

He was in a major hurry to catch his afternoon flight to Heathrow and then link to LAX with New Zealand Airlines later in the evening. The car was packed up with his luggage and Erin was waiting from him with the engine running at the end of the driveway of his mum's, but his mother had gathered up a farewell party in her kitchen with all his aunts, uncles and cousins and a 'Good Luck Taylor Superstar aka Gerard the Cousin of Liam Neeson' banner across the front of the house. He was mortified. To add to the effect, his father had been on the brandy from early and could be heard probably in the nearest town with his crowing and boasting of how "the boy had done good" on repeat.

"The boy has done good," he said to everyone who congratulated him. "The boy has done good. You can say what you like, but the boy has done good."

Taylor acknowledged their overwhelming pride and he really was delighted and if they had warned them of their plans to see him off with such rigour, he would have called a lot earlier.

"It's the least we can do," said Krystal, sipping a glass of champagne that Aunt Marge had brought over and blinking back the fizz. She nibbled a cocktail sausage and then clinked her glass with a spoon to grab attention. "It's not everyone who can say their son is set to be a movie star! Okay, speech time, speech time!"

"Mum, really I have to go!" said Taylor. He was very late now and Erin would be thinking he had been kidnapped.

"Ahem, I'd just like to say," said Krystal, oblivious to Taylor's panic and directly to her enthralled audience. "In the words of the great John Denver, my son is now leaving on a jet plane, and I don't know when he'll be back again!"

"Thanks Mum, but –"

"Oh, Taylor, babe . . . I love you so!" warbled Krystal. She gave Taylor an exaggerated bear-hug and a prolonged kiss on the cheek, then presented him to the gathered crowd. "My son, the actor! Hip hip?"

"*Hurray!*" said Aunt Marge and her cronies.

"Hip Hip!"

"*Hurray!*"

"Mum, I'm leaving –"

"– on a jet plane!" sang Aunt Marge into her glass and Aunt Bridie attempted to harmonise.

"Thanks, everyone," said Taylor and they broke into an enthusiastic applause. "Thanks but I really must go or the jet plane will be halfway across the Atlantic. Bye, Mum – bye, Dad. I'll call you as much as I can."

He wrestled past his overenthusiastic aunts.

"And don't forget to look out for *Priscilla Queen of the D*esert! Anyone at all. Even the guy who played the piano player or the gas-station attendant. Or even better, the aborigine! Anyone!"

"I will," said Taylor, not wanting to ruin Aunt Marge's thunder by telling her that Priscilla and her mates were more likely to be found in Australia than Los Angeles.

At the door, Darryl Smith gave his son a hug with tears in his eyes and escorted him out with the flock of fans following, waving and singing. Taylor left his father halfway on the garden path and jogged out to the car, but then stopped when he saw his brother come running up the road. It was possibly the first time he saw John running since Primary School in the egg and spoon race where he inevitably came last.

"Taylor! Wait!" said John, with a cigarette hanging

out of his mouth. He slowed down to a fast walk, and puffed and panted as Taylor waited and the posse of lovely ladies in the garden turned silent.

"Okay, bro. How's it going?"

"I – I j–just wanted to wish you good luck," said John with the stammer that returned to him when he was nervous. "I, well, you know I don't say much but . . . I'm going to m–miss you and I'm proud of you and all that."

Taylor felt choked. John was actually talking to him, man to man, brother to brother, without a sarky comment or complaint about something or other? And he had spoken in sentences, proper sentences which didn't involve a grunt or a moan or a "woe is me" condition.

"And I've set this up so we can keep in touch," continued John, taking another drag from his cigarette. "Well, Rita The Councillor set it up for me and she says she'll keep me right on how to use it. I hope she got it right. She was rightly pissed this morning when I opened the bar and, speaking of which, I better get back 'cos I've left her in charge."

He stubbed his cigarette out and handed Taylor a slip of paper with Rita's neat scrawl (she was always neat and tidy in every way, despite being full of booze as a bingo bus twenty-four seven).

Taylor opened it and read an email address and he beamed with delight! His brother was embracing technology and moving with the times. It was a baby step, but it was a step nonetheless.

"John4hoofhearted@hotmail.co.uk. Cool," said Taylor. John had actually set up an email address? Shit, this really was serious!

"Yeah, well, Rita said it's about time and with you going away for a while it sort of made sense."

"Excellent!" said Taylor. "That's a great idea. Good old Rita, but who or what is Hoofhearted?"

"Oh, she's a mare. 'Hoof Hearted.' She's tipped for big things in the Gold Cup this year and Rita said to pick a name I can remember easily."

"Okay," said Taylor and he put the piece of paper (a betting slip of course) into his wallet. "Look, I really must go now or I'm going to miss my flight but this is great, John. Keep in touch, eh? I'll miss you."

John looked back at his older brother in disbelief. "Yeah right! You don't have to say that. It's only an email address. Everyone has one, except me until now."

"But I will miss you, John. Strangely, I will miss you all."

He gave his mum, his dad, his Aunt Marge and a few familiar faces from the Millfield Players a final wave, then jumped into the car and watched Little Hollywood and all of its characters see him off.

They passed The Butcher's and The Post Office and The Chippy and The Stage Bar, then as they drove a little further out he saw The Community Centre where he had learned his trade, with it's homemade sign which read "*Millfield Theatre*" stuck above one of the doors.

"It will always stay with you, you know," said Erin, knowing he was feeling slightly nostalgic. "You'll never get rid of us. We're all in your blood."

Taylor laughed and drove on with a smile across his face as he left his home village and all of its small-town ways, but deep inside he knew Erin was right. In fact, he was missing everything about life in Little Hollywood already.

"So," said Erin. "This is it then."

They stood at the check-in area of Belfast

International, holding hands, face to face, and Erin fought with the urge to cry. She didn't want to upset Taylor. This was the biggest event of his life after all and she wanted him to leave content in the knowledge that she was fully behind him, no matter how much it might hurt.

Holidaymakers and weekend travellers and commuters skirted around them and the tannoy announced last calls for several flights but Taylor and Erin were oblivious to all of their surroundings. This would be the longest they had been apart in many years and neither of them wanted to face up to how they would cope for six months without seeing each other every day.

"I'll call as soon as I get there," he said to her, leaning in so that their noses touched. "I'll call you every day, I'll text, Skype, email, Facebook, you name it. It will be like we were never apart. I'll be your cyberspace stalker."

"Oh God, it's going to be so strange in the house without you. I was just getting used to your messy ways and the way you watch re-runs of *Scrubs* and play the X Box till I want to shake you. I'm going to miss you so much."

Taylor kissed her hard and they wrapped their arms around each other and stayed there for as long as they could.

"I wish you could come too," he said.

"So do I," said Erin, "but can you imagine the face of Ryan The Producer if I left them in the lurch? I would be swiftly replaced by a younger model, I'd say. Oh my God, you won't replace me with a younger model, will you? I'm stuck between a rock and a hard place here . . ."

"Don't be so silly. What would a young beach-blonde, leggy, perma-tanned, big-boobed Californian girl have on you?"

Erin smirked and hit him a light playful punch. "Suppose, when you put it like that I have nothing to worry about at all."

"Exactly," said Taylor. "Glad we got that straight. And don't you be running off into the sunset with Eugene Daly or the likes. They don't call it Little Hollywood for nothing, you know. "

Erin rolled her eyes at the thought and Taylor's flight was called for boarding but they ignored it and more silence followed and a final cuddle and then Erin couldn't stand it any longer.

"Oh, this is so hard," she said. "I hate long goodbyes so I'm going to go now before I become a blubbering wreck and ruin your new coat or I really do make you miss your flight. Good luck, Taylor. I know you'll be a cracking movie star."

She stepped back and wiped a tear from her eye.

"Thanks, babe. I'll speak to you real soon, I promise. I love you so much. Forever."

He walked away into the throngs of people then looked back and blew her a kiss and Erin walked out of the terminal into the biting cold February evening, wrapped her coat around her and made her way home without him with tears dripping down her cheeks. What was life in Little Hollywood without Taylor Smith?

She was just going to have to learn to live with it.

ACT TWO

The Big Time

Scene One

"Houston, we have a problem." Darryl Smith sat in his conservatory and ran over his director's notes and sighed from the pit of his stomach. "This *Musical Explosion* is slowly falling apart at the seams and time is running against me."

Without Taylor, Darryl's grand anniversary showcase was potentially in ruins and he was sure that Erin was undoubtedly out of his grand plans without her other half. Erin, on top of her talent, beauty and popularity in his productions, always managed to slip in a plug on her show on regional television, which he was confident she would still do, but there was no way she would take part without Taylor. No way.

Plus Darryl was in big financial trouble. The hire of The Community Hall had rocketed since the recent refurbishment, and without the bums on seats Millfield Players could potentially be out a fortune if they were to go ahead with their plans – but if he didn't go ahead,

The Players would fall apart and would lose faith in him forever. Without the appeal of Taylor in a leading role to pull in the audience it was bad. Without Taylor *and* Erin it was potentially catastrophic.

Krystal set a mug of extra-strong coffee down for her husband and slithered into the chair opposite him, hugging her own mug. She watched him scratch his head, calculate figures, re-jig the cast but he was getting nowhere fast. She had tried to help him all morning, but the very sight of her seemed to really irritate him.

"How about if you leave the *Grease* section out of it?" she suggested. "Would that make life easier? I mean, since Taylor can't play the part, who else are we going to find?"

Darryl took a swig from his coffee and almost choked on it as he shook his head vigorously.

"Leave it out? Leave it out! Of course I can't leave it out, woman! *Grease* is a timeless classic and it appeals to all generations plus I have planned half the buckin' show around it. It's one of the highest-grossing movie musicals and one of the most successful film soundtracks in Hollywood history and I can't think of one person who doesn't know the words to 'You're The One That I Want' or 'Go Grease Lightnin'". It would bring the house down. And how could I possibly tell those poor, hopeless teenagers that they won't be able to dress up as Pink Ladies and T-Birds after all? They would be gutted. They would never forgive me."

They both sat in silence, listening to the rain which pelted down on the conservatory ceiling and dripped down the sides so that they could barely see outside. It seemed that Millfield Players had come to a crossroads and that no one, not even Darryl, knew which path to steer them onto.

Krystal really did want to help though.

"Well, I know I may be a bit old, but with the right wig and –"

"That is not helping, Krystal! You cannot pass for a high-school student like Sandy!"

"Well, Olivia Newton John was no spring chicken either when she played the part. I can still hold a note and –"

"It's not happening, Krystal! That is a ridiculous suggestion and anyhow, maybe Erin *will* still take part. With Taylor away it might be just what she needs. We are jumping to conclusions. But we *do* need a new Danny Zuko. And we need him fast."

Krystal pursed her lips and raised her pencil-eyebrows. There really was no need for Darryl to be so abrupt. She was merely trying to help and she would love to squeeze into a pair of rubber leggings and a little black top for the part, but alas her husband didn't see it as an option. You'd have thought he'd love to push his nearest and dearest into the limelight. Chance would be a fine thing . . .

"What about Eugene?" she asked. "He is always lurking in the background and I don't believe you have ever heard him sing."

"*Eugene*! Eugene *Daly*?" Darryl was spitting now. "Really, you are making things worse with your pathetic ideas! My blood pressure is rising, I just know it. I can feel it. Don't you have any *constructive* advice to offer?"

Krystal didn't. She thought it would be nice to give someone like Eugene a chance. Granted, he was no

Taylor or John Travolta but he was so dedicated and was always shoved aside till he was invisible or else stuck backstage if Darryl could get away with it. He always gave the best parts to the same people every year, in and out. In fact, when it come to casting, Darryl treated Krystal with about as much respect as he did Eugene and she knew that if Darryl had his way, she wouldn't even feature in the productions at all. He preferred her at his beck and call as his bloody slave and one year he even forgot to put her name in the programme! How insulting! He handpicked his favourites all the time and he never auditioned. Never. The words "fair" or "deserved" or "audition" didn't exist in Darryl Smith's vocabulary . . .

"Oh my God, I've got the answer!" said Krystal and she jumped up from her chair in excitement. "No, this time I really do!"

"Oh Lord spare me!" said Darryl without lifting his head from his paperwork.

"Really! We can hold auditions, like real auditions where we publicly advertise for someone to play the part and see who comes forward.

"Auditions?" He dropped his pen and eyeballed her.

"Yes! You never know who we might find. Maybe . . . yeah, maybe that guy who runs the coffee shop in town has a singing voice – you know, the really good-looking guy with –"

"Millfield Players do *not* hold auditions, Krystal! It's The Director's choice. It's an inner circle. We do not need every Tom, Dick or Harry thinking they can mix with our elite group. They don't call this place Little Hollywood for nothing, you know. People have to *earn* their place on our stage!"

Krystal sat back down on her chair but her eyes were still dancing with excitement.

"Well, if it's good enough for Simon Cowell … *You* are the Simon of Millfield. You would still have the authority as Artistic Director to pick and choose who you give the part to and who you don't. We could have a judging panel, just like the real thing, and it would be great publicity for the show. Ah, come on! You have to admit this is the answer! It has to be!"

Darryl scratched his chin and stared out at the flowing rain. Could it possibly work? Would people actually come forward? He hated to admit it but perhaps Krystal was right. Maybe it was time to widen the net a bit, to open The Players up and introduce some new blood – perhaps even from further afield? He would never admit it to Krystal but she might have just given him a lifeline with her idea. He would sleep on it. Yes, he would and then he would come up with a way of pretending it was his idea all along.

Erin poured herself a glass of wine and felt her heart beat faster as the rich red liquid glugged into the round glass. She licked her lips and held it to her mouth and felt her pulse quicken as the wine flowed through her body and into her bloodstream, giving her the kick she needed to make it through the night.

She had managed to get through the weekend by visiting her mum and gran more often than she had done in months and she even called her friend Georgie who she hadn't spoken to in over a year. Georgie lived in Galway and was married with kids to a man twice her age and was treated like a lady of the manor. They had fun on the phone, catching up on days gone by and it had passed the evening nicely but now Erin couldn't think of anything else to do but sit down in front of the soaps with a glass of red for company.

She longed to speak to Taylor but it was noon over in LA and he had meetings all day. He promised to call her when he had a break and she was determined not to make him feel bad by constantly calling him for no real reason apart from wanting to hear his voice. She flicked on the television and curled her feet under her, careful not to spill her wine. She had sat the bottle on the floor where it would be within easy reach.

At times she found herself watching out for Taylor coming into the room or making his way down the stairs, and she would jump to hide the evidence of her drinking, but then she would remember that she was all by herself now and she could drink her way into oblivion if she so chose to. But even that didn't fill the gap that Taylor had left behind. The house was so empty.

Home was a place to feel contentment and a place for laughter and where you felt comforted and at your best. But Erin had no sense of home any more. She felt cold and alone and she was not used to her own company – home never felt like this.

She had taken to sleeping on his side of the bed and would change into an old checked shirt he used for doing odd jobs around her house when she found she missed him so much she needed to feel him near her. And when she got it really bad, she would listen to old voicemail messages from him on her phone and play them on repeat just to heal the pain of her loneliness without him.

The theme music of *EastEnders* played on the television and Erin found she was relaxing somewhat as the warmth of the red wine worked its magic. Ordinarily she loved a Monday evening in front of the box and she reminded herself that she was lucky to have such comforts around her and a late-night phone call to look forward to.

Her doorbell rang and she froze, checked the clock and set her wineglass down on the floor. She rarely had weeknight visitors and a chill ran over her. Was something wrong? She felt alone and afraid and vulnerable and then surprised when she saw Darryl Smith standing on her doorstep.

"Darryl! Is it Taylor? Is everything okay?" Neither Darryl nor Krystal had ever darkened the door of Erin's house before despite Darryl's promises to visit since his son moved in a few months ago. Erin felt bile rise to her throat with fear.

"No, no, it's not Taylor. I would like a quick work with you, if you have the time. It's about The Players. I need some advice."

Erin gulped. Advice? This was strange. Darryl Smith gave advice, he never asked for it.

"Okay, of course. Come on in and I'll put the kettle on," she said and she stepped aside to let Taylor's father into her home for the very first time.

She noticed how he took in his surroundings as he made his way through the hallway and into the kitchen which sat to the back of the house. It was thoroughly modern, with solid cherry wood set against stark white tile and stainless-steel accessories. A small selection of photos sat on a block shelf on the white walls and only a vase of cerise orchids gave the room its minimal splash of colour.

Darryl took a seat and Erin filled the kettle, still wondering what she had done to deserve the honour. Taylor would laugh if he saw her now, making tea for his father on a Monday evening without him to rescue her or to keep the conversation going. Erin had always felt awkward around Taylor's parents, especially Krystal, and this was probably the first time she would be in Darryl's company alone. The water flushed into the kettle over the silence between them and Erin prayed for conversation to come their way.

"So, have you spoken to Taylor much?" asked Darryl. "I'm sure he is never off the phone."

Erin brightened at the sound of Taylor's name and the opportunity to talk about him to someone who would miss him as much as she would, not to mention that Darryl's question broke the uncomfortable silence at last.

"Yeah, of course. He has settled in well. He said the hotel is comfortable and that LA is amazing, just as he had imagined. I'm happy if he is happy," she said.

"That's a healthy way to look at it," said Darryl. "I still can't quite take it in that my son is going to be on the big screen. Don't get me wrong, I am proud of both my boys and Taylor's television career was always steady, but this is just something else."

Erin watched as Darryl's eyes crinkled up with joy as he spoke and she set down a tray in front of him, delighted that she hadn't eaten the remainder of the Toffee Pops she had bought at The Corner Shop on her way back from work. She had been so tempted and

Darryl was lucky to have caught her before there was nothing in her biscuit tin but crumbs.

"It is so exciting," she said, pouring steaming hot tea into two cups. "I can't wait to hear what Malibu Beach is like and what the studios are like, not to mention what Sandra Bullock is like in real life. It's amazing, it really is."

Darryl shifted uncomfortably and Erin reckoned he was about to cut to the chase. She had absolutely no illusion that this was a social visit. Darryl and Krystal had never thought she was good enough for the legendary Taylor so they were hardly likely to take her under their wing at this stage of the game. If anything, they were probably praying that he would have a well-publicised fling with a beach bunny to get her off side.

"Erin," said Darryl, twiddling his thumbs as he spoke. "I'm in a bit of a pickle with the show now that Taylor has gone. Look, I know that you only take part now in The Players because of loyalty to Taylor and I just want to say that I hope we haven't lost you too from the group, now that he is gone."

Erin gulped back a swig of her tea and thought of her delicious bottle of wine which sat all alone in the living room.

"Em . . . well, to be perfectly honest, Mr Smith –"

"Please, call me Darryl. I hate formality. It makes me even more nervous that I am at the minute."

Nervous? Darryl Smith? Well, if he was telling the truth, then there was a first time for everything. Darryl Smith was normally as nervous as Katie Price in a room full of hot-blooded men. It was hardly likely . . .

"Okay, Darryl then. To be honest, I've barely had

time to think about this year's show and, yes, I have been taking part because it was something Taylor and I could do together. But I also take part out of loyalty to my community. My grandmother *was* one of the founder members of The Players."

Huh, she thought. Did Darryl Smith honestly think that his family were a dynasty reigning over Millfield's Community Theatre?

"Oh, and I totally respect that. Look, let's not get off on the wrong foot. I'm here in the hope that you will take on the role of Sandy, that's all. If you need a day or two to think about it, then that's fine but quite frankly if you can't do it, I may need to . . . I may need to . . . I may need to admit to Krystal that she is right and that we will have to hold auditions."

Erin thought she was going to burst into laughter. Auditions? In Millfield? That was totally unheard of and against the traditions of the group but she had to admit it was long overdue that they introduced some new faces. There was only so long that The Players could survive on the talent they had – as good as they were. But could she give Krystal the pleasure? Could she hell . . .

"I'll let you know tomorrow," she said and lifted a Toffee Pop biscuit from the plate that sat between them like a net on a tennis court. "Let me sleep on it and I assure you I will let you know if you need to audition for a new Sandy or not."

Darryl's face changed pink again and he stood up without finishing his tea. He straightened his trademark pastel jumper which hung around his neck by the sleeves and fixed his navy blazer.

"Wonderful," he said. "I cannot ask for anything

more than that. Sorry for disturbing you on this cold, frosty evening and thanks for the tea."

"Oh, that's okay. Could have been worse. Could have been the TV Licence man or worse, the bailiffs. Thanks for calling, Darryl."

She walked him to the doorstep where she stood with her arms folded, huddling back from the cool night air.

"I look forward to hearing from you," said Darryl and he pressed a button on his car keys which flashed the lights on his shiny silver Mercedes. "Don't leave me hanging too long!"

Erin laughed. "Oh, I meant to ask," she called out, her breath visible against the black sky. "Who is playing Taylor's role? You know, who will I be partnered with if I agree to take part? Who will be my new Danny Zuko?"

Darryl paused.

"Why, Eugene Daly of course," he said and he opened the car door as Erin's face fell. He looked back at her and quickly put her out of her misery. "I'm kidding! Believe me, I'm kidding. Well, sort of."

He zoomed off and Erin walked back into the house and closed the door, itching to get back into her red-wine zone and to think if she could really take part in the annual show without Taylor. But in her heart she already knew the answer, and Darryl Smith was not going to like it.

SCENE TWO

Erin awoke at the sound of her alarm and already she hated herself.

Her mouth felt like an Arab's sandal, her head gave an all too familiar throb and she could almost taste the red-wine stains that were glued to her lips.

She crawled out of bed and stumbled to the bathroom where she stood under the shower and urged all this to be a dream. It's not that she had declared herself to be on the wagon but she had made a promise not to over-consume on week nights for the sake of her job and her reputation, not to mention her very sanity. She was so disappointed in her lack of control and discipline and she prayed she wouldn't be caught out by Ryan The Producer who was now her new best friend on a daily basis.

"Fancy lunch – my shout?" he had asked her the day before. "It's the least I can do after the fantastic job you made of Friday's show."

Erin was thrilled with the suggestion. Apart from the fact that Ryan The Producer was as tight as a duck's ass when it came to matters of a financial nature, he had never, ever taken any of the team out to lunch on a one to one basis. This was truly a privilege and honour and just what Erin needed on her first day back to work with life "sans Taylor".

They had spent well over an hour in Giraffe on Stranmillis Road and Erin was pleasantly surprised at how easy the conversation flowed. Soon, business talk fell to the wayside and they chatted easily, covering all sorts of topics, from days at university (after they realised they'd both lived on the same street), to a surprising shared love of music and even the same taste in food when they ordered exactly the same dish. Erin told him of her love for her home village and of some of the characters she knew and adored, and those who made her life a misery at the very sight of them and he found some of her anecdotes quite hilarious and refreshing in comparison to his own life at the moment.

"I feel for her, I really do," he said when he spoke of his wife and how difficult things were at home since the new baby came along. "I know she has her hands full during the day and that I sometimes come home in foul form when all she wants is a helping hand. It feels like we are living on two different time zones, on two different planets almost."

Erin picked through the remainder of her Pesto Chicken and listened to him with sympathy.

"To be honest, I never was one for having children and now I'm afraid it might be showing. It's horrible, Erin, but I feel as if they are Melanie's children and not mine. God, I must sound like a monster!"

Erin looked into his sad eyes and knew there was no way that Ryan The Producer was a monster. He was a few years younger than she was – twenty-seven at the most – and he had worked his way up ferociously to be producer at *It's Your Friday* and she felt genuinely sorry for him. There was no way she would feel up to being in charge of a pet gerbil at her age, never mind two squealing infants. No, he wasn't a monster at all. He was saying what many others in his position were perhaps afraid to say and she respected him for that.

"My best friend has twin daughters," she told him, "and I love them dearly but I don't see all of that as part of my life for quite a while. This is a big lifestyle change for you and perhaps not one you had in your five-year plan, but it has happened and your bond with your daughters will grow. Don't beat yourself up over it. I think you're being too hard on yourself."

Ryan looked relieved at his confession and how it had been met with some sort of empathy. Erin understood that he could never admit at home that he felt that way and she could see a new spring in his step when they walked back to the television studios.

"Never mind the lack of sleep," she joked as they made their way into the offices. "Babies don't come with an instruction manual. It's not everyone who is cut out to turn into 'Parent of the Year' overnight."

Later that afternoon, Erin had been at her desk, up to her neck in a news piece on the latest political stance on policing (yawn!) as she had been asked to step in to read the evening news bulletin, when an email message popped up on her desktop.

"Thanks for chat today," it read. "Feel like a weight off

my shoulders. Ever considered counselling, lol? Trust you understand it was in confidence. Enjoyed the company. RTP."

Erin sat with her hand over her mouth at his signature, then composed herself in case he was watching from his office for her reaction. RTP! As in Ryan The Producer! She wasn't sure if it was a nudge at how she insisted on giving him his full title, or if he genuinely was nerdy enough to sign off as that on his own bat.

Nonetheless, she had most definitely seen another side to RTP and now, with her bloodshot eyes and her pale, blotchy skin and her bedraggled mindset, she was hoping she wouldn't see the Big Bad Boss come out on him again.

Fucking red wine!

"You'll never guess what," said Eugene Daly to his sister in a hurried phone call from his perch on the back of his bin lorry. He was on "runner" duty today and he hated it. He'd much rather be in the driver's seat but his Tuesday partner never let him win the toss.

"You'll have to speak up," said Sorcha. "I can't hear a word you are saying as bloody usual."

Tuesday was Sorcha's day off and she was still in her pyjamas and it irritated her that she couldn't hear her brother above the machinery in the background, yet he persisted on making calls to her at every flaming turnaround.

"Can you hear me now?" yelled Eugene.

Sorcha held the phone out from her ear. Yes, she could hear him now. He could wake the dead when he yelled like that in his girly high pitched voice.

"Darryl Smith was at Erin O'Brien's house last night. He begged her to take part in the next show. It's the talk of the village and everyone is on tenterhooks in case she says no, but Krystal is raging because she thinks he should have open auditions for the part."

"Who told you this?" asked Sorcha as she flicked through her tatty old school yearbook and traced a heart with her finger around Taylor Smith's pen-picture.

"Krystal, of course! She's been texting me flat out since our little tête-à-tête in the bar the other night and has made me privy to all the inner-circle secrets. Like, what does Erin O'Brien have that you don't have, Sorcha? Why can't he give the main part to you for a change?"

"I'll tell you what she has that I don't have," said Sorcha. "She has her own TV programme, she has a figure and a face that make men go 'gaga' and most of all, she has Taylor fucking Smith. Thanks for reminding me, brother!"

She hung up the phone and bit her lip to fight off tears as she stared at her photo collection of Taylor. She was heartbroken at his departure and was totally disillusioned about taking part in the new Players production. Amateur dramatics had never been her first love – to be honest, she preferred a kick-about on the football field when no one was around but in Millfield ladies' football was yet to take a leap into the twenty-first century and she would be called a dyke if she as much as held a football in her hand, never mind kicked a few points over the bar on the Gaelic pitch. She would give rugby a go too, given half the chance, and even though she could down a pint of Guinness as quick as the next man she knew in her heart that she was "all woman" and all she needed was to find a good man. And that man was Taylor Smith. No one else would do.

She remembered the very first day she saw Taylor Smith as if it was yesterday. It was the summer of 1990 and she was a nervous first year at the nearby college in her navy-blue uniform and white socks pulled up to her knees. He had jumped on the bus outside The Butcher's in the village with a confidence that Sorcha had never seen before and she nudged her twin brother so hard at the sight of him that Eugene still claimed to have the bruise to show for it.

Of course, Taylor never even acknowledged her existence back then no matter how many times she waited for him at the bus stop, or when she made sure she walked along the same corridors when she knew he was going to class, and one day she even dropped her tray in the canteen right in front of his eyes but instead of helping her (as was the plan, obviously) it was Eugene who came to her rescue. Taylor had jumped up to her aid and her heart soared with glee, but Eugene insisted that it was his duty and Taylor left her side and went back to the "cool corner" with the rest of the beautiful people. She hadn't spoken to Eugene for months afterwards. In fact, she may have been physically violent with him for being so bloody thick, if she recalled correctly.

And then she found out that he was involved in The Millfield Players and she knew she had found her ticket to moving closer to his heart. She went to the library and read up on all things dramatic – from classics like Shakespeare to modern Irish greats and she even paid attention in English literature when they were studying

Brian Friel's *Philadelphia, Here I Come*. She took a greater interest in drama and bagged a role in the school panto (as an Ugly Sister, but it was still a part) and eventually she picked up the courage to watch her first Millfield Players production. She bought a single ticket – not wanting to risk taking Eugene in case of embarrassment – and sat in the front row, gawping as Taylor took to the stage in a play called *The Field* where he played the role of Tadhg, the slow-witted son of the protagonist Bull McCabe.

Taylor was outstanding in the role and when he got a standing ovation, Sorcha thought she was going to burst with pride as she applauded him from her pole position right under his eye level.

From that day on, she knew that as long as Taylor could be found on stage, then she would continue to feed her obsession, even though nothing about the theatre came naturally to her. She learned where the "wings" were, what a "tech rehearsal" was, the difference in a lighting rig and a lighting plot, how to mark out centre stage, the difference in stage left and stage right – until the point where she was a walking dictionary of technical terms.

But it wasn't until she was in her twenties that she finally plucked up the courage to join The Millfield Players. She had heard it was a clique to be reckoned with and she had been warned by her cynical mother (a self-confessed "blow-in" to Millfield) that she would never be welcomed. Her heart pounded that cold February evening when she turned up at The Community Centre in a bid to impress Darryl Smith and when he approached her with a quizzical look on his face and a clipboard in his hand, Sorcha almost had cold feet.

"I'm . . . I'm Sorcha Daly," she had muttered, kicking herself for not appearing more confident. "I'm a keen dramatist and would love to be involved in your next production. I know all about the theatre. *Everything* there is to know. I have studied plays, monologues, musicals, technical terms. I know all my playwrights from A to Z, I have memorised the lyrics of all of Lloyd Webber's collection. I know about front of house, back stage, box office . . ."

Daryl had stared back at her and tried to get a word in and she still cringed at the memory of her ranting and raving and how he eventually folded his arms and let her talk so much she almost got herself in a spin. In fact she could swear that he was looking at his watch on occasion.

". . . so, basically, I feel that it's time I put my name forward. I'll do anything, I'll sweep the stage, I'll sell programmes, I'll make tea. I heard that a lot of the greats started off at the bottom, not that I'm saying that Millfield is the bottom or anything or that I even *want* to be one of the greats but I'm ready and willing and I'm all yours and here's my card."

She handed Darryl a home-made business card with her name, address and number and then before he had a chance to respond, she turned away and ran home as fast as she could and waited for days and days for him to give her a "callback".

But he never did.

In fact, Sorcha never heard from him until a few months later when she was working as a trainee on the nearby *Gazette* newspaper. She had been working on a story about a tractor pile-up on the Blackstock Road and her heart jumped into her mouth when she heard his voice. Alas, he wasn't looking for her in the capacity she had initially hoped. Yet, she still believed it was fate that he called when he did.

"Good morning, Darryl Smith here, Artistic Director of Millfield Players, the 'cream of community theatre' as once quoted in *The Belfast Telegraph*. I'd like you to run some editorial on my, I mean, *our* forthcoming production, please. Who am I speaking to?"

"Em, this is . . . this is Sorcha, Mr Smith," she stammered. "It's me, *Sorcha*!"

"Sorcha? Who? Sorry, do I know you?"

"Sorcha Daly! I spoke to you a while back. I live just outside Millfield and I gave you my card once because I have read up on all things theatrical and I'm ready and willing and –"

"Ah ha!" he had said. "Miss Daly! Of course, of course, how could I possibly not recognise your voice? Didn't I get back to you before now?"

"No, no, you didn't. I waited and waited but –"

"My mistake, my mistake. And I didn't know you worked on *The Gazette*!" He sighed a sigh that said "silly me", then continued. "Why don't you come and see me again, Sorcha? I may have a role for you in The Players after all. We are rehearsing tonight at seven thirty at The Community Centre 'stroke' Theatre. I'd love to see you there."

Sorcha had beamed at the invitation and despite Cynical Mother telling her as she gulped down her dinner that evening that Darryl Smith was just using her for her access to column inches in *The Gazette*, she had set off to rehearsals that night and was ever since a "stalwart" (by her own definition, mind) of The Millfield Players – and she had even managed to have so much fun with Taylor that she was now more in love with him than ever. She'd even dragged Eugene along and although he rarely got as much as a "hello" from Darryl of any of the other Players (apart from Agnes who loved everyone of course) he had stuck in there and enjoyed every moment of life as an am-dram type.

But now, as Sorcha sat in her bedroom staring at old programmes of plays gone by and press clippings of Taylor from days gone by, she feared her days at Millfield were coming to an end. Without Taylor's involvement in this year's production, it all felt a bit worthless really to be giving up her spare time to attend rehearsals when she could be . . . when she could be . . . well, she didn't really have *anything* else to do but that wasn't the point.

It wasn't as if anyone would notice if she didn't show up to rehearsals, now that she thought of it – 'stalwart' and all as she might be. Darryl paid her attention only when he wanted something and Krystal looked at her as if she was shit on her stiletto sole but this year she would show them that Sorcha Daly was a force to be reckoned with. This year, she would make them all see how much they needed her in the drama group. She might not have the appeal of Erin O'Brien or the youth of those teenagers who had wormed their way in just because he needed a few "crowd scenes" – but Sorcha Daly *did* now have control over what went into *The Gazette* since she had been appointed sub editor a number of months ago.

Oh yes, she could play hard to get too and if Darryl Smith wanted her, well then he would just have to come and beg her . . . just as he did with that stuck-up cow O'Brien.

SCENE THREE

Erin tiptoed past Ryan The Producer's office safely and checked her appearance in the bathroom near the admin section of the studios. Her face was still a bit bumpy and when she looked closely at her eyes there was no denying her state of mind and body. And why the hell did she wear black? It should be a rule that hungover people are not allowed to wear black – it drains the face. Or red – it can make you look flushed if you get a sweat attack. She fixed her hair behind her ears and thanked God it wasn't Friday. At least today she wasn't on air. If today was Friday she would be terrified of what Ryan The Producer might do. There was no way he would put her on live television looking like a wasted wreck and, even today, despite their new-found friendship and bonding over a lunch session, he might still feel pressured to give her the heave-ho if anyone caught on that she was reeking of booze and could barely string a sentence together. She sprayed some breath-freshener and an extra squirt of perfume and the combination of mint and flowers made her gag a little, so she waited until she was totally composed before heading to face the firing squad. She fixed her (black) jacket and (black) top over her (black) skirt and made for the bathroom door, to be met face on with Aimee from Entertainment who was her biggest, and probably her most realistic, competitor in the entire building. Great.

"Hey, Erin," she said in her cutesy baby voice. "Oh. Who died?"

Erin looked down at the smaller girl with her dinky little turquoise top and her white-blonde tumbling curls and her pink lipstick and she felt like Morticia from *The Addams Family*. 'Who died?' Was Aimee taking the piss?

"Em, well, it was my great-aunt," she said and waited for the other girl's reaction.

"Aw," said Aimee with a deep look of concern. "That is just like, so sad."

My God, she believes me, thought Erin.

"Is the funeral today?" Aimee went on. "Gosh, you must be so upset. Look at your eyes, you poor thing. You look like you've been crying for days!"

"I know, it's been a hard few days," said Erin, internally praying for forgiveness and promising to say a decade of the Rosary as penance. And then praying that Aimee would get a sudden rush of the runs to make her get out of her face. "She was old though. Very old."

"Yes, but sometimes," said Aimee with a tear in her beautiful green eyes, "sometimes the longer you have them the harder it is to let go."

Erin searched for an excuse to get rid of the Bambi-eyed mourner for her nonexistent dead great-aunt. She couldn't think of anything.

"Thanks, Aimee," she said, pushing past her and holding her vampire breath in until she reached the door and was at a safe distance to speak. "I'd better just keep my chin up and get on with my work. It's what she would have wanted."

"Well, if there's anything I can do. Anything at all, you know to just call on me. I'll keep an eye on you for the rest of the day to make sure you're okay."

"Thanks again, Aimee," said Erin, finally making her way out onto the corridor "That's very kind of you. Too kind, really."

Erin felt like a right rotten old liar. This was going to be a very long day and she hadn't even faced Ryan The Producer yet. What the hell had she let herself in for now?

"Mum, there's someone at the door," said Geri O'Brien but Agnes was too engrossed in her daily Sudoku to even hear her daughter call. Geri turned down the gas on the cooker and gave her pot of home-made vegetable soup a quick stir, then made her way to the front door to see who their unexpected midday caller was. You just never knew who would call at Number 5 Millfield Square these days. Agnes had a reputation of counselling everyone from locals to strays who got great warmth from her no-nonsense advice, her sympathetic ear and the fact that her cupboards where always full of comfort food – from biscuits and cakes to heart-warming Irish stew or, like today, delicious homemade soup.

Geri fixed her apron, flicked her hair and opened the door to find a rather dishevelled Darryl Smith at the door. He perked up when he saw Geri and she smirked when she saw that old twinkle in his eye. Darryl really was an old fox when it came to the ladies and he could charm the birds from the trees if the notion took him. Other times, he could be a right pain in the backside.

"Darryl, come in," said Geri, holding the door open. "Mum's in the sitting room. Mum! It's Darryl."

"Well, send him in," said Agnes and she gave a hearty chuckle. "To what do we owe this honour on this fine Tuesday afternoon?"

They made their way into the cosy sitting room where Agnes sat in her armchair, dressed in glamorous green with matching eye-shadow, her silver hair coiffed into a neat "set". Everyone loved calling with Agnes O'Brien and she never turned anyone away from her door. There was something about the home she shared with her daughter (and until recent years with her granddaughter Erin) that drew people in and made them feel safe and at home. The sitting room of the modest terraced house had a sheepskin rug on the floor and a marble fireplace which always had a roaring fire in its hearth and on the small glass coffee-table that sat on the rug, you were sure to find enough copies of *Ireland's Own* to keep you reading for a fortnight. And subtly, amongst the collection of family photos was a stunning portrait of a young Agnes in an elegant pose wearing a sash saying '*Miss Northern Ireland 1965*' and wearing an evening gown that would still pass as fashionable today.

"Agnes, hi – I mean, good afternoon," said Darryl and he took a seat on a soft pink armchair. "Sorry to disturb you. Sudoku, is it?"

Agnes took off her glasses and set her number game and pen to the side and clasped her hands on her lap.

"It is," she said. "I heard it keeps the old brain in gear and at my age every little helps."

Darryl guffawed. "My, my, Agnes, you could give any of those young girls a run for their money. Sure don't they say life begins at sixty now. Sixty is the new forty."

"They do? Well, that's good enough for me," laughed Agnes and she called to Geri to put the kettle on, knowing of course that her daughter would already have a tray full of goodies on its way.

"I've been to see Erin," said Darryl as Geri, right on cue, came in with a pot of tea and freshly baked butterfly buns on a floral tray.

"Erin? Why? Is everything okay? Is it Taylor?" said Geri, the tray wobbling under her nervous reaction. She was a constant panicker who always feared the worst in any situation.

"No, no, my boy is fine. Mingling with celebrities in Hollywood is hardly a chore, Geri love. No, I have been trying to gently convince Erin to stick with us at The Players this year. I have a horrible feeling she will pack it all in because Taylor isn't involved and, if that is the case, then I'm left with no leading lady as well as no leading man. I wonder can you work your magic and make sure she helps us out?"

Geri poured the tea and let Agnes do the talking. Agnes always did have more to say anyhow and it was much more likely that, if Erin was to be spoken with, it was her grandmother she would listen to.

"I'd be more concerned about filling Taylor's role," said Agnes. "Erin, I can work on, but what on earth are we to do without Taylor? I have to admit it has caused me the odd sleepless night but I think I may have an answer."

"Really?" said Darryl. "Well, let me having it. And I'm delighted with your confidence over Erin."

"Erin might at first say no, but she is like a lost soul without that boy and The Players is all there is to do around here, unless she wants to join the darts team!" Agnes laughed at the thought of her glamorous daughter throwing darts with the lads down the pub. "No, I was thinking that we should do a campaign to recruit more members, since it's our anniversary year, and with Taylor gone it makes even more sense. We need a new leading man. We're going to have to –"

"Audition?" said Geri with her hand on her chest. "But we never audition! I thought it was an unwritten rule that we only go on recommendation and . . . oh gosh, I don't know, Mum. I really don't know. It could all go terribly wrong."

Agnes threw up her eyes and leaned forward in her chair. "I have been with The Players every single step of the way, since our very first and very modest production back in the seventies and I know when it is time to move on. I won't take no for an answer. In fact, I'll get on the phone now to that design place in town to do us up some nice posters and we'll get this show on the road. We need a new leading man and we have no time to waste. Leave Erin to me, Darryl. That will not be a problem."

Erin kept her head low in the office and hid behind her computer, taking the odd sip from a bottle of flat Lucozade to help her keep her energies up. She was doing well so far, and on any sighting of the Milky Bar Kid, she would duck to the floor in search of an imaginary pen or pencil or hair-clip or whatever –

anything to make sure he didn't see her and frogmarch her to his office for some more Producer-to-Presenter bonding. Aimee was another problem, hovering around and bringing her cups of coffee with a forlorn look on her face and every time Erin glanced up over her computer station she could see the Blonde One, her head tilted and her big doe-eyes staring in her direction.

She opened her email and checked her Facebook to see if she could get any distraction from her hangover/mourning act and her mood lifted when she saw that Taylor was online. She checked the time. It was just after three in the afternoon which meant it was just after eight in LA so Taylor must be up and ready for the day ahead. She wrote him an instant message as quickly as her fingers could type for fear that he might log off again.

Good morning, honey. You're up early!

Hey, Princess, was hoping you might "pop" into my inbox.

Erin glanced around to be sure that no one could see her. Being on Facebook during working hours was the equivalent of calling the boss a wanker to his face. Not a good idea in any line of business.

How are you coping with all the sun and sea and celebrity? Miss me?

More and more and more . . . xxx

I have just told my colleague my great-aunt died. Don't ask . . .

Ah, yes. How sad about dear old Muriel. Silly old bat she was, though.

Thanks for the name. Was struggling. How did she die?

Pneumonia.

Of course. My brain isn't working. I have temporary memory loss due to shock. Aimee staring at me now again. Feeling v claustrophobic. Think I might punch her soon.

Refrain. Violence in workplace is sackable offence. Pretend you are crying.

Okay. I am. Shit, what did you say that for? She's coming over. Gotta go, bye xxx.

Aimee put her hand on Erin's shoulder and set a square box of pastel-coloured tissues in front of her. She smelt as sweet as she looked, whereas Erin felt like a right old bag lady in comparison. She would never, ever let herself down like this again. It was a miracle that her new best friend Ryan hadn't been lurking around but he had been in conference calls all morning and was out over lunch on a shoot with the show's roving reporter, so she had managed to avoid him all day so far.

"Ryan sends his heartfelt wishes," said Aimee, with her dainty hand still on Erin's shoulder. "I spoke to him earlier just after my mid-morning weather broadcast and he was so upset. He said that one of Friday's guests has cancelled so he will probably not see you today as he is trying to find a replacement, but he asked me to give you this. I got it for him on my lunch break." She handed Erin an envelope.

Erin opened it with the biggest rush of guilt she had felt in a long, long time. The card was a typical Aimee choice with pink flowers on a white background and in silver swirly writing it said 'In Deepest Sympathy' and when she opened it, tiny rose-shaped confetti fell out. She was surprised it didn't play the tune of In Requiem too.

"*So sorry to hear of your loss,*" it said in Aimee's handwriting. "*From Ryan and all the team. xxx.*"

"We didn't know the name of your aunt," whispered Aimee. "I'm sorry if it's a little impersonal without her name."

Erin nodded. She didn't know what to say. "It's . . . it's very touching. Very."

"What was her name?" asked Aimee. "I'm ordering a Mass Card today."

Jesus! This girl was unstoppable! She had a hangover, for Christ sake. How the hell did a hangover turn into a fucking wake!

"Er, her name was Muriel."

"O'Brien?" said Aimee.

"Yes. Yes, O'Brien." She really needed to shake this off.

"And, if you don't mind me asking," said Aimee in an even lower, more hushed tone, "how did she die?"

For God's sake, what was this girl? A bloody Ghost Whisperer!

"Pneumonia," said Erin. "Now, I'd better be off. I promised my mum I'd take her to the wake again this afternoon so please pass on my thanks and apologies to Ryan. You are all too kind."

She lifted her handbag and logged off her computer, then walked out of the offices and into the cool fresh air, feeling better already. She drove home to Millfield without remembering her journey, turned the radio in the car up, then turned it down, then back up again and when she pulled into her driveway her hands shook as she reached for the house key in her handbag. She pushed open the front door, flung her handbag and coat on the stairs and made her way to the kitchen where she poured herself a drink and downed it standing up, leaning on the counter. Then she breathed in so that her chest filled like a helium balloon and let it all out again.

And then she poured another.

Scene Four

Agnes and Geri made their way over to Erin's house, armed with fruit and chocolates and a bottle of her favourite red wine. Geri had made up a hamper with bubble baths and scented soaps and put in a few glossy magazines to go along with their impromptu visit. She loved popping round with little treats for her only daughter and surprising her when she didn't expect it, but this evening she had an ulterior motive behind her parcel of gifts as she was accompanying Agnes on her mission to make sure that Erin stuck to her traditions and took on the leading role with Millfield Players and, therefore, didn't let the side down.

It was a crisp bright evening and they had chosen to walk the short distance to the new housing development that Erin lived in, just off a steep hill on the outskirts of Millfield village. The clear air felt good in their lungs and they had chatted incessantly the entire way, commenting on the way the bright moon made the village's picturesque street even more beautiful and how the bare branches on the trees that lined the small promenade gave the place an almost majestic look.

They approached Erin's driveway, and admired how she managed to keep everything about the house so neat and tidy.

"I can't believe how much Millfield has changed," said Agnes as they shuffled to the door. "All these new houses and new faces are something we never thought we'd see around here. Our little village is really growing up, isn't it?"

"It is," agreed Geri. "To be honest I don't think Erin even knows most of her neighbours in here yet. Everyone keeps themselves to themselves, not like where we grew up on The Square, where everyone knows everyone else's business and visitors are two a penny. I have to say I would find this new lifestyle all a bit strange."

Geri knocked the door of Erin's detached home and waited for her to come to the door. It was just after seven and they had arranged to go and see her at a time when she would be relaxed after work and in the mood for a chat. Besides, it was good to spend time with her when Taylor was away as she was probably feeling the loneliness by now.

"She *is* here," said Agnes. "I can hear the television and there are lights on in the living room."

Geri knocked again. "Perhaps she's on the phone to Taylor?"

The two women took turns to peer through the stained-glass window.

"Oh, I *knew* we should have called her first," said Geri. "I'll go around the back and see if she is in the kitchen."

Geri handed the gifts to her mother and walked around the back of the house. She opened the gate that led to the rear garden and ventured towards the patio doors, then she stopped in horror at the sight she saw inside.

"Erin!" she said, knocking the door with a vengeance. "Erin, this is your mother! Let me in now!"

Geri was disgusted and shocked at the same time. What on earth had come over Erin? She sat slumped across her kitchen table, two empty bottles of wine by her side and a cigarette smouldering in an ashtray. Erin didn't even smoke. She hated smoking as much as she hated being on her own in that big empty house without Taylor. She had to get her attention but Erin was out cold. Geri banged on the glass door, fearing her knuckles might bleed as she called in vain for her darling girl to come around. She ran across the back garden to the boiler house where she knew Erin kept a spare key and when she opened the wooden door, her hands went up to her face when she came across a huge stash of empty bottles of wine, with another pile of still-to-be-opened bottles by its side, visible only slightly under a large sheet as if they were supposed to be hidden from view. She thought of the bottle of wine she had brought as a gift and her stomach turned sour as she realised that Erin's drinking habits might be a whole lot more than recreational. It was seven o'clock in the evening and Erin was already drunk. Geri felt like she was going to cry.

"Are you sure you don't want me to stay too?" asked Agnes, wringing her hands in concern. "I really don't mind and I'm sure you need the company."

They had made their way into the house with the spare key and found to their immense relief that Erin was conscious and able to respond, though utterly drunk. They moved her into her bed, undressing her as much as they could.

"No, Mum," said Geri. "You go on home to your own bed and I can look after things here. Now that Erin is in bed, I can rest easy and I probably would only keep you awake with all my fussing in and out to check on her all night. I'll call you a taxi to take you home."

Later that evening, with Agnes safely gone, Geri O'Brien sat down on her daughter's sofa and flicked through the television channels but nothing caught the attention of her wandering mind. She tortured herself with the idea that Erin's heavy drinking was something she should have noticed much earlier on. How many nights had her daughter been in such a state? How did Taylor not notice, and if he did, why didn't he say or do something about it?

Geri was angry and frightened and she didn't know how to react or cope with this new reality that had greeted her like a slap on the face. She considered that it might have been a one-off moment of loneliness but then when she thought of the mountain of bottles that were so evidently not supposed to be seen she felt a shiver run up her spine and she realised that this could be quite serious.

A few magazines sat on Erin's coffee table and she tried to concentrate on their content but again, her mind raced and the sense of fear would not go away. She hated feeling out of control. It didn't sit well with her and, yes, she was known to panic and take flight at the slightest hiccup but no one in their right mind would rest easy if they even contemplated their own child getting themselves into such a state on their own.

Geri stood up from the sofa and was just on her way to check on her daughter when Erin's landline telephone rang. She answered it and was delighted to hear Taylor's voice on the other end of the line.

"Taylor, love, it's Geri. How are you getting on?"

"Oh, hi, Geri! Gosh, this place is amazing. I am having such a ball right now and I'm being treated so well. Everyone is on a real high and we start shooting in just a few days and last night we had this huge party on the beach where all the cast got to know each other and the Director is like the coolest guy you could ever meet. He is so down to earth – in fact everyone is. It's even better than I thought it would be. Amazing. So how is life in Little Hollywood? All set for the big production?"

Geri swallowed hard. Taylor sounded on top of the world and she didn't want to burst his bubble with misery and worry, but she had to test his awareness of Erin's boozy habit.

"Em, well, not as smoothly as normal but that's not for you to worry about. The Players might be a very different set-up when you get back." She managed a giggle at the thought of a hoard of new faces treading the boards at the centre. "I – I just came round to visit Erin and, well, I won't beat about the bush, Taylor. I think she may have been drinking a little too much and I think she has been hiding it from us. Tell me I'm wrong. Please tell me I have got this all wrong and that I am making a fuss over nothing."

Taylor didn't answer at first and Geri held her hand to her throbbing forehead as she awaited his response.

"Taylor? Taylor, say something?"

"Oh God," he said, his voice cracking. "I should have faced up to this knowing it could only get worse."

"So you knew?" Geri knew her voice told him she was horrified. "Why didn't you at least tell me?"

"I – I suppose I was hoping it might settle down. I dunno, look, Geri, you know Erin as well as me. She doesn't like to be told what to do and I was afraid if I highlighted that I thought she was drinking too much then I feared she might have got even worse with the knowledge that I'd noticed. How did you find out? Is she okay? I only texted her today and she seemed in great form."

Geri walked up the stairs as she spoke to Taylor on the portable phone. Her voice dropped into a whisper.

"She probably doesn't want to annoy you with anything since you're over there, and neither do I, Taylor. Look, the most important thing now is that we are both aware of it and it's up to me right now to keep an eye on things and to see if I can gently bring it up with her so that she can let me help her."

She peeped into the bedroom where Erin lay in a stupor, and it saddened her heart to think that she might have been battling with alcohol for some time now. How was she ever going to approach it? What would she say to Erin the next morning? She had no idea. She was too heartbroken to even think straight.

Erin awoke with that old familiar feeling of dread in the pit of her stomach and a wave of panic hit her when she realised she had absolutely no memory of when or how she got to bed. She sat up straight and checked the clock on her bedside locker, then lay back down again and breathed in and out, in and out, trying to encourage the fears to sweep by her in the knowledge that she hadn't slept in for work.

It was just after six thirty and Erin normally awoke by the sound of her alarm at seven, so she turned on her side and closed her eyes but her rapid train of thought was keeping her awake. She knew she was still in her clothes, well partially, from the day before and she stank of cigarette smoke and the fumes of alcohol in the room were suffocating. She longed for the energy to get up and open a window but her body felt like a dead weight, sunken into the bed and she didn't have the energy to move it.

When her alarm rang at seven, its ringtone was met with the sound of her mobile phone and she answered it, trying to sound as chirpy as she possibly could.

"Hey, Mum. I'm just getting up. How are you?"

"I'm downstairs, Erin. I'm here, in your house."

Oh shit. Oh *shit*! She couldn't remember a thing. Had her mother come to visit last night? Jesus! What the hell was going on? Perhaps she should make light of it all. Maybe she had called round on her way to . . . yes, on her way to . . . fuck, where would her mother be going at this time in the morning? She didn't even open the hairdressing salon till nine and that was only if she had an appointment booked in. This was a nightmare.

"Well, can you give me five minutes? I just want to have a quick shower and then I'll be straight down. Put the kettle on."

Erin walked into her en-suite and caught her reflection in the mirror. What the hell had she become?

She looked and felt pathetic – dark circles of black makeup on a pale, blotchy face which felt like it was on fire, eyes stinging in deep sockets and a bedraggled look that was alien to the person she used to be. And now her mother was on her trail. Maybe this was the wake-up call she had been waiting for.

She stood under the jets of the shower and let the hot steam cleanse her soul and the fresh smell of lavender shower-gel invigorate her senses. She massaged fruity shampoo into her hair, letting the softness of the suds massage her scalp and then she held her face under the water to rinse the grit from her face and the heavy burden of guilt that lay on her shoulders. There was no point lying to her mother. Her days of lying and hiding from her problems were over now.

Erin entered the kitchen still in her bathrobe with a fluffy towel wrapped around her head. She glanced at the clock on the wall, already knowing that she was going to be late for work but she had a feeling that she was not going to get away without talking this through with her mum. Geri was at table. Her face was taut but her eyes looked sad and forlorn. Erin pulled out a chair and sat. She poured a coffee from the percolator, too ashamed to meet her mother's gaze.

"How long, Erin?" said Geri softly. "How long has this been going on?"

Erin bit her lip and stared at the table as feelings of relief and bungs of pressure mounted through her already fragile body. How long? She couldn't really say. She didn't know.

"A . . . a while," she mumbled. "I'm so sorry, Mum.

113

I don't like to let you down like this but I can't control it any more. I'm set to ruin everything I have because of the urge to have one bloody drink and then another and then another. I can't sleep without it, I can't sit down and watch TV any more without a glass in my hand and I get irritable without it. Please tell me Taylor doesn't know any of this?"

"He knows," said Geri. "Of course he knows but he loves you and he said he was dropping hints but you were ignoring him and he was so afraid that he might make matters worse."

"And Gran?" she asked.

Her mother nodded. "Yes. She was with me when I came here yesterday evening."

"Oh God, no." Erin hid her face in her hands.

"I sent her home after we had put you to bed but I stayed the night to keep an eye on you."

It was a nightmare of even worse proportions than Erin had imagined.

"Erin, love, are you worried about anything? Are you unhappy? Tell me . . ."

"It's . . . it's so hard to explain, Mum. I know I have nothing to be miserable about and sometimes I'm on top of the world and then other times I feel like I've fallen into this big black hole and the only way to get out of it is to have a drink so I can forget. But lately I've been aware of how this is taking over my entire life – my job, my relationship with Taylor, my interest in life in general and now I've let you and Gran down. I am a disaster. What a disaster!"

"Erin, don't say things like that!" said Geri. "Your gran is on your side. We *all* are but you have to get your

114

life back under control again because you want to, not because we have 'found you out' or because you don't want to let us down. You have to want to stop this, Erin. That is the only way."

Erin stood up and dug her hands into the pockets of the robe.

"I do want to," she said. "I really do. Look, thanks for staying last night and for looking out for me, even though I probably don't deserve it. I really have to get ready for work, Mum, but thanks for helping me live up to my demons at last. If you hadn't called when you did, I would probably continue to breeze around in this fog until it got me into real trouble."

Geri smiled at her beautiful girl. "Give Taylor a call, eh? He was so worried about you when he rang last night. He misses you terribly, you know."

"I know. And I miss him too. More than he will ever know."

SCENE FIVE

"Hold the ladder, for Christ's sake," said Krystal. "I'd love to know where and how I drew the short straw in this bloody arrangement!"

Darryl was distracted by a flashy car which had pulled in alongside The Bakery across the street. It was a black, new-model Mercedes and the driver was definitely not a local, and he had stopped to look at a poster – *their* poster which Darryl had just left in only minutes ago – in the window.

"I'll be back in a sec," said Darryl and he left Krystal hanging on for dear life halfway up a telegraph pole where she was pasting a new "*Auditions*" poster.

"Excuse me! Excuse me, sir!" said Darryl, scurrying across The Square in quest of the stranger's attention. "Are you interested in auditions? I'm the director of –"

His pathway was blocked by the whirr of a tractor which totally scuppered his vision and left a spray of slurry in its wake. The stranger in the Mercedes was now starting up his engine and by the time Darryl dodged the mess on the road, he was gone.

"*Shit!*" he roared and he marched back to where Krystal was gripping the sides of the ladder as if her life depended on it (which it more or less did considering the height she was up).

"What on earth are you playing at?" she screamed from her dizzy perch. "Don't you have any consideration for my safety? I'm practically dangling here!"

"I'd love to know who that young man was! Only for that damn tractor I could have cornered him. He looked at the poster. He actually *stopped* to look at it!"

"Darryl! That's what we want people to do, you moron. Now hold this bloomin' thing till I get my two feet back on solid ground. I am a vertigo-sufferer, you know, and this is not helping!"

Darryl reluctantly held the ladder as his wife dismounted and he pursed his lips then tutted in frustration.

"Damn tractors, that's what I say! He looked like he might be exactly what we are after, Krys. That was a near miss, I tell you. A shamefully near miss!"

Krystal felt like slapping her husband. He only ever called her Krys when he wanted to irritate her and by God it was working. She had sacrificed her entire morning to help him plaster every available space and every shop window with auditions posters and not a word of thanks did she get. Oh no, he couldn't even bring himself to acknowledge that this was all her idea, telling her that Agnes O'Brien and that mousey Geri one had came up with exactly the same thing.

"I've an idea," she said, clipping alongside him as he

carried the ladder across the street to the next lamp-post. "Why don't you camp here overnight and anyone who as much as looks at the posters, you can kidnap and threaten them and scare them off because if I saw you coming towards me the way you approached that poor guy, I would have made a quick getaway too. For God's sake, Darryl! Build it and they will come, isn't that the saying? We have set up the auditions, now it's up to people to come. Now, I'm starving. Why don't you treat me to a pub lunch?"

"Pub lunch? Pub lunch? Not a chance, me dearie. I have packed some banana sandwiches and a flask of tea in the car. We still have the neighbouring villages to do. Come on, let's crack on . . ."

Erin was suffering inside more than ever before. On top of all her usual hangover qualities, she also had a huge dollop of guilt on her shoulders, with a heavy dose of mortification and self-hate laid on top of it all for good measure.

She felt her skin crawl and every time she caught a glimpse of herself in a mirror or on a window or even the faint reflection on the screen of her computer monitor, her stomach churned. She didn't deserve to be given so many chances. She was on a one-track path to self-destruction and now that her mother sensed her troubles, she felt like running away and dealing with it all on her own.

"Can I get you a coffee, Erin?" asked Aimee in her little-girl voice. "You look really sad today. Do you want to talk?"

Erin looked up at Aimee's cherub features as she

nibbled like a squirrel on a cereal bar. Erin blinked heavily and shook her head.

"No thanks, Aimee. I'm just tired, that's all. But a coffee would be amazing. You really are too kind."

Aimee returned moments later with a steaming mug of milky coffee and a Kit Kat bar on the side. She left it on Erin's desk and then tiptoed out of her way and Erin sat in wonder as to why Aimee would pay her so much attention in what seemed to be a mood of genuine concern.

She took a sip of the froth that sat on the top of the mug and shivered. Then she glanced around to see if anyone was watching her and she opened her web browser and typed in the word "alcoholism" into the search engine, her heart thumping as she read what the page brought up. She clicked on "alcohol screening quiz" and set about answering the twenty questions the website asked to determine the dependency on alcohol in her everyday life.

Do you lose time from work due to your drinking? *Yes.*

Has drinking ruined your reputation? *Potentially, yes.*

Have you ever suffered memory loss due to drinking? *Hell, yes.*

Do you drink alone? *Yes. Nearly all of the time.*

Oh shit.

Is your drinking affecting your family life? *Well, yes.*

Has your ambition decreased due to your drinking? *Yes.*

Erin did not want to read on any further. She quickly closed down the window and sat with her head in her hands and ignored her mobile phone ringing from her handbag for the fourth time that afternoon. She just couldn't talk to Taylor about this. She didn't want him to think of her as an alcohol-dependent loser. Why should she ruin his life just because she couldn't manage her own?

She finished her coffee and stared at the computer screen, trying in vain to force herself to concentrate on interview questions for the guests on this week's show. They had a gardening feature planned on preparing your back yard for spring and had live music from an Irish soap star turned pop star who was apparently the next Michael Bublé. Normally she would be engrossed in research and up to her eyes with ideas for questions but lately she really couldn't care less. It was as if life had no meaning for her any more.

She lifted her head again and typed in a few keys onto a Word document, with "Gardening Feature" at the top of the page. Now, what would her viewers want to know most about at this time of year? Types of plants of course, when to plant them, how to prepare your garden for new features. Jeff, the series gardener, had prepared an allotment-style patch on the roof garden of the studios and she was overdue a visit to see his progress and normally by this stage of the calendar year she would be out there with him, making sure the area looked bright and inspirational for anyone at home who needed a seasonal boost. She drummed her fingers on the desk – gardening with kids perhaps might be a nice angle; or how about safe gardening for some of the elder viewers?

Soon, she found herself on a flow as the ideas kept coming and her fingers typed faster and faster on the keyboard so that she could barely keep up with the river that was flowing from her brain out onto the computer. She got an unexpected rush from the turn of events and, when she had filled two A4 pages, she printed them off and admired her efforts, then gasped as she noticed the time of day. She had spent over an hour on the feature and it felt so good.

"You seem in a much better mood," said Aimee on her way past Erin's desk, en route to the photocopier with a bundle of papers. She wore a bright-blue hair-band on her tumbling blonde curls and her long fluttery eyelashes reminded Erin of a summertime Minnie Mouse.

"Yeah," Erin said with a light smile. "Yeah, I am thanks. It's good to keep busy, eh?"

"It's the only way to keep your mind off things," said Aimee with a look that was way beyond her years. "This week's programme is shaping up well. I have some info on the soap star I could pass your way this afternoon if you want to let it take shape?"

"That would be great," said Erin. "Thanks, Aimee. You've been a great help to me as always."

On her lunch break, Erin drummed up the courage to call Taylor who had already left two voicemails on her answer phone expressing his need to talk to her. She dialled his number, her hands shaking both from the bitter cold outside the studio and the alcohol dying in her bloodstream. She listened to the international dialling tone and closed her eyes, waiting to hear his voice on the other end of the line.

"Erin! Are you okay? My God, I have been trying to get you for hours!"

Erin nodded as he spoke. "I'm sorry, babe, I've been so stupid. I don't know what I'm doing any more, but I will make this all better, I promise. You don't have to worry."

"I wish I was there with you. I hate to think of you being miserable and alone and drinking so much that it's affecting you so badly. Is there anything I can say or do? Please let me help."

"Really, Taylor I am going to beat this. I've had a surprisingly good morning – never thought I'd get so excited about spring gardening," she laughed. "I just need to keep busy and keep my mind active because I have taken my eye off the ball lately which is why I've ended up drinking so much. Believe me, I will be okay."

Erin could hear Taylor's production team in the background and someone spoke through a loudspeaker over the sounds of machinery and people chatting and laughing loudly. It sounded like a different world to where Erin stood now, outside the television studios on this bitter cold afternoon in Belfast.

"Look, I'm going to have to go real soon," said Taylor. "But I've been thinking . . . and I know you're not that keen, but is there any chance you'd consider taking part in the drama production?"

"No, thanks!"

"Seriously, please think about it. When the show is staged, it will be time for me to come home so the timing is perfect. Plus it means you will have fewer hours alone and it will really take your mind off things to be in such lively company. It will do you good. You know how much fun we have every year."

Erin could sense the desperation in Taylor's voice and she knew he was under pressure to get back on set. She couldn't live with the thought of making him worry about her when he was at the cusp of his career.

"Okay then, but I'm doing it for you and for you

only. Let me tell your dad. I was supposed to get back to him anyhow, so I'll pop in to the bar on my way home and have a chat with him. It will keep my own mother off my back too. You really are a genius, Taylor Smith."

"Yeah, and now I have to go to work with Sandra Bullock. It's a tough old game here in Hollywood."

They shared a laugh and said their farewells and then Erin made her way back into the warmth of the television studios. She pressed the button on the elevator and straightened her shoulders, determined that she would turn a corner in her life. She would not let negativity get her down. She was much, much stronger than that and she would prove it to anyone, but most of all, she needed to prove it to herself.

SCENE SIX

"Yes! Yes, you fucking beauty!"

John Smith gave a raucous cheer towards the television just as Erin entered The Stage Bar and his enthusiasm made her jump. She put her hand to her chest and made her way to the bar.

"Wow, I don't think I've heard you call me that before, John," she joked. "But if that's how you feel about me, well, you can join the queue . . ."

Her attempt of a joke went straight over John's head as he continued to stare at the plasma screen on the wall without as much as an acknowledgement of Erin's presence.

"Go!" he shouted. "Go on, ye bitch ye! Aw shit! No! Fuck, fuck, no!"

He put his hands up to the sides of his head, then covered his eyes and peeped through his fingers as the race came to an end and his horse came in third place.

"John?"

"Bastard!" he roared, and then he turned his attention to Erin and spoke in his usual mellow tone. "Sorry, Erin. What's up? Glass of red?"

"What? Er, no. No thanks."

Erin was used to John's sporadic outbursts at the television when horseracing was on, but she feared the rather handsome man who sat alone in the corner on his mobile phone wasn't. He was engrossed in conversation but he had to concentrate much more as he competed with John's decibels that would wake the dead.

Erin casually looked around her to take in his actions and her mind went into overdrive. He looked like something from a catalogue, but rougher round the edges and even though she couldn't make out a word he was saying, she could sense his passion in the way he spoke. She couldn't help but stare at him as he talked flamboyantly down the line in what she could hear was an American accent – or was it Canadian? Or Portuguese? She honestly had no idea.

"Who's your man?" she asked John, still unable to take her eyes off him. No matter how much she tried to strain her eyes to look in the other direction, her head bounced back to face where he was sitting as if he had some sort of magnetic force. He wore green army slacks with a white T-shirt that left little to the imagination (especially since it was like Siberia outside) and a navy baseball cap, and his physique was something else! She could see every ripple of hard muscle through his T-shirt and his arms were tanned and toned and not at all like a Millfield regular. She was intrigued.

"No clue," said John, not even looking in the man's direction. "We get the odd stray around here on their way to Derry or Donegal so God knows what his errand is. He's been on the phone since he came in, that's about all I know. And that he has some sort of weird accent shit going on."

Erin shook herself. Whoever this random visitor was didn't really concern her, she remembered, so she turned her attention to John who was dodging her to check the time of tomorrow's racing schedule. Yes, she had important business to attend to in the name of Millfield Players and in the name of her own sanity.

"John, I'm looking for your father actually. Is he around this evening?"

"Huh? Oh, Dad? Sorry, I've no idea where he is. He dragged Mum all over the place this morning putting up posters for those stupid auditions. I mean, auditions in Millfield? I really think this whole drama thing goes to his head from time to time."

Erin glanced back at the stranger who had now finished his phone call and was packing up his belongings. He had a notebook and pen, she noticed, plus a newspaper and an iPod and he packed all into a canvas rucksack and got up from his table. Then he gathered a black biker jacket and a helmet from the side of the booth where he had been sitting. His eyes lifted and met Erin's and he smiled a white beautiful grin, then took off his baseball cap and put it in his bag and Erin gasped when she saw the jet-black dark hair that had been hiding underneath it. She looked away, embarrassed. He had totally caught her staring at him and she felt her cheeks blush. She nervously looked at her watch and twiddled a beer mat to try and look busy but as he walked towards them she felt it hard not to steal a final glance.

"Thanks, mate," said John carelessly as the man walked out of the bar – John was still watching the television. "See y'again."

"Thank you," said the man, and he flashed Erin another smile before he left the bar. Erin felt funny inside. It was like his eyes had bored a hole in her soul and she felt shaken and a little dizzy.

"Wow, whoever he is, he sure has you in a state," said John as he aimed the remote control at the television. "Must remember not to tell Taylor that one!"

Erin gave him a cheeky look to show how petty he was being, but there was no doubt about it. Mr Strange Accent had enough sparks bouncing off his tight, taut body that she felt like she had just been electrocuted.

"So, where will I find Darryl?" she said, breaking out of her fluster. "I need to talk to him about the show. Would he be at The Community Centre? Or at home?"

John shrugged. "I'm not his keeper, Erin, and no one tells me anything round here, but, yeah, that would be a good place to start. One thing's for sure, he's not here helping me anyhow."

Erin threw her eyes up and left the bar, wondering exactly how many dead flies were hanging off John these days. He had as much get up and go as a tortoise and she was unsure if he could even say the word "enthusiasm" to say nothing of show it. He really was a lost cause.

The evening was bright for the time of year and, as she clicked open her car with her keys, she caught sight of Strange Accent again in the distance. He was wrestling with a motorbike on the side of the road and he looked like he was having some sort of trouble.

She got in, started her engine and indicated out of her

parking space slowly, still watching him hunkered on the ground, looking rather dishevelled, his bare arms working with a wrench at the wheel of the bike.

She drove towards him and, before she realised what she was doing, she pulled up alongside him and put the window down on the passenger side of the car. She leaned across and called to him.

"Are you okay? Is there anything I can do to help?"

He looked around and recognised her instantly and Erin noticed how he had a black streak of oil across his tanned face. He got up and leaned on the window.

"Ah, hello!" he said, slightly out of breath. "Is there a garage nearby? I have a flat tyre and I'm new round here so I'm a bit lost really."

His voice was thick and strong like black coffee, and she still couldn't put her finger on his accent which now sounded more broken and definitely European.

"Yes, there is, actually. You're not too far away from one. If you go to the far end of The Square and take a left turn onto Thomas Street, then down to the bottom take right at the lights and . . . oh sod it, I'm crap at directions. Can I give you a lift?"

"Sure. Thanks."

He wiped his hands on an old rag he took from his pocket but Erin didn't have the heart to tell him about the marks on his face. He picked up his gear and shot into the car.

She tried to ignore the fact that she had lifted an absolute stranger from the side of the road and was now driving with him in her car and he was wearing only a T-shirt, yet the heat she could feel from his body was mind-blowing. Yes, she was officially crazy.

"I'm Olivier," he said and extended his hand to hers, then withdrew it with a laugh when he realised he still had traces of oil on his skin. "This is very kind of you."

"I'm Erin," she said, her voice cracking as nerves set in. Jesus, what was she thinking?

"Nice name. Do you live locally?"

She could feel his gaze on the side of her face and the smell of oil and light sweat from him, mixed with pheromones and a hint of musky aftershave, was making it very hard to concentrate on the road. She sat poker-straight in the driver's seat, steering the car like a learner driver, her nose in the air with blind concentration.

"Yes, yes, I do," she said, deciding not to give any of her personal information to this stranger. She was already having palpitations at how risky she was being. The traffic lights came into view and she indicated right. It was not too far now.

"Do I know you from somewhere?" he asked. "You look really, really familiar. I have seen you before, haven't I?"

Erin felt her blood go hot in her veins and her heart pounded so hard she feared he might hear it and sense her fear. Where had he seen her? Oh my God, who the hell was he?

"I . . . I don't see how you could. Em, apart from just now, in the bar. What brings you around here anyhow?"

"I'm *really* sure I have seen your face before, but if you say no, then perhaps I am mistaken. I stay about five miles from here, in Ballyforte, but I travel through Millfield sometimes to meet friends or to pick up my gran from her travels."

"Your gran? Oh. Would I know her?" Erin was

surprised at how, despite her fear, she could still be incredibly curious – or nosey as the case may be. "Everyone knows everyone around here."

"I shouldn't think so," he said and they drove for a few minutes in silence. "She lived in France for a very long time so I doubt you would have come across her. Bernadette Laurent?"

"No, sorry. I can't say I do. That's not exactly a Millfield name!"

"No, no it's not," he laughed. "I'm very sorry to have put you to any inconvenience. You are very nice, Erin. I mean, kind. You are very kind, Erin."

Erin breathed through her nose and kept her eye on the road. The way he said her name was so erotic she felt her whole body sizzle inside. She had to get a grip on this, she had to wise up! This was a complete stranger! She slowed the car down and then stopped when she came to Pat Brannigan's cottage and she gave out a nervous giggle.

"So, this is it," she said. "This is a garage, Millfield style."

"Yeah," he said, peering out the window. He lifted his helmet from his feet. "This looks . . . this interesting."

He matched her laugh and shook his head, then put his hand to the handle on the door.

"Do you want me to wait to make sure he can help you?" asked Erin. "Old Pat works his strange hours and sometimes I'm afraid they don't match up to the outside world. I don't mind the wait."

He looked genuinely surprised and impressed by her generosity and his black eyes were like mirrors as she waited for his reply. She gulped and then looked away as her hormones did a Riverdance that would make Michael Flatley proud.

"Well, once again I am most grateful," he said, "and I would love to say no and that I'll be fine, but I'm afraid if I don't find Pat the mechanic then I may be even more lost than I was in the village. Are you sure you have time?"

"I have time," said Erin and when Olivier got out of her car, she sat in disbelief and silence, wondering what the hell was going on with her now? In just one day she had admitted to having an alcohol problem, acknowledged she had to change her attitude in her work life and had actually made progress, and now she had just befriended a drop-dead gorgeous Frenchman on the side of a road. Life in Little Hollywood was due to get a lot more interesting for Erin O'Brien, whether she wanted it to or not.

The knock on the car window startled her and she turned down the radio and then the window to where Olivier stood shivering in the cold.

"All sorted?"

"Yes, thanks," he said. "Pat is going to take me back to the village with his tools and he'll have a look at the bike and hopefully I'll get back home in time for dinner. Otherwise Gran will be very cross."

His smile was infectious and Erin returned his pleasantry with a smile, then lifted his jacket from the passenger seat and handed it to him through the window.

"You will probably need this," she said. "Irish weather is a bit unpredictable and it *is* February."

"You sure it isn't Christmas?" he asked with a

knowing wink. "I realise now where I've seen you before. On the television, of course. My gran is a big fan of your show."

"Oh," said Erin and she gave a loud laugh. "Oh, I am quite embarrassed about that Christmas glitch. Please don't tell me that is the only episode you have ever watched. I really hope not!"

"No, no of course not. I finish early some Fridays so I have actually watched one or two. It's a nice programme and it was really nice to meet you. And thanks again, Erin."

Erin felt her stomach twist into a knot as she waved him goodbye. She drove out onto the country road and looked into the rear-view mirror to where he stood watching her as she moved away. As soon as she got out of sight, she stopped the car and found her phone. She checked the time and although she knew Taylor would be on set, she just had to hear his voice. Something had happened between her and that French guy and she needed to grab onto a sense of reality, right here, and right now.

SCENE SEVEN

Darryl was delighted to see Erin and even more enthralled when he heard the good news of her commitment to *The Musical Explosion*.

"This is going to be spectacular," he said with gusto. "We just have this hiccup of replacing Taylor but I have a good feeling about these auditions. Tell me, would you by any chance do me the honour of sitting on the panel? It would be great to have someone of your calibre and talent at my side."

Erin was surprisingly touched by Darryl's request and sitting on the panel sounded like great fun, plus she liked how Darryl had commented on her calibre and talent. Even if he was an old charmer.

"I'd love to join you on the panel. Who else have you recruited?"

Darryl let out a deep puff-like sigh and rubbed his tummy. He smelled of cigars and cologne and his normally pale complexion looked rather flushed.

"Oh, Krystal, of course," he said," but she really

thinks she knows more than she actually does. You can be Dannii Minogue to her Sharon Osbourne! Yes, this is all coming together nicely."

Erin laughed with an air of dread. "Apart from the fact that Sharon left *The X Factor* because of Dannii? That's a great comparison, Darryl! I think you may be asking for trouble."

Darryl leaned across and whispered into Erin's ear. "Well, let's hope it mirrors the real thing and she walks too! There is a method to my madness. You know I'd love to replace her with a younger model and that Sorcha Daly one has given me the eye more than once, you know!"

Darryl guffawed but the imagery in Erin's head wasn't healthy. She had this awful flash of Darryl with his white, silky locks and portly belly and Sorcha with her pointy chin getting it on and it just didn't make for peaceful dreams. *Yuk*.

"So, when do we start?" asked Erin. "Do I need to bring anything? Like Evian water for the tables or some flowers to make the place look pretty? What do you think?"

Erin was being funny but Darryl thought she had just solved the world's greatest mystery by making her suggestion.

"That's a marvellous idea!" he said rubbing his hands. "You see, I would never have thought of anything like that. I am so glad I asked you to sit on the panel, no matter what Krystal says."

He walked away with glee and left Erin standing on her own, wondering how on earth she had managed to be talked into this palaver.

The first round of auditions was called for the Friday

evening and Erin found herself looking forward to them more than she could have imagined. She had spoken to Taylor more than normally on the phone every night and he shared her enthusiasm, delighted she seemed in a much better mood.

"Enough about me," she had said the night before while munching on a pizza. She'd had a refreshing shower and applied a layer of tan and in a new pair of cosy pyjamas she felt better than she had in a long time. "Tell me more about how you are living the high life over there. We are all so jealous. Everyone really misses you."

She could feel Taylor's beaming smile as he spoke to her of how he was enjoying his new-found lifestyle.

"Well, Malibu Beach is just something else," he said. "I mean, I've never seen such perfection – everywhere you go it's just full of beautiful people and it's not like real life at all. You go for dinner, you see movie stars, you have breakfast alongside people you've seen in magazines and the weather just makes you jump out of bed knowing that you are going to be working with people at the top of their field. I'm still pinching myself every day."

"That sounds amazing, honey. I am so glad it's all you hoped it would be."

"And more, Erin. It's so much more. I don't take one second of this for granted and I thank God every day for giving me this opportunity. You know what would make it even better though?"

"What?"

She heard him swallow and butterflies danced in her tummy.

"It would be even better if you were here to see it. I

can just imagine your face walking along Rodeo Drive and admiring all the sights around you – the fashion, the glamour, the people, all the absolutely craziness of it all. You would really love it."

"Some day . . ." said Erin, trailing off.

On Friday morning, she twisted her hair through her fingers and watched the world go by outside as she spoke to Taylor on the phone again. This time he had just arrived home from a party and it was four in the morning in LA. Erin felt refreshed and bright and ready for the day ahead, while her handsome boyfriend sounded drunk and giddy on the other end of the line.

"I am so pissed!" he sang. "What a night! What a fucking night! Shit, Erin if you had seen the size of the house we were in. It was like a hotel with huge, huge rooms and the sound system pumped music right throughout the place, even onto the terrace and the poolside and the food they served – not to mention the drink! They had every beer and wine and cocktail imaginable."

Erin loved to hear Taylor in such a happy mood but in this instance she found it difficult to relate to his joviality and drunken high. She had a television show to do today and then the auditions that evening and she had battled the night before with the urge to drink, but was on her own little high of pride now in the knowledge that she had gone to bed and resisted giving in to her overwhelming craving. It had been almost impossible to sleep at first, but she'd read for a while and listened to some soft music and eventually she must have drifted off but she felt so much better for it now. Taylor, she noticed, was not only in a different time zone, but he was also in a different mindset from her life and her problems right now. He hadn't even asked her yet how she was coping.

"And then Jimmy, right, he's the guy who works on sound and he's this big burly Brummie, well, he dived into the pool with his clothes on and before we knew it, half the party were doing the same. And all the time the host was asking everyone if they were having a good time and we were like, yeah!"

Erin watched out her window as a neighbour struggled to put her toddler and a newborn baby into her car, the postman walked past her window whistling in the early springtime sunshine and further down the cul-de-sac a young man was polishing a motorbike, his dark hair glistening in the mid-afternoon light.

It was strange how they all lived so close by but lived completely anonymous lives. Erin's grandmother said it was a sign of the times and the birth of a new Millfield lifestyle, unlike the companionship shared between neighbours in the older parts of the village. Her eyes skirted back to the man with the bike and then she moved closer to the window as he lifted his head and put on his helmet. Was it him? Could it be Olivier?

"Erin? Are you there?"

Taylor's voice sprang her back into reality and she felt guilty – as if staring at this strange man across the close was a form of cheating or betrayal.

"Gosh, yes, I'm sorry, Taylor, I'm here. The pool, yes. Sounds like you had a fantastic night."

"I sure did," said Taylor in a mock American accent. "Well, I guess you're probably trying to get ready for work so I'll let you go and I'll get some sleep. We have to be on set in less than five hours. I love you, Erin."

"I love you too, babe, and maybe someday I'll get to share such fun with you, but for now I have auditions in Little Hollywood to plan for and I get the feeling we might be in for quite a bit of drama on that front too."

Darryl wiped his brow with a towel and looked around The Community Centre. Yes, the room was looking very well. The modest stage to the back was clean and cleared of clutter and the wooden floor, though scored and worn, was as polished as it could be. He had even managed to convince the local playgroup who used the hall on a daily basis to put most of their soft-play facilities and sand-pits and the like into the storeroom on the promise that he would have them back in place for Monday morning, and The Youth Club's football nets had been pushed to the back wall. All he needed now were his fellow judges and he was ready to rock 'n' roll. Oh, and some auditionees too would be nice.

First to arrive was Erin O'Brien who looked more splendid than she had done in a long time. He heard her heels clipping across the floor. She wore a short multi-coloured mini-dress which sat well on her curvaceous hips over thick black tights and long high-heeled boots. Yes, Erin oozed glamour, just like her mother and grandmother before her and Darryl was in no doubt about what his son could see in her as a partner.

"Welcome to our humble theatre," said Darryl with open arms and he air-kissed Erin when she came to greet him. "This is exciting, eh? Now, don't panic, it's early days and Marjorie says that she has received quite a few phone calls this week with wannabe thespians hoping to audition."

Erin gave a beaming smile and took in her surroundings.

"Marjorie?"

"Yes, the priest's housekeeper – you know, Father Bob? Well, she said I could put her number on the posters as well as my own, since this is a parish fundraiser as well as a talent showcase and you know how enthusiastic Marjorie is."

"Oh, of course. Well, you sure have made an effort in this place," she said and Darryl nodded with pride. "I just hope we get plenty of interest after all your hard work. Did *you* get any calls?"

Darryl scratched his chin. "Did I? Yes, I did! Now, let's see . . . well, John called from the bar to say that . . . what did he say again?" He pondered for a moment. "Oh, yes, no, actually he was taking the mick. He called to say that he had a holding room for us to use if we needed it and that the place was swarming with wannabe John Barrowman lookalikes already. I told him to go and empty the bins or change the keg on the Guinness tank and mind his own bloody business."

Erin sniffed a laugh and took a seat at the desk which was laid out with three chairs, three sets of papers, three glasses and a bottle of Evian water each just as she had suggested.

"Well, that's just typical John, isn't it? And did Marjorie say who her callers were? Were they local? Or anyone new?"

Darryl pulled out a chair and sat on it back to front, folding his arms across the top with an enthusiastic wave.

"Yes, she did say. Well, the first one to call was

Gladys from the bakery to say that someone had torn down the poster from her window . . . and your grandmother called to see if she could sit in on the auditions which of course is perfectly fine but then she rang me today and said she would nip on out to bingo instead and . . . now who was the third? There *was* a third . . . Oh, that's right, it was just John again who thought he'd call us between horse races to wish us luck. I tell you, for a boy with no interest or ambition in drama, he does spend a lot of his time trying cause a drama by winding me up!"

Erin's disappointment about the lack of interest in playing her leading man was interrupted by the high-pitched squeal of Krystal who seemed to have run into some danger on her way into the main hall.

"*Darrrryyylll!!!! Come quiiick! Quuuiiiiccckkk!*" Her scream was like a banshee's wail and it echoed in the tiled foyer.

Darryl jumped to his feet, knocking down his chair, and Erin followed him out into the foyer where Krystal sat on the floor clutching her ankle.

"I'm injured, I'm badly injured, Darryl!" she said, rubbing her ankle. "I twisted my ankle! Well, don't just stand there! Help me!"

Darryl pulled her up from the floor and he could hear Erin stifle a snigger behind him – the worst thing was, he totally understood why she was sniggering and was dying to do the same.

"Krystal, those heels are like stork legs," he said, trying to disguise his giddiness. "Why on earth do you insist on wearing stiletto heels that are suitable only for women half your age?"

"It's nothing to do with my heels and you know it!" spat Krystal as she rose from the ground, smoothing down her mini-skirt and fixing her freshly blow-dried hair. "It was a fucking tennis ball!"

She held up a squashed tennis ball and Erin walked swiftly back into the main hall, unable to contain her laughter for any longer.

"This place is a death trap, a bloody death trap!" said Krystal. "Those youth club brats leave everything lying at their flipping backsides. If it's not tennis balls to trip you up, it's shuttlecocks that get stuck in your heel. They have no consideration for fashion at all. None! I would claim only I know The Parish hasn't a penny!"

Darryl held her as she hobbled inside and slowly took her seat at the right-hand side of the table, where Erin had been sitting previously. Rather than rock the boat, Erin sat on the other side and let Darryl take prime position in the centre. He cleared his throat, and shuffled his papers, then spoke with authority to his colleagues.

"Now, ladies," he said in a deep voice, "first of all, can we agree that this process is to be taken seriously and will be carried out fair and square? We must not use prejudice, bias or family reasons to select who is most suitable to replace Taylor in the musical, so no matter how well you know any of our clients today, we must treat them all as equal. And on that note, I'd like you to raise your glass of Evian water in a toast to an eventful and fruitful first audition session of The Millfield Players."

Erin smiled as she raised her glass but Krystal was too busy rubbing her ankle to listen to her husband. Despite not having smoked in almost six weeks, she was now in desperate need for a cigarette and the very sound of Darryl's voice was getting up her nose.

"So, when a candidate enters, I will lead proceedings," he continued, "with an introduction of The Panel and then we will all make a note of the person's name and contact details. After that, I will invite them to sing and we will each mark them with a score out of five, then discreetly place our decision in this box." He lifted a small shoebox with a slit cut in the top from the floor and placed it on the table. "However, do not put your own name to any of the sheets of paper. We are in this as a team, not as individuals, and it is only when the votes are being totalled by Marjorie who should have been here by now, that we will hear who received the most marks and who therefore should be granted a call back for a second round tomorrow. All clear?"

"All clear," said Erin checking her watch. *Coronation Street* would be starting soon and the idea of settling down for the evening with a glass of wine and a Chinese take-away was becoming more and more appealing, especially as Krystal's moans and groans grew louder as each minute passed.

"*Yoo hoo!*" Marjorie Bannon peeped her head round the door. "Sorry I'm late but Father Bob insisted on potato waffles for dinner and I had to step out to the shops. Shall I put the kettle on or where do you want me?"

"Oh, I'd kill for a cuppa," said Krystal. "And can you see if there is any ice in the freezer for my ankle? I stood on a tennis ball and sprained my ankle but no one seems to care."

Darryl threw up his arms and rolled his eyes at his wife. "You are such a drama queen!"

"Oh, no one could ever steal *your* crown, honey bunch! I'd like to see you go down on your knees for something more than your bedtime prayers!"

"I'll get the tea then," said Marjorie and she left them to it.

By seven forty-five, Erin was seriously considering calling it a day with the auditions. They'd had only one interested party so far and the end result of that was quite embarrassing to say the least.

"Your name, please?" said Darryl.

"My *what*?"

"Your name, please."

"Aw, come off it. What the hell is this? You know who I am. Aunt Krystal? Erin?"

Darryl signalled at the others not to speak. He put on his frameless glasses and squinted at the kid who was deeply humiliated in front of "The Panel" who all knew him since he was in nappies. He pulled at his sweatshirt and fiddled with his belt, clearly uncomfortable with the process, not to mention how Darryl was insistent on making it even more difficult for him.

"We have a procedure here, Stephen, and we must stick to it."

"There, you just said my name!" said the boy. "Why do you need me to tell you what you already know? I came here to sing, not take part in a kindergarten lesson!"

"Stephen, I don't like your approach and I'm sure your mother didn't send you here armed with so much teenage attitude and testosterone. Now, let's go through the registration procedure so that we have all the necessary information at hand when it comes to choosing the right candidate to represent us in this theatre!"

"Theatre? It's a fucking community hall," said Stephen, pointing at the football nets in the corner and the offending tennis ball that sat on the judge's table. "My ma said your head was up your arse, Uncle Darryl, but I didn't believe her. Stuff your theatre and stuff your stupid auditions!"

And that was that. Stephen had left in a puff of teenage angst and there had not been another entrant since.

By eight o'clock Krystal had begun to desperately search through her handbag, her heavy breathing grating on Darryl's nerves more and more as the clock ticked by and the hall stood empty. He was devastated. All he wanted to fill was one part!

"What are you staring at me like that for?" said Krystal to her husband.

"Because I can't believe I ever listened to you in the first place," he snarled at his wife Krystal, who had by now found a stray cigarette at the bottom of her handbag and as a result her breathing began to steady. "Bloody auditions. I should have known!"

"Excuse me!" squealed Krystal. "But what the hell are you blaming me for? When did this shambles become my fault?"

"It was *your* idea!"

"It was *my* idea until *you* decided it was Agnes O'Brien's idea and now that it's a flop you've decided all of a sudden that it's *my* idea again? How bloody typical! I'm away for a smoke!"

Darryl drummed his fingers on the table as he listened to the uneven beat of the injured Krystal's stilettos across the floor and Erin lifted her handbag from the side of her chair.

"I'm so sorry it didn't work out, Darryl," she said. "Maybe Millfield isn't ready for auditions after all."

She got up and hesitated at the sight of Darryl staring at the blank sheets of paper in front of him, totally deflated and disheartened by the entire process.

"Come on, Darryl. Let's call it a night."

Slowly shaking his head in remorse, Darryl packed up his belongings and walked with Erin towards the door.

"I even had it mentioned on the radio and the posters cost a fortune," he mumbled. Maybe my work here is done. Maybe Millfield Players needs a new leader – someone with their finger on the pulse, a more creative eye, new ideas and new vitality. Now that Taylor has made his mark on the drama world, perhaps that is my sign to 'hang up my dancing shoes' so to speak."

"No. Don't say that," said Erin and she put her hand on Darryl's shoulder as they walked. "You are the driving force behind this group. Without people like you, there would *be* no Players so don't ever think your work here is unappreciated. There could be lots of reasons why we didn't get a good turn-out this evening. It's a nippy cold night and, well, I hate to say it but maybe Millfield Players is a victim of its own success."

"How do you mean?"

"Well, we have a bit of a reputation for being cliquey and a little bit, well, smarter than the average bear when it comes to all our awards for drama. Perhaps outsiders find it just a little bit daunting to come along here and bare their souls only to be rejected by 'her off the telly' or 'that Darryl Smith fella whose son is in Hollywood'."

Darryl stopped walking and put his hands on his hips, then let out a deep sigh that oozed pride.

"You are probably right, Erin," he said, rubbing his forehead. "'*Onwards and upwards*', isn't that what they say?"

"They do."

"'Now for Plan B' . . . then Plan C and so on and so forth . . ."

"That's the right attitude."

"'*The show must go on*' . . . em, can you think of any other sayings?"

"Er . . ." Erin thought for a moment. "'*It ain't over till the fat lady sings*'?"

"And I couldn't have said it better myself!" said a voice from the doorway where Marjorie Bannon stood with her porky hands on her pinched-in waist and her feet standing wide apart. "It ain't over till the fat lady sings and I have not yet sung my song. Darryl, this fine gentleman wants to know if he is too late to audition and I told him we would wait all night for him if he wanted."

She chuckled aloud, then stood back and in walked Olivier – the handsome French stranger – with his biker helmet under his arm and a rolled-up scroll of papers in his other hand.

"Sorry I am so late. Bike trouble . . . again."

He shrugged his shoulders and his dark hair flicked over his black eyes. Erin thought she might faint. Just for a second. But she was okay now.

SCENE EIGHT

"Olivier?"

"Ah, Erin! I have to say I didn't expect to see you here but this is a very nice surprise."

"Ooooh! Do you two know each other?" asked Marjorie, her huge eyes rounded like saucers and a smile curled on her lips. "*Va va voom!*"

"Well, no, not really," said Erin as the sparks bounced off the walls around them. "We . . . not really . . . I . . . I gave Olivier directions to the garage. He had trouble with a flat tyre."

"Flat tyre?" said Darryl, puffing out his chest and extending a hand. "I have trouble with flat tyres too from time to time. Darryl Smith, Artistic Director of Millfield Players. Welcome to Little Hollywood."

Olivier smirked and darted his eyes from Darryl to Erin as he shook the older man's hand.

"I'm Olivier Laurent. Glad to meet you. I ride my grandfather's Harley to get me about and I have to say it is very old, but a very classy machine. Erin kindly showed me to the garage. It was a very cool garage."

"I took him to Pat's," whispered Erin and they all shared a laugh at the idea of Pat's tin shed being called a garage in comparison to some of the fancy, all singin' all dancin' one-stop shops available a few miles out of the village.

"It was good. He fixed me up," laughed Olivier. "Pat is a cool guy. A bit hard to understand, but cool."

"So," said Darryl. "You are here to audition. How wonderful! *Dansez-vous, Olivier? Chantez-vous?*"

Darryl said Olivier's name in a perfectly polished French accent. He spoke with his hands in an "*ooo la la*" way and Erin noticed him bounce on and off his tiptoes as he did so, like Olivier had released an inner passion for all things Français!

"*Oui, je chante et je danse et j'ai chorégraphié à Paris au Moulin Rouge depuis cinq ans avant que je suis venu en Irlande avec ma grand-mère.*"

Olivier spoke his native language at lightning speed and Erin thought she was going to explode with laughter at the look on Darryl flushed face.

"*Er . . . oui,*" he mumbled. "English is fine. Just fine."

"Aah!" said Olivier with a mesmerising smile. He shrugged and then reverted to English. "Yes, I do sing and dance. In fact I was a choreographer in the Moulin Rouge in Paris for five years before I came here to live with my grandmother."

Erin thought Darryl had died and gone to heaven by the look on his face. Marjorie was grinning from ear to ear and she had been joined by Krystal in the doorway who looked like she'd had a mini-stroke.

"So how did you find us?" asked Darryl with a slight stammer. "How did you get from Paris to, well, Millfield? This is almost too good to be true."

Krystal breezed into the room and commanded attention.

"How about we take a seat and get more acquainted?" she asked, having suddenly come back to life after her little trauma. She tried to walk normally across the floor in her spindly heels with her sore ankle but her efforts were as graceful as an elephant and her face was flushed with excitement at the fresh meat that had taken her fancy in the form of this young French actor.

They sat around the table, Krystal, Darryl and Erin on one side and Olivier on the other. He laid out some CVs and photos of him in action in some hot poses from his days in the Moulin Rouge – an array of black and white imagery of his toned physique in athletic movements mixed with carnival-coloured portraits. They were classy, they were professional and, most of all, they were damn sexy to boot.

"Oh my word, you can surely move," said Krystal, and Erin was sure she was dribbling saliva down her chin.

"I have danced since I was four years old. It's in my blood," said Olivier in a rich, lilting accent that made everyone take notice. "My mother, Dominique, was a ballerina so I had no choice. She taught me to dance as soon as she could encourage my father to let me. He always said she wanted a girl but got me instead."

"And . . . so you want to dance for us?" asked Darryl in a guffaw.

"I'd love to! Dance, sing, build sets, make tea. Anything, really. I would just like to be involved in any shape or form. If you will have me?"

"Why, this is . . . this is amazing . . . this is even more than I could ever have wished for," said Darryl and he looked at the two women by his side for agreement but they were lost in Olivier's smouldering presence as was Marjorie who had lingered at the door shaking her head with disbelief at this glorious vision who had entered their lives so unexpectedly.

"You really want to be involved in our humble little show?" asked Krystal. "Why?"

"Yes, I do, Madame," said Olivier. "You see, my grandmother is unwell and as I have a few months off work I thought I would come and stay with her. I arrived here only weeks ago and already I miss the theatre with its magic and warmth and atmosphere and when my grandmother noticed my withdrawal sufferings, she told me about your group. She says she went to school with one of your founder members, Agnes O'Brien . . ."

"Agnes O'Brien? Yes! That's my gran!" said Erin, realising that she sounded overly excited at the connection. She had really wanted to play it cool but it was almost impossible in the presence of such talent and power. "*Ahem*, that's my gran. Agnes O'Brien."

"How wonderful," said Olivier and he leaned back on his chair and crossed his arms behind his neck. "Small world, eh? We must reacquaint them. My grandmother loves to have company."

Erin gasped inwardly at the way Olivier looked at her. His eyes, she noticed, were extremely intense and when he spoke he made her feel like she was the only person in the room. She wanted to ask if it was him she had seen in her housing development earlier today but that would be just downright nosey. No, she must contain herself. She had to get a grip. She could investigate that later.

"Yes . . . yes, that would be nice," she said and fixed her skirt over her knees. "It would be nice to reacquaint them. So, Darryl, what do you think? Is Olivier our leading man? Is he 'the one that you want', pardon the pun?"

Darryl also composed himself and sat up straight in his chair, then cleared his throat. "*Ahem*," he said. "I do believe we have found our leading man. Olivier, I would be delighted to offer you a part in our show if it was in your interest, as I presume it is because why else would you be here if you weren't interested in taking part in the first place . . ."

"Oh for God's sake, Darryl, spit it out!" said Krystal. "Olivier, darling, you are very welcome to Millfield Players. Here is our rehearsal schedule and on behalf of our panel here, can I say it has been a pleasure to meet you and I hope you enjoy our humble efforts at entertaining the locals. It's a far cry from Moulin Rouge, but it's Little Hollywood to us."

Olivier's eyes darted from Krystal to Erin and back and forth and Erin sensed that he found the Smiths as overwhelming as the rest of the community did from time to time. She gave him a wink and then stood up and he seemed relieved that she had given him an exit plan.

"I look forward to working with you all," he said, gathering his photos and papers from the table. He rolled them back and placed an elastic band around them, then picked up his helmet from the floor. "I should listen to my grandmother more often. She always gives me the best advice."

He reached across to shake Krystal's hand and when he lifted it and kissed it, Erin sincerely thought she had wet herself with the way she crossed her legs in response, or else a kiss from Olivier Laurent was enough to do the whole business for an old cougar like Krystal. Darryl wasn't any more composed and when Olivier took his hand to give it a manly shake, Darryl closed his eyes and clasped his other hand on top of Olivier's, as if he was thanking the Lord for sending him such divinity. But instead of kissing Erin goodbye, he took a few steps back and blew her a kiss that hit her in the face so hard she thought she might fall over.

"*À bientôt*," he said to her and then he was gone.

"What did he say to you? What did that mean?" asked Krystal in a flurry of jealousy and utter nosiness. "If he is giving you secret code words, Miss O'Brien, my son will not be happy. If Taylor thought –"

"It means 'see you later', Krystal!" said Erin. "Calm your bloody well-jets, would you? And for the record, I'm not the one getting their knickers in a twist over him, am I? It's time you had a look in the mirror."

Erin marched out into the evening air and stopped on the top of the steps of the community hall to find her car keys. She longed now for a long, refreshing glass of wine to finish off her day and she knew that unless a miracle occurred, there was no way she was going to be able to fight off her urge.

"Lost something?"

She looked up and saw Olivier by the roadside on his bike watching her and her stomach gave a leap. She pushed her hair back from her face and shook her head.

"No, no, I'm fine. Just the usual search for my car keys. I did find the kitchen sink though."

"The kitchen sink?" he asked, puzzled. "I don't understand."

"It's an old saying. *'Everything but the kitchen sink . . .'*"

"Ah! Perhaps my English isn't as good as I thought it was. Sometimes I catch your humour here, sometimes it goes whoosh!"

He pushed his hand over his head and smiled widely, showing a row of white teeth that would make any dentist proud.

"Your English, I can tell you, is perfect," said Erin. "It's a darn sight better than my French anyhow. Ah, here, I found them. *À bientôt*, Olivier! See you at rehearsals."

"*Oui*," he whispered and as Erin walked away from him, across the short forecourt she wondered why he was still waiting. She could feel his gaze burn into her and she prayed she didn't trip and fall on her way to the car, or that her skirt wasn't tucked into her knickers or that she had a visible panty line. She glanced back and he started the engine on the bike but his helmet was hooked on the side of the handlebar. Yes, he was definitely waiting for something.

"Erin?" he called.

Erin stopped dead, then slowly turned to face him again. The way he said her name sent shivers down her spine. His accent made butterflies have a party in her stomach and her face flushed.

"Yes?"

His eyes crinkled and he stroked the back of his neck as he spoke, showing how nervous he was.

"I was wondering . . ." he closed his eyes, "would you like to . . . oh, I am so bad at this. I was wondering if you ..."

"Erin!"

Erin looked back to see Krystal bloody Smith hobbling down the three steps that led to the forecourt, her high-pitched voice more grating than usual. "Erin! I'm going to have to beg a ride home with you! Darryl is staying behind with Marjorie and there is no way I can walk up the road on my ankle. I'll have to see Bridie Nugent about the cure. It's badly sprained. Very badly."

Erin glanced from Olivier to the pathetic sight of Krystal in her short skirt and goose-pimpled fake-tanned legs and she let out a sigh.

"I'm sorry, Olivier," she mumbled. "I have to, you know . . ."

"It's okay," said Olivier, with a wink at Erin. "Some other time perhaps."

"Some other time for what, Erin? What exactly are you two planning?"

Erin shook her head but Olivier spoke before she had a chance to.

"Mrs Smith, you just ruined my moment. I was just about to ask the lovely Erin if she would like to have dinner with me tonight. I would offer you a lift but I would never risk a lady's safety when she has no helmet. I'm a safety kind of guy."

Erin's eyes widened. Oh no! Shit! What the hell did he have to say that for? About dinner?

"That's very good to know, Olivier," she mumbled.

154

"That you're a safety guy and think of things like helmets and the like, but you should also explain that the helmet, I mean, the dinner offer was merely a thank-you. Because I took you to the garage, remember? You were just trying to show thanks, that's all. It's a French thing, isn't it? Doesn't mean it's like a date or anything."

"Oh, is that right?" spat Krystal, then a smirk grew on her face and she turned to Olivier, her voice changing to a seductive tone. "Well, I'm not sure if the lovely Erin told you or not, but the lovely Erin is very much attached to my son who is in Hollywood at the moment, so she is unavailable, you could say."

"Hollywood?"

"Yes, Hollywood. But don't worry, Erin. Mummy won't tell her precious boy that while he is making a name for himself in Movieland, his girlfriend is making out with Mister Moulin Rouge!"

"I . . . I didn't even . . ." Erin wanted to slap her face. This was right up her street!

"I am sorry. I did not mean to cause trouble," said Olivier. "I didn't know. This is not Erin's fault. Erin, I apologise. I just wanted to say thank you for helping me to the garage, that is all. I meant no harm."

"You weren't to know," said Erin, and she glared at Krystal. "And that's very kind of you, Olivier. Come on, Krystal. I'll take you home."

"Only because I am injured."

"Whatever. Good night, Olivier."

"Good night, ladies," said the Frenchman and he mouthed "Sorry" to Erin as they walked away.

She took one final glance back at him and when she saw him place his helmet on over his dark hair and start up the

155

engine on his bike, she got a feeling inside she knew she really shouldn't. This was not what she needed right now.

Erin slammed the front door behind her and threw her coat and bag on the stairs. The phone was ringing but she ignored it and went straight to the kitchen where she found a bottle of wine she had carefully hidden under the sink a few days ago, then she corked it and poured a small glassful.

"It's only a small glass," she said inwardly. "Only a small glass to relax and it's Friday and everyone has a glass of wine on a Friday night. Everybody does. It's perfectly normal and why should I be any different? Even if I am talking to myself as a matter of convincing . . . yeah, who am I explaining myself to? Fuck it! I can drink a glass of wine on a Friday night if I want to and no one can stop me. No one will know."

She took it into the living room and sat on the sofa, curling her feet under her, then flicked on the television. This is civilised, she thought. I can control this. I can sip this as I watch television and I am not doing anything wrong.

The telephone rang again and she answered this time, hoping it was Taylor so that she could explain the Olivier story, or non-story as it was, to him before his mother put her viper-like twist on the tale. But no, it was Kizzy who seemed in distress.

"Is Kizzy in a tizzy?" she joked, taking a second sip of her wine. See, this was normal. This was fine. Glass of wine in hand, television on in corner for company and a conversation with her best friend on the telephone. Perfectly normal. Perfect Friday night.

"As usual," said Kizzy in a whisper. "I swear, Erin. If I don't get out of this house soon I am going to spontaneously combust. I have a bad dose of cabin fever, the kids have a dose of the diarrhoea and I am so bored I am almost rocking back and forth here. How did I end up like this? Why can't I settle myself and enjoy my responsibilities instead of feeling like I will burst with boredom?"

Erin relaxed back in the armchair, her phone nestled under her chin and her glass of wine resting on her thigh.

"Where's Dermot?" she asked.

"Dermot who?" said Kizzy. "Oh, let me think . . . that's right. I used to know someone by that name. Yes, I married him. Is that the one you mean?"

"Oh dear . . ."

"Never marry," said Kizzy in a hurried whisper. "I know there are days where I felt smug and all settled while you are still acting like a teenager and I know we argued about who had the best lifestyle, but believe me, you have. *Yours* is better. Don't do it, Erin. Not even if he takes you to the bloody banks of Venice or gets down on his knees on the Champs Élysées, say no. Do you hear? No way. That lazy fucker doesn't deserve me and I'm learning it all too late."

Erin breathed in and waited for a gap in the one-way conversation. This was so unlike Kizzy to bad mouth 'My Dermot' as he was fondly known. It was 'My Dermot' says this, 'My Dermot never does that', and Erin's favourite, 'My Dermot the Ledge'. (Teen talk for 'legend' for those who don't know. She heard it on *Hollyoaks*.)

Now, poor Dermot had been relegated to "that lazy fucker" and he wasn't even there to defend himself.

"So where is he?"

"Where is he? Where is he? He joined a fucking darts team, that's where he is. Like, *darts*! Who the hell plays darts nowadays? Poker clubs, yes, I hear they're all the rage, or the odd game of five-a-side soccer at The Community Centre – I could live with that, but no. That lazy fuck couldn't be bothered lifting his arse any further than from here down to the pub and the only exercise he gets is by using his arms to lift a pint and throw a dart, lift a pint and throw a dart. Fuck me!"

Erin felt a giggle and she walked to the kitchen on auto-pilot and refilled her glass. Sure, one more wouldn't do any harm.

"Is he at The Stage or did he venture further?" she asked.

"Nah, he's at The Stage probably talking to that fucking grump John Smith – no offence."

"None taken."

"It's his bloody fault for starting up a darts team. I mean, it's not as if Dermot Parks doesn't spend enough time in that bar. He can't walk past it these days without going in for a flutter on the horses or for a hot whiskey to take the edge off the man flu he is all of a sudden suffering, or 'cos his fucking ma says he looks pale so he needs a pint of Guinness to give him a bit of iron. Like, hasn't he heard of a good feed of liver and onions? An iron bar round his arse that's what he needs!"

Erin sipped her wine. "Where are the kids?"

"They're in bed sleeping sound. At least that's one good thing, I suppose. God but I need to get my head cleared."

"Can you get a baby-sitter?"

"Suppose I could try."

"Right, well get your ass over here and we'll have a girly night with *X Box Lips* and you can pick up a curry on the way."

Erin heard Kizzy give a high-pitched intake of breath with delight.

"You're an angel," said Kizzy. "I'll call our Michelle right now to come and sit with the kids. She owes me for doing her spray tan the other day. If she says no, I'll murder her."

"Excellent! It's a date."

SCENE NINE

Sorcha Daly put on her pyjamas and sat on her bed. She could hear her parents argue downstairs but so far she hadn't made out what the topic under dispute was on this occasion. It could be anything really, from serious issues such as money and the lack of it, to trivial time-wasting topics like whose turn it was to close the curtains. It had been the same all her life. Ever since she was a tiny child she would hear muffled sounds at night from the sitting room as she battled with sleep and the muffles would turn into heated debates which would mount to raging arguments and would always, always end up in tears. Sorcha's tears, mostly.

Sometimes at night her brother would make his way into her bedroom and they would sit together in silence as the war between their parents broke out from downstairs. When they were very small, Sorcha would sing to Eugene to try to block out the sounds from below, as voices reached fever pitch and tempers rose to the boil. And now, it was no different. The same old story, time and time again.

She sat back on her single bed with her laptop on her knee and typed "rental properties Millfield" into the internet search engine. Moving out was long overdue and at twenty-five years old, she was thoroughly sick of living under her parents' roof and putting up with their strict house rules and petty arguments.

"Come on!" she said as the internet speed slowed down. She had spotted a really nice terraced house for rent right in the heart of Millfield village and she wanted to check out the price they were after. Maybe Eugene would come too and they could both make a fresh start, still in the village they loved so well but far enough away from their parents' farm and rundown house that held so many horrible memories.

There it was. Five hundred and fifty pounds a month? Well, between them they could probably afford it. Her salary on the newspaper was fairly decent and she didn't have to travel too far to get to her work, so her living costs could be kept fairly low. And with Eugene's contribution they would be able to live fairly comfortably in the modest two-bedroom house – anything would be better than this torture every time her father had a drink or two.

She took a note of the estate agent's details and checked her bank account online. Yeah, she could manage a deposit. Then she checked a savings account she had opened with her First Holy Communion money and had never really kept an eye on and her stomach fluttered with delight. Her savings account was much higher than she thought! All of those random twenty-pound lodgements she had made down the years had amounted to a tidy sum and now she had enough to make a fairly decent start on a New Scene in her life. She was pleased with herself for only a few moments because, as usual, when something went right for Sorcha Daly and she felt high, something in the back of her mind niggled at her and brought her back down again. You are not good enough, said the little voice. You will never succeed. Look at you. Twenty-five years old, working on a dead-end rag of a newspaper, still living with your sparring parents, protecting your hapless brother, you have nothing going for you, Sorcha. Not even a pretty girl, are you?

She looked up at the giant poster of her heroine Marilyn Monroe on the wall facing her bed. It was a classic black and white Marilyn pose but her pouted lips were red and she always seemed to advise Sorcha on what to do. Tonight Marilyn looked sad and Sorcha felt the same.

She gripped the duvet by her side and closed her eyes tight. Go away, she thought. Then she covered her ears from the sounds of her parents' horrible voices and rocked back and forth on the bed. Seconds later she scrambled to the side of the bed and pulled out the year planner from school she kept within arm's reach. She flicked through the pages – one, two, three, four, five. Second row, middle column. Yes, there he was. Taylor. Her Taylor. How she wished he was hers! She stared at his photo, into his eyes and pleaded with him to rescue her from her lonely existence. But the voice in her head laughed. As if Taylor Smith would look at you! Why have a burger when you can have steak at home! Ha ha ha!

Sorcha slammed the book shut and threw it onto the floor. She ran to the mirror and stared at her tearstained face. She was horrible. Everyone at school and at university had been right all along. Sorcha Daly with the turned-up nose, the pointed chin and the straggly hair. *Sorcha Daly looks like a witch, Sorcha Daly is a bitch!* The chant ranted in her head and she breathed in and out, in and out, trying to control the rage that bubbled inside her but it wouldn't subside. She lifted a photo frame from her dressing table and slammed it against the wall, taking momentarily pleasure in the smash and destruction she could make when she wanted. Then she lifted an old piggy bank and gave it the same medicine. She felt better already as the adrenaline that pumped through her veins began to settle and her pulse regained a steady pace. Then her eyes widened as an idea flowed through her brain and gave her inspiration that she should have thought of much earlier! Yes! That was the answer!

She rushed across to the laptop and looked up flights and accommodation and as soon as she had entered her bank details and the dates and clicked to confirm, she let out a gasp and then a burst of laughter. What the hell had she done! She was so full of excitement she felt she might explode and the madness of what she was about to do projected a huge smile onto her face, so wide that it almost hurt.

If Mohammed would not come to the mountain, the mountain would come to Mohammed. Sorcha Daly was going to Hollywood where she would make Taylor Smith sit up and take notice of her, once and for all.

"Curry, check! Vino, check! Sanity, check!"

Kizzy hauled a takeaway that would have fed a small

country in through the door of Erin's house and sat everything on the kitchen table with gusto.

"It's been way too long since we did this," said Erin who had laid the table and was finding Kizzy a wineglass before the girl died from alcohol cravings.

"I know, I was just saying to our Michelle before I left the house that there is no reason for me to be cooped up in that house twenty-four seven just because I am married with children. I should have some 'me' time. Everyone deserves some 'me' time, don't they? Jesus, it's not too much for ask for, is it?"

Erin stopped. Was Kizzy crying? Her voice was crackling and she was doing that wobbly thing with her lip that most people did when they were fighting back tears.

"Kizzy? Kizzy, is there something else you want to tell me about? What has got you into such a state?"

Kizzy gulped and wiped her eye with the sleeve of her pink fleece. "Ignore me, ignore me. Please just ignore me. Now, give me that wine for God's sake."

"Kizzy, you know you can tell me anything. Are you depressed? Are you feeling down? This is not like you at all. Talk to me."

Erin scooped out heaps of Pilau rice onto each of their plates as Kizzy sat at the table sniffling and shaking her head. The hot steam from the Chicken Tikka Masala filled the air with an aroma of spices and Erin felt her stomach growl but, until Kizzy composed herself, she didn't think they would be eating.

"Let's eat first and then no doubt when my tongue loosens with a few glasses of wine and a full belly, you'll be sorry you even asked."

"Okay," said Erin. "That's okay. Food first is always a good motto to live by. Now get stuck in!"

It was after ten when the two friends finished eating and their mood had relaxed somewhat, with the help of Norah Jones dulcet tones in the background as they chatted about everything from days gone by to what might be around the corner.

"Leave them!" said Erin when Kizzy made a move to do the washing up. "Really, it's only two plates for goodness' sake. They can wait. Let's go in to the fire and talk some more."

They pushed the couch up further to meet the dancing flames of the open fire in Erin's tasteful sitting room and Erin moved Norah and her "Come Away with Me" soothers into the same room so they could continue on the same level with the same relaxing ambience. It was so good to have company for a change and she found herself drinking at a much more enjoyable and manageable pace than the way she gulped it back when she was on her own.

"Tell me more about Taylor," said Kizzy, her eyes brighter now that the wine had begun to take effect. "I can't believe you are not rushing out there to be with him. I think I would if I was in your shoes."

Erin shrugged her shoulders and let out a gentle sigh. "Would you?"

"Too damn right I would! I would be on a plane as quick as you could say 'Sandra Bullock' and I would be her new best friend, shopping with her, hangin' out on set and down on Sunset Boulevard, staying in the Regent Beverly Wilshire . . . gosh, I think I have watched *Pretty Woman* once too often. I've always wanted to stay there

165

ever since I saw Julia Roberts look so glamorous as she lay in that luxurious bubble bath with Richard Gere."

"Sounds like it!"

Erin fell quiet and she fiddled with the stem of her wineglass.

"What's up?" asked Kizzy. "You don't like *Pretty Woman* any more? We always loved *Pretty Woman*? Erin?"

"You know, I can't believe I am saying this, Kizzy. And I would only ever tell this to you because I know it will not go any further, but I don't think I am missing Taylor as much as I thought I would. Oh God, I can't believe I just said that out loud!"

Erin clasped her hand over her mouth and her heart gave a leap. She'd had too much wine, that was all. Where had such an outrageous statement come from?

"Erin? What?"

"Forget it. I'm talking nonsense. I don't know where that came from. Of course I miss him. I miss him terribly and if I didn't hear his voice every day it would drive me insane. I've had too much to drink."

Kizzy's eyebrows were arched and her eyes were wide with shock.

"Erin, may I remind you of the sex god you are in a relationship with? May I remind you of how you once said you would walk over hot coals to even have him notice you and now you are coming out with this drivel?"

"It's drivel, I know. I said forget about it. I was just having a moment of madness."

"Good."

"Yeah."

"Okay. Now, tell me all about him."

"No, tell me all about you," said Erin. "You were in tears earlier and you said you would tell me what was wrong. I hate to see you feeling so miserable, Kizz. You never were the life and soul of the party, but you're always the one who makes me laugh and giggle again like a schoolgirl and listens to me when I am down so if I can't help you when you're feeling a bit glum, who can?"

Kizzy waved her hand, forgetting she was holding her glass of wine and it threatened to slurp over the edge of the glass and onto Erin's polished wooden floor.

"Whoops, clumsy me!" she said and composed herself. "I am over it, Erin. Like you said, I was just having a moment. Probably just hormonal or something. Yeah, that's it, I'm full of raging hormones."

Erin watched as Kizzy fumbled over her words. She was hiding something. Something big.

"You're not . . . you know . . ."

Erin glanced at Kizzy's midriff and then back to her face.

"Don't even go there! I swear I'd better not be pregnant again. Jesus! No – no, there is no way. We have been careful. We are not ready yet. It's way too soon. Oh shit . . ."

The pair sat in silence for a while as Kizzy shuddered at the very possibility at being pregnant with her third child. Erin could see the terror in her friend's glazy eyes as she stared into her glass, a million tiny question marks floating through her head.

"Kizzy?"

"What?" said Kizzy, still staring into the rich red liquid.

"Are you having an affair?"

Kizzy's entire posture changed and her mouth twitched but no words came out. She fiddled her hair and tried to speak, then drank more wine and tried again.

"Don't be ridiculous," she stuttered. "Who the hell would have an affair with me? The postman, the milkman, the bloody window cleaner?"

Her voice was bitter now, angry even and she stood up in the middle of Erin's floor.

"I mean, look at me! Look at me and then look at you! I bet you have hundreds of offers from all sorts of high-flying men, but why or how would anyone look at me? I spend my days covered in baby sick and mashed banana and I couldn't tell you when I last had a decent haircut! And even if I did I don't think Dermot would bloody notice. I feel invisible, Erin. I feel old and past it and my God, I just want my life back!"

And then the tears came back again but this time they weren't the hidden gentle sobs that she had almost disguised earlier in the evening. No, these were heavy, bitter, heaving tears that almost drowned out every other sound in the room including Norah Jones who was still warbling away from the CD player in the corner.

"Kizzy, Kizzy, come on!" said Erin and she wrapped her arms around her best friend. "This is not like you at all. I can't believe I'm hearing this. Where is my vivacious and confident, bubbly friend who makes me laugh with her witty charm and positive glow?"

Kizzy heaved a huge snottery sigh and fought back her tears.

"I don't know her any more, Erin. I really don't. She has been replaced by a miserable, sloppy, invisible old woman who spends most nights talking to old boyfriends on the internet in search of some sort of fucking link to her glorious past."

Erin led her rather tipsy friend back onto the armchair and she sat on the arm of it and stroked her hair. On the internet? To old boyfriends? *Kizzy*? This didn't sound right at all . . .

"So, what old boyfriends? Who exactly?"

Kizzy sniffled more and slumped her shoulders. "Well, when I say 'boyfriends' plural, I mean only one. Oh God I can't believe I am admitting this! It was just curiosity at first and I looked him up and then later he added me as a friend and I got a tiny rush of excitement. Soon we got chatting and now it's like this everyday drug that keeps me going and gives me something to look forward to. He is so complimentary and we talk about old times and it makes me feel young . . . I know, I know, it's stupid and it's dangerous and it has to stop."

Erin slunk across to the settee where she had been sitting originally and sat, curling her feet underneath her again, her wineglass resting once more in her hand.

"Name, please."

"What does it matter," sighed Kizzy. "It's all a pile of balls really."

"Name!"

"I mean if he even caught a glimpse of me now with my baby belly and my smocky clothes and my – "

"Who the hell is he, Kizzy? Tell me his name!"

"It's Niall," groaned Kizzy and she looked at Erin

through squinted eyes, dreading her reaction. "I know, I know. Please don't kill me."

Erin looked like she was chewing a bitter lemon or as if she was sucking a pickled onion.

"No, Kizzy! Not Niall! Anyone but him!"

SCENE TEN

Taylor's voice on the line sounded more distant than ever when he rang the following morning, just after eight. Apart from her familiar throbbing head and flashbacks from the night before when Kizzy had left in a terrible state of confusion, Erin felt like she was a different person and Taylor obviously sensed it, despite the carnival that was going on in the background of his latest late-night party.

"So, aren't you going to ask me how filming is coming along?" he said, over a thumping reggae beat and the sounds of laughter and fun. "We have been on the phone for twenty minutes and you have barely said a word."

"Sorry, Taylor. Sorry, I am just a little bit fragile," said Erin, rubbing her head. She recalled her conversation with Kizzy's reincarnation with the horrible Niall McGrath and it was making her skin crawl. "And you are at a party. I didn't think you wanted to talk about work but, hey. How are you getting on? How is all the gang?"

171

"The *gang*? Look, it doesn't matter." His voice cracked. "Yes, I'm at a party but that's what we do over here."

"Cool. Well, go party, then. Don't let me hold you back."

The sounds of girls, probably scantily clad girls with plastic but perfect figures, giggling in the distance reached her through the throb of the background music was churning her insides.

"Erin! Were you drinking again last night? I thought you said –"

"I had a few drinks, so what!" she snapped. "It was a long week and Kizzy called around and we had a good chat over a few glasses of wine. What's the big deal?"

"A few? How many is a few?" he asked and she heard him shuffle further away from the hubbub where he could hear her better. "You really need to slow down, Erin. How do you think I feel at the other side of the bloody world while you drink yourself into oblivion at home without me?"

Erin sat up in the bed, her hangover temporarily numbed by Taylor's accusations.

"Taylor, how dare you? I am not drinking myself into oblivion. Yes, I have been a bit rough with the old vino for a while but I have acknowledged that and Kizzy needed me last night. It was a sociable few. I was in control. I can handle this."

She could hear Taylor's frustration as it rattled down the phone.

"I don't see you handling it! You are in trouble at work, your mother is going off her head with worry about you and now you are using Kizzy as an excuse to get pissed on a Friday night. Get a grip, Erin!"

Erin clasped the telephone and squeezed it tighter and tighter. She did not need lectures from Taylor. Not now. Not ever. Not when he was living it up in the Sunshine State while she battled misery and pain in rainy Ireland.

"Taylor, I'm sure you have much more to worry about than what I get up to on the weekends. You're in LA, for God's sake! As if you really give a shit!"

Taylor fell silent and then he spoke slowly and quietly. "That is unfair and you know it."

There was an extra long pause between them and Erin closed her eyes and tried to think.

"I'm sorry," she said. "Maybe I'm not handling this well at all. I am so mixed up right now and . . . God, this place seems so empty without you and maybe I *am* throwing myself into booze to numb the pain but I think . . . I think I'm trying to protect myself from the inevitable by somehow blocking you out of my mind for now."

Erin knew by Taylor's short silences that he was horrified by what she had to say, yet she couldn't lie to him. She had a horrible gut instinct that his life in Hollywood would drive them apart in the long run.

"You know what, Erin, I can't believe this is happening," he said. "This is exactly what everyone else thought would happen, but something I thought you and I knew never would. I never wanted this to come between us, but it looks like it will no matter what I do. I'm sorry it has to be this way."

Erin slumped back onto her pillow and held the phone to her ear and her hand to her forehead. What was happening to her? First she allowed her drinking to threaten her career and now it was fogging her feelings for Taylor, the one man she had fought long and hard to find. The one man she would always have laid down her life for. The one man who knew her inside out and loved her with every flaw and every ounce of ambition she used to have. She was losing the run of herself and she couldn't keep up.

"Taylor, don't . . ."

"Don't what, Erin? Don't what?"

"Don't listen to me. I'm sorry. I am being silly and childish and . . . just . . . just . . . oh God, I don't know."

She could hear a voice calling for him in the distance, back into the party with the pool and the barbecue and the Barbie dolls. She felt sick.

"I'll be right there!" yelled Taylor to his new friend. Then he lowered his voice and spoke to Erin again. "Do you have any idea know how much this scares me? I am petrified that any success I have out here will threaten what we have at home but when I call, I don't get the same feeling from you at all. What can I do to make you realise that this won't change anything between us?"

Erin felt like her head might explode. She couldn't think straight.

"Just be you," she said. "Please don't change, Taylor."

"I won't," he said and then the American voice called to him again to come back to the party. "Do you believe me, Erin?"

"Yes," she said, but she wasn't so sure. She could hear Taylor's voice but she didn't recognise it as his at all. He sounded different. His words were just like those Taylor would use, but they didn't register with her like they once did. She needed to shake out of this.

"Have a great time, Taylor. Have the time of your life."

"I'm trying to," he said. "I'll call you later?"

"Yeah, later," said Erin and she hung up the phone and lay down to surrender to more sleep.

Erin awoke at eleven with the bleep bleep of a text message drilling through her brain and the blinding light of a winter sunshine which beamed through the bedroom window and into her eyes.

She fumbled to find her phone and squinted as she read the contents of her inbox. She had two messages – one from Taylor and one from Darryl Smith. She turned around on her side and clicked open Taylor's message.

Hey, honey. Chin up. Hold on for me, please.

She cuddled the phone to her chest and closed her eyes, then reached across to the empty pillow beside her. Shit, this was torture. He loved her – he really did, so why couldn't she just accept his word and push her paranoia away from her muffled mind? How could she protect her own fears of being hurt, without pushing him away?

She scrolled down to read Darryl's message and sat up on the bed with a jolt when she did.

"Fuck! Shit!"

She raced to the shower and stood under the steaming-hot jets, trying to wash the cobwebs from her mind. They were waiting for her at The Community Centre for rehearsals! She was over an hour late. Shit!

She pulled on a grey jumper dress, leggings and boots and a spray of perfume. A quick rub of foundation and some mascara was all she had time for, then she ran from the house and into the car and had reached the centre within five minutes.

"I am so, so sorry, Darryl!" she said when she walked into the fusty hall. "I had totally forgotten about this morning. I don't blame you if you are really angry with me."

Krystal sat on the edge of the makeshift stage, filing her nails and glancing at Erin in distaste. Her ankle was bandaged now and she was lapping up sympathy from her fellow-cast mates on how much she had suffered with the excruciating pain of it.

"Nice to see this show is top of your priority list, Erin," she said. "Some of us refuse to get above our stations around here, some of us are just wrapped up in ego and making a late entrance." She blew the ends of her nails and smiled up at Olivier who was standing nearby, a flock of teenage girls staring at him adoringly from a little huddle on the floor.

Erin ignored Krystal's nasty swipe and took a seat to the side of the hall, a deep lonely feeling in the pit of her stomach. She searched around the room for someone she could tag along with until she was needed but all she got in return were glances and whispers and she suddenly felt so out of place in an environment which was always like a second home to her. Without Taylor, she realised, she really didn't know anyone that well and she felt tears prick her eyes.

"Isn't my mum here?" she asked Eugene Daly who was busy lugging a cage across the floor as a prop for a scene from *Joseph*. It was a bad day when even Eugene didn't pay her even a tiny bit of attention. He was normally like a fly around shit when it came to all things "Erin".

"Oh, Erin. Didn't see you there. Your-your-your

mum was here earlier. She's gone with your g-g-gran to look for some costumes for the leper scene in the *JC S-S-Superstar* scene. Think she was trying to call you earlier."

"Oh," said Erin and she clasped her hands in front of her, trying not to fidget and show off her discomfort. "That's okay, thanks, Eugene."

She smiled at him and he blushed as he tugged the giant cage across the floor to show Darryl, just to make sure it met his approval.

"What is that?" yelled Darryl.

"It's the c-c-cage for the J-J-Jo-"

"It's hideous. Take it away, Eugene. My God, if you want something done around here . . . Erin, I'll be with you in a few minutes," said Darryl in his "under pressure" voice. "Just let me finish off this piece with Joseph and then I'll have a chat to you about your scene. I had to re-jig the schedule at the last minute when you weren't here at ten, so I'm afraid you may have to wait a while."

"No, no that's fine," said Erin, a lump choking her throat. "I can wait."

She looked around the hall and noticed how everyone else was either busy with a job to do, or gathered in small groups having a giggle as they waited their turn to practise their nominated scene for the big show. She was a fish out of water in her own hometown. The "girl off the telly" she heard one of them whisper but no one came to say hello or to welcome her into their company. She felt her confidence drip off her body and onto the floor. Is this what she was without Taylor? A self-deprecating, alcohol-dependent, alienated mini-celebrity who no one felt an urge to talk to or even acknowledge with something more than a nod?

Her wallowing was interrupted when she felt someone sit beside her. She stared at her hands, not wanting to look up in case she might cry, such was her lack of self-esteem at that very moment.

"You look sad," said a voice.

Erin looked up to see the warm, handsome face of Olivier. She smiled automatically as she met his dark, deep eyes and white smile but she didn't know how to answer him.

"You have clothes on," she said.

He sat back in amazement. "I do. Why, have you seen me in any other condition that I am not aware of?"

"I mean, oh God. I mean you have jeans and a shirt . . . sorry, I'm just more used to seeing you in leathers and boots and today you are . . . well, you look nice."

"Phew!" he said and the way he lifted his eyes when he said it almost blew her away. "I thought you had been spying on me, or perhaps I had been sleepwalking naked."

Naked. Olivier naked . . . The very words sent a rush of energy through Erin's veins as she got a mental image of what he might look like underneath his clothes. His tanned, handsome body . . . his jet black hair that he had to push off his face, his . . .

"I met your gran this morning," he said and she blinked back to reality.

"Oh?" Yeah. She's a nice lady. And your mum is too."

"Gosh, you have been a busy boy," said Erin. "Soon you'll know more people around here than I do. I feel like a sort of stranger today."

Olivier looked around the room. "I think they are mesmerised by you," he said. "You are Erin O'Brien. Television star. Other half of their other hero, Taylor Smith. I, on the other hand, am a *true* stranger and the one they think is going to try to steal not only Taylor's place on this stage, but his place in his woman's heart."

Erin was sure her heartbeat had been amplified and it felt like it was competing in a sprint, such was its pace. The way he looked at her was so amazing. His voice was sincere and sad almost and she realised that he felt much more unwelcome here than she did.

"Oh Olivier, I am sorry everyone is being so presumptuous. How dare they jump to conclusions like that?"

"It doesn't bother me, really, but I thought you should know. I don't want to get you into any kind of trouble. I hope we can be friends and I would never, ever try to move in on another man's woman. It just isn't my style."

Erin blinked and then gulped back the lump that was still lodged in her throat.

"Well, as long as you and I know that, then to hell with the rest," she said. "I think we should flirt wildly to feed their imaginations. Give them all something to chew on, the pile of nosey –"

"Olivier! Erin! Can I have you, please?"

Darryl rolled his tongue when he said Olivier's name and the room went silent as the two leading stars of the show made their way to the Director's desk in the centre of the floor. Erin felt Olivier's hand lightly brush the small of her back as they approached the place where Darryl sat and they took their places in front of him.

"So, it's a scene from *Grease* then?" asked Erin. "I'm sure we can make that work pretty easily."

"No, it's not any more," said Darryl, shuffling scripts and papers around his desk. "I've changed my mind since we have found such a gem in Olivier and I have decided that you two kids will perform that beautiful song from the film *Moulin Rouge* where Satine and Christian sing together in a magnificent display of passion and romance. I want you to work on 'Come What May' and I know, I just know it will be pure magic."

He handed them a script each and Erin's hand shook as she took the pages from Darryl who looked like he had just put the icing on top of a very large cake or a cat that had been dished out with a double helping of the proverbial cream with his huge satisfied grin.

"'Come What May'?" said Erin. "But that's mine and Taylor's song . . ."

She could feel Olivier shuffle beside her and she regretted saying anything that heightened his discomfort but she couldn't help herself. What was Darryl thinking? This was the very first song she and Taylor had performed together and it was the one that brought them together, the first time that Taylor Smith properly noticed that she even existed. How could Darryl do this to her? How could he choose this song?

"Don't be silly," said Darryl. "It's no one's song. It's a classic piece from a very popular score and it is the one I have chosen for you and Olivier. Now speak to your mother about costumes when she gets back and you two find a corner to have a practice so we can hear you before we close for today."

Erin looked at Krystal who pursed her lips as she

tried her best not to show the dirty smirk that crept over her face. What a meddling, evil bitch! She would place money that this was all her idea.

"Fine then," said Erin. "If you are happy, then I am happy. Are you happy with the song change, Olivier?"

"I am happy," he shrugged, only half-aware of what he was being dragged into.

"Great. Let's practise."

"Oh, and Olivier?" said Darryl. "You did say you'd help the others with choreography, didn't you?"

"I would be delighted," said Olivier. "So . . . which would you like me to do first?"

"Em, let me see . . . do Erin first," said Darryl and Olivier gave Erin a light smile at the suggestion in Darryl's choice of phrasing. Darryl handed them both a lyric sheet and gave Erin a CD of the song. "Yeah, do Erin first."

"I will go do Erin now," he said and Erin rolled her eyes with a smile. Perhaps she could make this fun. Yes, she could have fun with Olivier it seemed. A lot of fun.

Scene Eleven

Erin led Olivier into a small rehearsal space at the back of the hall which was normally home to tennis rackets, a volley-ball net and some play equipment from The Mother and Toddler Group.

But at this time of year, it was cleared out to make room for the many practices that would be packed into the calendar as The Millfield Players prepared for their annual showcase. The room smelled of mothballs and sweaty sports gear and Erin raised a smile at its familiarity and the many memories she held from watching her mother and grandmother practise songs from many musicals down the years when she was a small child, to admiring Taylor Smith from the corner of the room when he was a young teenager who oozed charisma and talent, to later years when they would flirt with each other from opposite sides of the room.

It seemed very, very strange to be standing in this tiny room without him.

"You look like you don't want to be here," said Olivier. "I'm not sure what that was all about out there, but I take it you have a history with the song that Darryl has chosen."

Erin sat down on a plastic chair and bit her lip. "Yeah, I do. But hey, that's not your problem. I mean, it's only a song, right?"

"It obviously means a lot to you," said Olivier. "Do you want to talk about it?"

He pulled a chair from beneath a small wooden desk and watched her as she battled with raw emotion when she put the CD of the song into a small music station that had been set up for them. The opening notes of the song came on, and he noticed her flinch in her seat. She pulled at her sleeves and shook her head.

"It was mine and Taylor's song. It still is, I suppose. We . . . gosh, I feel like a teenager telling you this . . ."

"No, go on," said Olivier.

"Well, we have known each other since we were kids," she continued. "Taylor is five years younger than me so I was never really in his company as friends or anything growing up, but we would have spent time together after rehearsals as my mum and my gran stayed behind with his parents to go over the finer detail of the shows. Then when I was about twenty-five, we found ourselves mixing in the same circles, especially here when it was show time. We hung out, you know? And we realised that we had so much in common. Our parents have always been so absorbed in local theatre and we would joke about their antics and share memories of some of the muck-ups that were made, or nights when the audience were on their feet. Then Darryl cast us alongside each other to sing this song for a one-off variety show he had put together for a local charity and it was the start of the most amazing relationship. We started practising together, right here in this room, and then . . . well, the chemistry was like – wow!"

Olivier's eyes brightened and he laughed with Erin.

"And the rest is history, as they say?" he suggested in his gorgeous voice.

"So they say," said Erin, pulling at her sleeves again. Then she sighed deeply. "But now he's in Hollywood, destined to be a big star and here I am right back where I started, sitting in this room, singing this song . . ."

"With me . . ."

Erin looked at Olivier in apology. "No, no, that's not what I meant. This is hardly your fault, Olivier. It's just Krystal and Darryl playing games with me. I know Krystal can't stand me. She's probably praying every night that Taylor runs off with Sandra Bullock so she thinks that by shoving me in your direction – 'cos, let's face it, you are pretty easy on the eye – that I will forget about Taylor and she is watching out for any connection between us like a hawk! She is so desperate for him to make her proud and she thinks I will stand in his way."

"And will you?" asked Olivier.

"No way! I mean, I'm finding it all really hard but I would never, ever stand in his way and Taylor knows that with all his heart."

"Well, tell her to butt out, then."

Erin laughed and Olivier looked embarrassed.

"What? Did I say the wrong thing?"

"No, no you didn't. It's just . . . it's just funny the way

you say things like 'butt out' with your accent. It sounds so sweet."

Olivier scratched his head and shrugged. "What can I say? I spent way too much time here as a child. The lingo rubbed off on me."

Erin felt her heart warm at Olivier's honesty and how sincere he was to help make this as easy on her as possible.

"You seem like a nice guy, Olivier. I can see it in you."

The song in the background faded and they sat in silence for seconds which seemed like an eternity. Awkwardness filled the air and then Olivier took to his feet.

"You know what, Erin? I have so many ideas for this show," he said with a new-found enthusiasm. "I realise I am going to have to be so careful not to push my ideas too far because I know Darryl likes to steer this ship and keep control but I have this really hot salsa routine I think some of the kids could pull off. I think it would really put some passion into this place and rock things up a bit."

He spun into a sexy, hip-thrusting move and Erin's eyes almost popped out when his shirt lifted up over his jeans slightly to reveal his tanned torso and she swallowed hard.

"Yeah, yeah. Gosh, is it hot in here or is it just me?" she laughed. "You really can move, Olivier. Maybe that's what we all need around here. A little bit of Moulin Rouge in Little Hollywood."

Olivier lifted his shoulders then held out his hands for Erin to join him.

"Come on," he said. "Let me teach you."

Emma Heatherington

Erin shook her head and sniggered. "No way. Not a chance! I can sing, but there is no way I can dance like you."

"Come on, Erin. Let me be the judge of that." He waved his hands for her to join him and her stomach went into knots. The way he said her name . . . ooh, it was like it melted on his tongue like hot chocolate. She felt her skin prickle as a pulsing lust pumped through her for a glorious moment. He seemed genuine. He seemed harmless. Should she?

"Well, okay then, but don't say I didn't warn you." She stood up and fixed her jumper dress, then tucked her hair behind her ears and her eyes met his.

"Do we need music or shall we just learn the steps first?" he asked, his voice dropping to a whisper. She was mesmerised as she took his hands and he began to move in a rhythm she never even knew existed.

"Learn . . . the steps. Learn the steps first. Yes . . ."

Good God! She felt perspiration rise and dampen the back of her neck as she rocked with him back and forward and then he twirled her around and she couldn't believe when she landed back in exactly the same place, just under his chin. She looked up and breathed in and out slowly, then stepped back.

"Wow!" she said. "I've never done anything like that before."

"Well, isn't that just flaming fantastic!" A round of applause sounded from the doorway and Krystal Smith stood shaking her head in mock delight. "Not sure if that's what you were *supposed* to be rehearsing, but it's clear you two are working off your very own script in here. Darryl will see you now. He wants to hear the

186

song? You know, the song that you have obviously not been practising?"

She turned and limped away and Olivier brought his hands to his face.

"Oh my God, I am so sorry!" he said. "What is it with that woman?"

"No, no, don't be sorry," said Erin slowly. "She's not worth it. And that is exactly what she *wanted* to see. Exactly."

"And now let's hear a rough run through of our scene from the hit movie, *Moulin Rouge*," said Darryl, ruffling his pages at his director's desk. He sat back in his chair and crossed his legs. "You know I can't emphasise enough how much I love this song . . ."

A light groan whimpered through the gathered cast.

". . . and can I also say what a treat it is to have Olivier Laurent join us here at Millfield Players this year. To have someone with his experience, all the way from the bright lights of the Moulin Rouge is a fantastic honour. It really is. Now let's hear how he and our very own Erin got on today."

Erin felt like she might choke. They had only listened to the CD. Surely he didn't expect them to perform together in front of all these gazing eyes and pricked up ears already?

"Darryl, I don't think we're performance-ready as yet," she said. "We only had about twenty minutes to practise together. It's not the same with a new partner."

"Oh, just a quick run through with the pianist, Erin. Come on, just a taster. I know it won't be perfect but we have to start somewhere. I don't expect a 'performance' as such."

She glanced at Olivier who seemed willing to take her lead.

"Do you even know the words?" she whispered to him. "I was so busy babbling on earlier I didn't even ask if you had as much as heard the song before!"

"I know them almost back to front," he said under his breath. "Come on . . . let's show them how it's done. I will if you will."

Erin pushed her shoulders back and nodded at the pianist in the corner who was almost asleep at this stage.

"Come on, Nellie, chop chop!" said Darryl. "We don't have all day. Get tinkling on those ivories."

Olivier leaned one arm on the side of the piano and held the lyrics out in front of him, giving Darryl the impression that he was reading them as he prepared to sing. Erin stood by his side, her back against the piano so that she was in full view of Krystal who was poised like a peacock, waiting for the grand crash and burn as Little Miss Hollywood met Mr Moulin Rouge.

"Is there a dance to this song?" asked Krystal, her chin tilted forward and her nose in the air. "It's just that when I went in to call you two, you were dancing? Fancy that!"

"Oh, all will be revealed in due course, Madame," said Olivier. "Let's just see what we make of the vocals first, and then we can show you our moves."

A group of young teenage girls let out a loud "woooo" from the scattered audience and the first few notes of the song was played by Nelly on the piano. For a doting old bird, she could still play to perfection.

The room fell silent and tension filled the air as everyone waited to see what Olivier and Erin had to offer as a musical duo. Olivier took a deep breath, glanced at Erin and then down at his lyric sheet and he began to sing . . .

His voice was like magic and he sang every word like he had written each word for Erin as he looked into her eyes. Then, when it was her turn, you could have heard a pin drop and her heart soared when he joined in and they harmonised to perfection. It was like there was no one else in the room and when Erin closed her eyes she could see Taylor standing beside her, she could feel him with her and it was like she was right back to those early days when she only had to look at his gorgeous face or brush past him to feel the butterflies join a carnival in her stomach. She opened her eyes as they burst into the crescendo of the last line and a tear fell from her eye, then the song reached its dramatic finish and she was back in the room with everyone staring at her. The entire cast were speechless, and after a brief but stunned silence, they burst into applause.

"Well done," said Darryl and he fixed his cravat. "Well done. That was . . . that was, well . . . em, maybe Erin you could work on your . . . em . . . yes, no. Very good. Now let's move on. Where are the cast from the *Grease* scene?"

"Thank you, Darryl," said Olivier and he and Erin walked back to the side of the hall, not knowing if they were free to go or if they were needed again. There was a strange atmosphere now and they sat together, as a team against everyone else in the room. Erin felt Olivier's hand reach for hers and squeeze it tight.

"Thanks," said Erin when he let go. "I thought that was pretty good. What about you?"

"Amazing," he whispered.

"Me too."

"I'd do you again anytime if it's going to be like that! Wow!"

They both giggled and then Erin caught sight of Krystal's warning glances.

"Oh, fuck you sideways," whispered Erin. "No, not you, Olivier! I'm talking about old Vinegar Tits over there. She is not missing a beat. Boy, but we showed her up, didn't we?"

"I think we did," he said. "Hey, what do you say we get out of here and grab a bite of lunch? I could murder some pub grub and a pint."

"Now you're talking!"

Erin stood up and lifted her handbag from the floor, making sure that Krystal could see her smiling and laughing with Olivier. She would rub the snotty bitch's nose in it. If she wanted gossip, she was going to get it by the absolute bucket load.

SCENE TWELVE

Sorcha Daly couldn't believe her eyes. Erin O'Brien had it all. She had the looks, the career, the money and the man and still it wasn't good enough. There she was, cavorting in the corner with that new French guy and they looked so good together it turned her stomach. Him with his dark, sexy looks and her with her stunning smile and silky hair – they were like something from a bloody catalogue and the way he stroked his hair when he spoke to her spoke volumes. Plus she was sure she had seen Monsieur whatever his name was squeeze Erin's hand and the chemistry between them when they sang earlier had been nauseating. And now they were leaving together! She would have to interrupt.

"Hi, Erin," she said, marching towards the two star-struck lovers as they made their way to the door of The Community Centre. "How is Taylor getting on in LA? I'm sure you're missing him terribly?"

She looked both of them up and down as she spoke and she couldn't hide the bitterness in her voice. Imagine doing the dirty on someone as wonderful as Taylor Smith. What an ungrateful bitch!

"Yes, yes, I am," said Erin, moving a little further away from Olivier's side.

She was caught and she knew it. At least she had the grace to blush.

"Nice singing earlier," she said to Olivier. "I had my doubts about you, but it looks like you will be able to fit into Taylor's place better than I thought."

"Er . . . thank you," said Olivier. "I *think* that was a compliment?"

"Yeah. Well, Taylor is a big loss to us all around here. We all adore him. It's sort of like when someone you really like leaves your place of work and then when their replacement starts and you take an instant dislike to them, just because they aren't you know, the other person. I didn't like you but you seem okay, I suppose."

"Tell it how it is, Sorcha," said Erin, and she tried to brush past.

But Sorcha dodged her so that she blocked her path. She put her hands on her hips.

"I'm going to see him," she said.

"What? Who? What are you talking about?" said Erin.

"Taylor," said Sorcha with a wide grin. "I'm going to Hollywood to see him on Monday courtesy of *The Gazette*. They want an interview on set and I've it all arranged."

Her heart soared with delight when she saw the sheer horror on Erin's face. This was priceless.

"*You* are going to Hollywood? To interview Taylor? On the set of his *movie*?"

"Yup. Exciting, isn't it?"

"Oh . . ."

Sorcha's grin was unstoppable. She swallowed and then delivered her bombshell.

"I was speaking to him on the phone just this morning. He says it is so wonderful to have support from home, well, from an old friend like *me*, because no one else is really that bothered at the moment. I can see now what he means."

"*Taylor* said that?" said Erin, panic rising in her voice. "Sorcha, be careful what you say. Taylor and I go back a long, long way and if you start twisting things around and making up little stories to tell back and forth, well, you are messing with the wrong person."

"I'm not making anything up," said Sorcha. The fear in Erin's eyes was fierce. "I am simply doing my job and if that makes you angry or jealous then that's your problem. But if you ask me, you seem to be getting on pretty well without Taylor."

She looked at Olivier and then back at Erin who was now seething.

"That's the thing, Sorcha. Nobody *is* asking you. Now keep your nose out of my business and I will keep mine out of yours. Come on, Olivier. Let's go and have lunch."

"That nosey little cow," said Erin, marching along the footpath so fast that Olivier was finding it difficult to keep up. "She's had her eye on Taylor ever since she could talk and now she's going to start meddling and spreading rumours and God knows what else she'll make up by the time she gets to LA. I mean, why the hell is a local rag like *The Gazette* sending her all the way to Hollywood when they could wait and speak to him when he comes home. He *is* coming home, you know! I think everyone forgets that from time to time. He is only away for a while. He will be home."

She stopped dead in her tracks and her face crumpled. Don't cry, don't cry, she told herself.

Olivier put his arm lightly around her. "He would be mad not to come home to a beautiful girl like you who loves him so much. He will come home."

Erin stared ahead but she couldn't see a thing in front of her. "But what if he doesn't? What if all his partying and sunshine and beautiful people out there make him want to stay? What the hell do I do then?"

"He will come home to you," said Olivier. "He will. Now, let's go and have some food because my tummy thinks I'm teasing it at this stage. Come on."

Erin calmed slightly as they drove out of the village and into the nearby town where they pulled up outside a small hotel that served up a delicious hot lunch. Heads turned as usual when she walked inside and she could hear her name whispered as other diners recognised her from the television.

"Oh, I feel like I'm with royalty," said Olivier and his eyes crinkled when he smiled. "Everyone is staring at you. That must be very strange."

"I suppose it is strange," said Erin as she took off her coat. "It's why I like to keep my roots firmly in Millfield. It keeps my feet on the ground. Honestly, if there is one place on earth that won't let you believe your own press, it's there!"

Olivier laughed and a waitress made her way over to the table.

"Hello, Erin," she said and then clasped her hand over her mouth. "Oh my God, I can't believe I called you by name! How embarrassing! I don't know you and you don't know me so just pretend I didn't say that and I'll do my best not to appear all 'stalkerish' and star-struck. It's just I watch your show and I've never met you before. And now, here I am serving you and you probably think I'm some sort of wacko! Sorry!"

"It's perfectly fine," said Erin to the waitress. She was a very pretty girl with dark auburn hair that reflected the light and she had an infectious smile. "What's your name, now that we have become acquainted?"

"It's Molly. I'm Molly. And you are Erin, yes, I know that. Oh God, here I go again! I'm a jibbering wreck!"

Erin looked at Olivier who seemed to be drinking in every word the girl said. He was watching her with a wide smile and he seemed mesmerised by the very situation.

"Well, Molly. This is my friend Olivier. Olivier, Molly. Molly, Olivier."

"Oh, you are so nice. You know, you're even prettier off the telly than you are on it," said Molly. "I should really just shut up now, shouldn't I? I should take your drinks order and leave you to look at the menu."

"Great, I'll have a glass of Merlot, please, Molly," said Olivier.

Erin was sure the girl was physically shaking now that she had heard Olivier's fantastic accent. She nodded at him with bright eyes and then looked at Erin, glanced back at Olivier, then at Erin again.

"I'll have the same," Erin said and instantly regretted it but she didn't want to make a fuss. She could have one, though? Yeah, she could have one glass with her lunch. Just the one . . .

"Okay, I'll be right back," said Molly and off she went with a spring in her step.

"She's pretty," said Erin as Olivier's gaze followed the waitress until she went out of sight.

"Yeah, she is," he said with a smile. "Cute how she was so nervous talking to you. I must text my friends that I am having lunch in Ireland with a celebrity. They will be so impressed."

"I wouldn't go so far to say 'celebrity'," replied Erin. "Though imagine what it will be like for Taylor when he comes back, especially when the movie is released. It's going to be crazy."

She thought she noticed a slight discomfort in Olivier when she mentioned Taylor's name again.

"He's going to be noticed a lot," said Olivier. "You really do love him, don't you?"

"I do," said Erin and she blinked back emotion. "I'm just so scared that he will find this all too small-town when he gets back and that by opening this fantastic new scene of his life, he will have to close the rest and leave it behind. And that includes me."

"I don't think so," said Olivier and he leaned his chin on his hands and looked into her eyes. "You obviously are a very strong couple. Everyone seems to talk about you as a twosome and all I have heard since I came here this morning is how fantastic a guy he really is. They all really do have him up on a pedestal, don't they?"

Erin shrugged. "Yes, I suppose they do. And unfortunately that pedestal is sometimes a little out of my reach."

Molly the waitress interrupted them and Erin was almost glad of the break in the conversation. She didn't want to bore Olivier with how much she missed her boyfriend. Olivier was a stranger from a different country and she should be making him feel welcome, not burdening him with her tales of woe. She would change the subject. Yes, she would find out more about him. It was only manners.

They ordered steaks and fries and Erin couldn't believe how relaxed it was, considering how they were still virtual strangers but there was something about Olivier that made her feel totally at ease in his company.

"So, tell me more about what brings you here. Tell me about your gran," she said. "I can't believe she and my gran were such good friends. It really is a small world."

"Yeah," said Olivier. "It is. My gran is a wonderful lady. She has always been spritely and young at heart, a bit like Agnes is, but since my grandfather died she has become very introverted, very lonely and she seems to have aged overnight. I used to spend summers here when my mum was on tour in France and we became very close, so when I had this break in my schedule, I knew I wanted to come and keep her company. She's great fun when she has company around her. I think she has brightened up already and she's delighted I'm taking part in this show. Gives her something to brag about when she's getting her hair done in town!"

"Ah, that's so sweet," said Erin. She really was impressed with Olivier's reasons for coming to Ireland.

"I love it here," he continued. "I love to come and switch off from the crazy lifestyle I lead in Paris. I swear, if my friends could see me now, sitting in a cosy country hotel, having lunch with a pretty girl, having a glass of wine and basically chilling out, they would never believe it."

"Really? Why?"

"Because it's just not me at all," he whispered. "Well, not how they know me. At home I am this manic workaholic who never takes a day off and I'm always rushing here, there and everywhere. I can be quite highly strung and I'm a bit of a perfectionist over there, whereas when I come to Ireland I manage to switch off completely."

"Funny that," said Erin. "You leave the Moulin Rouge and you end up in Little Hollywood. That's quite a different lifestyle, all right."

"Aha," said Olivier. "That's something I've heard this place being called quite a few times. How did it get that nickname? It *is* a nickname, right?"

Erin paused as a smiling Molly placed their food in front of them, and the smell of the sizzling steaks mixed with the aroma of fried onions filled her senses and made her mouth water.

"Enjoy!" said Molly.

"Little Hollywood . . . yes," said Erin when Molly left. "It is a nickname but it's been around for quite a while. You see, Millfield is a hive of talent of all levels. We have actors obviously, television presenters including me, we have an award-winning playwright and a published poet but, he died last year, and the butcher's daughter is a radio presenter. It seems that you can go back generations and find a host of people who were successful in the arts. I don't know who gave it the name, but it has stuck."

"And now your Taylor is going to make sure it really is on the map. Cool. It's a very nice little village. I'm glad I found it."

"I'm glad you did too," said Erin as she tucked into her food. "It's nice to have someone new in our midst. Sometimes it can be a bit cliquey so it's nice to shake the dynamics up a bit."

"That's sweet of you to say that," said Olivier. "And this food is amazing too. *Bon appétit,* my new friend. We should do this again some time."

"We should," said Erin and she felt her heart race when their eyes met across the table.

With looks and a personality like Olivier's, Erin knew that he could shake up a lot more than dynamics in the village if he really wanted to – and she had a feeling that whether he intended to or not, that was exactly what was going to happen.

SCENE THIRTEEN

"Five, six, seven, eight! Five, six, seven, eight!"

Erin watched Olivier teach the chorus a dance piece as Darryl looked on with pride. The young girls were picking up the steps quite easily and with Olivier's easy charm and charismatic teaching methods they were all in their glory. Erin noticed how they giggled and joked with their new choreographer, who had them all eating out of his hands as he walked them through their steps, then raised the temperature through the roof when he put the steps to music.

"Come on, Sarah, wiggle those hips!" he said to one of the girls as he shimmied around the group. "Give it a little bit more, you at the back! Let's feel the music!"

Erin couldn't help but smile and Olivier winked across at her when he took one of the girls by the hand and spun her around on the floor. They'd had such a lovely time over lunch and Erin was starting to believe she had found a true friend in Olivier, even though they had really only just met. There was so much more to him than the looks and the bike and the delectable French accent. He was a down-to-earth, multi-talented man who was fantastic company and a treat to be around. And he made her laugh. She loved to laugh.

"He really is something else, isn't he?" said her mother who had popped back into The Community Centre with clean tea towels and a box of goodies for some of the children. The place was buzzing and the atmosphere was heating up as everyone busied around in preparation for the show.

"He's a great guy," said Erin, watching as Olivier swivelled his hips in the centre of the floor. "We had lunch together and he told me all about his life in Paris. He's an exotic creature, I tell you. Mesmerising, almost."

"Be careful you don't get too close, Erin," said Geri in her "mother knows best" voice. "You're pretty vulnerable at the moment and you don't want to be doing anything silly. I noticed how he looked at you earlier . . ."

Erin took her eyes off Olivier and turned to her mother. She took the box of goodies from her, shaking her head.

"Oh, you really are a wise old owl, Geri O'Brien," she said. "But don't worry, I'm a big girl. I don't know where this assumption has come from, but it seems that everyone has paired Olivier and me off together already which means I can barely speak to the guy without everyone jumping to conclusions. We actually get on quite well, and I don't think Taylor would have a problem with that, so everyone else can just butt out."

Erin giggled in remembrance to how Olivier had used that same term earlier and Geri rolled her eyes and followed her daughter across the room towards the kitchen.

"Fair enough, fair enough" she said. "Just don't say I didn't warn you."

They made their way into the tiny kitchen where Agnes was wiping around worktops with a bleach spray as if her life depended on it. She looked so glamorous in an effortless way and even in her apron and rubber gloves, she oozed style and a youthful appearance.

"Just the very person," she said when Erin made her way in. "I was hoping you might turn up soon. You'll never guess what."

"Er, what is it?" asked Erin. "You have found the secret to everlasting youth and you want to pass it on to me?"

"Not exactly," laughed Agnes. "But I have a date for your diary. This Monday evening at seven o'clock the three of us have been invited for dinner with an old friend of mine. Gosh, I really can't believe we are to meet up after all this time. And she only lives up the road. People are just too busy these days to keep in touch. Modern times, eh?"

Geri looked at Erin and then at Agnes who was well and truly excited about her big news.

"Is this Olivier's grandmother?" asked Geri.

"Yes, it is. How exciting!"

"And she wants the three of us round? Why not just you?"

Agnes dried her hands on a tea towel and then folded her arms.

"Bernadette and I went to school together," she said. "When we were teenagers she went skiing in the Alps with her family and she met the love of her life – a French man called Garrett Laurent. She went to live with him in France and spent many years there but then she moved back when she had her family reared and has been living only about ten miles away ever since. We have been meaning to meet up for so long and now with Olivier being around here so much, she sees this as an opportunity to stop talking about it and do something. I think she wants to show him off to all of us!"

"Hmmm, I can see why," said Geri, peeping out through the kitchen door to get a look at Olivier in action. "God, but he is handsome!"

"Mother! Control yourself," joked Erin. "So did she call you today? How did this invitation come about?"

"She called me just now," said Agnes. "I gave her grandson my number this morning and he obviously passed it on straight away. She tells me you two had lunch together today. Very cosy."

Erin took a deep breath and looked at her mother who shrugged.

"People will talk, Erin," said Geri. "People will talk."

"Well, if going for lunch with a friend is a crime, then I am guilty. Hands up, I surrender to the Lunch Police on this occasion. My God, we talked about Taylor most of the bloody time. Olivier is a sweetheart and I will not be kept away from him because of jealous busybodies in this village!"

"And right you are," said Agnes. "Well, then, you will be glad to know that I have accepted Bernadette's invitation and we are to get directions to her home from Olivier before then. Erin, can I leave that in your capable hands?"

"That you can, dear grandmother. Permission to talk to a member of the opposite sex, please, Mother?" she joked.

"Granted," said Geri. "Just don't get too close."

The rehearsal session ended on a high later that afternoon and Olivier seemed exhausted after all his teaching and the fun he'd had with the chorus dancers.

"They picked everything up so quickly," he said to Erin as he put on his biker jacket. "I have to say, today has been so much fun. As much as I love my grandmother's company, it's fantastic to have this wonderful community spirit just around the corner so that I can get my fix of all things artistic."

Once again, Erin could feel the glare of Krystal Smith on her back as she spoke to Olivier. The woman really did have it in for her but Erin was much stronger than that.

"Speaking of just around the corner," she said. "I believe we have a dinner date on Monday evening?"

"Really? We do?"

Olivier looked a tad confused and Erin was sure she saw a flash of excitement in his eyes.

"Well, there are five of us in total. I believe. Your grandmother has invited my family to have dinner with yours," she said. "It is so kind of her to do so. I'm really looking forward to it and my own grandmother is like a child at Christmas. She seems to have very fond memories of Bernadette Laurent."

Olivier zipped up his coat and leaned closer to Erin. "My heart actually skipped a beat just now," he said. "I honestly thought you were going to ask me out."

"Oh!"

He held his hands up. "Not that I would have expected it. And I know it is totally out of bounds but for a brief millisecond there now, I . . . well, maybe I was hoping for the impossible."

Erin could feel her face flush and she glanced around her to see who was watching. Oh yes, just as she had anticipated. Everyone was.

"So, dinner at my gran's then," said Olivier as she scrambled to get her breath back. "Sounds good. I look forward to seeing you then, Erin."

"Me too. Oh, hold on. Before you go can you give me directions or an address at least?"

She could feel her heart pump inside her as adrenaline surfed through her every vein. He took out his phone and punched in her name.

"I'll text you. That's if it's okay to give me your number. Perhaps I am being presumptuous?"

He laughed as he said the word and Erin flicked back her hair. To hell with them all. If you're going to be a bear, be a Grizzly, she thought. Might as well be hung for a sheep as a lamb and all that. She chanted out her number and he nodded at her and put his phone back in his jacket pocket.

"I will be in touch. *Au revoir* everyone," he said to his adoring fans who were lapping up his every move. "That session was '*fantastique*'. I look forward to Wednesday already."

Geri gave Erin a knowing look but Erin was smiling too much to care. She wasn't doing anything wrong, was she? My God but some people lived in the Dark Ages. What harm was it to befriend a stranger to the community? She would do the exact same if Taylor was here. Yes, of course she would. . .

The evening passed gently for Erin and she was proud of herself that she had not succumbed to the urge to visit the off licence on the way home from rehearsals. She settled into a pair of comfy jammies after a hot bubble bath and flicked through the television to find some entertainment to while away the hours till bedtime. She thought about Taylor and what he might be doing now, so far away from her.

It was afternoon over there, so he was probably enjoying some downtime with his new friends in the sun. Perhaps they were at the beach or at a pool or a barbecue. She wondered if she was even on his mind right now. When her mobile rang at that moment and she saw his name on the screen her heart soared and she got a hug of reassurance, knowing that they were thinking of each other at exactly the same time.

"Hello?" she said, cosying into the sofa so she could enjoy the sound of his voice in the greatest comfort. "Hello?"

There was no reply. She could hear background noise and a mixture of accents and music. It was outdoors.

"Hello? Taylor? Can you hear me?"

Then she heard a voice in the distance. "Hey, Taylor. Come on! You promised!"

"I'll be right there, Belle. Two seconds. I never break a promise."

Erin froze, then gulped and her blood ran cold, sending shivers right through her.

"Taylor?" she said into the phone, but he couldn't hear her. He had dialled her number by accident. She held the phone away from her ear and her thumb hovered over the button as her heart told her to hang up. But her head said no. She had to hear more. She put the phone to her ear again and closed her eyes shut, waiting for another insight into Taylor's Hollywood lifestyle.

"He said he'll be right there, Belle," said another man. "My God, that kid has it bad for you."

"Tell me about it," said Taylor. "What she was whispering into my ear last night. Holy shit! It has nearly kept me awake since. Jesus!"

"Well, go and play, man," said the voice. "You're in Hollywood. Go get your prize."

Erin's heart sank and she hung up the phone and threw it on the floor. She couldn't listen to any more. Suddenly she felt cold and lonely all on her own. How could he? How could he do this to her? After all that they had built up over the years. How could he throw it all away because of some damn holiday romance that he would forget about once he landed back on home soil?

She sobbed on the sofa, not knowing what to do and hugged her knees. So her fears were true after all. All her deepest fears and instincts rushed to the surface and a river of emotions washed through her – disappointment, fear, guilt with how she had perhaps felt about Olivier, but most of she was so, so sad.

This was going to force some decisions her way that she never wanted to face. She would have to end it with Taylor. If you love someone, set them free, she thought, and she went to the kitchen and scrambled in the cupboards until she found what she was looking for.

Sorcha Daly put the finishing touches to her suitcase,

checked her passport details for the third time and let out a satisfactory sigh. She kept replaying the scene in her head when she had told Erin O'Brien her news of her big trip. Oh, how the mighty have fallen, she thought. Erin had appeared so smug and confident as she strolled out with the handsome French newcomer, but Sorcha had pulled the rug from under her feet.

She closed her eyes and pictured the moment when she would meet Taylor in Hollywood. He would be tanned and gorgeous, his white smile beaming when he saw her and his beautiful face would light up especially for her. He must be so lonely over there with all those strangers and a visit from home would no doubt brighten up his day.

Of course she had added to her story when she was speaking to Erin. Taylor had absolutely no idea she was flying out to him and nor did *The Gazette* but a few lies here and there wouldn't hurt anyone. It was a working holiday, she had convinced herself, and the interview she would have on set with Taylor – and who knows, maybe even Sandra Bullock if she played her cards right – would earn her brownie points not only with *The Gazette*, but also with the entire newspaper group. If Taylor couldn't accommodate an old school friend to a scoop, then who would?

She looked up at Marilyn on her wall and she was sure she gave her a wink with those famous, fluttering dark eyelashes.

"I know, Marilyn," she said. "I am *so* doing the right thing. I can just feel it in my bones."

She zipped up her case and got into bed, delighted at last that the house was silent. Eugene was in his own room, superglued to his video games as usual and her father was at the pub. All hell would break loose when he got home, no doubt, so for now Sorcha was going to make use of the peace and quiet and try to get some sleep. She closed her eyes, snuggled further into the duvet and urged her mind to drift to the sunshine in California where she would be reunited with her beloved boy.

Erin looked at the clock and squinted. She needed more wine. She had to get more but there would be nowhere open apart from The Stage Bar and it was too far to walk. She had searched every cupboard, every nook, every cranny of the kitchen to where she usually hid the odd bottle but everything was gone. Even in her fuzzy state of mind, she knew all of the places to look. The medicine cabinet, behind the bin under the sink, at the back of the corner cupboard where she kept tins and other dry foods – all little hiding places where no one else would think of stashing their booze. Her wine rack was empty but it had been for days now, and the mini-cellar she had made out in the garden shed was cleared out by her mother.

Damn you, Taylor, she thought as she stumbled out into the hallway. Damn you and damn Hollywood! Why oh why oh why? She lifted a photo from the hall table and stared at him, her head nodding gently under the influence of the alcohol.

"I hope she's worth it," she slurred to him. "I hope she makes you happy 'cos I obviously didn't. You liar! You fucking liar!"

She dropped the photo frame onto the floor and it

smashed into smithereens. Sniffing as she walked away, she fetched a brush and made a feeble attempt to clean up the glass which was strewn across the floor in tiny, winking slivers that shone under the light.

She bent down to scoop them up and wobbled as she stood again, but then a familiar sound made her ears take notice. Was that the sound of . . .? Could it be?

She walked to the front door and opened it wide behind her, then a wave of excitement swept through her when she saw Olivier get off his bike and stroll to the door of a house across the road. She had an urge to call for him, but didn't, instead choosing to watch from afar, wondering who his friend in this housing development was. He hadn't mentioned anyone. Could it be a woman? As far as she could figure, he was unattached and available and flirtatious and oh so sexy!

He knocked the door of the house and Erin stepped back slightly as he glanced around while he waited. He was certainly a late visitor and whoever lived in that house must not be expecting him at this hour. When it was safe to do so, she peeped back out again and her stomach knotted when she saw a young lady. She greeted him with a kiss and a hug on her doorstep and then ushered him inside.

So *he* was a smarmy rat too then, she thought, and she slammed the front door shut then went into the living room and slumped down on the sofa, wondering how her life had become so damn complicated.

SCENE FOURTEEN

"I think Dermot is having an affair," said Kizzy the next morning when Erin called in to her to be comforted.

Erin hadn't even had a chance to tell her about Taylor when Kizzy blurted it out as she waited for the kettle to boil.

"Probably is," said Erin. "Sure aren't you having a semi-affair yourself with that ugly beast Niall McGrath? I really can't believe that out of all your exes, you end up reacquainting with *him*. I mean, we used to call him Dumbo. Isn't that enough to put you off?"

Kizzy put one hand on her hip and pointed at Erin with a teaspoon.

"Looks like you got out on the wrong side of the bed too this morning? Hungover again?"

Erin shrugged. "Maybe I am. Maybe I have good reason to be. Maybe I should have a fucking affair because all the rest of my nearest and dearest seem to be doing the dirty. Maybe I missed the bloody memo to inform me that it was 'secret lives and lovers' season!"

211

"Erin," said Kizzy, "I have no idea what you're on about. And before you accuse me of having an affair with Dumbo, can I remind you that I told you in confidence –"

"Don't lie – you told me because you were drunk."

"Okay then, I told you in drunken stupor that I had flirted with Dumbo online a few times and that he wanted to meet up. But I did *not* meet up with him and I *will* not meet up with him." She paused. "Especially now that you have reinforced that horrible nickname in my brain. I'd forgotten that. Were his ears really that big?"

"Massive."

"Gross," said Kizzy. "Anyhow, forget about him. I'm talking Dermot here and his new shoes. He went out the other day and bought himself a pair of new shoes and a Robbie Williams CD. Like, *hello*? Smells like an affair to me."

Erin, despite her bad humour, couldn't help but laugh at Kizzy's detective work. She took the cup of coffee from her friend and sat down on the two-seater sofa in Kizzy's kitchen.

"Sorry, I don't get it. Is there a website that says if a man buys new shoes *and* a Robbie Williams CD at the same time that he must be having an affair? Shoes plus Robbie equals infidelity?"

Kizzy rolled her eyes. It was a running joke that she Googled everything in life so she couldn't argue back on that one. It was partly true.

"No, I didn't find that theory online. No website could be so accurate even if I do say so myself," she said. "But I did find a site that said to look out for signs such as new behaviour or new interests. First of all came the darts – I still am not over that one. Then he buys himself these really expensive shoes that look like something from the Next Directory and are so shiny you can see your chin in them when you're talking to him. Now, before you speak, remember that Dermot hasn't bought himself a stitch since I started going out with him. Not one stitch of clothing in ten years and that is no exaggeration. His mother did it for him before I came along. He is clueless."

Erin wanted to laugh but she couldn't. Kizzy was taking this very seriously.

"So where does poor Robbie come into the mix? Doesn't Dermot buy CDs either?"

"CDs? No way! Never! I'm telling you, Erin. I can count on one hand what Dermot has bought since the day and hour I met him. He buys cigarettes, Red Bull, chewing gum, beer and . . . no, that's it. Four things. He wouldn't even know the difference between Robbie Williams and Ronan Keating, I swear!"

Kizzy was determined that something was going on. She had done her homework over the weekend and had turned around from being a bored wife tempted to have a secret rendezvous with her big-eared ex to a suspicious wife who was convinced that her husband was having a fling with a girl who liked darts, shiny shoes and Robbie Williams. What a difference a day makes!

"Anyhow," said Kizzy, "I'm going to confront him when he gets home from Mass in half an hour or so. Imagine him dragging his ould ma up the aisle to eat the altar rails every Sunday while I slave over a bloody roast beef dinner, when all the time he's seeing some young thing behind my back!"

"Lovely. So I'll make myself scarce then. Can I finish my coffee first?"

Kizzy plonked down on the arm of the sofa and swung her feet around onto the seat so that she was facing her friend.

"Gosh, I'm sorry. Right, go on. Tell me . . ."

"Tell you what?"

"Tell me your tale of woe now that I've burdened you with mine. You were drinking again last night and what's this I hear about you going for lunch with that new French guy?"

Erin's eyes widened in disbelief.

"Jesus Christ, where the hell did you hear that? Is there a game of Chinese Whispers going on in this village or what?"

Kizzy made a face. "Wooo! Looks like I may have touched a wee nerve."

"No, you haven't touched 'a wee nerve' at all. I just think it's ridiculous that people feel my lunch-time routine is a conversation topic. We went for lunch. So what!"

"Calm down, love! I'm just *saying*. My mum heard it when she went round to your mum last night to have her hair done. They were talking about this big Players show and he came up and then incidentally so did you. So what's going on? Has he said '*voulez vous coucher avec moi*' yet?"

"No! Fuck off!"

"Well, then what is it? You look flustered and bothered. It has to be Taylor then, right?"

Erin fiddled with her bracelet in silence for a moment. "Unfortunately, yes, it's Taylor. "Hey, did you hear that

The Gazette is sending Sorcha Daly over to see him in Hollywood? Like, I just don't get that. I work on a television show and they wouldn't have the budget or the inclination to do that for me. Why does she get to go and I don't?"

Kizzy stood up again and lifted a piece of Lego from under her behind, then sat back down.

"Yeah, I heard that too from the same source – it was all the gossip last night at your mum's," said Kizzy. "Biggest pile of nonsense I've ever heard in my life. She's kidding nobody but herself, poor girl. I feel kind of sorry for her and her brother. If that's what makes her happy, then let her go on about her business. Is that it? Is that what's bothering you?"

Erin paused and thought about what she had overheard the night before. "No, of course not. Oh, why are all men such bastards, Kizz? Why isn't there one decent man around who is honest and faithful and who can love us for who we are for longer than the honeymoon period? I just don't get it. I am totally convinced that Taylor is flying his kite over there in LA. Totally."

"I'm sorry, but the mood I'm in with Dermot and all men in general, I can't even defend him. I hear you, sister," said Kizzy and she got up to see to one of her twins who had just woken from their morning nap. "But at least you don't have the weight of a wedding band on your finger. You can walk anytime you want, my friend. But unfortunately, it's not that simple for me, is it?"

Erin was turning the key in her door when she caught a glimpse of Olivier's black motorcycle out of the corner of her eye. It was still parked outside her neighbour's house. Oh-oh. Surely he would have mentioned a girlfriend when they'd spent so much time yesterday talking about Taylor? Yes, it would have been a fairly natural thing to lead into. And why all the hints that he wanted a date with her? Was that just meaningless flirtation? But how could he have established a relationship in Millfield so quickly? On the other hand, from what she'd picked up from him to date, he would be a pretty quick mover if he was interested in someone.

It was none of her business anyway, she told herself, and she walked into the hallway. She had other fish to fry like an errant boyfriend and his bloody Californian babe "Belle".

She threw her keys down on the hall table and noticed the lack of glass on the photo frame which she had smashed the night before. Temper, temper, she thought and the fear of not remembering doing it filled her with dread. This latest bombshell with Taylor would be the perfect excuse to dive into a drunken haze for a few days but she had a big week ahead with a political scandal having broken in the Province and she was sure she would be drafted in for support in the news team at work. No, she would be ultra-sensible on this occasion and focus on the real world. A world without Taylor because that's what the future held, or so it seemed.

She hadn't heard from him which was even more worrying – to say nothing of even more frustrating. She longed to challenge him and her mind had raced all morning with how she might broach the subject when he did eventually call. Which he would, she had no doubt.

Perhaps she should play it cool and ask politely about how everything was going, then ask in particular who he was chums with since she had been accused of being disinterested previously. Or, she could go straight for the jugular and ask him what the fuck he was playing at with some bimbo called Belle at a poolside party when he was too pissed to know that he was calling her at the same bloody time!

Breathe, she thought. Breathe in and out and don't panic. He may have a perfectly sound explanation for it all. Maybe he had indeed won a prize. Maybe they'd had a raffle or a bet and he had one and Belle was minder of the prize which could be anything from a cuddly teddy to a bottle of champagne or a nice box of truffles? Yeah, right!

She picked up the phone and dialled her mother's number.

"Were you at Mass?" was the first question her mother asked her. Not, how are you or would you like to come for dinner or how did you spend your Saturday night. Oh no. Straight to the point was Geri O'Brien.

"Em, no, I was on my way, you see, and I just remembered that I had left something at Kizzy's the other day so I went round to get it. I did say a decade of the Rosary on my way home to make up for it though."

"Hmmm," said Geri and Erin could just imagine her fiddling with her hair as she watched *Something for the Weekend* with *The Sunday Life* on her lap. "I just don't know any more. Since Taylor left . . . oh, it doesn't matter. Are you coming round for dinner? Gran has a nice roast on and it's almost done."

"Suppose," said Erin.

"Well, if you don't want to, that's fine. I mean, if our company isn't good enough . . . maybe you'd prefer to have lunch with Olivier again. Honestly, it's the talk of the village."

Erin counted to three. One, two, three. She could say so much right now . . . but she wouldn't.

"Tell Gran I'll bring a rhubarb tart. I'll see you in five."

She hung up the phone and lifted her mobile, purse and keys and walked back out through the front door where she heard the rev of Olivier's bike. She froze, not knowing whether to let him see her or not. He had no idea where she lived and if he did, he hadn't said. She didn't want him to know that she knew of his secret sleepovers at her neighbour's house. She stood there, facing the door and her heart picked up pace as she heard the bike come closer and then slow down to a stop behind her.

She fidgeted with her keys, pretending she couldn't find the right one and kept her head down. Shit.

"*Bonjour*, Erin," he called from beneath the visor on his helmet. "I didn't realise you lived here."

She turned, flicking her hair back, and walked towards him, trying to appear surprised and ever so casual.

"Um, yeah. This is my humble abode."

Now, you tell me why you've been staying here, she thought. But no, he didn't. He just reached into his jacket pocket and took out a piece of folded paper.

"Directions," he said. "For tomorrow night. Like you, I'm not very good at directions so I asked my friend to write them out, rather than me attempting to text you and have you get lost. I'll see you tomorrow night?"

Your friend – interesting, she thought. She could barely see him beneath the helmet and she got a sudden rush of romance and excitement. There was something about him that could potentially make her do very, very dangerous things.

"You will," she said, her mouth quivering. She gulped and he gave her a beaming smile.

"I am looking forward to it."

At that he, revved up his engine again, leaned forward on his bike and flicked the visor back down on his helmet then zoomed off into the distance.

"Oh holy God," said Erin. "What the hell am I going to do?"

SCENE FIFTEEN

"You seem distracted," said Aimee in work the next day. "Did you have a nice weekend or is your mind lost in the hills of Hollywood, you poor thing?"

Erin looked up at Aimee's angelic youthful face which was always so caring and attentive. How could someone possibly be so bloody kind and compassionate all the time? Aimee really did have the face of a cherub and the body of a goddess. She only had to walk through the offices to have men almost falling at her feet.

"I actually had a . . . let me see . . . you know, it was quite mixed you could say. Good points, bad points but nothing I couldn't handle. So what's on the agenda this week? Have you heard anything about extra news coverage needed? I'm so up for extra work this week to take my mind off things."

"Oh," said Aimee and put her tiny porcelain hand to her mouth. "I thought you might have heard by now. Gosh, this is embarrassing . . ."

"What?" said Erin. She stood up from her chair, walked around her desk and leaned her behind on it. "What's embarrassing?"

"Maybe you should talk to someone in the newsroom," whispered Aimee, barely able to meet Erin's eye. "I don't want this to come between us, Erin, but they have asked me to do some on-air work this week, just on a trial basis. You know, to see if I'm up for it . . . and I might not be. But it means that you probably won't be needed. I'm so sorry."

Erin felt like someone had blocked her windpipe and the room went fuzzy for a few seconds.

"Oh," she said, lifting a paperclip and twisting it around her little finger. "Well, that's . . . that's fantastic for you, Aimee. Just a bit of a shock for me but great for you. Ah well, you win some you lose some. It was never really 'mine' to start with so I can't really complain."

Aimee looked well and truly heartbroken. In fact, Erin was sure she might even be a bit teary, but maybe that was just her.

"I could say no and they would come straight to you," said Aimee. "But it's what I've worked towards for two years now. It might be my only chance to impress them. You see, I have looked up to you all along and this might give me a tiny, tiny glimpse into what it's like to be . . . to be, well, like you."

Erin squinted at the younger girl and laughed uncertainly. "You don't want that, Aimee. Believe me, you really don't."

"I do! Ever since I first started here, even before I started here, I used to watch you as you climbed the ranks from weather girl to newsreader and now you

221

have your very own show. You have your very own show, Erin! Do you have any idea what I would do to be in your shoes? It's my dream. It's always been my dream."

Erin sat back down on her chair and pursed her lips. It was surreal to hear that someone actually admired her in such a way. Yes, she knew she was recognisable at a very local, provincial level and that her job had the odd perk such as free make-up trials and the opportunity to meet so many people but she didn't ever realise that she was living someone's dream. She really did take things for granted sometimes.

"Well, in that case," she said. "I wish you the very best of luck this week, Aimee. You go for it, girl. I hope you blow them away and if there's any advice you need from me, you know you can ask any time."

"Really?" said Aimee, her doe-eyes widened. "I . . . I don't know what to say. I was terrified that you might not like me after this but . . . wow! Thanks, Erin. You really are as nice as everyone says you are. Thank you so much."

Aimee walked away back to her own side of the huge office space and Erin looked around her in a muddle. Did people really like her here as much as Aimee had said? God, she really had been living in a bubble lately. Maybe she should take Ryan The Producer out for lunch and show some enthusiasm for the wonderful opportunity she had in her day job. It might not be Hollywood, but it was small-screen gold and she knew she could do so much better if she believed in herself just that tiny bit more.

By evening, Erin's mood had lifted to a new high and she found herself fantasising about her dinner date with

Olivier and his grandmother. What should she wear? Should she ask her mother to blow-dry her hair for the occasion? What should she bring as a thank-you gift? Her head spun with so many things and combined with the action-packed programme of ideas she had given to Ryan The Producer at lunch-time, her brain was a hive of creativity.

"You seem to be slowly getting back to your old self," he had told her over a Pizza Express. "I'm delighted to see some of your old spark back."

"Well, sometimes it takes a bit of competition to wake you up," she said. "I'm delighted for Aimee. She deserves a chance as much as the rest of us. It's not all fun and games where I am right now, but I've got a sudden rush of positivity today and I don't want to let it go."

"Glad to hear it," said Ryan. "It's nice to see you so bright-eyed and bushy-tailed on a Monday morning. No offence!"

"None taken," said Erin.

Now, she had dinner to prepare for and it was only when she was shopping in her local Sainsbury's for some flowers for Olivier's gran that the whoosh of sickness came like a whirlpool in her stomach again. Oh Taylor, she thought. Where are you and why aren't you calling me to explain what is going on?

She paused by the flower stall and let the stabbing pain pass through her as images of him with another woman flooded her mind. She had managed so well today and although she couldn't understand it, the wave of new-found energy and interest in her work that came from Aimee's breakthrough had carried her up to this point. But now the doubts were back again and the power of the heartache she was in for was pulsing into her brain.

She called Kizzy, who was elbow-deep in the bath with the twins.

"Should I call him? Just tell me now. Should I?"

"Yes, I've been telling you to do so all along," said Kizzy. "Ow! Sorry, but my darling daughter decided I needed suds in my eyes. Look, babe. You know Taylor, as lovely as he is, can be a teeny bit stubborn just as most people can be and he could be holding out for a call from you. Didn't you say that your last conversation was a little bit edgy?"

"Yeah, but . . ."

"Yeah but there you go. He's licking his wounds and waiting for your call."

"As long as that's all he is licking . . . gosh, I can't believe I said that. Oh God, images in my head now please go away!"

"Settle your wee head Erin and give him a call. Give him the benefit of the doubt at least and then take it from there. It's not like he has even defended himself and you may be jumping to conclusions about his liaisons with this Belle babe. She could be a pure dog for all you know."

"Hmmm," said Erin, and she lifted a bunch of daffodils from the bucket in the supermarket. "What else could I bring? Daffodils and what?"

"To where? Oh God, that's right! Oh, the excitement that is your life, Erin O'Brien! If only we could swap places for just one day. I swear, you come round here and make Dermot his cabbage and bacon and I'll go and stare into that dreamboat's eyes. I would actually pay you to swap with me at this present time. All I have to look forward to is a double whammy of *Coronation Street* and the sound of Dermot snoring on the sofa."

Erin shuddered at the very thought. No harm to Kizzy but she would probably have a nervous breakdown if she was living such a miserable existence. So much for two-point-four children and a white picket fence with your childhood sweetheart! Did such a lifestyle even exist?

"Well, I'll let you know how it goes. In fact, I'll call Taylor after dinner in case it turns into an epic and puts me off going to Olivier's at all. I wouldn't like to let my grandmother down just because my boyfriend is having so much fun in La La Land and I can't cope with it."

"Attagirl," said Kizzy. "Now, I want all the juicy details when you get home so give me a call too. You know I'll be there for you if this doesn't work out?"

"I do."

"But chin up, babes. Somehow I don't think that you have anything to worry about where Taylor Smith is concerned. He is prime-time in love with you! He'd be crazy if he wasn't!"

Sorcha Daly adjusted her oversized sunnies and checked out her reflection as she walked through the busy terminal at LAX. She felt like a celebrity as she sauntered through the buzz and the atmosphere that spelt Californian life. All around her were super-skinny, suntanned beauties drinking healthy juices and nibbling on fruity snacks and everyone looked famous or wealthy. This is the life, she thought and she pulled her modest Asda suitcases along behind her, feeling a bit tatty amongst all the Louis Vuitton and Versace luggage that sped past her.

"Er, the Andaz Hotel, West Hollywood," she said into a cab that pulled up to the sidewalk. She loved all the American terminology like "sidewalk" and "boulevard" and "vacation" and just seeing the familiar signage that she had seen on television and in the movies gave her a buzz that she had never, ever experienced before. It was magical.

"Welcome to the City of Angels, baby," said a man on the street who was selling new copies of the *Hollywood Gazette* and the *LA Times*.

"Why, thank you, kind sir," she said back and, having put her luggage into the boot, she got into the cab, suddenly feeling every inch the princess that she intended to be during her brief visit. She had scraped up a few thousand pounds and transferred them into dollars for spending money and she had prepaid her accommodation and flights so the world was her oyster. Meeting Taylor on set at Universal Studios or on location at Malibu Beach was her main mission, but she had a few hoops to jump through to make that happen so she made sure to have enough cash with her so she was sure of a good time, interview with Taylor or not.

The cab drove along the 405 Freeway and Sorcha caught her breath when she saw the famous Hollywood sign on her right-hand side. Her mouth dropped open as the familiar surroundings of the Hollywood Hills came into view under a hazy blue sky and her heart raced at the fact that she was really here. She had so much to do and see and she couldn't decide where to start. She wanted to visit the grave of her lifelong heroine, Marilyn Monroe, she longed to taste a hotdog from the famous Tail o' the Pup stand that she had seen in many movies, she wanted to put her hands in the prints of the stars on the Hollywood Walk of Fame – but first of all she wanted to shop on Hollywood Boulevard and make herself beautiful.

She opened her purse to pay the driver and found the envelope that Krystal Smith had given her on the Saturday afternoon at rehearsals. She had forgotten all about it, but Krystal had said it was in exchange for all of Taylor's Hollywood contact details. She would open it when she got inside.

The Andaz Hotel boasted the highest rooftop garden in the Hollywood Hills and Sorcha was warmed by the balmy sunshine that fell on her shoulders when she stepped out of the air-conditioned vehicle. For early March, it was remarkably warm yet she noticed passers by wore clothing more suitable to weather at home. She couldn't wait to get changed into shorts and T-shirt and top up her tan as she explored what the movie capital of the world had to offer.

The outside of the hotel was stunning with its glass front and palm trees at either side and she breathed in the Californian air. She took her suitcase from the cab driver and had only walked a few steps when the concierge took her two cases and led her into the hotel's lobby where she couldn't take the grin off her face as she walked up to the check-in desk.

"Miss Sorcha Daly," she said in her most polite voice.

"Five nights, Miss Daly?"

"Yes, that's right. Five nights."

A few clicks on the computer later and Sorcha was greeted by her hotel host who led her to a bar where she was offered a glass of wine on the house.

"Don't mind if I do," she said and reminded herself not to sound so bloody desperate. The host returned with the wine and joined her in the lounge where she explained all the tours and guides available and a few insider tips on how to make most of her stay in Movieland. The excitement she felt was nothing like she had ever experienced before. She was in Hollywood, baby! She thought of the dull, loveless, grey life she had left behind in Millfield and it seemed like she was now on a different planet. What she would give to never have to return to that misery with her squabbling parents and her lonely existence! If only she could escape to a sunshine life like Taylor was experiencing right now. She would never go back. Never.

When her host had made her feel more than welcome, she was brought to her room on the third floor and, with every step she took, she was discovering more and more why she had made the very best decision to come on this spontaneous adventure. She opened the door to her double room and gasped at the views out over the rusty rooftop views of houses nestled in the leafy hills which some of the most famous people in the world called home.

"I love you, Los Angeles!" she said and then she fell backwards onto the soft, white cotton sheets of her king-size bed, her arms spread out and her spindly legs up in the air, and closed her eyes and listened. She could hear the faint sounds of Hollywood life in the far distance and it soothed her mind and let her relax into a place in her mind that she had never been before. No arguing from downstairs, no Marilyn on the wall to look at her and determine her mood, no feeling like a leper when she walked down the street, or a failure when she was still stuck writing about weddings and wakes on *The Gazette* after three years. No, this was Hollywood and in Hollywood she could be whoever she wanted to be.

She found her purse once more and tore open the envelope from Krystal, making sure once again that it was for her and not a private message for Taylor. No, it said on the outside – 'Sorcha – *do not open until you arrive. K. xxx*'

Well, that was pretty clear. She lifted out a folded piece of notepaper and out dropped a hundred-dollar bill. The note said in block capitals:

TAKE TAYLOR OUT FOR COFFEE ON ME. FIND OUT AS MUCH AS YOU CAN – YOU KNOW WHAT I MEAN. WE WILL MEET WHEN YOU COME BACK TO DISCUSS. KS.

"Oh my, my, my!" said Sorcha. "Guess who else isn't Erin O'Brien's biggest fan. Tut tut, Krystal. Tut tut!"

With that, she slipped the hundred-dollar bill into her purse and lifted the phone to order room service. Yes, she fancied a long cool fruity cocktail as she planned her evening with the pleasure of knowing that she had so, so much to do.

SCENE SIXTEEN

Geri had been quiet the entire ten-minute journey to Olivier's neck of the woods while her mum and daughter gabbled continuously about how nice it was to be invited for dinner on a Monday evening.

"I normally would do a bit of turnip on a Monday evening," said Agnes from the back seat. She leaned in to make sure she could be heard over Erin's choice of music. "I like it fried in the pan with the juice of a slice or two of bacon which is really not what the doctor would recommend at my stage of life, but sure you have to have the odd vice, that's what I say."

Geri piped up out of her daze to join in the conversation.

"I hope this old friend of yours isn't going to feed us full of grease," she said. "I thought the French were healthy eaters. There's no fat on that Olivier boy, anyhow. Oh and I meant to ask you, Erin – what do you think of this blouse I have on? It's not too young, is it?"

"It looks lovely, Mum. Honestly, it does," said Erin

but her eyes were fixed on the road as she indicated into the old-style housing development where Olivier and his grandmother resided. It was a zig-zag of little two-bedroom bungalows mixed with terraces of taller three-storey homes with neat gardens lined with trimmed hedgerows. "Now what number does it say on those directions? I don't want to look myself for fear of running over a small child or someone's cat."

"Sixty-five," said Geri, holding the piece of paper out from her face and squinting at the lettering. "He writes like a girl though, doesn't he? Do you think he might be a bit gay with all that dancing around?"

Erin let out a deep sigh that turned into a groan and she pulled into a parking space not too far from where Olivier's motor-cycle was mounted on the pavement.

"The directions were written by a friend of his who happens to be a girl and I don't think it is very broadminded to assume that, just because he can dance, he must be gay. Really, Mum, I thought better of you."

They got out of the car and filed up the narrow pathway of the little bungalow. It was as neat as the other houses around it and a lilac window-box with bluebells and snowdrops were a welcoming addition to the tiny windows. A border of flowers lined the pathway and a modest garden bench sat along the wall. It was a low-maintenance home which suited a lady of Bernadette Laurent's age but seemed way too small to house someone as tall, dark and handsome as Olivier.

"Do you think we've brought enough gifts with us?" whispered Agnes as they waited for someone to answer the door. "I'm really quite nervous, you know. I haven't seen Bernadette in many, many years."

231

"Relax, Gran," said Erin and she coiffed her grand-mother's curls at the back while they waited. "Oh, here she comes now. This is exciting."

Bernadette Laurent opened the door of her modest house with a warm smile that would have made any stranger feel at home. She was a tiny lady with her white hair tied back into a neat bun and even though, as Agnes had reminded everyone at every possibility, she was Irish born and bred, she had a certain air of French chic about her that made her seem glamorous and elegant for a lady her age.

"Bernadette!" gasped Agnes and the two women embraced in the doorway.

"Just Bernie," said the lady. "And this must be Geri. Oh you do look like your mum. And wow, I can't believe I am having Erin O'Brien over for dinner! Come in quickly before the neighbours see you or they'll be round for autographs."

Bernie led the O'Briens into her little sitting room which they all noticed was quite minimalist and much more modern than what they would have imagined the house to look like on the inside. A tasteful wooden floor formed a base for a décor of creams and soft brown and beiges and on the pale marble hearth sat the only photograph in the room – a professionally shot black and white image of Bernie with Olivier and his parents and her own late husband. It was breathtaking how beautifully happy they all looked in their pose and both Geri and Erin tried their best not to stare.

"Olivier is in the kitchen, just through there," said Bernie. "Now, have a seat and let me fetch you some drinks. What can I get you? Wine? Orange juice?"

She reached for the drinks for her guests from a pre-prepared display of bottles and glasses on a side table which sat just under the window.

"Just orange juice for me," said Erin. "But I'm sure Mum and Gran will sample some wine?"

"Don't mind if we do," said Geri like a giddy schoolgirl. She couldn't help but take everything in. An unobtrusive CD of classical music hummed in the background and the smell of herbs and spices filled the air. It was a relaxing, tranquil setting which beat Agnes's normal turnip and bacon or her own normal Monday-night soap fest.

"So, Olivier is in the kitchen? He can cook too?" said Agnes. "He really is a talented boy, your grandson. You must be very, very proud."

"I am," said Bernie. "Ah, here he is. Olivier, come in and relax. We should have everything under control in the kitchen, shouldn't we?"

"*Bonjour*," said Olivier with his trademark smile and a hush fell over the women in the room. "I am so delighted you found us."

He made his way into the living room and Erin tried not to blush at the sight of his beauty. He looked different again and she couldn't put her finger on why. He wore faded denims, a loose white shirt and Converse trainers and he looked serene and even more handsome than before.

"Delighted you invited us," said Geri, suddenly forgetting her earlier reluctance to bother with this date at all. "And what a lovely treat on a Monday night. You know, most people have dinner parties on the weekend but there is very little to do on a Monday night, you know. Great idea. Thank you."

Erin sensed her mother's nerves from her unexpected rant and she decided to step in. She could feel this magnetic connection between Olivier and her and she almost expected him to give her his full attention or sit with her just like he had done at The Community Centre a few days before. Maybe she believed the rumours that had started already in the village? Yes, she was being influenced by idle gossip. She would treat Olivier as the person she knew, which was a stranger with whom she shared a common denominator: their grandparents.

"It is our pleasure, isn't it, Grandmère?" he said. "Erin, can I squeeze in beside you? I'm afraid we don't have a lot of space to entertain, but we will do our best."

Erin moved along the settee closer to her mother and Olivier sat beside her. It was, in fact, a tight squeeze. She could feel three pairs of eyes on them, each with different expressions. Geri had a warning look, Agnes was cautiously envious and Bernie was overjoyed.

"I just can't believe that on Friday I watched you on my television set, and now here you are sitting on my sofa," Bernie said. "This will give me something to talk about at bingo tomorrow night."

"Ah, do you play bingo?" said Agnes. "I used to play bingo but could never really take to those snazzy new halls they have in town. Is it easy to follow, Bernie? I'd love to pick up on it again."

Olivier gave Erin a secret smile and she returned it as the three ladies became engrossed in talk about bingo-pens, computerised numbers and the way things used to be when it was the Parish Priest calling out numbers in The Parochial Hall for a jackpot they called "The Snowball".

"Want to give me a hand in the kitchen?" Olivier said to Erin. "I think there are a few things we could find to do?"

They slipped out and when Erin walked into the kitchen she gasped in delight.

"Wow, Olivier. Did you prepare all of this for us? It looks stunning!"

Olivier shrugged. "It is no bother. I just thought I'd make an effort. It's not often we have visitors for dinner so let's say it is a novelty and I couldn't resist."

The small kitchen had been transformed into a candle-lit haven with a tasteful tablecloth and a single flower as a centrepiece. The room was cosy and warm and Olivier's personality oozed within the four walls. It was . . . it was so, so appealing, so welcoming and it made Erin feel so special that he had prepared all of this for her. And her mother . . . oh, and her grandmother, of course. She would not get too carried away.

"So, what can I do to help? Do you want me to wash up, or is there anything else I can do?"

"No, of course not," he said with a smile and Erin felt her heart flutter. "This is your seat, across from mine. Why don't you sit down and enjoy your drink while I prepare the starter and then we can interrupt the bingo ladies and get this party started?"

"I like your thinking," said Erin and she sat at the table and rested her elbows under her chin. She watched him move around the kitchen, humming as he prepped the first course and every now and then he would catch her eye and smile. He was mesmerising to look at, music to her ears to listen to and when he looked at her that way she felt her whole body melt before him. A voice inside her warned her not to let this happen. She was emotional and vulnerable and hurt by her fears of what Taylor was up to in his faraway existence. This isn't real, she thought. This is fantasy. This is not what I need to be thinking right now.

But the way he looked at her bored right into her soul. There was a strong connection between them like a wildfire that both of them knew was raging their way. She wanted to ask him about his friendship with her neighbour. Who was she? Why hadn't he mentioned her before? He referred to her as his "friend" but he stayed in her home, he kissed her goodbye. They had to be more than friends.

"So, is there anything you *can't* do, Monsieur Laurent?" she asked playfully. She tucked her hair behind her ear and looked up at him, her face slanted downwards but her eyes directed into his.

He dried his hands on a tea towel and then leaned on the table in front of where she sat and she heard her heart boom as his dark hair came so close to her face it almost touched her.

"I can do most things," he said. "Well, at least I will try to."

He stayed there and she was afraid to breathe out, he was so close. Think of Taylor, she told herself. Think of all you have with Taylor and how it will be okay and this is just a lustful temptation that you don't have to follow through. Think of the girl across the road who he might stay with tonight again. Think sensibly, Erin. Just think.

She sipped her wine and leaned back slightly in her chair, needing to breathe and break the intensity between them.

"Shall I call the others in now?" she said, her voice

cracking. The heat in the kitchen was unbearable and she needed some air. She needed to break the mould that was building around her and this strange but wonderful man.

"*Oui*," he said. "It's about that time."

Erin scraped back her chair and brushed past him, inhaling the fresh smell that lingered on his body. His full lips opened and closed like he was about to say something, but he stopped and just smiled instead.

"What?" she asked.

"Nothing," he said. "I must be . . . I must be very sensible, Erin. I . . . were we flirting just now?"

Erin felt a wave of heat rush right through her from her toes to her face which burned into a hot blush.

"Em . . . I . . . I don't know," she gulped. "I'll just go and get everyone . . ."

She closed the kitchen door behind her and stood against it, feeling her chest heave up and down as she caught her breath. What was happening to her? Where was Taylor in her mind? No matter what she feared, he was her long-term boyfriend and they had a lot of communicating to do so why was she lusting after a handsome stranger?

"Erin, what on earth are you doing? You look flustered. I'm just trying to find the bathroom."

Geri had her busybody-hairdresser face on and she looked at her daughter with an accusing stare. Erin braced herself, straightened her shoulders, flicked back her hair and smiled at her mother.

"Dinner's ready," she said. "I'll go and tell Gran and Bernadette. It looks delicious."

She could barely find her breath.

"Just like the chef?" said Geri, an eyebrow raised in suspicion.

"Yeah, you're absolutely right, Mum," said Erin with a cheeky smile. She would tell the truth. "Delicious, just like the chef, and you'd have to be deaf, dumb and blind not to notice just how adorable and delicious he really is."

Bernadette kept the conversation overflowing as much as the wine was over dinner, and the way she and Agnes were able to remember the finer details from their schooldays and teenage years was heart-warming.

They shared stories over duck spring rolls and mango dressing, laughed as they enjoyed succulent fillet of beef bourguignon and giggled over home-made meringue nests with fruit coulis and sweet whipped cream.

"And now here we are, kicking the ass of seventy and still thinking we are young spring chickens!" said Bernadette. "Oh why should we have to grow old? In my mind I am back in those days when we were carefree and running through the village as if we owned it. I don't want to be old. In fact, I refuse to be old."

"That's the right attitude, Grandmère," said Olivier. He had set out a platter of mixed olives with feta cheese and crackers in the centre of the table and they were going down a treat as a finish to their sumptuous meal. "Live life to the full and stay young in the mind. It's the only attitude to have."

Bernadette leaned across and put her wrinkly hand on top of Olivier's tanned, manly arm.

"And having you here with me keeps me so focused and very, very young indeed, my son. Oh, girls. What will I do when my Olivier leaves me? He makes my day."

Agnes stepped in, sensing that her old friend was feeling a little emotional. Olivier really was a sensational young man who had been one of the most impressive hosts she had ever come across and the love between him and his grandmother was evident. He had been so attentive to all four ladies, but there was a tension between Erin and him that hung in the air and it was the only sense of discomfort in the whole evening.

"I'm only ever a short time away from you, Grandmère," he said. "Whenever you need me I can hop on a plane and be here with you within hours. You know that."

Bernadette wiped her eyes. "Oh, I think I've had too much wine," she said, dabbing the sides of her mouth with a napkin. "One glass is enough for me, but I have to say I thoroughly enjoyed it this evening. We must do this again."

"We definitely will, but next time, it's my treat," said Agnes. "Although I doubt if I will be able to match Olivier's fine cuisine and attention to detail. That really was something else, young man. You will make someone a fine husband one day."

Bernadette beamed with pride, Geri stared at Olivier with lust-filled eyes and Erin stared at the table, afraid that if she caught his eye once more her loins might get up and dance with delight such was the incredible chemistry between the two of them throughout the meal. The way he glanced at her, just tiny glances as he ate or the way he asked her the odd question was so intense she was feeling quite claustrophobic and out of control. Plus, because she was driving she could have only the one glass of wine and she was longing to have another and relax in his company with the soft, mushy feeling that alcohol could give her.

By the time they had coffee in the sitting room it was getting late and Erin was afraid they would outstay their welcome.

"We should probably go soon," she said, giving her mother the eye to back her up. "Pity it wasn't a weekend and we could have stayed for longer, but some of us have to get up for work in the morning and it's getting late."

"That's right," said Geri. "I have Marjorie, the priest's housekeeper in for a rinse at nine in the morning. She's going to some big do at the Parochial House on Thursday and she likes to have her hair set and coloured a couple of days before, so it's an early rise for me."

Well played, Mum thought Erin. She couldn't bear this sexual tension any longer and the fact that her mother and her cronies were here made it all feel a bit icky. If this is what Olivier could do to her in a room full of their relatives, what did the future hold when they had to dance and sing that heavy, romantic song together? What would it be like in the rehearsal room? She had to control herself. She had to go home.

"Well, it has been an absolute pleasure to have you all," said Bernadette. "I loved entertaining in Paris but I never seem to do it here. It was Olivier's idea and he did all the hard work, but I really enjoyed the entire evening so all credit goes to him. He really is my delight."

"Grandmère," said Olivier. "Please, I am blushing. I only prepared dinner, I didn't win a Nobel Peace Prize. But thank you for your kind words."

"Thank *you*, Olivier," simpered Geri.

In the course of two hours, Erin noted how her mother had once again transformed from a glaring, warning monster mum to a love-struck puppy who was putty in the hands of such fine male company.

"Once again, my pleasure," he said and he lifted Geri's hand and kissed it and then did the same to Agnes.

Erin had a memory flashback to that first day in The Community Centre when he had done the same to her fellow female company but blew her a kiss instead. And now, once again, he didn't extend the same farewell to her. She felt her heart sting. What was he playing at?

They walked to the door and Erin could barely lift her head, she was so confused and in a way angry that Olivier was so intense with her all evening and then would leave her out in the cold by not saying goodbye the way he did to the others.

"Goodnight, Erin," he called to her as she walked down the pathway towards her car. Her feelings of sobriety and hurt were not a pleasant mixture so she just managed a wave and then realising that she was being rude after all his fine hospitality, she grunted a light goodbye with a quick glance in his direction. Seeing him stand in the doorway, his tall handsome figure so drop-dead gorgeous as it filled the entire space and the way his hair flopped down so that he had to push it back from his face made her insides jump around once more. Think of Taylor, she told herself as she turned her ignition. Think of Taylor and don't think of Frenchmen who will only break your heart.

But then Taylor was perhaps about to do that too.

SCENE SEVENTEEN

Sorcha stretched out in her king-size bed and welcomed the morning sunshine into her hotel bedroom. What a night she'd had last night and the fun was only beginning! It was such fun being alone and anonymous in a city of dreams and she intended to live up to every moment of it. She had sipped cocktails by the pool on the rooftop terrace until almost midnight, and then watched some television in her room while nibbling on pretzels and drinking a large vodka and lime mix that Luka, the bar waiter, had made up especially for her, having complimented her extensively on her gorgeous green "emerald eyes". Sorcha had never been complimented before and her head still buzzed from the sensation she had felt when he kissed her goodnight. Just a light peck on the cheek, but a kiss was a kiss . . .

Now, she had a full day of excitement ahead and after breakfast she planned to go shopping on Sunset Boulevard, grab a bite of lunch on the terrace at Jeri's

Deli and finish the afternoon by the pool on the terrace again where she hoped to bump into Luka and see if he was really as good-looking as she had thought the night before after her cocktail feast. Then, when she had built up the courage to do so, she would send Taylor a text message and hope and pray that he replied with the answer she had been hoping for – a one-to-one interview with him on the movie set. She was so excited she could barely contain herself.

She yawned and stretched again and, after a quick refreshing shower, she answered the door to the room-service call with a crooked smile.

"Why, thank you, sir," she said to the young waiter and she tipped him with a confident wink. She waited while he laid the tray on her table and then she sat by the window and tucked into an ultra-healthy breakfast of oats, fruit and freshly brewed decaffeinated coffee. Her white dressing gown and clean body made her feel new and revived and she sat back in her chair and nibbled grapes as she watched Hollywood wake up through her window.

Yet every now and then, just when she was feeling on the crest of a wave with this wonderful Hollywood high, she would realise how she had spent so much of her lifelong savings on a whimsical few days that she could never buy back. She thought of her sad, downtrodden mother dodging arguments like bullets around the kitchen at night when her father came home from the pub. She thought of Eugene lying in bed with his iPod turned up high and his puny body curled up in a ball, trying to block out the sound and not having the courage to go down and face the real music which played like a thumping heavy-metal beat from beneath his bedroom floor. She thought of how after she had fulfilled her last-minute fantasy, she would have to go back to it all again, and the very notion of it made her feel sick to the core. But for now, she would try not to think of reality. She lifted the phone and dialled through to the in-house beauty salon and made an ad hoc appointment to have a facial, a blow-dry, a manicure and her make-up done, plus a spray tan to give her a true Californian glow. Then she finished her percolated coffee, pulled on a pair of denim shorts, a baby-pink vest top and a pair of flip-flops and made her way out into the elevator where she prayed she would be transformed into a beautiful swan by the time she came face to face with Taylor Smith.

Erin was getting worried now. It was getting late and she still hadn't heard from Taylor and no matter how much she tried to reason in her mind that he might be genuinely busy, she knew in her heart that there was something badly wrong.

She took the phone in her hand and stared at it, willing it to ring. A text message would be enough to let her go to bed and have some sleep but her inbox was empty and there were no missed calls for her to return. Come on, Taylor, she thought. Please, just a sign to say that you still care for me. Just one sign. Give me one glimmer of hope so I can work at getting our life back on track.

She couldn't stand it any longer. She scrolled through the address book on her phone and clicked on his LA phone number. It rang and rang and rang but there was no answer. Then she dialled again, but still no answer. And again, and again and again until the sickness in her stomach burned like a volcano. Something wasn't right at all.

"Hello, Taylor, it's me," she said to his answer phone. "I'm not sure what is going on here but I'm really worried. Why haven't you called? Are you okay? I really need to talk to you."

She hung up and sat down on her settee, clutching the phone in both hands, and she stared at the ceiling. Perhaps I should have a drink, she thought. No, no, I won't, I can't. I could call Kizzy and see what she thinks I should do now?

She looked at the clock and realised it was way past Kizzy's bedtime. Plus, she was afraid to call anyone in case Taylor tried to get through and she blocked the line. She would use her landline. No, he might call there first. Her mind raced with possibilities of what might be going on with him so far away in a life that she knew she was no part of. Was he with that girl? Was he hurt or injured, or was he simply having too much fun to even think about her? She had no idea what to do next.

Sorcha Daly! Yes, that's what she could do. She could call Sorcha and see if she had tracked him down yet. She had her number somewhere. Moments later she was dialling Sorcha's mobile number and waiting for her to answer.

"Hello. Sorcha Daly speaking."

"Sorcha!" She tried to compose herself. "Hi, Sorcha. It's Erin. Just wanted to check you had arrived safely in LA?"

There was a long pause. "Since when did you care about anything I got up to? What are you really calling for?"

Erin walked around the sitting room in circles. She should have known Sorcha would make an issue of what should have been just a very simple and quick enquiry.

"Okay, I'm wondering if you'd managed to locate Taylor as yet? Just, well, I'm having trouble tracking him down and since you are lucky enough to be over there I was wondering –"

"Not taking your calls, is he?" Sorcha snorted. "Gosh, that's strange. Maybe he's heard about your dangerous liaisons with the mysterious Olivier? It can't be easy for him working his ass off out here, living his dream job, only to be plagued with images of his loving girlfriend in the arms of another."

"Sorcha, stop playing games with me. I am asking you, woman to woman, if you have been speaking to him since you arrived. Come on. I have never wronged you before so why do you feel it is necessary to behave like this?"

She heard Sorcha sigh and then she must have covered her phone for a few seconds as she spoke in a muffled tone.

"Sorry about that," she said with a giggle. "I was just ordering another Hollywood Slut. It's a drink with vodka, rum, cranberry and pineapple, though I'm sure the real deal is to be found aplenty in this town. So, you were saying . . . Taylor, no contact? What do you want me to do? Play Cupid?"

"No, I don't want you to play Cupid, Sorcha. We are not teenagers," said Erin, regretting her call. "All I wanted to know is whether or not you have seen him but I take it that you haven't. Thanks for all your help. I appreciate it and I will remember it if you are ever in a situation where you need some help –"

"Hold on," said Sorcha. "I haven't seen him but, yes, I have spoken to him. About an hour ago."

"Oh God, is he okay? How did he seem?"

"He seemed pretty chirpy with me, but then he always is. He is thrilled I made the effort to come over and tomorrow we are having dinner at Ago. It's a restaurant owned by Robert de Niro. You should Google it. Sounds divine."

Erin's face fell into a frown and she felt her bottom lip push out like a disappointed child. So he hadn't fallen under a bus or had a freak accident or lost his phone or . . . He just didn't want to take her calls. She was heartbroken.

"Oh . . . well, tell him . . ." She wasn't sure what to say. "Will you tell him that . . ."

"Quickly, Erin. You're costing me a fortune here. I hope you aren't calling from a mobile phone – we're not all wealthy television presenters, you know."

Erin gulped back tears. "It's okay," she said. "Don't worry about it, Sorcha. Have a nice time in Hollywood."

She clicked off the call and let her arm fall, so that the phone dropped onto the floor. She sat down on the settee and leaned her elbows on her knees and let her tears flow down her face as images of a life without Taylor unfolded in her mind. She thought of their first date, how they giggled in anticipation before they shared their first kiss, how they'd shared secret nicknames and code words and private jokes that no one else could ever have translated. This was the beginning of the end of all that. She remembered their first weekend away, how they couldn't wait to spend a whole night together for the very first time and how he told her that he loved her as they shared an ice cream on the pier the next morning and her stomach had given a leap when she looked into his eyes and saw how much he meant it. She had been the happiest girl in the world.

She lay down and brought her knees up and she hugged them and shivered as she realised that she might never feel his touch again. How he'd whisper to her as she drifted off into a sweet, satisfied slumber, how he'd stroke her hair as they watched television in comfortable companionship, how he'd rest his hand on her lap as he drove with her as his passenger. A host of memories past and a future of possible new memories were all slipping through her fingers and she didn't know where to begin to make it better. Taylor was drifting away, further and further just as she had feared and she had no idea how she would cope without him.

A knock on the door startled her and she froze on the settee, wondering who on earth could be looking for her at this hour. She wouldn't answer. She closed her eyes and wished them away but the knocking continued and a deep fear arose and shook her from within. Then her mobile rang and she didn't recognise the number but she answered it, glad of the contact with someone who could maybe come to her aid.

"Hello?" she said, the nerves and sadness she felt reflecting in her voice.

"Erin, it's Olivier. Please answer your door. I need your help. Please!"

She stumbled off the sofa onto her bare feet and made her way quickly out into the hallway and to the door. When she opened it, he charged inside, his handsome face crumpled and his hands trembling as he spoke.

"I need your help," he said. "Please tell me you can come with me now."

All thoughts of Taylor and Sorcha and Hollywood went out of her mind as she looked into Olivier's eyes. He was desperate and she needed to do all she could to help him, whatever it took.

SCENE EIGHTEEN

He lifted her coat from where it lay at the bottom of the stairs and handed it to her.

"Please, we have no time. Just come as you are."

Erin looked down at her bare feet and her slobby pyjama bottoms under her coat. She reached for a pair of slippers and grabbed her keys and followed Olivier out onto her front lawn and across the road to the house on the other side of the cul de sac. What was going on? Why did he need her help?

"Are you good with babies?" he called to her as he marched across the road. Then he stopped and caught her hand so she could keep up with his pace. It was only a hundred yards away but it felt like they were running a marathon.

"Um, well, not really. I can change a nappy if I have to," she said with a nervous giggle. I can change a nappy? Where the hell did she get that from?

"Good."

Olivier pushed open the front door and the sound of a baby wailing came from upstairs, while another much more distressing sound came from the sitting area. She followed Olivier inside where a girl lay propped up on a makeshift bed on the couch, her pale face sunken and a light fluff of downy hair peeping out from a multi-coloured headscarf.

"This is Róisín," he said. "Róisín, this is my friend Erin I have been telling you about. Erin will sit with Baby Joseph until I get you to hospital. Is that okay, my love?"

The girl looked up at Olivier with huge adoring eyes and a smile that would have broken a heart of stone crept across her sad face.

"Thank you," she mouthed at Erin but no sound came out.

Erin looked at Olivier for reassurance. What was wrong with Róisín? Was she going to die? Where was her baby's daddy?

"I'll go and get Joseph now and get you two acquainted and then I'll take Róisín to hospital. Her temperature is fierce and I can't get it to come down no matter what I've done. I'll be a minute."

He raced up the stairs and Erin didn't know whether to stare at Róisín or the television that was turned down low in the corner of the room. She noticed a few of Olivier's belongings scattered around the room – his scarf, his leather jacket – his helmet on the floor. Then she unwittingly caught Róisín's eye and she saw that the girl was waving her to come closer, too weak to call out her name.

"Yes, yes, love? What is it?" asked Erin. She was

never good in such situations, always preferring to let professional carers take over, but with Róisín she found herself easing a little, wanting to do all she could to help. "Can I get you anything? Some water?"

Róisín shook her head gently and her smile came back, her heavy eyes falling, then opening again, then falling.

"He likes you," she whispered and her eyes fell closed again, but her smile stayed the same. "He told me."

Olivier arrived back in the room with a little boy in his arms. Erin guessed he was a little older than Kizzy's twins but not by much – he was perhaps about eighteen months – and he sucked hard on a dummy and rubbed his tired eyes, then nuzzled into Olivier's shoulder.

"This is Erin, look, Joseph. Erin is going to look after you just for a little while so I can get Mummy all better."

He leaned forward so that the boy was within Erin's reach and she cagily took him and held him, then marvelled at how warm and cuddly he felt, and when he put his soft blonde head on her shoulder, her mouth dropped open in disbelief.

"He likes you," said Olivier, and Erin and Róisín shared a secret smile. "Look, we won't be long. This is fairly routine but I'll explain more when we get back. Joseph should go straight back to sleep if you just want to flick through the channels and keep the lights low. His room is the first at the top of the stairs. Thank you so much, Erin."

He leaned across and kissed Erin on the cheek and she felt like she had been hit by lightning, then he scooped Róisín's frail body up from the settee and made his way outside and into her car in a manner that made

Erin feel insanely proud of him as if he was hers in the first place.

They were gone within seconds and it was only then that Erin realised how different the reality of this situation between Olivier and the girl with the headscarf was from her first impression.

"Hey, little man," she said to the cherub who had taken to her so easily, much to her surprise. She had virtually no experience of babies or small children and the very thought of being left alone with a toddler had always been enough to give her the shakes, but here she was, in a stranger's home with a child she didn't even know and it felt . . . well, it felt quite good. She lay back on the armchair and rubbed his little head until they both settled into a restful sleep with Erin for the very first time in her life worried about something much more than work, love life or where she was going to get her next drink. She reached over the back of the chair and pulled a throw over them and rested into a peaceful slumber.

Erin was awoken by Olivier's whispers as he made a phone call on his return. She opened her eyes to see him stand by the window, holding his forehead as he spoke and nodding when he didn't. Little Joseph was still sound asleep on her shoulder and it seemed like he had barely moved. His arm rested on hers and his gentle snores warmed her heart as she kissed his head and gently rubbed the curve of his spine.

"How is she?" whispered Erin when Olivier hung up the phone. "We have both slept since you left. Sorry for being a bad baby-sitter and not putting him to his cot but we were so cosy."

Olivier's face broke into a wide beam and he tilted his head to the side.

"Ah, poor little man," he said. "Isn't he so good? Here, give him to me and I'll take him upstairs, then I'll fetch you a hot drink and tell you all about it. I'm sure you are terribly confused."

"A little," said Erin and she felt empty and lonely, not to mention a little more cold when he lifted the babe from her arms. She heard him soothe Joseph as he climbed the stairs and by the time he had come down again, she had composed herself and was much more awake.

With a cup of cocoa in their hands, Olivier and Erin fell into deep conversation, and all the while she was becoming more and more impressed by what she learned from this very endearing man.

"Joseph is my godson," he explained. "My best mate, Jacques, came over here with me to spend a few weeks a few summers ago. He met Róisín in a bar in a town about twenty miles away and they hit it off immediately. I knew he would never come home and he didn't. He was smitten and so they married three years ago and had the little man and everything is happy and sweet. But Jacque's job takes him around the country for nights at a time, and unfortunately Róisín has been very unwell since the baby was born."

"Gosh, that is so sad. Is it serious?" asked Erin. The steaming mug of cocoa was like medicine as it went down and she didn't care that it was well after midnight. She could sit up all night and listen to Olivier.

"They thought it was ME at first – you know, what they used to call 'yuppie flu'. She was constantly tired and she started to lose her hair, the poor thing, then she slumped into a depressive state. Her energy levels are now nil, she is sore all over and she has these raging temperatures that knock her off her feet, just like you saw now. She has leukaemia, Erin."

Erin shook her head and felt tears well up in her eyes. To think that she worried about such minor details in her life, like what to wear, where to go for lunch and with whom, how she should fill her evening without Taylor to talk to her – she really had no idea of what it was to live in the real world with real-life issues and worries and now, here was a young girl who lived across the street from her with an illness that was taking over her life, taking away her life, and Erin had no idea she even existed. Her mother was right. She did live in a bubble.

"And what did they say when you brought her in? Will she be okay?"

"Oh yes, she is fine for now. They settled her temperature and she's all tucked up in bed and fast asleep. Jacques is back in the morning so that's me off duty. I promised him I'd stay when he is not here so I can keep an eye on things but this is the first time anything like this has happened and I guess I panicked. I am so grateful to you for giving up your sleep to help me out."

Erin swallowed. He looked so sincere and full of gratitude and she wanted right there and then to go over and hug him and tell him how the world would be a much better place if there were more people like him around.

"You are such a good person, Olivier, and I am only too glad to help you in any way that I can, day or night. I only wish I could do more for Róisín and help her get better. It's so sad for her to have to live this way and be so dependent on others when she has a little boy who needs her. It's heartbreaking."

She handed him her cup and he took it to the kitchen, then she stood up and made her way to the door. She could feel him behind her, his height towering over her and his strength warming her back as she walked even though he was a few steps away. When she got to the doorstep, she waited for his farewell greeting, but once again, there was nothing. She felt that sense of hurt again and it bubbled at her so hard that the words just flooded out.

"Why don't you ever kiss me goodbye?" she asked. "You kiss everyone else, yet you never . . ."

Her words trailed off and a rush of embarrassment raced through her veins. Why oh why oh why did she have to ask him that?

"Because, Erin," he said and then he glanced away into the sky. "Because I really think, Erin, that when it comes to you, one kiss would never be enough. I would crave more and more and more so I'm trying to protect myself, and you, from wanting something that we both know we can't have."

He wet his lips and looked at her and she felt her breath leave her again, just as it had on so many occasions before when he spoke to her with such intensity and meaning.

"Oh . . . I see. Oh . . ." She didn't know what to say. "That's . . . well, that makes sense, I suppose. Goodnight, Olivier."

"Goodnight, Erin."

And once again she left him with a heavy heart and her mind in a daze of confusion, with a longing in her body that she wasn't sure she could control.

Scene Nineteen

When Taylor called Erin early the next morning, her sense of relief was soon replaced with one of sheer frustration.

"Where the hell have you been? I have been worried sick about you. I haven't heard from you in nearly two days!"

Once again when she spoke to him he was being called away by someone in his company and the irritation crept over her like an uncontrollable itch. She was running late for work but he obviously hadn't even thought of that when he called the landline in her house. Why hadn't he called her mobile so she could talk to him as she travelled into the city, just like he would have done if he had been working on a job at home?

"I have been incredibly busy, baby, and to be honest I slept most of yesterday because I wasn't needed on set. I needed it so much. I didn't wake until late afternoon and then we had this dinner thing to go to and I was running late."

"So who did you sleep with? Belle? Or did you have another prize to pick up?"

Taylor fell silent. "I . . . I don't know what you're talking about, Erin."

"Yes, you do. Belle. You know the one who, let me see how you put it – oh yeah – she almost kept you awake a whole night by the things you had whispered into your ear? Or, how about when you were told to go and get your prize when she was calling you? You did phone me, Taylor. Unintentionally, mind, but you did call me. Thanks for that."

Again she was met with silence.

"I . . . look, it's not like that at all, I swear. We have so many people here, scurrying round after us, practically stuffing dollar bills down our pants when we are out and about. There's a group of them and, yeah, I was flattered but it's all so false and shallow . . . you mean more to me than that, Erin. I promise."

Erin lifted her keys and threw them into her handbag, then flung her coat over her arm and marched out into the spring sunshine.

"Stuffing dollars where, Taylor?"

"What? Into my pants . . . I mean, my trousers. What difference does it make?"

Erin looked over at Róisín's house where the curtains were still drawn and Olivier's bike sat out in its usual parking place. Hollywood and its sunshine and its bungalow bunnies were a million miles away from real life as she knew it here in Millfield.

"Why don't you call me back when you have taken your head out of the fluffy clouds?" she said. "Give my regards to Belle and her babes. Like they say where you are, 'have a nice day'!"

She hung up the phone and jumped into the car, then locked it into reverse and when she arrived at the television studios just after nine, she realised she couldn't remember one step of the journey she had just made because she had been so damn angry.

"Erin! Just the lady I was looking for. Oh my God, you have a face like thunder. Who died?"

"My cat."

"I didn't know you had a cat," said Ryan The Producer, taking tiny steps at the speed of light with his little short legs in a bid to keep up with Erin's pace along the corridor.

"I don't. I lied. No one died. There I'm a fucking poet too into the bargain!"

She pushed open the glass doors that led to the shared office space and continued to march towards her desk. Then, in one fell swoop, she took the three photos of Taylor off her desk and dropped them into the waste-paper basket, wiped her hands and looked up at Ryan The Producer with a painted smile.

"So, now. What's up?"

Ryan The Producer looked like he was afraid to speak.

"Bad mood?"

"No shit, Sherlock."

"Thought so. Maybe I should call back in say, ten minutes? Or would you like to talk about it? Quick Starbucks on me?"

His Milky Bar Kid glasses steamed up as he glanced around the office space and made jerking movements towards the door. Erin imagined a Tazo Chai tea with its spicy cinnamon taste and she felt calmer already. Yes, Ryan The Producer. You are so with the programme.

"You're on."

They sat at their usual table by the door and Erin stared into the black peppery cup of tea as Ryan made small talk in the build-up to her problem-fest.

"I call her Martyr Mum," he said with a snigger. "She hates it but it's true. Ever since the baby came along, she has to do everything her way and her way only. Not even her mother's and, believe me, her mother would scare the pants off you."

"Pants. You see, that's what really got me. When he said 'pants'," said Erin. "Why not just say trousers like he always did? He knew it too because he corrected himself."

"I swear, I only tried to change the child's nappy last night to give her a hand, but oh no. I was doing it all wrong."

"Taylor wouldn't have the first idea about babies . . ."

"And then she had the cheek of accusing me of letting him cry for too long! I only had sat down and I didn't literally have time to get up again unless I had sat on a giant spring! She is impossible. Impossible."

"It's impossible to go on like this. Did I tell you about Belle?"

"No, who's Belle? Is she a Martyr Mum too?"

They stared at each other, realising that neither had listened to a word the other had said. Then they sipped

260

their drinks and watched the world go by outside on Botanic Avenue and wallowed in their own problems. Ryan The Producer was feeling useless and surplus to requirements in his home life which was sodden with toys, nappies and a very controlling wife, while Erin was wracked with mixed emotions of despair, guilt, anger and frustration at her feelings for both Taylor and Olivier.

"Shall we go?" she said and Ryan was already on his feet.

"Feeling better?" he asked her as he opened the door of the coffee shop.

"Yes. Yes I am, thanks," she said. "Thanks for listening."

He laughed and they walked together in equal steps this time and didn't speak again until they were back in the office block.

"Now," said Erin. "Let's start this working day all over again. I refuse to take my personal problems into the office. What's on the agenda today? And please don't say it's anything to do with handsome Irish actors or hunky French dancers."

"I can assure you not," said Ryan in a stern tone. "But we are considering doing a feature on the Moulin Rouge to mark Bastille Day in July, now that you mention it."

Erin gave him a glare which warned him not to go there.

"Oh, it's a long way away, my dear Erin, so you needn't worry about it yet. It's not until July in fact. Now, about this week's show . . . we're talking Monkeys, and I'm not talking the ones you find in the zoo. It's that band . . . oh, what's their name again? Something to do with snow?"

"It's Arctic, Ryan," said Erin. "I think you mean Arctic Monkeys. Oh my word!"

Night-time in Hollywood could be one of two ways, Sorcha noticed as she settled into Californian life. The residents went to bed extremely early in preparation for their health kick the next day, which began when most of us are turning over for a second sleep, but tourists had a range of things to do and see and the place was hiving with star-spotters at night. There was a range of nightclubs and restaurants to choose from, and Sorcha had explored all her options before deciding to take a stroll up towards Chinatown where she marvelled at its ornate buildings and came across a film crew at the famous Old Chinatown Plaza.

This is the life for me, she thought, as she compared what she was doing now with what she would be doing were she at home in Millfield. Probably sitting on her bed, browsing through social network sites, listening to the same music over and over again and wondering why some people had it so lucky while her life had turned out to be shit. But maybe that was all about to change now that she had spread her wings a little and made the most daring, spontaneous decision that she had ever made.

She couldn't help but smile when she thought of her conversation with Erin O'Brien over the phone earlier. It wasn't that she had a particular dislike of the girl. Oh no. It was simply seething, green-eyes-monster, dirty rotten jealousy that got beneath her skin. Erin was a lovely girl, a darling in the community who was almost untouchable and unapproachable through everyone's admiration for her, but Sorcha had detected a weakness in her, and that weakness was her fear of letting Taylor come here to Hollywood. Erin loved Taylor very much, but his move to Hollywood threatened everything she stood for.

But nobody loved Taylor Smith the way Sorcha Daly did. Nobody knew as much about him. Sorcha was his biggest fan and one day he would understand how much he meant to her.

She sat down on a bench on the Plaza and braced herself to send him the message she had been planning in her head since her arrival. If only what she'd told Erin had been true, but in her mind it nearly was real, she had dreamed about it so often. She imagined them at dinner together at that posh Robert de Niro restaurant, sitting under the trellis in the villa courtyard amongst the grapevines and bougainvillea. They would share a bottle of the finest Italian red wine and Taylor would choose from the menu for her. She could hear him laugh in her little scene in her head and he would tell her how she was so beautiful and he would throw his head back and say "How did I miss out on you for so long?" and she would nod shyly and say it didn't matter because now they were together and that was all that mattered.

She lifted her phone and began to type in her message:

Hi Taylor. It's me. Sorcha. Sorcha Daly. Eugene's sister?

Shit, no, that sounded too needy already. She deleted it and started again. She had to play this very casual or he would know that the only reason she was there was because of him and it would scare him off. How about . . .

Hey Taylor. I'm sure your mum told you I'm in Hollywood right now . . .

Yeah, that was better. The more casual the better, but not too casual. She wanted a result out of this and that was to snare a meeting with him. A dinner or even a lunch date would be incredible, but she would start low and hopefully he would bite the bait.

"Well, it would be cool to meet you for a coffee. I'm in town until Friday. Sorcha Daly x"

There. That was perfectly cool, wasn't it? Maybe she should remove the x at the end? No, she would leave it like that. You never know, it could be just what he needed – a little kiss at the end of a message was friendly and heart-warming. It was nice for someone to show interest, not that Sorcha could really relate to it. She had never even got past first base with a boy and the only fumble she ever had was many moons ago – about seven years ago to be precise and she learned years later that the boy in question only did it for a dare. Yes, she knew she was aiming way out of her league with Taylor, but if you didn't ask, you didn't get and with Taylor Smith this was her big opportunity to ask. She hadn't come all this way for nothing and it was probably her only chance to get his attention without his gorgeous girlfriend snooping around – all through the years at the Millfield Players she was there, hanging around. Then again, if he shot her down she would be totally devastated. More than devastated. She would be . . .

Her phone bleeped and she thought her heart had been stabbed such was the pain of the excitement she was experiencing right now. It had to be him! She felt a rush she had never felt before but one she would welcome with open arms on any given occasion when it came to Taylor Smith. Taylor fucking Smith! She

Since You've Been Gone

couldn't believe she was communicating with him so directly. He might be nasty like the other boys at school had been when she had tried to be nice to them or feel part of the gang. But this was Taylor. Her Taylor. Please, let him at least be pleasant and not blow her out.

She closed her eyes and opened the message, then took a deep breath and looked at it, not knowing what to expect.

Hey Sorcha. Wow! No, Mum didn't say you were comin over. Haven't called home in few days. Can I call you later? Am still on set. Look forward to catchin up. Taylor. X

Oh good God! Sorcha read it again. And again and again. Then she read it for a fourth time and she screamed. Yes, she screamed out loud with the biggest smile on her face but she didn't care who heard her or told her to calm down or be quiet. Taylor Smith texted her back! And he said he was 'looking forward to it!' And he put an x at the end! This was the best feeling ever. She didn't need any more entertainment for the evening. Oh no. She was going straight back to her hotel where she would order another Hollywood Slut and watch her phone with her eyes peeled as she waited for his precious call.

Sorcha could feel herself becoming more and more pissed in a thoroughly pleasant way as she sat with her feet in the pool and her new favourite drink in her hand. Her new best friend Luka the waiter had served her up not one but two sneaky cocktails on the house and she was feeling super sexy and confident for the first time in her life. Yes, for the very first time in her life. She kept admiring her nails and checking her make up in her

265

handbag mirror and the more cocktails she downed, the more she thought she looked good enough for Hollywood. Good enough for Hollywood but, more importantly, good enough for Taylor Smith.

She was getting butterflies every time she thought of his name or pictured his face and she had saved his message and read it so many times she could now recite it by heart.

Hey Sorcha. Wow! No, Mum didn't say you were comin over. Haven't called home in few days. Can I call you later? Am still on set. Look forward to catchin up. Taylor. X

X! What if he decided to take her out tonight? She gasped at the thought and couldn't control the smile that was now hurting her face, it was so wide. This was the best feeling in the world. She was so far from home, in a world of her own and she was absolutely loving it. Millfield seemed like the tiniest dot on the tiniest map and she was in this vast landscape of excitement and she couldn't describe the feeling of ecstasy that pumped through her right now. Please don't let this bubble burst, she prayed inwardly. Please just give me a tiny bit of happiness for once in my life. Just this once let me be the bride and not always the bridesmaid.

She stared at her mobile phone and willed it to ring.

"Come on, come on. I can't wait for this. Please, please, please!" she chanted. What if he had forgotten? What if he had changed his mind or decided to do something else? No, Taylor would have let her know if he had. He was kind like that. He would have let her down gently, not dumped her unceremoniously the way other men would. He would call. She knew he would. She really, really hoped he would.

Perhaps staring at her phone was an unlucky omen? Yes, maybe she was trying too hard to let it ring. She would put it in her handbag and think of something else like where she would go shopping next, or she could look around her to see who was wearing the most glamorous poolside outfit. Or maybe she should read a chunk of that trashy novel she had bought at the airport? Yes, that was better. She would try and take her mind off it for a while.

She had just nipped to the loo to fix her make-up when her phone finally rang and she scrambled furiously in her handbag to find it, pulling all her belongings out one by one and eventually tipping the entire contents into the sink – lipstick, compact foundation, mascara, the works, all came slapping out over the gleaming white sink – and eventually she located it and answered it, trying her best to play it cool, but she could hardly breathe. She really could hardly breathe.

"Sorcha speaking," she said in the most natural voice she could find, but to her horror it sounded like a squeaky mouse and the dreaded paranoia she suffered from started to seep through her skin and up into her brain.

"Sorcha, hey girl! It's Taylor. I really can't believe you've brought me some Little Hollywood out here. How on earth are you?"

Sorcha's mouth went dry but she was extremely glad she had consumed a few cocktails to gain a bit of Dutch courage and she was only shaking ever so slightly at hearing his voice. Normally, she would have to stop at "hello" when it came to Taylor Smith and even saying that took great effort and practice on her behalf.

"I'm . . . I'm good, I'm having a ball . . . it's amazing out here . . ."

"Good on you! Yeah, this is the life! Who are you out with? Your brother?"

She could lie and for a split second she thought she should, but she didn't want to complicate things so she opted for honesty.

"No, no. I'm on my own," she said. "I was sent here by *The Gazette*, you know the local paper I work for?"

Well, that was only a *tiny* white lie.

"Cool, so how are you fixed this evening? We could meet up?"

Oh sweet Jesus!

"I have some downtime starting now," he continued, "and it would be a crying shame if I couldn't make some room in my schedule for a familiar face from home."

She tried to unscramble the flurry of words in her brain.

"Unless you have other plans?" he said.

Sorcha couldn't speak. She felt like she was a young 'brace-faced' teenager who was too shy to open her mouth in case the boys taunted her for having a mouth full of metal. She heard the chants of them all on the school bus – calling her ugly and teasing her brother – and she shook her head, urging them all to be quiet. Taylor wasn't one of that gang. He never had been and perhaps that's why she had carried a flame for him all these years. He was quieter and she could remember how he would look at her and Eugene with pity and apology. There was no way he could have stood up to all the others on his own, but the way he would give her a knowing glance, as if he fully understood what she felt there and then was enough for her to believe he was on her side. Remembering this gave her the courage to answer him with just a hint of confidence.

"That would be . . . that would be just fantastic," she said, trying not to listen to the voices that were telling her he was taking the piss, or that he was only seeing her because he felt he had to. "Where . . . where would you like me to meet you?"

Taylor, on the other hand, had no problems with confidence. He was brimming with it and rightly so with his major success, his kind open ways and his stunning good looks.

"I dunno. Your shout? Have you eaten yet? It's never too late to eat in this town and I am starving. Go on, what do you fancy? Chinese? European? Italian? You can decide."

Could she say it? Could she say the name of the place that she had dreamed of? Could her dream really, really come true?

"Er . . ." She bit her lip. "I've heard of this nice Italian place. I actually looked it up online before I came here."

She couldn't believe this was happening so she literally pinched herself and left a huge red welt on her arm which she instantly regretted.

"It's er . . . it's called Ago?" she muttered, hoping she had pronounced the name of the place properly. How embarrassing would that be?

"Ah, yes of course. Ago. De Niro's place! Yeah, I know it. Look, give me half an hour and I'll meet you there. Great. I'll go get freshened up. Thanks for looking me up while you're here, Sorcha. Means a lot, it really does."

He hung up and she leaned against the bathroom units and hugged her phone to her chest. Was this really happening? She checked her call log. Yes, he had texted her earlier. Yes, he had just called her. A burst of raw energy bounced through her body and sent electric shocks all over her skin. She wanted to scream, she was so happy. Her feet kept moving with excitement so she did a dance in the middle of the bathroom floor – it was a mixture between an Irish jig and a hand jive and it was all on her tiptoes.

"Oh yeah!" she said.

She danced some more.

"I'm going for dinner," she said in her broad Norn Iron accent to a stretched-face fifty something who had made her way into the bathroom. "With Taylor Smith. *Me*! Can you believe it? Can you *fucking* believe it?!"

"In this town," said the blonde, "in this town I would believe anything, honey. You go enjoy yourself. Life is for living and this is Hollywood."

SCENE TWENTY

Erin had itchy feet. She was on her own again and the house seemed so quiet that she could almost hear the walls whispering even with the television on. She hated being on her own, especially at night, and she was craving some of Taylor's laughter and silly jokes to fill the emptiness she felt in her heart right now.

Where had this all gone wrong? She flicked through the channels on the television and stared at the screen but its colours just mixed in her head and she knew she should just go to bed and at least try to get a good night's sleep but the thought of lying in her bed all alone was the least inviting thing she could think of right now.

She found her phone in her handbag and found Taylor's number and her finger hovered over the button, then she closed her eyes and pressed it and closed her eyes as she heard the international ring tone. She concentrated on her breathing, not knowing whether she was ready or not to talk to him when he answered. Not sure of what she wanted to say. Where would she start?

She heard Olivier's motorbike go past her house and something inside her longed for him to stop and come in to her and take away this horrible empty fear she felt inside. But it was wrong to cling to someone like Olivier when she really wanted Taylor. She wanted her Taylor back home and that was all there was to it.

The phone clicked on to Taylor's messaging service and Erin's stomach sank just a little when she realised he had changed his greeting.

"Hey, it's Taylor. Sorry I can't take your call but I'm either on set, on the beach or hangin' with Sandy and the gang. Yeah, I know. It's a tough life. Have a nice day!"

Sandy and the gang. "Sandy" as in Sandra Bullock. And "the gang". Erin knew in the back of her mind that one day not too long ago, she would have found that greeting a little bit funny. She could just imagine Taylor recording it and laughing to himself as he did so but right now it irritated her to bits that he was having such a bloody good time without her. Since when did he know Sandra fucking Bullock as "Sandy". That's what people like Hugh Grant called her, not Taylor Smith from bloody Millfield in the middle of nowhere in Northern fucking Ireland!

She hung up the phone. Then she lifted it again and redialled, her lips pursed with anger and frustration at how things with Taylor seemed to be slipping further and further away. He might as well be in Outer Mongolia for all the contact they were keeping. His newly toned Norn-Iron-meets-LA twang rhymed off his oh-so-funny message and she took a deep breath, and then spoke in an acerbic tone that would have made a bitter lemon taste sugary.

"Hey, Taylor, it's Erin. Remember me? Yeah, well, I'm not hanging with Sandy unfortunately. Nor am I on the beach, nor on set, nor with any gang whatsoever. I'm sitting here on my own, in my fluffy pyjamas that you once loved, on a sofa where we used to snuggle up and watch Sandra fucking Bullock movies and . . . and . . ."

She felt the tears spring from her eyes and her mouth twisted as she fought them back but it was too late. She tried to speak again but her voice was distorted and sniffly. She wiped her nose on the back of her cotton sleeve and pulled herself together.

"I think I've lost you, Taylor. I really do. I hope you are having a good time and that you prove me wrong. Bye."

At rehearsals the following evening, Olivier was late and Erin found herself helping out with some of the teenagers, putting them over their steps and practising chorus parts. She felt better when she was surrounded by people and the youngsters were proving to be quite good company with their up-to-date lingo and their enthusiasm that was tangible to all involved in the showcase. They were rehearsed to within an inch of their life and Olivier had choreographed a stunning routine, the like of which Millfield or indeed some of the professional theatres in Belfast, would never have witnessed.

The conversation jumped from "What's it like being on telly?" to "Are you always being asked for autographs?" to "Can you get me to meet Westlife?"

Erin was surprised at how she fitted in with them and it gave her a boost of confidence when she was literally surrounded by them, all looking at her with a hunger for information and, for the first time in a long time, she actually felt like she belonged here again. But when the conversation steered, as it inevitably did, to Taylor's life in Hollywood, she found that she was quite stuck for answers.

"Has Taylor met, like, loads of celebrities?" asked a young girl with freckles and braces on her teeth. "Like, who is the most famous person he has met so far? Like has he met anyone from *Twilight* or has he met like, the Jonas Brothers? Oh, I would *so* love to meet the Jonas Brothers!"

Erin was sincerely warmed by their eagerness and interest in how Taylor was getting on but the questions still flummoxed her. If only she knew enough about Taylor's lifestyle to tell them. Instead, all she knew was that he partied a lot, was having a ball with a girl called Belle and didn't seem to have much time to call her these days. And he had changed his voicemail message to reflect that he was a million miles away from Millfield and having the time of his life.

"Do you think when he comes back I could get my picture taken with him?" asked a skinny little Bambi-like creature.

"Oh can you ask him to bring me back Sandra Bullock's autograph? I *love* Sandra Bullock."

"And Liam Neeson's too? My mum loves him."

"I'll see what I can do," said Erin and she pressed play on the CD to try and get them back to work as their excitement was becoming somewhat out of control. The opening night was just around the corner and, although this was one of the stronger groups in the production, there were a lot of loose ends to tighten up, not to mention how much she needed to rehearse on a one to one with Olivier. These days he was always late for practice and when he got there he seemed distracted, or else Darryl had him pulled into another area of the room to choreograph another routine. She knew it wasn't entirely his fault, but these days at rehearsals he seemed to have no time to practise with her so she found herself helping Darryl manage the wide range of acts more often than rehearsing her own scene.

She heard an intake of breath from some of her group and then the giggling and whispering started and she knew that Olivier must have put in an appearance at last. She looked behind her and there he was. His hair was wet from the rain, his leathers were soaked and his very presence changed the whole atmosphere in the hall. Olivier had such charisma about him that even the hardened Millfield mob of actors who formed their little cliques around the rehearsal room stopped to take notice.

"Olivier, darling! You are soaked through," chirped Krystal, rushing towards him, followed by Marjorie the Priest's Housekeeper. "You'll catch your death of cold."

"I'm not soaked through at all," he said. "Just give me a second and I'll get out of this gear."

He looked sullen and moody and Erin felt a stirring inside, a strange sensation that she longed to control but she couldn't. He brought out emotions in her that she had never felt before and in a way she hated him for it. It was like he heightened every part of her vulnerability and pinpointed it so that it was more obvious to her than it had ever been before. She caught his eye and he looked away and she felt her heart sink, but then he glanced back in her direction almost immediately and her heart rose again when she saw a light smile grow on his face.

"He is such a ride," said one of the teenagers and Erin felt her cheeks burn. "I think he just looked at me. Did anyone else see that? He looked at me! OMG."

Olivier slipped into the bathrooms and Erin pulled herself together.

"OMG? What on earth does that mean?" she asked when she turned back to face Olivier's adoring fan club.

"It, like, means Oh My God! OMG! We say it all the time to each other when he comes into the room. We follow him around the village and everything. He is hot, hot, hot! Unreal!"

"Yeah," said the girl with the braces. "One day we followed him into the corner shop and he bought an ice cream with a flake and a packet of salt and vinegar crisps so we all bought the same. We are like his biggest stalkers!"

Erin sensed that Olivier was making his way towards them when she heard her mother swear from the stage. Her mother never swore. Ever.

"Fuck, sorry!" she said. She was sizing Eugene for his costume and accidentally stuck a pin in his leg because she was so distracted by Olivier's wet hair and the black T-shirt that clung to his body, showing every contour of his manly physique.

"That's okay, Geri," said Eugene in a high-pitched voice, grasping his thigh. "It wasn't really all that sore."

"Hey, everyone," said Olivier and the group of young girls swooned. "Sorry I'm late, Erin. I'm sure you thought I had packed this all in."

"It's okay," she said and she felt her heart beat a little faster.

"No, I really do apologise," he said and he made direct eye contact with her. "I was really busy this evening and I lost track of time. I had to sort stuff with Róisín. She is having a bad day. I'm sorry."

She looked at him and could see the pain etched on his tired face and she got this strong urge to hold him close and tell him it would be all right. Oh and also because his arms were so goddamn sexy that she wanted to see what they felt like. She had a thing for strong arms.

"Poor you," she mumbled, realising that her eyes gave her longing away.

"No, poor Róisín," he said with a shrug and he clasped his hands together. "She is the one who is very ill. I'll be okay. Erin, you and I need a while to work on our scene so when you are ready, I will be in the small room. Your little room at the back."

He smiled and nodded towards the little room at the back of the hall where they had last rehearsed their song. It seemed so long ago, like so much had happened since then and she felt a mixture of excitement and discomfort at the thought of being alone with him. He was quite an intense creature. Deep and meaningful in the way he looked at her, in the way he spoke to her, in every way he moved and the way he made her feel like jelly inside.

"What a handsome boy!" said Geri and gave Eugene another poke in the leg with her needle. "Really, Erin. There are so many times I look at him and see what you see, but be careful, my lovely. Please, be careful. He is the Adam to your Eve. Forbidden fruit is only sweet for a very short time."

Erin felt dizzy as she watched Olivier walk down The

Community Hall, greeting people as he did so and leaving a trail of swoons in his wake.

"Yes, be-be-be careful," stammered Eugene as he rubbed his leg. "Don't mix up what's in Little Hollywood with what you have over in the real Hollywood, Erin. B-but if you ever need anyone to talk to or if you're feeling lonely, I can give you my number."

"Thanks, Eugene," said Erin, trying not to laugh. "That's very kind of you but trust me, I'm a big girl. I know exactly what I'm doing."

Olivier was flicking through the CD on the sound system when Erin made her way to the little rehearsal room. He was hunkered down with his back facing her and she stopped at the doorway to watch him for a moment. He wore a black T-shirt that crept up over the back of his blue jeans, showing a strip of tanned flesh that drew her eye like a magnetic force and no matter how she tried to look away, her eye was drawn back instantly. He pressed play and mumbled something in French on realisation that he had hit the wrong number on the player, then feeling her presence he swung around and stood up, his eyes matching hers with such intensity she felt the walls close in to meet her.

"You look really nice today," he said as he made his way towards her. The introduction to the song began and she gulped when he took her hands, still looking into her eyes with a curved smile on his face. He was so damn sexy and he didn't even know it.

"Thank you," she mumbled. "So, talk to me. We have so much work to do on this song it's not even funny. Are you sure you're in the mood for this?"

"I'm always in the mood for you, Erin," he said and she waited for a punch line, for him to crack a joke or to laugh and nudge the tension that hung in the air but he didn't. He just let go her hands again and walked away, then pressed pause on the CD and sat down.

"Aren't we going to practise?" she asked, joining him when he patted the seat next to him. "It's only a few weeks to the show and I'm starting to feel a bit nervous."

"Nervous? Why?"

"Well, we've only ever sung it once together and I have no idea of what you have in mind for choreography. You've been spending most of your time with the chorus group or with Krystal and her posse and I'm just wondering if you're going to take our song seriously."

"Erin? Are you . . . are you . . .?" He covered his mouth with his hand and his forehead creased into a frown.

"No, I am not jealous – I am worried," she said, reading his mind. How dare he assume that she was jealous! She felt her cheeks burn and she faced forward, staring at the door.

"Phew," he said. "I don't mean to make you feel that way and I am taking this seriously. Very seriously indeed. I've just been pulled in all sorts of directions since Darryl got his hands on me and maybe I have neglected our scene together, but it wasn't intentional."

Erin felt a tug of emotion and she tried to curb it but it wouldn't settle. What had come over her? She had no reason to be angry with Olivier. It was only one song. But she couldn't help herself.

"It's just that when Taylor and I have a scene

together, we rehearse and rehearse and rehearse and –"

"And I'm not Taylor!" said Olivier and he stood up and looked away from her. An awkward silence fell in the air and then he met her eye again. "I'm sorry, Erin. That was insensitive of me. I just . . ."

Erin felt her hands shake and she clenched them together on her lap. This was not his fault. She was taking her frustration out on a man who had shown her nothing but kindness.

"I know you are not," she whispered. "And I don't expect you to be. I'm sorry."

"No, I am sorry," said Olivier and he held his forehead. "I shouldn't have burst out at you like that. I just feel like I'm constantly being compared to a guy who I can never live up to. In every way, they expect me to be like him and I don't think I can."

Erin felt a nervous giggle warm inside her. "Burst out at me? That's a new one."

"You know what I mean."

"I do," she said. "I don't expect you to fit in where Taylor left off in any sense of the word. As much as I miss my boyfriend, and believe me I really do miss him right now, your company makes me very happy and I'm glad I got to know you like I have. You don't need to be anyone else, only Olivier. I mean it."

He licked his lips and leaned forward..

"You really love him, don't you Erin?" he said and she could have sworn she saw pain in his eyes.

"I . . . I do," she nodded. "But . . . there is a 'but' when it comes to my love for Taylor, I'm afraid."

"You don't have to talk about it if you don't want

to," whispered Olivier. "But if you do, I am a very good listener."

He looked at her and she couldn't help but smile.

"I feel like I can talk to you, you know. Call me mad but I feel a connection between us. Maybe it's because I was the first person you met from here. I feel like you were my . . . like you were my friend first. God, that sounds a bit crazy, doesn't it?"

"No," said Olivier. "I know exactly what you mean. We do have a connection. A very beautiful one but I promise you that I will not read that for anything more than friendship while you are still in love with your boyfriend. That's just not my style. It never has been."

Erin nodded at him, knowing exactly what he meant. There was no doubt about it. They had this growing chemistry between them that was almost electrifying at times, and if she was not in a relationship the sparks would have flown between them and they would have given in by now. It was almost terrifying sometimes how much the entire world could stop and she wouldn't notice when she was with him like this.

"Do you . . . do you have someone waiting for you back home?" she asked. It was a question that had bugged her for some time. How could someone so beautiful not have women crawling over each other to get a piece of him?

He didn't answer for a second. He looked at the floor in thought and then he pushed his damp hair back from his face.

"I . . . I find it very hard over there," he said. "It's not hard, it is virtually impossible to sustain a relationship in the business I work in. You have no idea."

"Tell me," she said, wondering if she truly wanted to know.

"Well, I work on this huge production and the cast changes very often. It's so easy when you are working so closely with people, practically living with them all, to get extremely attached to some of them and then when you find out that as soon as their time with the show is up, their time is up with you too, it can be very hard to swallow. That has happened to me too many times and now, well, now I just keep myself to myself. I never want to go through that again."

Erin wanted to reach out and touch him. He looked lonely and sad and she had no idea his exotic life in Paris and the Moulin Rouge could be so lonely.

"It's a false existence, Erin," he said, looking at her now. "It's a goldfish bowl lifestyle and once the show is over, the bowl cracks and it is the loneliest feeling in the world. To be honest, it's part of the reason I escaped here while I'm on my break. I just couldn't face that deep, dark plunge into life without that crutch of showbiz again. I would swap that whole existence for what you guys have here in a heartbeat. I really would."

Erin heard every word he said loud and clear. She recalled how Taylor had promised he wouldn't change, or that life in Hollywood wouldn't change him so to speak. But he was in that goldfish bowl now and she wasn't part of it. Life in Little Hollywood was mundane, boring, real life and he had been bitten by a bug that was so out of her reach. Olivier was right, but he had seen both sides of the lifestyle Taylor was now experiencing and she admired his honesty and his maturity for how he saw right through it.

"Would you really give all that up for a life here?" she asked. "So many people would give their right arms to live your life and all that comes with it. Why here?"

"Because this is Little Hollywood," said Olivier. "And sometimes Little Hollywood is big enough for all of us."

They ran through their song only twice as time was ticking on.

"Tomorrow is another day," said Olivier when they decided to call it quits. "Even though we spent most of our time talking, I think that went pretty well."

"So did I," said Erin. She could still feel his touch in her hands and his hands on her waist from the routine he had choreographed. Although subtle and romantic, the way he held her made her pulse throb and at one stage she had to stop just to control her urge to kiss him. It was overwhelming and her mother's words about forbidden fruit echoed so loudly in her ear that she just had to restrain herself.

"So, what are your plans tonight?" he asked as they packed up. "Doing anything nice?"

"Not really," said Erin. "Probably another night in front of the telly, maybe read a book, I dunno. A 'party for one' again. It's not all glamour, you know, this whole business, but who am I to talk?"

She gathered her belongings – her script, her handbag and her mobile phone and gave him a smile as she did so.

"Well," he said and he looked at the floor, "I am free all evening."

Oh good God, she thought. Oh please don't ask me

to join you because I don't have the power to say no. Please don't.

"If you wanted," he said, "and please don't take this the wrong way, I could call around to keep you company and we could possibly manage to get through this song another few times. I have a feeling the choreography is a tiny bit bland so I will work on it. But only if you are comfortable with that?"

Erin felt her heart glow and she could hardly breathe. If that was bland, then she was in for a spiced-up feast of forbidden fruit and she just couldn't resist it! She loved the idea of Olivier calling on her but her mind was still playing a game of moral tennis which delayed her answer.

"Forget I even mentioned it," he said, holding up his hands. "What would the neighbours say, and all that? We can practise here again tomorrow. No worries."

"No," she said. "I mean yes! Yes, I would love you to call later. I couldn't bear another evening of re-runs and reality television. What time will you be there? I could cook us something?"

She spoke as if she was on speed and could see his eyes brighten as she did so. When he put on his jacket, a huge smile beamed over his face.

"I . . ." He gave a nervous laugh and the way he looked at her was mesmerising. "I am . . . I'm . . ."

"What?" she asked, biting her lip. She could feel perspiration tingle all over her as the urge to hear what he had to say became the most important thing in the world. What was he going to say?

He put his hands in his pockets and lifted his shoulders, then breathed out and looked at the ceiling.

"I'll bring a takeaway," he said, shaking his head, telling her that he had chickened out on what really was on his mind. "You go home and relax and do your thing and I'll see you at seven. How does that sound?"

She had never experienced anything like the sensation she felt at that moment. Her heart felt like it was going to explode and a rush of energy pumped through her with such intensity that she felt she could run a marathon right there and then. What was he doing to her? What had he really wanted to say? This was so frustrating!

"That sounds just perfect," she said, unintentionally dropping her voice to a whisper. "I'm looking forward to it already."

"So am I, Erin," said Olivier. "So am I."

He left the room, pausing only to look at her and smile and she was sure he was going to kiss her hand just as he had done to so many others when he greeted them or left their company, but no. He kissed her instead with his smile and left her wanting more and more and more.

SCENE TWENTY-ONE

Sorcha was fashionably late. She had deliberately booked her cab for the time that Taylor had booked the table, just so she could walk in knowing he was there. Being in the hotel roof bar on her own was one thing, but there was no way she fancied sitting at a table in Ago waiting and fearing that she might be stood up by one of Hollywood's rising stars.

She looked good and she knew it. She wore a slinky black dress with silver accessories and her hair was tied up in a loose bun with tendrils of loose curls falling around her face and she looked as close to Audrey Hepburn as she ever could. Even her pointed chin was less obvious in LA. But maybe it was the five Hollywood Sluts that she had consumed that made her feel that way.

She walked down the stairs of the hotel and was sure that heads were turning in her direction. Oh yeah, this felt so good. People were staring. They were impressed. They were in awe. Then she caught her reflection in one of the long mirrors in the lobby and she was horrified. Oh sweet Jesus!

She slipped into the nearest bathroom and stood up against the door and tried to stop the urge to cry. They were strangers, they didn't know her, they would probably have forgotten by now.

She waltzed to the mirror and fixed herself. Her mascara had run in the heat and her face resembled a baby racoon. She looked hideous. Think positive she chanted inwardly as the dark thoughts came flooding back.

"Who do you think you are?" laughed the voices in her head. "You don't belong here. Go home to small town, Ugly!"

"No," she said, blocking her ears. "No, I am going to meet Taylor. He is waiting for me. He is waiting for me at Ago and we are going to have dinner together. My cab is waiting."

"You don't belong here," whispered Marilyn Monroe into her ear.

"And you certainly don't look like me!" laughed Audrey Hepburn.

Then they all cackled a chorus of laughter and when she closed her eyes she could see them all on the school bus. She could see the school uniform she despised so much and she saw Marilyn and Audrey in the back seat with the popular set. Then she saw Taylor and he was laughing too. Audrey was stroking his hair!

"No, Taylor, no!" she pleaded. "You said you would meet me tonight."

She remembered to breathe and she sucked in a gasp of air, praying that the panic attacks she had suffered for years would not come to visit her right now. Breathe in long and hard, then blow it out so that your shoulders drop. She did it again. And again. And again and slowly she felt herself coming around. That felt better. Yes.

She rustled for her phone which bleeped a message and her heart lifted when she saw Taylor's name flash up in her inbox. Then the fear that he might be cancelling hit her like a blow to the head but she made herself open the message and read it.

Just getting some drinks in. You on your way, babe?

Her eyes widened. Babe. He called her babe. She traced her finger over the screen and touched the word, feeling like she was touching his beautiful face. See, this was real. She gave herself one last glance in the mirror, double checking for any faults, tidied her hair and stuck her nose in the air as she walked out into the hotel lobby and out through the revolving doors.

Just as she had hoped, no one recognised her as the girl with the racoon eyes. She got into the cab and rested back on the cool leather seats, taking in the palm trees that lined the street and the beauty of it all. She was truly anonymous here. She could really stay here forever. If only she could . . .

Melrose Avenue. Ahhhh! Even the sound of the taxi driver saying it gave Sorcha a real rush of excitement. She looked out of the window and saw the place she had dreamed of meeting Taylor, ever since she planned this trip to Hollywood.

The faded yellow wash on the outside gave it a truly authentic Tuscan feel and the wooden windows that opened out onto the courtyard and the bougainvillea and vine plants were just what she had imagined.

She composed herself and walked towards the doorway, then entered the bright airy restaurant with its buttery walls and fresh airy feel to it. She took a deep breath. She was in Hollywood. She was looking for a table for two. She was searching for that intimate table for two where Taylor Smith – yes, *The* Taylor Smith – would be waiting for her, glass of red wine in his hand, ready to give her a few hours of his undivided attention. She pinched her left arm. Yes, this was real.

"Ah, here she is everyone!"

She heard Taylor before she saw him and the familiar accent was like a hug to her. But "everyone"? Who was "everyone"? She walked past the huge Italian vines and tried to hide the horror on her face. She gulped, then smiled as Taylor stood up to greet her.

"Belle, Rod, Mattie, Princess, this is Sorcha, an old school friend of mine from home. Make her feel welcome, won't you?"

The maître d' took her coat and she was seated at the top end of the table whereas Taylor was dead centre, and all attention was focused on him. She felt a little bit queasy as the disappointment surged through her insides. Taylor picked up a story she had obviously walked in on and the entire table was drinking in every word he was saying. She felt like a spare prick at a wedding, a fish out of water. She wanted to go home. Right now.

"So are you in the industry?" asked the girl whose name was Princess.

Sorcha longed to ask if that was her real name, but she had a feeling it really was. She looked like a

Hollywood princess, with her lollipop frame and her bleached blonde hair and pumped-up pout and chest and she twiddled with her curls as she spoke.

"Er, no, I'm a . . . I'm a journalist actually. Back home, in Ireland."

"Ooooh!" said Princess in a high-pitched tone. "Do you write about people like me then? Can you write about me?"

Sorcha wanted to slap her Botox-ridden face. Why the hell would the readers of *The Gazette* want to read about her? They were much more interested in dog fouling and litter on the streets and breaking news like town planning and what went on in the Council Chamber.

"No, I can't actually," she said. "I have no idea who you are."

The table fell to a hush and Princess shot her a disgusted look. Even Taylor came to attention and glared at Sorcha like she had broken a golden rule.

"Sorcha," he said, "*Princess* is David Lawlor's niece. You know, David Lawlor?"

"Sorry, no, I don't," said Sorcha, knowing she was dreading on dangerous territory as the silence grew more deafening. She could feel her cheeks burn. "Should I know him?"

Rod or Mattie – she didn't know which because they both looked exactly the same with their pretty-boy looks – let out a nervous cackle. Gosh, she really had committed a mortal sin.

"David Lawlor is the executive producer on our movie," Rod/Mattie said. "He is like, he is like God to us. How can you say you don't know him and, even worse, that you don't know our beautiful precious Princess?"

He pronounced the word "producer" like "prod-oo-cer" even though Sorcha was sure he was from Wales or somewhere near there and she took an instant dislike to his pompous ways. His other half (Rod or Mattie, she didn't know which) put his hand on top of his and they shook heads in disbelief.

"I'm new to here," she mumbled. "It will take me a while, I suppose, to know who is who, but I'm sure I'll learn. But . . . I'm just here on holiday."

"On *holiday*!" said Belle, who looked extremely comfortable in her prime position next to Taylor. She had a similar size-zero/monstrously-big-head figure like Princess had but her hair was died within an inch of its life in stark black. She looked like an unhealthy version of Angelina Jolie and, again, Sorcha didn't take to her at all. "How cute! Don't you mean you are on *vacation*?"

"Tomayto, tomato," said Sorcha and she took a gulp of the champagne that sat in front of her. Shit, she was quite drunk already. Perhaps she should slow down. Fuck it, she thought and she downed it. "Potayto, potato."

She caught Taylor's eye and he was staring at her with a look that spelt fright and disgust. She was like a time-bomb to him, she realised, but her disappointment in the way he had changed and the way Belle with the big head and skeletal frame with two watermelons attached was staring at him was making her violently ill.

"Shall we order?" asked Taylor, running his eye over the menu before him. "We have work to do tonight so best make this a quick one."

Sorcha's stomach churned with a mixture of distaste and alcohol over-consumption and she scanned the menu with her mouth twisted. This was the exact opposite to what she had hoped for tonight to be and she was beginning to regret the moment she set foot in Hollywood.

Sorcha excused herself and made her way to the Ladies'. So far, she had learned that Rod and Mattie had met on set as extras and had widdled their way into the inner circle because Mattie (from Wales – he let it slip that he had once appeared in *Gavin and Stacey*) and Rod (who was David Lawlor's love child) had fallen madly in love and had befriended Princess who was undoubtedly the Paris Hilton of the group. Belle was a Boulevard Bunny or hanger-on and seemed obsessed with Taylor (until now Sorcha wouldn't have faulted her for that) and Taylor, with his direct link to the A Listers and matching accent to Liam Neeson, was indeed the leader of the pack.

Not once had he mentioned or asked about life at home. Not once had he talked about how Sorcha and he had any sort of history other than that they had "gone to school together" when he introduced her, and strangest of all, not once had he asked about Erin or how she was getting on back home without him.

Sorcha sat on the loo contemplating her actions. Why was she suddenly swapping sides in the love affair of her idol Taylor Smith and her nemesis, the incredibly beautiful and talented Erin O'Brien? Why was she repulsed by what she had witnessed at that table of starlets and actors with their fickle outlook on life and the way they adjusted their accents to suit the company? And why was she sitting on a toilet in one of the best restaurants in West Hollywood, feeling like she would much, much rather be back at home playing darts in The Stage with Taylor's younger and much more grumpy brother John? It just didn't make sense.

She realised she had been residing in the cubicle for a lot longer than she should when she heard the clip-clop of heels come into the bathroom and the distinctive transatlantic accents of Princess and Belle when they called her name.

"Sorcha?" they called in chorus but it was in a sickly, sing-song way that nipped at her. The way they said her name – Sorrrr-kaaa. *Eugh!*

"Honey, are you okay?" asked Belle. They sounded like and looked like Disney characters with their prissy names and over-the-top voices.

Still she didn't answer. She just sat there, her expensive underwear still at her ankles and a bunch of toilet roll that probably cost a lot more clenched between her two hands.

"She must have gone out for a cigarette," said one of the Little Mermaids. "I'm sure I saw a pack of Marlboro peeping from that horrendous handbag she was carrying. I have to admit, this time last year I would have gone for that, but that's before I learned the meaning of style, you know?"

They cackled and Sorcha felt her nose twitching in anger. Horrendous handbag? That had cost her the best part of a hundred-dollar bill! Granted that was peanuts to those two, but back at home that price would have been quite a head-turner for the guys down at The Stage.

"Never mind her," said Princess. "Tell me . . . how are you getting on? I can see you are trying, baby, and I have told you, keep working on him. He will come your way, I just know it. You have to concentrate on the two most important words in the business. Just keep them to the forefront of your mind at all times."

Sorcha's ears pricked up. The two most important words in the business? She wanted to know them too. Not that she wanted any part in their sordid business, but the nosiness had got the better of her.

"Awards Season."

"Awards Season," repeated Belle and both girls gave a gasp. "It's just around the corner, honey, and I have my eye on my prize. Do you think he will bite again? Do you really?"

"Well, he bit before, didn't he? I just hope you showed him enough to impress him at Uncle David's party to make him gag for more."

"Oh I did," said Belle. "I really did. And if Taylor Smith doesn't come back to me tonight for extras, then I have failed you and have failed everything we stand for. I want to make a name for myself and if he is my ticket to fame, I will go after him with every inch of my manicured body!"

"That's the spirit!" said Princess. "But tell me one thing and then I will never ask again."

"Ask me, angel!"

"Was he good? He looks mega fit, but sometimes new boys like Taylor Smith are hard to break in."

Sorcha heard an intake of breath and she pinched her nose as she felt a sneeze coming on.

"He was just . . . he was sort of, I suppose . . ."

Sorcha concentrated as hard as she could. If she sneezed now she would miss the punch line and as a hardened journalist who wrote obituaries on *The Gazette* with aspirations for bigger and brighter things – much bigger and brighter – she just couldn't afford to miss this one.

"I'm late," said Belle. "I am fucking late."

Princess didn't answer. Sorcha didn't sneeze.

"You are late? No! No, baby, no. How late?"

"Look, I'm not panicking yet," whispered Belle. "You know me, I hardly eat. In fact I am going to get rid of that salad now, so being late is something I suppose I should be used to, but I have this niggling fear that after the other night with Taylor, it . . . it just might be."

Sorcha held her breath and the toilet roll in her hands became clammy with perspiration. She felt sick. She felt like she was a child who was overhearing her parents again with nitty-gritty detail about their marriage and its problems that she didn't want to or didn't need to hear. But she couldn't stop listening now. How could she? They weren't exactly whispering *that* much and they had no idea she was even there.

"Well what the hell are you going to do? What about the dress you have been measured for? Belle! This was not part of the plan!"

"I know it wasn't but don't worry. I'm not worried. It's probably nothing. Jeez, I wish I hadn't even mentioned it. If it is what I dread to think it is, then I'll pop down to the clinic and get back to normal again. I'm twenty-three years old and I have a career in this town. I'm not stupid, you know."

Sorcha heard shuffling in handbags and the smell of way too expensive perfume filled the air. Then she heard both girls move into the cubicles at either side of her and the sound of retching made her gag. She pulled the flush on the toilet, walked out to the sink, washed her hands, fixed her hair and made her way out into the busy restaurant and bade farewell to Taylor Smith and his life in Hollywood.

SCENE TWENTY-TWO

Erin tried to call Taylor but again there was no answer. She tried not to let her worries and fears destroy what had been a very lovely evening with Olivier as they practised their song in her living room.

Olivier was in the bathroom now and they had gone over the song until neither of them could bear to listen to it again and she had poured them both a glass of wine as a finale, warning herself not to overindulge in front of him. She tried Taylor's number again. Still nothing . . . just that silly voicemail recording with that stupid accent that made her stomach churn inside.

She contemplated leaving a message but a voice inside her told her not to. He still hadn't responded to the last one and when she had bumped into Krystal at rehearsals that afternoon, she talked about everything from the weather to the price of fish – but not a mention or a question on her darling son.

Still, Erin ached inside to hear from him and until she

knew any different, she would fight for her relationship and pray that things got back to normal as soon as he got home. But somewhere in the back of her mind was Olivier and all that he stood for. He was almost too good to be true with his mannerly ways and the way they shared such explosive moments. She couldn't deny the strong connection they shared every time she saw him and every time they sang together a fire burned inside of her. It's lust and longing, she told herself. Just longing for Taylor and lusting for a man to hold her and love her. It would pass. It had to.

Olivier came back into the kitchen and she handed him the glass of wine. He held it out towards her. He looked different now, softer perhaps, and his dark hair shone under the light of the room and the candles that burned gave off a sensual fragrance.

"I would like to propose a toast," he said, his dark eyes burning her inside as they always seemed to do. "I would like to propose a toast to you, me and happiness, if that is okay. And to life in Little Hollywood. The very best place to be."

She clinked her glass against his and a rush of emotion surged through her. She had to fight against her feelings for him. She was lonely and vulnerable and she couldn't mistake that for true feelings. She couldn't speak. She didn't have to.

"This is fucking hard," he said, throwing his eyes to the floor. "My God, Erin. If things were different . . . if things were different I would . . ."

Her heartbeat danced inside her. Oh God, what was she getting into? She longed for him right now. She longed to fall into his arms and give in to the sensation that rippled through her that urged her to express the feelings she had for this wonderful man. She wanted to hear what he had to say but the fear she felt wouldn't let her question what her heart was pushing her to hear.

"Don't do this to me," she mumbled. "I don't know that I can resist this, Olivier. You know why I can't do this."

He took a step back and she felt like a mountain had grown between them. He looked deflated and rejected and she longed to climb over the mountain and tell him that, yes, she felt it too, but her mother's warnings flashed in her head and she thought of Taylor and the promises they had made to each other before he left. No matter how distant she felt from her Taylor, she couldn't betray him until she knew it was over. It just wasn't over with Taylor. Not yet.

Olivier lifted the bottle of wine and poised it over her glass. She shook her head. She couldn't drink any more, not until he left and then she knew that she would rummage in her kitchen until she found her latest secret stash and down it till her heart and mind was numb from all this confusion. But he filled it anyway and she drank it down like sweet milk, not letting her eyes leave his. They were magnetic. They always were.

"You okay?" he asked.

"I think so. You?"

"I can't think of anywhere else I would rather be right now."

Erin took a deep breath and leaned against the worktop opposite the place he was standing. She took him in. Good God, but he was a model of pure masculinity. The way his shirt clung to his body and the bottom button lay open just enough to give her a glimpse of what lay beneath his clothes. She could . . . she really could. As the wine warmed her veins and filled her empty heart, she let herself relax into the moment with him. She put some music on and she saw his body move to the tempo, so precise, so goddamn sexy. She wanted him. She needed him.

"Dance with me, Erin," he said and he set his glass down then reached his hands out to join hers. She met with him like it was the most natural thing in the world to do. She felt tipsy, a little dizzy, but she wasn't sure if it was the wine or the effect he had on her. Perhaps it was a combination of both. Nonetheless, she found herself in his arms and the heat that radiated from his body was so intense she felt like she might burn.

The music was slow and full of meaning and they moved together on the one spot, her head nestled on his strong shoulder. She blanked out all her feelings as his arm rested on her waist, his other hand in hers. She breathed him in. All of him and then he lifted her chin and looked at her, looked through her. A hundred images flashed through her mind: her mother, Taylor, Krystal, rehearsing with him and singing with him for the first time, the way he made her feel when she saw him that first day on his bike, the way he smiled at her when he left her at the garage. This wasn't real, she reminded herself. She was replacing Taylor with his body, she was replacing the need for the touch of a man, for the love of a man. She pulled away.

"I'm so sorry, Olivier."

Saying his name sent ricochets right through her. She wanted him. She needed him. She looked for her glass of wine and it was empty. He poured her another and before she knew it, they were dancing again.

Make this stop, she pleaded inside. Make me see sense. Make me feel like I need to feel but don't let me do this to Taylor. But there was no denying it and when he placed his hand under her chin again and lifted it to his face, then slipped his hand around her neck so that she felt shivers, she had to give in and she kissed him, long and slow. And God, but it felt good.

The next morning, Erin awoke with a familiar feeling of confusion and a throbbing head. Gradually as she lay with her head nestled into her pillow, the events of the night before fell into place. She had kissed Olivier. She had kissed him in the kitchen and then they had moved into her sitting room and lain on her sofa and she had felt his strong body on top of hers. They had stopped and drunk more wine, and then they had danced more and talked more and then . . . well, she couldn't remember what had happened after that. Oh God no! She reached for her phone and scrolled through her call log – she had a text message. Could it be from Taylor?

What had she done? She had been unfaithful to Taylor. She had kissed another man. She had kissed him and wanted him and longed for him and she was a cheating partner who no longer could look at herself in the mirror without feeling wrecked with drunken guilt and hazy memories of something . . . something that had been oh so good. Something that no matter how hard she fought it was always going to happen in the long run.

She was in her pyjamas. Thank God, she thought.

That was a good sign at least and when she opened the text message she was surprised that it was not from Taylor, but from Olivier.

Erin, last night we shared something I never, ever thought could happen. But it did and I can't deny any longer what I feel for you. However, I understand your commitment to Taylor and therefore I will go before we get in too deep. Good luck for the show. Remember, the show must go on, Erin. But I can't do this any more for as long as you belong to another. All my love forever. Olivier.

Erin sprang up in the bed and her phone rang before she had time to absorb the message. She checked the caller display. Shit! It was Taylor! Such perfect timing.

"Hey," she said. "Long time no hear."

A burst of nerves exploded inside her as the guilt rippled through her. She gulped and rubbed her throbbing head. Why couldn't she have controlled herself last night? Why couldn't she have told Olivier that drinking wine was a thing she had no control over?

"I'm a bit drunk," said Taylor. "Well, I'm a big bit drunk. Big, big, big . . ."

She heard a female voice in the background and her stomach sank. Then laughter. Lots of laughter.

"Taylor? Taylor, can you please tell me what the fuck is going on?"

She knew as she said it she reeked of hypocrisy. She knew she had kissed another man but she had a feeling that Taylor had gone much, much farther. She had tried to reach out to him. She had tried so many times but he had drifted so far away from her.

"It's not you . . ."

Oh shit! What a fucking wuss! No, she couldn't listen to this. She just couldn't.

"You are drunk, Taylor. Call me back when you are sober enough to talk to me. I deserve at least that. Jesus, Taylor, what the hell has happened to us? We said this wouldn't happen. You promised. I promised."

She felt tears spring in her eyes and she wasn't sure if it was disappointment or fear or guilt but a mixture of emotions surged through her. This was Taylor, her Taylor who she had planned a future with and now they were both making such a mess of it. And yet, no matter how he would answer her, she longed for . . . she longed for Olivier. But he was gone.

"I am . . . I am so confused now," he said, then he covered the phone and mumbled, "No, not now! Gimme a second. Just a second."

"Taylor," said Erin. "Taylor, what are you doing? Taylor!"

She was in hysterics now as the realisation that she and Taylor were no more filled her head and the reality sank in. It was too late to save it. He had gone too far. And so had she.

"I'm sorry, Erin. Believe me, no matter what happens, I am so, so sorry."

And then he was gone too.

Sorcha packed her bags with a heavy heart and ignored the stream of phone calls that were coming through from Krystal Smith. She could not lie to the woman. She wanted juicy gossip, she would get it but it was not in the way she would have anticipated. Yes, Taylor was fooling around. Well, he was a fool and by the sounds of it he had sure been around, which is what Krystal was hoping for so that she could shake Erin off, but it was more his personality change – he had gone from small town hero to a macho wannabe who reeked of ego and self-glory. The way he had made her feel the night before in that restaurant was a way she never wanted to feel again. It was just like the old days and she couldn't handle it any more. All her hopes of being with him, all her weak obsessions were long gone and deep in the pit of her stomach, somewhere amongst the deep disappointment, was a sense of closure at long, long last. He was human with weaknesses and faults just like anyone else. Yes, he was on his way to becoming a Hollywood superstar, but that was so flash in the pan and she was now convinced at last that Taylor Smith was just a man. He was just a man. She would go back to her life in Little Hollywood, safe amongst familiar surroundings and she would seek out that little house she had her eye on and work on her obituaries so that she could prove herself to her boss that she was a proper journalist who could report on stories like she always dreamed of. If that was about dog-fouling or littering or what went on in the Council Chamber, Sorcha didn't really care any more. She was going home. She would go home where the hurt was, and where her heart was, and she was going to move on in her own life in her own way. Taylor Smith could do his own thing in his own way and she was relieved that at last she really didn't care.

Erin's frustration was heightened by a knock on her front door. It was Sunday morning for goodness sake and anyone who knew her would realise that she cherished a Sunday morning lie-in more than life itself. Apart from that, she was reeling from the shock of her graphic conversation with Taylor and the sound of that squealy bitch in the background and what happened with Olivier and the underlying want and need she had for him was swimming through her head. She didn't know who she was any more; she didn't know what she wanted any more. She didn't know who was at her fucking door at this time of the bloody morning!

She pulled her dressing gown on and checked her face in the mirror of her dressing-table. Oh dear. White face, black eyes and red-wine stains around her lips were not a flattering look. She took a cleansing wipe and gave her face a quick rub, then applied a quick dash of tinted moisturiser on to her skin before making her way downstairs.

She took one last glance in the mirror before she answered the door. Oh yes, she looked horrendous but whoever was knocking on her door was not going to give in. She looked through the stained glass and didn't recognise the figure of the person who was wanting her so badly.

"Hello?" she called from the other side, hoping she would recognise the voice at least or hoping that he would let her know his identity.

"Erin, can you open the door? It's Jacques, I'm Róisín's husband from across the road? I need a quick word."

Oh shit! No! Something had happened to Róisín! She swung open the door, forgetting her appearance totally and the face of a crumpled man met her eye. Oh sweet Jesus! That poor woman! That poor baby boy!

"Jacques?" she said, without recognising her own voice. "Is she okay? What can I do?"

Jacques stood on her doorstep with his hands in his pockets.

"It's not Róisín," he said.

Erin shook her head in confusion. "I don't understand? What's wrong?"

"Erin, Róisín asked me to come quickly and let you know what has happened. I'm so sorry but I have bad news. It's Olivier. There has been a terrible accident. We both thought you would want to know."

ACT THREE

After the Big Time

SCENE ONE

Erin felt numb. She stared at the hospital bed and didn't recognise the figure that lay before her. The beautiful man she had got to know was crumbled, lying on sheets of white and hooked up to machines with his eyes heavy and sore. The medical staff explained to her that she had five minutes and five minutes only and not to encourage any conversation with Olivier but she longed to just get one word from him. She had no real idea how they had left things, apart from the precious text message that she had now saved on her phone which declared how he truly felt for her.

She had called into work sick for three days now, unable to face reality and choosing instead to sit by Olivier's bedside for five minutes at a time, or keeping his dear grandmother company as she pined for his recovery. His parents had come over from France and some of the dance troupe from his Moulin Rouge act had sent flowers and greetings, but apart from that and the odd visit from Jacques and Róisín when she was able for it, Olivier was lying in a strange place in a strange country and Erin just longed to be with him.

He hadn't spoken since the accident, which had happened on his way home from her house that night. How she wished she could turn back the clock and make him stay with her, rather than take his bike after having a few drinks. She had wrecked her head for answers as to how they had parted but once again, alcohol flurried her memory and she couldn't recall much more than their brief argument and the passion that flared between them. He had drunk a few glasses, that was for sure, and the few miles to his gran's home was far enough to cause this "almost fatality" that she was witnessing now.

"Talk to me," she whispered into his ear as his eyes reached out to her. "Just say my name. Say anything, Olivier. Please."

But there was no response. There hadn't been since that morning when Jacques came calling at her door. Poor Jacques and poor Róisín with their little Joseph. They'd had enough troubles and worries and now Olivier who had helped them through so much had been struck down under such tragic circumstances.

Erin cursed herself for that night. She cursed how as always she couldn't remember the detail. She cursed the alcohol, she cursed the moment but she couldn't curse the strong longing she still felt when she looked at him, or the memory of that precious kiss they shared.

She stared at his face. It was failed and sunken and his eyes were empty but behind the void she could still hear his voice, she could still hear him singing and she could still feel his arms around her waist as they had danced in her kitchen that night. She longed to turn back the clock and to tell him how she really felt for him. She longed to tell him that Taylor was far back in her mind now. He was a different person in a different land and the love she had carried for him was fading fast since this tragedy had happened.

But Olivier didn't respond. He couldn't. The nurse peeped around the curtain and nodded that her time was up, so she lifted her handbag and made her way down the lonely, clinical corridor and into the family waiting room where his grandmother sat reading her Bible.

"Any change?" asked Bernadette, just as she did every time anyone came into the waiting room from having seen him. It brought tears to Erin's eyes when she saw the hope the older woman was clinging to and she wished she could bottle it and keep some it for herself. Bernadette had Rosary beads wrapped around her fingers and as Erin flickered through magazines absentmindedly, the gentle chant of Bernadette's prayers soothed her somehow. A clock on the wall ticked the seconds by but they seemed to last minutes, minutes like hours and hours like days. She knew she didn't have to be there for such lengths of time but she was afraid that he would wake up when she was gone.

His parents didn't say much. They kept themselves to themselves and whispered a lot, and his mother wept in silence every time she returned from Olivier's bedside. They were making arrangements to have him transferred to a hospital in Paris as soon as he was able to be moved and they spoke in French most of the time which frustrated Erin even though she knew it shouldn't. But Bernadette had all time in the world for her and kept her up to date with anything she felt Erin should know.

"The brain is a very complex organ," said Bernadette out of the blue. She was staring into space, clutching her beads and rocking ever so slightly in her chair. "It's amazing what they can do nowadays. He is in the best hospital here. No need to move him at all, that's what I say but they won't listen."

Erin put her hand on Bernadette's and nodded. She couldn't understand why Olivier's parents were so keen to have him moved from a hospital like the Royal Victoria. It had such a fine reputation and the doctors were hopeful but not confident that Olivier would make a full recovery eventually. It was a miracle he had broken no bones but the head injury he suffered when he came off his bike was severe enough to cause grave concern right now.

"I think if they could just be patient, it would be best for Olivier to stay here. They have to think of what is best for him."

The waiting room door opened and Erin's heart lifted when she saw Kizzy come in, armed with magazines and bags of sweets that would rot your teeth just by looking at them.

"Holy Good God, look at the set of you," said Kizzy and she plonked down on a squishy chair beside her best friend. "Sorry, I'm Kizzy. I'm Erin's friend and I had absolutely no idea where she has been for the past few days until I called her mother. I'm an internet addict, you see. I don't go out much."

Bernadette shook Kizzy's hand and then covered her mouth as she started to giggle.

"What's wrong, Bernadette? Are you okay?" said Erin.

312

Bernadette hunched over in kinks of laughter and then let out a long sigh.

"Sorry, love. I'm sorry. It's just the way … what did you say your name is? Kizzy?"

"Aye," said Kizzy. "Well, it's Kathryn really but my mother was a Roots fanatic back in the day and the priest wouldn't christen me after a black slave like she wanted him to so she had to stick Kathryn on the birth certificate just to save him having a stroke. But no matter, how is Oliver? Is it as bad as it sounds?"

"Olivier," said Erin. "Not Oliver."

"Sorry."

"There has been no real change since the accident," said Bernadette, back to her solemn self now. "He is just lying there, looking at us, but there has been no response as yet. I feel so guilty. If it wasn't for me he would never have come here to stay. He would never have taken an interest in that bike and he wouldn't be lying there on that hospital bed. What will I do without him? What will I do without Olivier? It is all my fault."

Bernadette broke down into a sob and rummaged in her handbag for a tissue as the tears fell down her slightly wrinkled face. Kizzy handed her a fresh one from her bag of tricks that contained everything from baby wipes to Band Aids and Bernadette nodded in gratitude, unable to say even a simple thank you.

"No," said Erin rubbing her shoulder gently. "Please no, Bernadette. Olivier loves it here. He told me so many things that he has got up to down the years, spending summers with you and the way you both used to sit in the garden and sing as you lay on sun loungers, or how he used to go fishing with his grandfather and they would disappear for hours and you would be cross when they turned up, soaked through and starving but late for dinner. He loved it here. He still does love it here. In fact, he said he would give his whole life in Paris, all the glitz and the glamour, to come and settle near you in Millfield. This is his Little Hollywood now. This is where his heart is."

Bernadette's tears continued to flow but Erin could see a change in the lady. It was like Erin's words had raised her spirits and her hopes even higher than her God had as she prayed to him constantly. She gripped Erin's hand tight.

"Thank you, Erin. I honestly never, ever thought he felt that strongly about here, not in that way. I . . . I always knew he loved to come and visit so he could switch off, but I never thought that he felt like that. It means so much for you to have told me that."

"Would anyone like a Bull's Eye?" asked Kizzy, offering a white paper bag full of the black-and-white boiled sweets.

"I would absolutely love one," said Bernadette. "Can we keep her here, Erin? I'd really like to keep you, Kizzy."

They shared a laugh and Kizzy rolled her eyes.

"Tell my husband that and he will cut you a deal. He'll even pay for you to take me. And I am not joking. Name your price and I'm yours!"

"Okay, spill the beans," said Kizzy as she and Erin sat at a Formica table in the hospital canteen. "How did you and this Olivier go from being Torvill and Dean, i.e. working partners, without the ice of course, to bloody

Sonny and Cher? And where the fuck does Taylor fit into all this? I thought my wee humble life was scrambled with my lazy shit of a husband and an online lover who thinks I'm still nine stone. But you!"

Erin stirred her coffee clockwise and then anti-clockwise and blew onto it. How could she explain? She had no idea where to start.

"Did you sleep with him?" asked Kizzy. "I never really got a really good gawk at him at all, but from the talk around the village he is one hot piece of gear. There's something about a man on a bike that just gets my engine running. I think it's the leathers and the helmet or maybe it's a bad-boy thing. Why the hell didn't I marry a bad boy instead of that useless sofa-hogging, dart-playing git I did? Why didn't you say to me, 'Kizzy, do you really want to be superglued to a computer in quest of romance while your children pull the cornflakes from the cupboard?'. Like, didn't you know?"

"I thought you said he might be having an affair. Remember? The Robbie Williams CD and the new shoes?"

"Pah!" said Kizzy, waving her spoon in the air. She had treated herself to a heated muffin with ice cream and was still marvelling at how it only cost £1.99. She would seriously consider coming to this canteen for a night out. "I don't think My Dermot would know the meaning of the word 'affair'. It would take too much out of him to try and ride another woman. Sure he can't even be bothered to sort me out at the best of times. Too busy adding up darts scores in his head."

She hoofed a spoonful of muffin and ice cream into her mouth as the thought of Dermot 'riding' anyone was giving Erin a mental image that she'd rather forget. Dermot wasn't a bad-looking fella but he looked more like your rounded cousin than a potential sex god. Plus, he really did have the personality of a goldfish. There was more craic at a wake than when Dermot was around.

"Well, 'my' Taylor surely knows the meaning of the word affair, and hell, it looks like I do too. Do you count it as an affair when he is shagging stick insects in Hollywood? I mean, does this account for an affair, now that I am on a vigil by Olivier's hospital bed and couldn't give one flying fuck of how many Playboy Bunny types he has stuck to him over there? What do you think?"

"Apart from the fact that this muffin and all its deliciousness is really distracting me from what you are saying right now, I did catch some of that and I would say that the answer is no. Unless you slept with Olivier first which you still haven't answered me on, because in that case, then you cheated on Taylor and you are as bad as . . . shit, you're as bad as me, I suppose."

"With Niall 'Dumbo' McGrath? Nah, Kizzy. You wouldn't. Would you? Oh Jesus Kizzy, did you?"

"No! Not that way," said Kizzy. "No I didn't. I wouldn't. I don't *think* I would. Well, *he* wouldn't anyhow if he saw me now. That's why I still haven't put a profile photo of myself up on Facebook. He still talks about how I looked the night of our school formal in my little purple dress that was only a size eight or something! I was six-bloody-teen but I told him I can still fit into it. Jesus, what was I thinking leading the poor man's head astray? What I didn't tell him was that I could just about manage to fit one leg into it. That would soon ruin his illusions, wouldn't it?"

"You need to talk to Dermot about this," said Erin more seriously now. "You have two beautiful children who need their mummy and daddy to sort things out before you really do something you can't go back on. All me and Taylor will have to sort out is who owns the plant in the hallway because that's the only thing he ever bought for the house and it only cost six quid in Asda. You know, I don't honestly think Taylor would even be able to look after a plant . . . I never really thought of that before . . ."

Kizzy licked her spoon and stared at Erin as she drifted away in deep thought.

"And what about motorbike man up the stairs there? Could *he* look after a plant? I *think* I'm following you here. I *think* I am."

Erin gulped and then stood up as if divine intervention had just struck her.

"Kizzy, you know, he could. He really could."

"Good," said Kizzy, glad to have established that but not sure why.

"Olivier is the one for me, Kizzy. He really is. I'm sick of life being all about ambition and careers and how many people you can step on to get to the top. I want a life with Olivier and he wants one with me. I'm going back up to that ward and I am not budging until he comes around and then I am going to tell him that he was right. We are meant to be and that's all there is to it."

She swung her handbag over her shoulder and marched away from the table as Kizzy shoved the last spoonful of her muffin in before she followed her.

"What was it? Was it the plant that did it for you? Is

he green-fingered? My God, I think you are losing the plot here, woman. What has looking after plants got to do with the price of . . . the price of a muffin and ice cream?"

They strode along the corridor, dodging patients, visitors and medical staff who wore a mixture of green and blue and white uniforms. Erin stopped dead in her tracks as a stream of people threatened to bump into her.

"I want to be with him," she said. "I want his babies and I want to – oh my God I can't believe I am only realising this now! Yes, it's Olivier I want to be with. Olivier who makes me melt when he touches me, who cares for people when they are sick, who can look after little toddlers as if they are his own, who loves his grandmother enough to spend months on end with her, who has enough talent and charisma and sex appeal to light up my whole life without aspirations for things out of reach. It's him I want, not Taylor. And I am going to tell him right now."

SCENE TWO

Kizzy slipped into the waiting room as Erin marched her way towards Olivier's side ward on the neurosurgery floor of the Royal Victoria Hospital. Erin was smiling, yet she knew that when she saw Olivier, the fear that he mightn't fully recover from this terrible accident would return and she would crumble by his side, now that she was totally sure of how she felt for him. She stopped at the door of the room and peeped in through the glass square so that she could see the lower part of his body. His parents were with him, so she turned around and leaned on the wall next to the door, determined to wait until her turn came.

She said a silent prayer that he would be okay. It had been three days now and the doctors were reluctant with information when she asked, insisting only on releasing it to next of kin and when she did ask questions and they asked what her relationship with the patient was, she didn't know what to say. But now she did. Now she would say that she loved him and that he loved her and that on the night that this happened, he had been so hurt and distraught at how close they had come to being together, but they'd known that because of Erin's loyalty to Taylor it wasn't to be just then. But it was now.

She heard the door handle move and Olivier's parents came out of the room, his mother as always with her head bowed and his father, who Olivier spookily resembled in every way, with his hand on her shoulder and the other protectively at her waist. They were a couple who were incredibly strong and fiercely in love and Erin admired that in them, even if their closeness made them seem distant to others.

"Any change?" asked Erin, realising she sounded like Bernadette, with that slight glimmer of hope in her heart and in her voice.

But Olivier's father gave her an apologetic shrug and escorted his beautiful wife down the long lonely corridor.

Erin pushed the door open and moved quietly into the little room where Olivier lay. A stream of light filtered through the flimsy curtains and rested on his hand by his left side. She sat down next to him, not once taking her eyes off his face, and she clasped his hand into hers. It was warm but his palm stayed open, no matter how tightly she gripped it.

"Olivier," she said. "Olivier I am so, so sorry about what happened the other night. I wish I could turn back the clock and kick myself into realising that you were so, so right. I have never, ever felt like this before. I have never connected with someone like I have with you. I barely know you yet you complete me and I can see in your eyes when you look at me and feel it in your hands when you hold me that you mean every word you say. If only things were different now. This is so typical, that it would take something so tragic for me to finally realise what has been staring me in the face for the past few weeks since you came into my life."

She closed her eyes as thick, salty tears dripped from them and down onto her hand. She clumsily wiped her face with her other hand and inhaled deeply and when she opened her eyes again she saw Olivier blink. He blinked incredibly slowly and she stared at him, wondering if he was trying to give her a sign. Then, like an electrical current had run up her arm, she realised that he was holding her hand. Her face crumpled with emotion and then she smiled and slowly, very slowly, he returned the expression as a faint smile crept across his handsome face.

"Oh Olivier. Oh my God, Olivier! I don't know what to say. I have to get your parents. I have to get Bernadette!"

The way Olivier's parents whispered and nodded to the medical team in the corridor and she and Bernadette sat just out of earshot unnerved Erin at first. She knew she shouldn't be feeling so overprotective of his wellbeing and she had no right to do so anyhow, but a dread lay inside her that told her she had something to be concerned about. These concerns were verified when Mr and Mrs Laurent came into the waiting room.

"We have come to a decision," said Mr Laurent as his wife clutched his hand and leaned into his side. "With Olivier's progress, doctors have agreed to move him to hospital in Paris by the end of the week. He will make a full recovery at home where he belongs."

Bernadette gasped and Erin did not know where to look. All the joy she felt from Olivier's steps to recovery was pulled like a rug from her feet and she felt like she really didn't belong where she was right now, amongst this very tight family who were making decisions that she had no say in, but wished she had.

"But he is in the best place here," said Bernadette, her voice in a quiver. "Why have him moved when he is getting better here and we have some of the top neurologists' right on site. I don't understand . . ."

Olivier's parents sat down opposite them.

"I think I will leave you all to it," said Erin with a lump in her throat. "This is family stuff and I don't think I should be here right now. You barely know me. I have stayed for too long."

"No, stay," said Bernadette, her frail eyes pleading with Erin. "You and Olivier are such good friends and I want you to stay . . . with me."

Erin licked her bottom lip and looked at Olivier's father for approval. He held out his hand for her to take a seat again.

"He told me . . ." said Mr Laurent slowly. "He told me just last week that he had met an amazing Irish girl and that he was falling in love with her. He told me all about you, Erin."

Erin felt tears prick her eyes. "He did?"

"He also told me you have a boyfriend and that no matter how much he tried to fight it, he couldn't hide his feelings any more and that he was going to tell you. Did he tell you?"

"He did," said Erin as the tears fell down her face. "He told me. He told me just the other night."

"Olivier has a long road to recovery, Erin, and you have some trouble to clear up with your partner. That aside, my main concern right now is for my son's full recovery and I truly believe that my colleagues back home can help him get there. The team says he will be ready to fly on Friday and I trust them in their knowledge. Erin, I know you are sad but if you and Olivier love each other as much as you think you do, then this will not make any difference in the long run. I don't want you to feel like we are taking him away from you. Just take this time to think about what it is you really want."

Erin felt Bernadette's protective but dainty arm across her shoulder as her head dropped down with fear. She knew she and Olivier could still make this happen, but the thought of losing him right now, just at the moment she had realised how much she really did love him, was blocking her vision of any plans for the future.

"He will get better, won't he?" she sniffled. "I mean, he will be back to normal soon. Oh God . . ."

She was surprised when his mother answered, behind muffled sobs.

"Pray for him," she said gently. "Pray for my boy . . . and please give him his time to recover."

Erin kissed Olivier's forehead and clasped his hand as she did so. His eyes smiled at her and when he tried to speak, she hushed him, willing him to reserve his energy as much as he could.

"I will be back very soon," she whispered to him. "Don't go anywhere."

She rubbed her hand gently across his jaw line, feeling the light stubble beneath her fingers and she kissed him again on the lips this time, but so lightly that she wished she could do it again and again.

"Bye," he whispered so faintly that it only just caught her ears and he gripped her hand tightly before releasing it and then letting her go.

Bernadette was waiting for her in the corridor and they made their way down the long corridors of the Royal Victoria Hospital, across the glass-walled walkways with their colourful and attractive gardens below, and down the escalators until they reached the bright light of the springtime afternoon that awaited them.

"I cannot thank you enough for how you have kept me company all this time," said Bernadette. "I know my son and his wife can be very proud people but it's their culture and it's their personality too. I think Olivier inherited more Irish qualities than my son ever did, and that's why he and I have always been so close."

"He certainly loves you very much, Bernadette. He really does."

Bernadette stopped just before they stepped onto the zebra crossing and she waited to compose herself. Erin linked her arm and waited for her. She was in no hurry.

"I am going to miss him so much, Erin. I have become so used to having him around the house, and even when he is helping Jacques with Róisín and little Joseph, I always know he isn't too far away. We had another month together and I took that for granted. I can't believe this is all happening. I don't have the energy to travel to France, but if I did, I would go back with them, whether they want me or not."

Her moment was disturbed by a familiar voice from across the car park. Erin looked up to see Darryl Smith, his rounded figure and smartly dressed attire shuffling towards them, flanked by an uber-glam, mutton-dressed-as-lamb Krystal clip-clopping behind him.

"Erin, just who I was hoping to bump into! How is he? How is Olivier?"

Krystal was carrying a bag from Marks and Spencer and Darryl rattled his keys as he spoke, stopping when they both reached the side of the pavement where Erin and Bernadette stood.

"Darryl, Krystal, this is Olivier's grandmother Bernadette. I'm not too sure if you know each other or not?"

Krystal's red lips quivered into an Oscar-winning, heartbroken expression as she shook Bernadette's hand.

"Darryl speaks highly of you, Bernadette. He remembers you of course from the early days of The Players. I can tell you now that no one is as sorry as Darryl is for what has happened to poor Olivier. I just hope the rumours are not true. Darryl says —"

"Darryl can speak for himself," said Darryl, shooting Krystal a look to keep her mouth shut and Erin watched their every move, wondering what on earth the rumours might be that Krystal was referring to. That was the only downside of living in a goldfish bowl like Millfield. You couldn't take a piss but the town and country knew what colour of knickers you had on.

"He is making slow progress at last," nodded Bernadette. "It really has been touch and go and the doctors are astounded that he has no broken bones, just a chipped collar bone and a lot of internal bruising. But it was the head injury that has caused the main concern. Today he finally showed some reaction, and he even spoke to Erin, albeit only to say goodbye."

Krystal threw Erin a look that would have turned milk sour.

"Well, from what we have heard, Erin is –"

"Krystal!" said Darryl. "Not now!"

"No, do go on," said Erin tartly. She was ready for this. She was ready to take on Krystal Vinegar Tits Smith with her hooked nose and made-up face.

"This is neither the time, nor the place," said Darryl, tightening his cravat. "We are here to see Olivier and show him our support on behalf of The Players, not to get down and dirty on personal issues or grievances."

"Down and dirty?" said Erin. "Would someone like to explain just what the hell you two are on about?"

"I saw Olivier's bike at your house," said Krystal. "I was calling to you to talk about Taylor. I have been worried sick about my son because we have not had any word from him in days and I thought that you just might be worried too. But from what I saw in through your living-room window, you couldn't give a toss about Taylor! You are the very same, man-eating, cheating little trollop that your mother was!"

Erin gasped as if she had been stabbed in the chest. She longed to slap Krystal's orange face but her hands were trembling so much that she didn't have the energy or strength. She looked at Bernadette who had her hand over her mouth and she linked her arm again, for fear that if she didn't she just might strike out. Krystal took a step back and leaned into Darryl but he shrugged her off.

"Taylor is on his way home, Erin," said Darryl, straightening his posture. "His flight left this afternoon from LA and he is due back in about two hours' time. We will meet him at the airport and bring him home – wherever he decides that 'home' is. I thought that at least, no matter what else was going on, you might want to know that he was on his way back early. I don't know what his reasons are, but perhaps you do. Goodbye, Erin. Goodbye, Bernadette."

Erin and Bernadette crossed the road in silence and Erin paid for her parking while still on auto-pilot. So Krystal had witnessed her brief encounter with Olivier. Taylor was on his way home early. Olivier was going home to Paris to recover from his serious injuries. And he told his father that he loved her. She didn't know where to begin. She didn't know how it would all end. She didn't know anything any more.

SCENE THREE

Erin's heart was racing when she got to her front door. Taylor was coming home. Tonight. He was coming home tonight and yet he hadn't even told her so. She just couldn't understand it. Despite how her feelings had grown for Olivier, she hated that things with Taylor could end like this. They had so much history together, so many memories, so many years behind them and no matter what, she had always believed they would be together forever. But now, everything had changed.

She opened the living-room door and saw her mobile phone on the mantelpiece. She marched across for it, realising that in all her hurry to leave the house earlier to see Olivier she hadn't even brought it with her. She had four missed calls and a host of messages – all from Taylor.

"Erin, I am so sorry," he said in the first one. *"I've been so stupid and I've ruined everything, I know I have. The movie is set to wrap much earlier than we*

thought and I'm pretty much done so I'm coming home. I'm coming home today. To you, if you will still have me."

Hearing his voice stirred her emotions and with every message that he left on her voicemail, she heard the real Taylor again – the Taylor who she knew inside out and had always loved more than anyone else in the world.

Then she pictured Olivier, holding her close in his strong arms, the heat she felt from his body and the gentle way he listened to her every word and the way he totally understood her. The way they connected . . . the way she knew he could love her, and the way she knew she could really love him too.

But no, she told herself. No. Taylor was coming home. She must give him a chance. She would clean the house, she would prepare dinner, she would make her home welcome for the man she had loved for years. Yes . . . Taylor had made mistakes. But she should give him a chance, shouldn't she?

She sat down on the sofa and her thumb hovered over the text button as she wondered what or how to respond. She looked at Taylor's texts and re-read them, then she thought of Olivier again. Her heart wanted him so much, but her head told her that Taylor was the one she should focus on. Taylor was the one she had failed by becoming involved with Olivier in the first place. If Taylor had been here all along, she wouldn't even have glanced in Olivier's way. Would she? *Would* she?

No – she loved Olivier. She loved Olivier but she had so much left to sort out with Taylor.

She slumped back on the cushions and her head spun with a range of emotions that made her feel nauseous inside. Taylor. Olivier. Taylor. Olivier. The names ricocheted in her mind and through her body, as her head and heart fought for her to take sides.

She wrote her text. Then she closed her eyes and pressed send. Her head had won. She would go to the hospital and say goodbye to Olivier. It was what she had to do. It was the right thing to do.

The room was silent as always and Olivier lay there, sleeping peacefully. Erin took a sharp breath when she saw him and her hands longed to touch him, her lips longed to kiss him and the taste of her tears took her by surprise.

She sat down quietly by his bedside and watched him, his chest rising and falling as he slept.

"So you're heading home then," she whispered and pushed back a strand of his hair that had been blown across his face from a fan at his bedside. She let her hand rest on his forehead for a moment. "I hope they look after you well over there. Your dad seems to think so and I know that he wants nothing but the best for his only son."

She felt her voice choke her and she concentrated on breathing again.

"Olivier, I don't if you can hear me now, and for some reason I am finding it even harder to talk to you than I thought I would. Even if you can't hear me or can't answer me, I have to say what I am going to say."

Erin breathed in and out, in and out and when a nurse came into the room to check Olivier's chart, she was glad of the distraction. She didn't want to talk to him when she was in such a state.

"It's very upsetting, love," said the nurse as she scribbled on her clipboard. "He is making excellent progress, though. Wait till you see, by Friday he will be talking in sentences again and sitting up. I just know he will. I've seen it all before."

Erin rested her hand on his arm. "He's going back to Paris on Friday," she said. "Life around here is going to be so empty without him."

The nurse smiled and rested her clipboard on her hip. "He's a bit of all right, really, isn't he?" she said with a chuckle. She was almost retirement age and Erin knew she was being facetious. "We tell him that all the time and he smiles back at us. His parents are so, so proud of him. I'm sure he will leave a lot of broken hearts behind."

"He will," said Erin with a smile. "He definitely will."

The nurse left and Erin leaned her cheek on Olivier's arm, looking up at him in his dreamy state. His long, dark lashes sat under his eyes and she longed to reach up and touch them, but she didn't want him to wake up just yet. She had too much left to say. She rested there for what she thought was only minutes, but when she opened her eyes and looked at the clock, she realised that almost an hour had pasted.

She sat up, fixed herself and was slightly startled to notice that Olivier was awake and was watching her.

"Hey, you," she said to him. "I must have fallen asleep there. Gosh, how embarrassing! You look . . . you look happy. Well, *happier* considering."

"Seeing you," he mumbled and his eyes dropped heavily. "It's seeing you."

Erin felt her heart swell. She glanced at the clock again. It was after six and Taylor was due home in just under an hour. But she couldn't leave Olivier, not now.

"You are looking so much better," said Erin. "I am so happy to see you like this. Every time I see you, you take a tiny step forward and it's just so heart-warming. They will look after you well in Paris. I know they will."

She noticed his expression fall slightly and he tried to shake his head.

"I love you," he said and her insides fluttered.

She swallowed and put her hand on his. Why did this have to happen? Why did Taylor have to come home?

She shook herself. She shouldn't be thinking that way. It was wrong to curse Taylor's return home when it was what she had longed for since the day and hour he left her. When she saw Taylor it would all come flooding back, she just knew it would. She had to ignore her heart and its silly ways of wanting someone else.

She couldn't take this any more. She had to think things through and sitting here with Olivier was making her want him more and more. She stood up, leaned across, and gave him a gentle kiss on the forehead, knowing that her lips rested there much longer than was necessary. His eyes pleaded with her to stay and she shook her head as tears fell again.

"I know you love me, Olivier, and I am sorry. I am so sorry. I really think I love you too, but . . . but Taylor is back. He came back early and he wants to try again. I have to . . . I am so confused, but I think I have to give him a chance."

She let go of his hand slowly and sniffed back tears and sorrow, then she turned away and left him and when she got to the door she stopped and closed her eyes tight, trying to be sure that she was doing the right thing.

"Goodbye, Erin," she heard him whisper and her heart sank to the floor. "I hope everything works out for you. I hope you are happy."

She couldn't look back at him even though she knew he was watching her leave. She had to do the right thing and right now that meant going home to meet Taylor. Her relationship with Taylor deserved at least that much, didn't it? They had both promised that they would not let Hollywood come between them. She owed it to Taylor to give it a chance.

Erin heard Darryl's car in the driveway and she checked herself in the mirror before she opened the door to welcome her boyfriend home. She looked, well, not *that* bad, considering she felt like she had been dragged through a hedge backwards. Her hair was perfect, glossy and loose just like Taylor always told her he loved it. She had topped up her make-up and changed into a fresh outfit of casual jeans and a white shirt and she looked natural and effortless. So why on earth was something as simple as smiling proving to be such an effort?

She made her way to the door and painted on her best grin, ready to greet the love of her life, or at least the love of her previous life. What the present held, she still wasn't sure, but she wanted to love Taylor and she wanted him to love her. She really did. She repeated it to herself to make sure she did.

Darryl was first out of the car and Erin wasn't surprised that Vinegar Tits didn't move from her perch in the front passenger seat. She knew better than to even

333

as much as make eye contact with Erin. Darryl made his way to the boot of the car and then, after seconds that seemed like hours, Taylor emerged from the back seat and Erin drew her hands to her face.

"Oh my God," she whispered and she froze to the spot. It was Taylor. It was him. Taylor was home from Hollywood, but when he looked at her and made his way towards where she stood she saw a complete stranger. She had no idea who he was any more.

He reached out for her and she leaned against him, her eyes closed as she fought the feelings of negativity bouncing around her entire body. She clasped her hands around his neck and looked at him, directly into his eyes but she saw nothing she recognised from before.

"I've missed you," he said and he kissed her mouth and she tried her best to respond but it was like kissing someone she didn't know very well. There was no intimacy, no chemistry and as her tears fell and wet her cheeks, she felt guilty that they were not tears of happiness, but tears of sorrow for the emptiness she felt inside.

"Let's go inside," she said and broke away from him.

Darryl was waiting below the doorstep, flanked by Taylor's huge suitcases.

"Love's young dream rekindled at last," he said with a guffaw, but even he knew that there was an awkward tension in the air, which hadn't been helped by Krystal's grunting and groaning the whole way back from the airport about Erin's "distant behaviour lately".

"Thanks, Dad," said Taylor after they carried in the suitcases. "I'll pop down to the bar later to see John and some of the lads. Maybe we can have a chat over a pint?"

"Sounds great, son," said Darryl and Erin was sure she saw a teary glint in his eye. "It's great to have you back. Well, I think so anyhow."

Erin's guilty heart skipped a beat. She was used to Krystal's nasty gripes and snide comments but to think that Darryl was on a similar wavelength was really quite a bit more gut-wrenching.

He left, closing the front door quietly, and the silence that hung in the air was deafening.

"House looks nice," said Taylor moving into the kitchen. "Did you do something different while I was away?"

"No," said Erin. "It's exactly the same. Sorry to disappoint you."

"I didn't say I was disappointed, Erin. I was just passing a comment."

He looked at her and they both were thinking exactly the same thoughts. How had this all happened? There was virtually no connection, no common ground and both of them were equally sorrowful and equally terrified.

"Look, are you okay with me being here? I could have stayed at Mum's but she was already doing my head in on the way down the motorway. Really, I'd hoped we could try and pick up from where we left off but I think we both know already that is not as simple as it sounds."

Erin felt her skin burn and prickle at the thought of Krystal blackening her name. She wouldn't please her by sending Taylor back so soon.

"No, I think we should at least try," she said. "You packing off to your mum's just because we haven't fallen into each other's arms like we first thought we would, isn't good enough reason to give up at the first hurdle. We have a lot of ground to cover, but yes, I think you should stay here. Face the music, so to speak."

He folded his arms and leaned against a worktop while Erin busied herself around him, rearranging things like vases and a mug tree and dishcloths and then putting them back in their place. She attacked the tea-towel drawer next, taking everything out and refolding them again.

"Aren't you going to get that?" she asked when Taylor's phone rang from his pocket. She could see fear in his face as the phone buzzed and vibrated from his jeans.

"It will keep," he said. "I have more important things to talk to you about."

"Like?" she asked, knowing her tone was as sharp as the contents of the knife-block just beside her.

"Like where the fuck this has all gone wrong – would that be a good starting point?"

"You tell me," she said and she eyeballed him, wondering how the hell she was going to control the psychotic urge to use one of the knives from the wooden block – and not to chop vegetables.

He chewed his lip then breathed out a sigh. "It's just . . . it's just a different world over there, Erin. It's like . . ." He paused and shook his head, then looked down at his feet.

Erin wanted to choke him now. She knew. She just knew. "I just hope you have left your ego in the hotel lobby when you checked out," she said and folded the last tea towel, then slammed the drawer shut. "Now, I'm hungry and I don't really feel like cooking, funnily enough. Get freshened up and we'll go out for a bite. Before I bite your bloody head off, Taylor Smith."

SCENE FOUR

"The prodigal son has returned at last," said John from behind the bar at The Stage when Erin and Taylor made their entrance over two hours later. He flung his red-and-white checkered tea towel over his left shoulder and made his way round to greet the couple. "Good to see you back, bro'. What's occurin'?"

"Still obsessed with *Gavin and Stacey*, I see?" laughed Taylor and the two brothers shared a very brief hug.

"No need to act like poofs," said John in a mock Welsh accent. "No need."

"Hey, that was good!" said Taylor. "I just know there is a thespian within you, John. It will come out eventually, you know."

"Over my dead body," said John. "Now, what can I get you two to drink?"

"A red wine," said Erin. "Large."

She noticed how John and Taylor shared a look when

she said it but she didn't give one shit what they thought any more. Dinner had been a mixture of awkward silences and nit-picking rows and the food itself had been the only saving grace in a damp squib of an evening – that and the knowledge that they were hitting the pub straight after it. Erin had refrained from having wine with her meal but right now she just longed to get absolutely sloshed and forget all about everything – Taylor, work, and her growing urge to be with Olivier. She missed him so much it actually hurt her physically. She had never experienced that before. Not even when Taylor was away. She had never missed him like she missed Olivier.

"So, how are rehearsals going?" asked John as he poured their drinks. "I am asking merely to make conversation, as you know. I could not give a monkey's about what goes on in those incestuous circles masked as 'Community Theatre'. A cover-up for swingers, that's what I think it is."

Taylor and Erin both laughed at John's observations. He had a point. Well, not really, but it was fun to think he had.

"I hear you've lost your leading man, Erin. Does that mean that you're out too? I'm telling you, Taylor, your eye was nearly well and truly wiped!" John laughed aloud and shook his head. "Everyone, and I mean everyone was obsessed with Olivier. The whole village. Isn't that right, Erin?"

As opposed to Darryl's, Krystal's and her own family's comments on her closeness to Olivier, she knew that John's were not malicious. He was so wrapped up in his cocoon of The Stage Bar, horseracing and repeats of *Gavin and Stacey* that his only knowledge of Olivier would be what he had heard from his punters. He would have had absolutely no idea of Erin's close friendship with him.

"He's a very nice guy," she said, taking a sip from her wine. It tasted so good. She took another, more generous sip this time.

"He is a fucking legend," said John and Erin almost choked. She looked at John in bewilderment.

"What?"

"He's a legend. Nearly was a dead legend, mind you, but yeah . . . I have ultimate respect for the guy. He looks shit cool, he acts shit cool, yet I dunno. There's something really, really sound about him. Like he would be a really good friend. We had some great chats here when he would call in from time to time. Yeah . . ."

John smiled and nodded as he spoke, lost in his own little dream world as he reminisced about some of his deep and meaningful chats with Olivier.

"John?" said Taylor and he nudged Erin in jest. "You don't fancy him, do you? Do you fancy the French guy? Do you, John?"

"Go to fuck!" said John and he humped away down the bar. "Go back to Hollywood and don't come back!"

Taylor chuckled and laughed, then downed the remnants of his pint of beer, but Erin just stood there, lost and confused, in a world where she was back in Olivier's arms. She had never felt so lonely in all her life.

"Give us a fucking fag, for God's sake," said Erin to John when she made her way out to the smoking area at the back of the pub.

"When did you take up smoking again?" asked John,

handing her a Silk Cut. He blew out a long puff of smoke. "Mr Hollywood won't like that, now will he?"

"I won't tell if you don't," said Erin and they shared a smile.

She felt sorry for John sometimes, she really did. He was so obviously the black sheep of the family with his opposing views on everything from politics to religion, to sport to music but she admired him for sticking to his own ways and not going with the flow for the sake of it. Darryl and Krystal weren't exactly parents of the year and she knew what John had meant when she referred to the theatre group as a "swingers club". It was common knowledge that both Darryl and Krystal had, let's say, "enjoyed" the company of others down the years but secrets were sometimes covered up well in a small place like Millfield. Like they were approved secrets that should not, nor would not be discussed.

"If I say something, will you promise not to bite my head off, even if you want to?" asked John, blowing out another long line of smoke.

Erin leaned across and he clicked his lighter to ignite her cigarette.

She shrugged. "Go for it. I won't bite. I won't bite quite simply because I do not have the energy to bite right now."

"Okay," said John and he flicked his ash into a steel bucket that sat by his feet. He drew a breath and then shrugged. "What the hell, I'm going to say this. You and Taylor . . . it's over, Erin, isn't it?"

Erin's eyes widened. Her first reaction was of defence and denial. "John! Where the . . . why are you saying that? No!"

"Admit it, Erin. The two of you are standing in there with a gap between you as wide as the Grand Canyon. It's so obvious that something has happened to you both over the past few months and I know I don't normally say much, but I can see that his mind is in Hollywood and yours is . . . yours is right here . . . in Little Hollywood . . . in Millfield . . . and it's not on Taylor but on Olivier. You know I'm right, Erin. You just have to admit it to yourself."

Erin realised that she had her hand on her hip and one foot pointed out to the side in a dramatic stance. She tried to respond to John's observation, to react as she should react after being told her true feelings by her boyfriend's brother who normally only spoke to jockeys on a television screen. She opened her mouth to tell him that no, he was very, very wrong and how dare he say such a thing. She wanted to be matter of fact and tell him to stick to pulling pints instead of handing out advice to his clients and, worst of all, his near family. She grunted again but no words would come out. Then she heard a crunch on the gravel pathway that led to were she and John stood, eyeballing each other like gladiators in a ring.

"Erin, you're smoking? That's disgusting!"

Taylor took the cigarette from her hand and threw it onto the sand in the steel bucket. She didn't respond, still trying to digest the words that John had said to her as a million reasons to tell him he was wrong spun through her head, yet nothing would come out.

"I'll leave you two to it," said John. He flicked his cigarette away and he walked back inside.

Erin couldn't even look at Taylor. She just stood

there, motionless, stoic, and she sensed that he was doing the same.

"Your mum's in there. In fact they all are," he said. "Looks like an impromptu welcome-home party is in the making."

He kicked a stone as he spoke and she looked at him at last. He was a beautiful creature, there was no doubt, and she had no dislike for him, no matter what had happened when he was in Hollywood. It was just like a fire had gone out inside her and she suspected that it had gone out for him too and it saddened her to think that all her hopes and dreams with Taylor were over. Yet she couldn't bring herself to admit it. Not yet.

"You want to go back inside?" he asked and extended his hand to her.

"Yeah, let's go back in," she said and, instead of taking his hand, she linked his arm and laid her head against him as they walked slowly back into the warmth of the bar, both thinking exactly the same thing, both equally saddened.

"Here he is!" yelled Krystal and the bar erupted with cheers and the sounds of glasses clinking when Taylor and Erin moved back into the pub's cosy fireside lounge.

"Oh, you two!" said Marjorie from The Players as she scurried towards them. "I remember the very first time I realised you were a couple. It was the most magical and the most natural thing in the world. Our two little stars and now you are reunited. I'll drink to that tonight!"

"Thanks, Marje," said Taylor. "Let me buy you that drink."

Erin left his side and found her mum and grandmother

who were contentedly sipping their usual tipple in their usual seat.

"Ah, come and sit down, pet," said Geri. "I thought you would have called in to me today, at least to get your hair done if nothing else. I would never have known about all this excitement if I hadn't gone over to The Butcher's when I did. The town and country knew Taylor was coming home before I did. Have to say, it was a little embarrassing but not that that matters now. He's home, you're here, we're here. Oh, how's Olivier?"

The sound of his name made Erin's stomach swirl. She pictured him lying on that cold hospital bed, his long dark hair so stark against the white sheets and his deep intense eyes that stirred her insides when he looked at her and told her he loved her.

"I need a drink," said Erin and, like magic, John appeared at her side with a glass of wine.

"Thought you did," he said with a wink and he whispered into her ear. "You do know, Erin. I'm here if you need me. If you ever want to scream or shout or just moan a little when things aren't going your way, I'm here. I may not say much, but I've learned to listen and when I do say something, I say it for the best."

Erin smiled up at John and then squeezed his hand. "Thanks, John," she said. "That's really, really good to know. You're a very nice guy and some day very soon I know you'll meet someone who appreciates you for everything that you are. You deserve it. Thank you."

"Aw, he's turned a corner," said Erin's Gran. "I never knew he could really speak at all, that boy. All I've ever heard is the odd grunt or groan or complaint. Just goes to show you, doesn't it?"

Erin watched across the bar as people flocked around Taylor, quizzing him about Sandra Bullock and movie sets and Malibu Beach and Sunset Boulevard. He was in his glory, telling stories of who he had met, who he had brushed past in restaurants, the people he had partied with and she knew he was reliving the one thing she knew he loved the most. And it wasn't her.

She ordered a round of drinks and then they had another and another and before she knew it, two hours had passed and not once had Taylor looked her way. She was tipsy now, more than tipsy, but the evening was young. She could get away with staying in the bar for hours more, but she felt dead inside as she watched him flaunt his stories and impress his oh-so-attentive audience.

"Load of shite, really, isn't it?" said a voice and she knew it was too high-pitched to be John, even though it was what he always said about everything. She turned around to see Eugene Daly and his sister Sorcha, the hatchet-faced journalist, at the next table.

"Oh, hi, Eugene. Hi, Sorcha," she said, expecting the usual tongue-lashing version of a "hello" from the younger girl who had always despised her because of Taylor.

Erin almost fell off her stool when Sorcha gave her a smile.

"It really is," said Sorcha. "It really is a pile of shite. Eugene is right."

"I have no idea what you two are talking about. Oh, how did your trip go? I was thinking about you the whole time. Did you manage to track Taylor down?"

"I did," said Sorcha, sipping her cocktail. It looked a

little exotic for something served up by John but she seemed to be enjoying it. "Yeah, I did."

She glanced across at Taylor and rolled her eyes. Then she slurped more of her cocktail and met Erin's eyes as she sucked through her straw, never stopping until the glass was drained of its strange-coloured concoction.

"It's a new cocktail," said Eugene with excitement. "I think my sister will start a new craze. It's called 'Sorcha' after her. You should try it. And no, it's not as bitter as you think it would be!"

He laughed out loud, a snorty, high-pitched laugh and Sorcha waved her straw in the air as if she was conducting his pitches and his snorts.

"Ha bloody ha," she said. "It's actually sweet on the inside, just like me. Can I get you one, Erin?"

Erin was cautious for a number of reasons. One, she didn't think she should actually drink any more alcohol in that particular sitting and two, she didn't have the best history with Sorcha Daly so why should she trust her?

"Another two?" asked John from the bar.

"Please, John," said Sorcha and Erin lightened up when she spotted a faint sign of chemistry between the two of them, even in such a simple interaction. "Two Hollywood Sluts. Otherwise known as The Sorcha."

Eugene held his hands up and giggled. "She left a virgin and came back a slut, what more can I say?"

"Eugene! Don't say that about your sister," said Erin, not knowing whether to join in on his laughter or look terribly shocked, but Sorcha didn't seem too bothered. She looked quite pleased in fact.

"He's right," she said, raising her eyebrows. "I had a

ball in Hollywood, but not with the people I thought I would. All you need over there is a rooftop bar, a tiny ability to act and you are sure the time of your life, if that's what you're into. I learned a lot over there in just a few days, but it's enough to let me know that I love life in Little Hollywood, much, much more than I do the real thing."

Erin watched in awe as Sorcha openly flirted with John when he delivered their drinks to the table.

"This could be your lucky night, John Boy," said Eugene who was presented with his trademark tap water and lime cordial with extra ice. "She's gagging for it. She's a proper little slut but she's buying her own house soon so you should stick with her."

Erin's hand shot to her mouth but then she realised that neither John nor Sorcha had noticed what Eugene had said, nor did they seem to care.

"Can I ask a favour?" said Erin to Eugene.

"Anything for you, my lady," he replied.

"Can you take me somewhere? I need to be somewhere else right now, but it's quite a bit away. I'll give you the petrol money if you'll drive me there."

"Shall we slip off now?" he said. "I think love's young dream will flicker on for a few hours more and no harm to her, but that Hollywood Slut drink is potent rubbish. She won't be fit for a snog let along anything heavier in an hour or two."

"Well, I promise to have you back again before it gets to that stage," said Erin. "Come on, Eugene. We'll go and for some strange reason, I don't think anyone will even notice we've gone."

They left the bar individually and Erin did a double

take when she was just about to get into Eugene's car. At first she thought it was the wine making her hallucinate, but she squinted and looked again and, yes, it was definitely her. It was definitely Kizzy skulking around the pub car park, glammed to the nines and looking extremely suspicious.

"Oi!" called Erin, very unladylike but that was her intention. "What are you up to? You'll get a fine reputation hanging about here in a short skirt like that!"

Kizzy looked extremely guilty as she shuffled across the car park towards Eugene's yellow VW Beetle. She was dressed in a hideous black-and-white striped mini with a low-cut V-neck that was so tight it made her cleavage resemble that of her breast-feeding days.

"Oh Erin, I just can't do it. I can't. I was supposed to meet you know who for a swift drink in a pub out of town but I chickened out and decided to come in here instead and meet Dermot after his darts practice but then I thought Niall might be in there too and now I don't know where to go and what to do."

Erin felt sorry for Kizzy. Her little bout of boredom was finally coming to an end as she realised it just wasn't in her nature to floozy around with men from her past.

"You could go home to your babies," said Erin and she opened the door of the car and pushed the seat forward. "Or, you could come with me and Eugene on a little *Thelma and Louise* style road trip? We'll be back before you know it!"

"You're a legend, Erin O'Brien. I may be dressed like a fat zebra and I may not have the guts to go through with an affair, but I have always wanted a spin in a convertible Beetle. I have just one question."

"Hit me."

"If I'm Thelma, you must be Louise and then . . . well, does that mean Eugene is Brad Pitt?"

"Please?" said Eugene, his hand clasped in prayer.

"Of course it does," said Erin. "Now, come on quickly before I chicken out."

Erin felt adrenaline pump through her veins as Eugene circled the car park on the lookout for a space. She drummed her fingers on her knees, lifted her handbag from the floor, put it back down again, lifted it again.

"Look, if you want to jump out here, I'll find a space and we can come and get you or meet you at the door, Erin."

"Good idea," said Kizzy. "You're bouncing around there like a hen on a hot bloody griddle."

"Maybe I should," she pondered. "Yes, stop. I'll run in and you can get me at the door. I'll only be a few minutes."

Erin jumped out of the car before Eugene properly came to a halt and tripped up a few times before she reached the revolving doors. She pushed her way through and marched down the familiar corridor until she came to the elevators but they didn't come quick enough so she took the stairs and climbed the five floors until she was out of breath.

When she reached the final set, a smile swept over her face and she felt joy in her heart like she had never felt before. She couldn't wait to see him. She couldn't wait to tell him that, yes, he was right and that she would wait for him forever if she had to. She had to tell him to his face. She had to let him know.

The ward was eerily quiet and Erin slowed her pace down to a tiptoe when she had gone through the security doors. It was just before visiting hours finished for the evening and she knew she was cutting it fine but what she had to say would take only minutes.

When she got to the little side room where Olivier had been laid up since the weekend, her heart pounded in her chest in sweet anticipation. She felt her chest swell as she pushed the door open. She couldn't wait to see him. She couldn't wait to tell him.

She walked inside and like a slap on the face and a blow to the stomach she stopped dead. His bed was empty. His room was cleared. Olivier was gone.

"They left about an hour ago," said an auxiliary who had followed her into the room. "All very sudden really but then they are a funny pair, his parents. Couldn't wait till Friday, they said – best get the boy home now. I didn't get to say goodbye myself and he was such a sweetheart."

"Did he . . . did he know where they were taking him?" asked Erin. "Did he even want to go?"

She felt anger bubble inside her. Why wasn't she told? Why wasn't she given the chance to say goodbye?

She felt her body crumble and fold and she wrapped her arms around her waist and slid down the wall onto the floor.

"Olivier," she mumbled. "I want you so much, Olivier. I need you. I just wanted to tell you . . . I just wanted to tell you . . ."

FINALE

Three weeks later

The buzz of the audience entering The Community Hall was almost enough to give Darryl Smith a heart attack and all joking aside, if it had happened right now, he would have died a very relieved man. Krystal was getting on his wick as always with her clucking back stage and complaints about her costume being too tight and the green face-paint ruining her complexion but that was the least of his worries. Taylor and Erin were touch and go about doing their scene from *Moulin Rouge* but if they couldn't pull it off for the sake of one night then the whole show would go down the tubes.

He'd had a fine job convincing them in the first place since Taylor had moved back home. Yes, they spoke to each other in a civilised manner and it seemed to be an amicable enough split, but singing together? Well, that was a very different story. It was now a case of will they or won't they? and the local media had spun a few excellent pieces on Taylor's movie success and how he was to save the day at The Players as a gesture of thanks to where his career all started. Now, all he needed was for that to come true . . .

He felt sweat sit on his forehead and he loosened his cravat. It was a tough job being The Producer, The Director *and* The Father of the Leading Man. He didn't know where to turn and he really missed Olivier's opinion and advice right now. There hadn't been a word from him or about him since he was whisked back to Paris by his parents and his poor grandmother was going round the bend according to local rumours.

"Ah, Erin, just who I was looking for," said Darryl, rubbing his hands. "All set? I know it's awkward and not exactly the plan we had hoped for, but the show must go on as they say. You will pull this off, won't you?"

Erin fixed the strap of her bag on her shoulder and looked Darryl in the eye.

"I can do this," she said. "It's acting for goodness sake, and Taylor is fine with it too. Don't worry, Darryl. The show will go on and there won't even be as much as a hiccup. There never is. Now, go relax and let the cast and stage management take over. You have done all your hard work. It's up to us to do you proud."

A television news crew pushed their way through the crowd, taking vox-pop comments from the audience, and Erin gave one of them a wave.

"I'm proud of you two," said Darryl and his cheeks turned a light shade of pink as he spoke. It wasn't easy for him to talk about relationships or matters from the heart. "You both have handled this entire fiasco with such dignity and pride. That means a lot, you know.

Keeps things nice and, well, friendly, I suppose. You have been part of our family for a long time, Erin. That won't just change overnight."

Erin patted his arm. "Thanks, Darryl. Me and Taylor will be fine, you know that. We were friends before any of this and hopefully we can always keep that going. Hollywood was just too big and too powerful for us to survive, I suppose, but we know that now. Me? I'll stick to life in Little Hollywood and tonight I promise to be the star of the show."

She made her way towards the side entrance that led backstage and Darryl drew a long deep breath as he watched her stop and greet her TV colleagues en route. She was a good kid, he thought. No matter what happened, he would always like Erin O'Brien, even if his wife thought otherwise.

Erin spotted Aimee chatting to some Taylor Smith fans at the side of the stage.

"Oh my God, he is so hot!" said a teenage girl whose lip-piercing was dangerously distracting. "I swear, if he even looks my way I will faint. I am so going to try and get his autograph."

Aimee wrapped the interview and turned to face Erin with a huge smile. Her baby-blonde hair was tied back in a loose bun and she wore false eyelashes which made her even more doll-like than ever before.

"Erin, honey! You all ready to tread the boards for your big night?"

Aimee's voice was like syrup and her sing-song voice that used to annoy Erin so much was now quite tolerable since she got to know the younger girl properly.

"I am. Well, I think I am," said Erin. "Oh God, Aimee, I won't lie to you. This is going to be so, so hard. When I think of the way it should have been, with Olivier, you know? And then how things have changed so much with Taylor and me. It's awkward to say the least."

"You'll be fine," said Aimee, taking Erin's hand. "You'll be fine. Still no word on Olivier at all?"

Erin shook her head. "Nothing."

"Maybe it just wasn't meant to be," said Aimee. "Maybe tonight when you and Taylor sing together, those old feelings you had between you will come fluttering back and things will spark off again. Fate has a funny old way of handling things, you know."

"Aimee, love . . . Taylor and I are never going to be back together. I know that's not what you or my mother or my grandmother or anyone else who cares for me wants to know. Unfortunately, my heart belongs to someone who is so far away from me right now and that is something that I will have to deal with within myself. It sucks, you know? It really, really sucks."

"Have you tried to contact him lately? I mean, really tried?"

Erin nodded and fought back a gulf of emotions that had been lodged in her throat for the entire afternoon. The very thought of getting up on stage and singing what was ironically a song she first sang with Taylor with anyone but Olivier was enough to make her cry a river.

"I've tried everything," she said. "Bernadette has gone over to see him – she has been so frustrated at the lack of contact from her own son. I called his landline to ask for him and his mother spoke in French and hung up. What is it with me and mothers? Am I really that bad?"

She laughed but Aimee looked at her with a serious expression.

"It's not your problem, it's theirs," she whispered. "Men like Olivier and Taylor Smith are pretty hot stuff. Their mothers adore and idolise them to a point where they don't think any girl is good enough for their blue-eyed, or in Olivier's case, brown-eyed boy. What they don't realise is that with you they have found the most talented, beautiful and adorable girl who people like me only wish they could be some day. Olivier saw that in you too, Erin, and if he really wants you like you want him, he will find you. And no pushy, protective mother will stop him."

Erin looked around the hall and saw Bernadette, clutching a programme in her hand, take a seat in the hall. So Bernadette was back? How nice of her to come along when Olivier was no longer involved. His name was still listed in the programme as both choreographer and in the role of Christian in the scene from Moulin Rouge, though, but Erin couldn't even bring herself to look at his name in print, nor could she look at the photo of him that sat alongside it as it brought back too many memories of that wonderful day they spent together after the photo shoot.

She knew she should be backstage already and if any of the other cast members had been spotted out front so near to curtain up, she would have been first to tell them off but the thought of going into the changing rooms and pretending she was as enthusiastic as the rest of them was almost too much to bear. Plus, her scene didn't feature until near the end anyhow so she had plenty of time to get changed and into make-up.

"I suppose I should go and make an effort," she said to Aimee. "Thanks for all your support over the past few weeks. You did such a great job covering for me the week of Olivier's accident and I will never forget it. You're destined for big, big things Aimee. Very big things."

The young girl's eyes glowed as Erin left her and opened the shaky little door that led into the wings.

"It's show time," she told herself. "Come on, Erin. It's show time!"

Taylor sat back stage holding his mobile phone in both hands, staring at the screen in a blanked-out daze. He hadn't changed yet either and was glad to have found a quiet corner where he could switch off from the growing bunch of "Taylorettes" who now followed him around every inch of The Community Centre, staring at him with adoring adolescent eyes. He really didn't want to be here right now. He didn't want to sing with Erin. He didn't deserve to. He had let her down and he felt sick every time he thought of how he had behaved in Hollywood and how he had allowed himself to get caught up with all the hype and girls who just wanted to use him as a stepping-stone to the silver screen. He had grown up a lot since he had returned home and next time, if there was ever to be a next time, he would play things a lot differently.

"Funny old world, isn't it?" said Erin and she sat down beside him. They were huddled in a dark corner, just behind the costume cupboard and totally out of sight. "I know you so well that when no one else could find you, this is the first place I looked. The show is about to start."

Taylor nodded and smiled at her, then turned his gaze back to his phone screen.

"You don't want to do this, do you?"

"Not really, But the show must go on, Taylor. Plus, your dad would have a coronary and I simply couldn't live with that on my conscience."

"Who'd have thought it, eh? That neither of us want to sing the song that once meant so much to us? A few months back we would have told them they were mad."

He sniggered a little, but it was a regretful laugh tinged with sadness. A stream of light touched his forehead and Erin could have gasped at how truly beautiful he really was.

"You were always too good for this stage, Taylor. You knew it, I knew it and your parents knew it. Go spread your wings and follow your dreams like you always wanted to. You don't need to feel guilty about us any more."

"But I do, Erin. I messed everything up by believing my own press. It's a hard lesson to learn, believe me."

Erin rested her head on his shoulder and breathed in his familiar smell. Taylor Smith would always be special to her, no matter what happened in her life.

"So you fucked up," she said and just as she thought, he laughed.

"You really don't suit saying that word. You never did."

"Yeah, well, sometimes good girls say bad things,"

she laughed back at him. "Come on, Mr Hollywood. Stop staring at the phone and come and get ready. Whoever you are waiting for will call you as soon as you put the phone away, believe me. We can do this, Taylor. You know we can."

"Of course we can, Erin," said Taylor and he kissed her forehead. "Let's go and show Little Hollywood what we are made of. Oh, and please, please rescue me from that lust-filled gaggle of teenage girls. Please!"

Erin extended a hand to help Taylor from his hiding place and shook her head with a smile.

"Oh no, no, no," she said. "Do you think you're gonna be the next Johnny Depp without bunches of adoring fans chasing you everywhere you go? I have housewives following me around Tesco every time I go in for milk. Get used to it, kiddo. Now come on and face the music."

Erin squeezed into the communal changing area where her mother, Krystal, Sorcha Daly and the teenage chorus were battling for space and using every last second before they were called on stage to put those all-important last-minute touches to their overdone faces.

"At last!" said Geri O'Brien. "We were really worried. We thought you had bailed on us. We really did."

"Maybe you should just forget about it," whinged Krystal. Her face was painted a sickly shade of green yet she suited it perfectly. It made her hooked nose look even bigger.

"Maybe I should what, Krystal? Forget what? Singing with Taylor?"

"Well, it obviously pains you very much to do so," she said. "I remember a time when you would have walked over hot coals to be with my son. Then, the first whiff of romance with a handsome stranger and you forget he ever existed."

"Don't you dare speak to my daughter like that!" said Geri. "This is between Erin and Taylor and you have no idea what you are talking about!"

"My Taylor did nothing wrong!" yelled Krystal, her troll-like face scrunched up in a bitter twist. "All he did was follow his dream to Hollywood but you couldn't even wait for him, could you! While he was slogging it over there, you were throwing yourself at Olivier Laurent like a bitch in heat!"

"Krystal! That is enough!"

"Oh wind your neck in, Geri! She's a little trollop just like you were! Don't think you can sit there now with your 'butter wouldn't melt' expression and your silly costume with that silly look of defence on your face! I know you have always thought you were the next big thing just because you were on *Top of the fucking Pops*! The apple hasn't fallen far from the tree, has it? At least I know my son wasn't messing around! At least I know I raised my son to have respect for his partner, even if she isn't worth the dirt on the sole of his shoe! My son is not a cheat!"

The changing room fell silent and the "Taylorettes" in the corner were watching everything with their mouths wide open. Geri was crying now and Agnes stood up, make-up brush in hand, and walked slowly over to where Krystal was, her green face all smudged with bad temper.

She raised the huge brush, which was covered in white powder, above her head and as if she did so in slow motion, tiny particles of sparkly powder filled the room and Agnes shoved the brush into Krystal's face. The Taylorettes cheered.

"Oh, and for the record," said Sorcha Daly, taking to centre stage in the middle of the dressing room, "I'd watch what you say about your son's respect for his partner if I were you. You asked me to get you some gossip, Krystal. You asked me to find out something that might ruin Taylor and Erin. Well, you didn't need to because Taylor was too busy ruining it all by himself by whoring about with a group of Beach Barbie dolls with silly Disney names! I really do wish things had worked out for Erin with Olivier and I'm glad my own teenage crush on your son has come to an end at last. He's just a man, Krystal. Taylor makes mistakes just like any other man. He isn't as perfect as you make him out to be and, in case you have forgotten, you have another son sitting out in that audience who is funny and smart and adorable too. It's about time you noticed John for once!"

Erin was taken aback. Sorcha had just defended her? And John was in the audience? He had actually managed to drag himself away from the bar and come to see a show? Miracles really did happen!

"John? Is here? Tonight?" she said.

"Yes," said Sorcha. "He is here to see . . . he's here to see me."

Erin was delighted and she couldn't hide it at all. The look on Krystal's face – mortification, guilt, humiliation – was an image she had longed to see for a very long time and it took a wallflower, well, an ex-wallflower, like

Sorcha Daly to bring it on. She could have hugged the girl. In fact, she did.

"What's that for?" asked Sorcha, a wry smile on her face.

"For – well, for being you, Sorcha. I hope you and John are very happy together. You both deserve it very much. Now, come on everyone. It's time to take up your positions in the wings. Let's keep the rest of the evening's drama for our paying punters."

"Not so fast," said a voice at the door. "Erin, I have something for you."

Erin looked towards the door where Eugene Daly stood. He presented her with a huge bouquet of flowers and Erin was truly taken aback.

"Why, thank you, Eugene! I – I'm thrilled. What on earth have I done to deserve these? You're too kind!"

She felt tears prick her eyes. Eugene was a gentle soul and, after that night at the hospital when she discovered Olivier was gone, she had spilled her guts out to him and he had listened to her every word. He knew how hard it was going to be for her tonight and his generosity touched her deeply.

"Erin . . . the flowers are not from me. I'm sorry to disappoint you but I couldn't afford a bunch of daisies on my measly salary . . . but why don't you read the card and see what it says?"

"What's the hold-up, everyone?" asked Darryl Smith in a gruff, flustered tone. "The audience is waiting! Come on, get a move on. This is not up to standard. Not at all."

"Oh give over, Darryl," said Krystal from beneath her newly applied green face. "I may be a bitch, but I'm a nosey one at that. I want to know who got Miss Prim here the flowers as much as the next Wicked Witch from the West would."

"Open it, darling," said Geri and she clasped her hands together.

Erin opened the tiny white envelope as all eyes in the room waited with bated breath.

"Yes," she said and her heart did a dance in her chest. "Yes, yes, yes! Thank you, God, thank you!"

"Tell us," said Agnes. "Is it him?"

"Yes, tell us for fuck sake," said Krystal. "Jesus, you O'Briens do like to drag the arse out of a good drama!"

"They're from Olivier," said Erin, biting her lip as tears fell down her face. "He's feeling much, much better. Oh, and he says hi to you all too and, well, break a leg of course."

"Great! Excellent! Bravo! *Voila*!" said Darryl. "Now let's go and do just that! Break a leg before I break a . . . oh just come on! Act One, Scene One! Let's go!"

It was the last scene of the show and Taylor and Erin stood in the wings at opposite sides of the stage. She could see he was nervous, she knew it by the way he stood, the way he paced backstage, holding his head in his hands. Then he saw her and he gave her a huge smile and a thumbs-up sign. She hadn't pressed Sorcha for any further information on what she knew of Taylor's liaisons in Hollywood, nor would she ever want to. She knew there would always be part of her that held a flame for Taylor Smith, but it was more in a proud, older sister kind of way. She couldn't hate him, even if he did sleep with that skinny bitch Belle in Hollywood. She truly wished him well.

The opening bars of the song from *Moulin Rouge* played and the lights went down on the stage so that a red, smoky atmosphere was created for Taylor's entrance. The piano was beautiful and Erin closed her eyes as Taylor began to sing, but all she could hear was Olivier's voice in her head. The music built and built to a crescendo and Taylor sang it to perfection as the crowd applauded, equally moved by his stunning vocals.

Erin entered stage left and joined him and the audience rose to their feet, then sat back down again as they harmonised to perfection. The mood was electric and when the string instrumental boomed out over the auditorium, Taylor leaned towards Erin and kissed her lightly.

"He's here, Erin," he whispered and Erin drew a light, sharp intake of breath. "He's here for you."

She couldn't look. She couldn't think and when the music came to a breathtaking climax and the audience stood once more, she glanced down into the audience and she saw his beautiful face staring up at her with immense pride.

Olivier was back. He had come back for her.

"Jesus Christ, Erin, that was just amazing!"

Kizzy met Erin at the stage door, aka the entrance to The Playgroup Area and enveloped her in a bear-hug.

"He's here, Kizzy. Olivier is here! He sent me flowers and I saw him in the audience. I have to go and see him."

"Go-to-fuck-no-way!" said Kizzy. "You do know I have never yet laid eyes on him? Come on, get out and snog the face off him. I won't stand in the way of true love, even if I am shaking like a leaf after hearing you sing like that. It was just mind-blowing."

They made their way out into the throngs of well-wishers and Erin scanned the crowds to try and find him but she couldn't see him anywhere. Taylor was surrounded by autograph hunters and the Taylorettes were helping him try and make some sense of it all as they filed the fans into orderly queues.

"Erin!" called Taylor and he waved her over to him. "Erin, I need to talk to you, quickly."

Erin felt panic rise inside her as she searched and searched for Olivier but he definitely wasn't there. She questioned her vision from earlier. It was him, it had to be him and even Taylor had seen him. But why had he left again? Why hadn't he stayed to see her after the show?

"What's wrong, Taylor?"

Taylor left the pushing and shoving and took Erin's hand. He squeezed it gently and kissed her on the cheek.

"I just wanted to tell you how wonderful you were tonight. How wonderful you have always been to me. I know this is the end for us, Erin, and I want to wish you all the happiness in the world with Olivier. He is a very lucky man."

"Thank you, Taylor. Unfortunately he doesn't seem to have hung around so I'm not sure what way I stand, but that means a lot to have your blessing."

Taylor shrugged. "I'll be out of your hair again in a few weeks' time. You know the way I was watching my phone earlier? I was waiting to hear from my new agent in LA. He has this amazing audition for me lined up next week so I'm Hollywood bound again, baby. This time, I won't behave like a Paddy on holiday. I learned my lesson the hard way. Good luck, Erin."

"That's fantastic news, Taylor. I want you to always, always follow your dreams. It's what we all need to do from time to time," she whispered. "Now, get back to your fans and I'll go and follow my own dream, before it's too late."

Erin walked outside into the night sky and tried to remember where she had parked her car. She stood at the top of the steps of The Community Centre and searched for her car keys, hoping that when she'd click the button, she'd see the flash of the car lights as a giveaway from the height where she stood. But as usual she had to rummage beneath make-up, bills and even an old script from work to try and find them. She found her phone and pressed it to shine a light into the darkness of her handbag.

"Lost something?" said a voice from a short distance away and she looked towards the sound to see Olivier at the side of the road on a motorbike in exactly the same place where she had seen him on the day of the auditions. "Or perhaps you have found the kitchen sink?"

"Are you a glutton for punishment?" she called to him as she made her way down the steps. "I thought you and bikes would be over by now? I would ask you for a ride, but you're a safety kind of guy, right?"

"I am when it comes to you," said Olivier and his accent filled her heart with joy. "But beneath this surface I'm a thrill-seeker who wants you more than ever right now. There are a lot of things you don't know about me . . . yet."

"I look forward to getting to know all about you. Oh, I've missed you, Olivier. I tried to contact you in every way but I couldn't find you. It's been horrible not knowing where you were or how you've been."

As much as she knew she loved him, she couldn't help but feel tiny pops of anger burst beneath her skin.

"I know, baby. I have been in long, quiet recovery and my parents have been a nightmare. I had this date in my head and I thought that when Taylor came home I should give you a chance with him but nothing would have allowed me to miss you tonight. You sang like an angel. You are my angel. I do love you, Erin. I love you very much."

He put his hand on her waist, pulled her close to him and kissed her lips with such a hunger that any anger she felt was dispersed and replaced with raw, uncontrollable passion.

"I love you too," she said when they finally parted. "I love you too. But I have a question for you. A very serious question . . ." She slid her leg around the back of his bike, tucked her body in behind his, and wrapped her arms around his waist, leaning her head on his back. "Are you ready for life in Little Hollywood? It can be fairly trying sometimes."

"I'm ready," he said and he leaned across to the side of the road where he lifted a shiny black helmet and he handed it to her. "But let's play it safe for now, and leave the thrill-seeking till later in the night."

"Well, let's go then," she said to him, pulling the helmet over her head. "I've had enough drama for one night. Take me somewhere far away, Olivier."

"I was thinking of taking you home," he said as he revved the engine of the motorbike. "I think we have unfinished business in your living room, don't we?"

Erin thought of her house in River View and the urge to go there with Olivier and feel warm and cosy and at ease filled her heart with happiness that she had never felt before.

"I think we do," she said and snuggled in tight to him, closing her eyes as the bike took off. "That sounds like the ideal place to go. Take me home, Olivier. Take me home."

THE END

If you enjoyed *Since You've Been Gone*
by Emma Heatherington why not try
Playing the Field also published by Poolbeg?
Here's a sneak preview of Chapter One.

Emma
Heatherington

Playing
the
Field

POOLBEG

PROLOGUE

Cara's rusting Fiat Uno grumbled along the country road, its wipers scraping the windscreen as the English summer rain finally subsided.

"Crap!" she said aloud. Was it right then left, or left then right? She couldn't remember.

She pulled the car in alongside a neatly trimmed hedgerow, turned off the engine and scrabbled in the depths of her handbag for the typed list of directions to Wimbledon that the recruitment agency had given her a few days before. Whoever her new boss was, she would not be impressed if her new "domestic assistant" was late.

List in hand, Cara turned the key in the ignition and the car spat back. Not a kick.

"Oh no, please don't do this to me now," she said, patting the dashboard and looking around her for help. She wanted this job. She needed this job if her career break was to work out as she had planned. Her glasses had steamed up and she took them off, gave them a quick wipe with her sleeve and said a silent prayer that she wouldn't be late.

She turned the key again and, as if the car had just been giving her a warning not to doubt its capabilities, it shot forward. Cara clung to the steering wheel, her eyes pinned to the road ahead. Then the car slowed down to its usual struggling pace.

Indicating right she took off again, chugging along the road and surveying her surroundings for another few miles, until she saw a huge set of gates that matched the recruitment agent's written description. Then she saw chimney-pots towering over trees far in the distance and she knew this had to be her new workplace. Yes, there was the name: Summer Manor. She slowed down further, glanced in her rear-view mirror and took a right turn through the gates.

"Oh holy shit!" she said as she made her way through sprawling lawns up a winding drive which led her to the front of the house, a modern home based on an old design. Its sandstone walls were a background for tall Georgian windows and a huge red door which was framed with ivy. Who lives in a house like this, she wondered, and she fought an involuntary urge to let her mouth drop open.

She wound down the window when she saw an older man who was watching her approach with a friendly smile.

"Ah, hello there," he said, leaning on a spade next to a mass of greenery. A black Labrador circled his feet. "You must be the new start."

The man's skin was a weather-beaten brown and his face was framed at either side with soft white curls that looked like candyfloss. If everyone at this "Summer Manor" was as friendly, Cara reckoned she would feel right at home. He looked so cute in an old-man sort of way that she could have put him in her pocket.

"I'm Cara," she said, extending her arm out through the car window. "Cara McCarthy."

"Cara McCarthy. Well, that's a pretty Irish name," said the man. "I'm Sam Potts, and this old scamp is Buster. He belongs to the man of the house but sometimes he thinks that's me."

"Lovely to meet you, Sam," said Cara. "And you too, Buster." The dog wagged his tail and panted up at her and Cara reached out to pat his shiny black head.

"He likes you," said Sam. "That's you off to a great start. Now, why don't you park up and I'll show you around?"

Cara surveyed the magnificent landscape once more and realised that whoever lived in this glorious home would hardly appreciate her hunk of junk standing out like a sore thumb.

"No doubt my trusty little motor will blot the landscape around here but it's the best I can do at the moment. I'll just park between these two beauties, then?"

"No, no, better not park there!" called Sam but Cara was already nosing her way between a nifty MG and a BMW jeep.

She locked the Uno into reverse and tried to straighten up the tiny lump of green metal, feeling dwarfed among such grandeur and wealth.

"Is that okay?" she panted, wishing for power steering, which evidently hadn't been invented in the land of Uno pre-1997.

"Sort of," said Sam, his blue eyes wrinkling into a smile. "Your new boss likes to have plenty of room to manoeuvre in and out of here when it suits her. Best to stay well out of her way in future and park down the side of the house. But I don't think she'll dock your wages for parking in the wrong place on your first day."

Cara stepped out of the car and squinted in the morning sunshine. "Honestly, I'm normally an excellent driver but I guess I'm just a bit, well . . ."

"Nervous?" asked Sam.

"Yeah. Nervous." Cara shoved her hands in her pockets and then took them straight back out again, hearing her mother's "tomboy" remarks echo in her head.

"Don't be nervous," said Sam and he signalled at her to follow him towards the sprawling home. "There are a lot more rules to remember than parking your car in the correct position around here, but you'll soon get the hang of them, don't worry."

Cara closed the car door gently and followed Sam and Buster.

"I'm afraid I'm not very good at playing by the rules, Sam," she said as they made their way to the entrance of the magnificent home.

"Well, then that makes two of us," said Sam, opening the huge ornate red door. "Now, let's go inside and I'll introduce you to Sophia and Dylan."

"Sophia and Dylan?" said Cara. The names sounded somewhat familiar.

"They live here. Well, this is Dylan's home but his girlfriend Sophia moved in only a few weeks ago and already she's making her mark by making lots of changes around here. You, my dear, are one of them."

Cara followed Sam in through the front doors and into a wide, marble hallway which was the size of a small ballroom. Sophia and Dylan. Sophia and Dylan. She rhymed off the couple's names in her head. The house had a faint smell of summer fruits to it. Sophia and Dylan. Their names went together like tea and toast. They sounded all too familiar and then, like a slap on the face, the penny finally dropped.

She stopped in her tracks and stared at the gigantic framed photo at the top of the stairwell and gulped in realisation. A striking black-haired girl lay with her head on the lap of her Adonis boyfriend and her eyes glared confidently in Cara's direction. Her brand-new boss was none other than Sophia Brannigan, the all-new high-maintenance, highly strung girlfriend of Premiership footballer and babelicious hunk in a pair of trunks, Dylan Summers.

"Yes, that's our Sophia," said Sam and he threw his eyes up towards the portrait, laughing at Cara's reaction. "She wasn't here five minutes till she had that portrait commissioned."

Cara let out a nervous giggle and pushed her glasses back on her face. Dylan Summers and Sophia Brannigan. She was going to work for Dylan Summers and Sophia Brannigan!

Oh holy, holy, holy shit.

1

Don't You Step in my Red Suede Shoes

"*Cara! Cara!*" The sound of Sophia's screeching tone pierced Cara's ears from the intercom that linked one room to the other at Summer Manor.

"Yes, Sophia?" Cara wriggled her way out from a pile of laundry in the utility room, wondering what the hell the demanding cow wanted now.

"Just an observation," called Sophia who was pinning her long, raven hair into a trendy twist in her dressing room, "that you have been here for weeks now and I am absolutely no further on in my career as a celebrity." She finished the look off with a pale pink neck-scarf and admired her own beauty, almost kissing the mirror. "To say I'm disappointed is an understatement." When Sophia was in a mood like this, her Liverpool accent became a little more posh.

Cara wondered how Sophia's celebrity career, or lack of it, could possibly be her fault, but then remembered that when Sophia went into a "poor me" rant, the world and his wife were to blame. Or the nearest person to hand: usually Cara. Fly in her chardonnay? Blame Cara. Lost lipstick? Cara again. War in Iraq? Cara, how could you be so cruel?

"I have to say I don't really understand what that has to do with me," said Cara as she folded the laundry, rolling her eyes as the intercom light flashed before her. "As you keep reminding me, I'm just your cleaner."

She could sense Sophia's frustration a mile off. It was one of those days when her boss would argue a black crow was white and no one would convince her otherwise.

"Well, you wouldn't understand," said Sophia. "You see, I am using your arrival as a yardstick of my success and if I do not make some progress soon, it can only mean one thing."

"Which would be?"

"That you are simply not a good omen."

Cara nodded to herself. She was not a good omen. She could live with that. She'd been referred to as frumpy, clueless, hopeless, useless and any other word with "less" at the end of it as a daily punishment-beating for just, well, breathing since she took on her job at Summer Manor. Being a bad omen was merely a minor flaw.

"I had hoped that by hiring you to keep this house on its feet I would have more time for social networking and extending my contacts, but to date there has been no progress on my commercial success at all. Nowt. Nada. Nothing."

The intercom flashed off and within minutes Cara heard Sophia's stilettos march towards her. Then she appeared at the door, all dressed up to go out.

"I have some shopping to do for tonight," Sophia ranted. "So, don't expect me back too soon and if I were you I would start praying that some sort of miracle occurs in the near future that gains me the profile and publicity I deserve. Oh, and by the way, if my package from Belle's Boutique arrives, leave it upstairs outside my dressing-room. Goodbye."

Cara felt like the weight of a rhino had been lifted from her back when she heard Sophia's car vroom away from the house. "Don't expect me back." Those were her favourite words of all time from Sophia and they were normally only said once a week, whereas "do not go into my dressing room" had been drummed into her repeatedly since day one.

She looked at the clock. It was eleven o'clock. Sophia's shopping trips were usually all-day events so she would give herself an hour before she made her way up the stairs to see if she could get a peep at what all the fuss was about in the dressing room. Sophia always locked it when she went out, of course, but by now Cara knew where she kept the key.

Yes, curiosity about what lay at the other side of that door had haunted her during her brief employment as general dogsbody to Sophia Brannigan and now she was about to give in to temptation. Like a forbidden fruit hidden on the second floor of the luxurious residence, the room was calling to her, daring her to open its heavy, gilded doors, assuring her that no one was around to find out she had broken the rules in her brand-new job.

Come lunchtime, Cara tightened her pony-tail and glanced outside to make doubly sure the coast was clear, then took a deep breath and climbed the winding staircase. She retrieved the key from a drawer in the master bedroom and made her way to the dressing room. Her heart pounded and adrenaline pumped through her body as she turned the huge knob and pushed the doors open.

"Wow!"

She gave a ballerina twirl across the fluffy, cream-coloured shag-pile carpet, into the centre of a room which was even more lavish than she could have imagined.

It was huge. At least five times the size of the family sitting room she had been reared in back in Donegal and it was shelved from ceiling to floor with not an empty space in sight. The entire room smelt like new leather, with railings of clothes on hangers labelled by designer and boxes and boxes and boxes of shoes. The ceiling had so many lights that the room was almost floodlit, and a deep cream podium made a magnificent centrepiece in front of a floor-to-ceiling mirror.

Cara looked out through the window onto the extensive lawns of the house. She took a deep breath, longing to pinch herself back to reality but allowing herself just one more moment of fantasy where all of this was hers . . . A haven of luxury that was so out of her reach it was almost impossible to believe she was standing inside it right now. And she was getting paid for it. Not paid to stand around of course, but when the cat was away and all that . . .

She imagined the man of her dreams waving to her as he finished a game on the tennis court at the far end of the manicured walkway. She imagined her top-of-the-range sports car – no, actually, a Space Wagon – sitting on the golden stones of the gravel driveway, with baby seats for her adorable twin baby boys who were the spitting image of their father. Yes, in this dream she drove a top-of-the-range Space Wagon with tinted windows and a key code that would open the huge electronic gates of the big house especially for her.

She pictured herself chilling out in the heated, kidney-shaped swimming pool, after a hard day's shopping, or lounging in the extensive drawing room that was never used. She dreamed of choosing outfits for charity dinners and awards ceremonies, where she stood right now in the long rectangular dressing room.

For a few precious hours every day, Cara McCarthy truly loved her job. As she scrubbed and cleaned her way around its nooks and crannies with no one to disturb her, she would allow her imagination to run wild and pretend that she was the true lady of Summer Manor. Tucked away in the country-style suburb of Wimbledon Village, where rolling hills and country hideouts hid the fact that the bright lights of London were only a stone's throw away, its private grounds were a nest of tranquillity and the perfect space for a dreamer like Cara who could easily lose herself in a world of peace and luxury.

She allowed herself to run her hands along the Prada section, she tried on a Galliano scarf and put it back exactly where she found it. Then she felt brave enough to go a little bit further by trying on a pair of Sophia's high-heeled shoes which luckily were just her size.

"Where did you get those shoes?" she asked her reflection, then stumbled and fell into a clumsy bundle before pulling herself together again.

She stared in awe at how dainty her feet looked in the full-length mirror and how lean her calves when she didn't try to walk, or move or breathe. The shoes were blood-red pure silk, with a fine, real-platinum slinky heel and a pretty red bow which sat on the edge of dainty peep toes.

"I think I've discovered fashion," she laughed, realising she was actually enjoying herself more than she had in a long time. "Have I really been missing out on so, so much?"

Cara didn't normally talk to herself, but then again, she didn't normally try on shoes either unless she really had to. Unlike most women, Cara McCarthy had always viewed clothes as one of life's necessities rather than an adrenaline-inducing passion. In fact, if push came to the shove and her life was in danger, she would actually confess to preferring hiking boots to high heels.

But these shoes were different. These shoes had beckoned to her from beneath their bed of soft, cream tissue paper. She'd even taken a quick peek at the label which was still stuck on the box and had almost choked at the price tag. To own only one of them she'd have to live on Super Noodles for at least a month and hobble to work because she wouldn't be able to afford petrol for her clapped-out motor car, let alone afford the match of the shoe.

"Perfect, just perfect," she whispered, wishing she could keep the glorious beings in her possession forever and take them home to the poky apartment she shared with her friend Natalie. She would never, ever wear them outside of course, but would just stare at their beauty on a daily basis as they lay in their shiny box, and when she'd feel like it, maybe once a month or so, she would put them on and dance around in the safety of her own apartment.

Hell, she wouldn't even show them to Natalie and she always made sure she showed every item of clothing to

Natalie. As her best friend and fellow "let's spread our wings and see the big smoke" buddy, Natalie was the one who had eventually told Cara that navy and black didn't go and that horizontal stripes made you look like a fat zebra, unless you had a frame like Kate Moss.

Feeling foolish, but brave, Cara maintained her balance and opened the heavy doors that led back onto the landing of Summer Manor. She made her way towards the stairs where the sassy drumbeat of a Girls Aloud song called to her from the kitchen.

Pretending she was as tanned and gorgeous as Cheryl Cole, Cara shimmied down each step of the spiral staircase in Sophia's stilettos to the beat of the music and made her way in the direction of the succulent aroma of her roasting chicken which filled her senses and added to her good mood.

She made her way carefully across the reflective white tiles of the hallway, through the double doors that led to the dining room and through a huge open-plan area that brought her into the kitchen, allowing her mind to drift into a world of glamour, perks and parties where everybody knew your name and everybody wanted to be your best friend.

Into a world where the biggest daily dilemma was which shop to visit on which day of the week, where your diary was bursting at the seams with parties and where the man of your dreams played a poncy ball game for a living in return for a salary that would feed a small nation for the rest of their days. Into a world where jotting down a few remarks on other celebrities' fashion sense made you a "columnist" in a weekly magazine. She could be a "columnist." Not even a fecking problem.

But this wasn't Cara's world at all. This was Sophia's world. This was a WAG's world. But, right now, for a few stolen moments on a Thursday afternoon in August, Cara "Cleaner to the Stars" McCarthy was living it – and she was loving every flippin' minute of it.

Even her rubber gloves and checked apron didn't feel out of place when she slipped them on and continued with her chores in the kitchen. She turned the volume up to the max and allowed herself to feel the music as it took over her body. The shoes had become so comfy she would have forgotten she had them on only for her tendency to look down and admire how delightful they made her feet look, approximately once every ten seconds.

With a dramatic *whoosh* she wiped down the draining board, and then let out an "Ooh!" as she dusted the dresser. She felt her heart surge with excitement as the gentle clip-clop of the heels kept to a rhythm on the ceramic floor beneath her.

She lifted a photo from the solid oak dresser in an over-exaggerated sweep of her arm.

"I'll just give you a quick facial," she joked to it as she ran the duster over Sophia's glowing face. Sophia grinned back at her (it was an old photo – Sophia didn't smile any more in real life – she pouted) and she found herself giving the glass on the frame a little more elbow grease than she normally would with just a tiny pang of jealousy added in for good measure.

For Cara knew that the shoes she wore, the shoes that fitted her so well and introduced her to the dizzy heights of haute couture didn't belong to her and they never would.

They belonged to the real lady of the manor – the one

person who could make Cara McCarthy feel like scum on her gorgeous shoes with just one sly comment or degrading cackle; the person who paid her a measly cleaning salary that was less than her own humungous weekly clothing allowance; the girl whose claws were so deep into her footballer boyfriend's existence that Cara could almost smell the gloss of the magazines she planned to sell her wedding to, if he ever proposed.

"Shallow cow," she said, vowing she would stop muttering as soon as she took off the shoes, which she would do in a few minutes of course, and she gave Sophia's rare grin another extra-hard polish. "Lucky, lucky, shallow cow."

The sudden crunch of tyres on the gravel from outside the house made Cara's heart skip a beat as she gave an extra fast dance spin on the kitchen floor. Who the hell was that at this time of day? Sophia didn't normally attract visitors. She didn't appear to have many friends.

"Jesus – shit," she stammered, glancing around and trying to decide on which direction to run. Sophia couldn't be back . . . could she? Cara clip-clopped over to the window and peeped out to see her worst fears come true. Sophia was back early.

Her pinched face framed by a long ebony mane and clad in oversized sunglasses was all Cara could see as she drove down the side of the house, yapping nineteen to a dozen into a tiny phone. Her personal number plate was emblazoned across the front of the car, just in case anyone would happen to forget just who she was.

She was early and Sophia was never early. Not from a shopping trip.

And she was coming in through the back door. And the back door led through a cloakroom that led into a hallway that led to the kitchen, where Cara stood in Sophia's red shoes that still had the price tag on them. A price tag that was the length of Cara's mobile phone number. Shit, shit shit!

Cara glanced down at her feet and dropped the duster into her apron pocket, then made a mad dash for the main hallway and towards the stairs, praying that Sophia's telephone conversation might hold her back and give her a few minutes' grace.

"Shit – bitch," she said, not knowing which word to use first. "Shit, shit, shit, shit, shit," as she took the stairs, two at a time. Sophia would sack her on the spot if she found out that she had as much as sniffed her brand-new shoes. Hell, she only let Cara use the cooker because she couldn't be arsed to use it herself and had a terrible fear of everything domesticated and electrical unless it could straighten her hair.

Cara opened a window at the top of the stairs and listened briefly to Sophia's conversation from below as she to-ed and fro-ed from the house to the car in a bad temper.

"But, honey, you promised!" she heard Sophia shriek into her cellphone as her heels clicked across the patio. Sophia didn't call her phone a "mobile". No way. That was too UK. "I have everything organised and we simply *have* to work on your profile, whether you like it or not."

Cara heard the car door open and then slam. That would be to fetch her shopping. A mountain of shopping. Cara hoped it would take her ages to unload it without her help, which Sophia was sure to scream for any second now.

"With the Beckhams gone Stateside everyone wants to park their pert little bottoms on their vacant thrones," said Sophia, "and this party is the ultimate opportunity to show the country that we have arrived." A pause, then an ear-splitting yell: "*Cara! Cara!* Come immediately and help me with all this!"

The intercom let out a shriek on the landing and Cara raced towards Sophia's lavish dressing room, silently complimenting herself on how she had learned to run so easily in such glorious footwear. To hell with cat-walks and premières, these shoes should be promoted as road-runners.

"Shit," she said again as she opened the dressing room doors. Then she reached down to take off the shoes. Her right foot felt naked without its new companion but she had no time to sympathise. She had to be cruel to be kind.

But, as she reached to slip off the left shoe, she lost her balance and bounced off the doorframe, then wobbled back into an upright position. She pushed the doors of the dressing room open further and hobbled quickly towards a chair. Faster than lightning she swooped down to remove the other shoe but suddenly her heart stopped.

It didn't skip a beat this time. It stopped.

For Jimmy Left Choo was now injured. Fatally injured. And Cara thought she was going to die too as the heel broke from its base and fell into her hand.

If you enjoyed this chapter from
Playing the Field by Emma Heatherington
why not order the full book online
@ www.poolbeg.com
and enjoy a 10% discount on all
Poolbeg books
See next page for details.

POOLBEG WISHES TO

THANK YOU

for buying a Poolbeg book.
As a loyal customer we will give you
10% OFF (and free postage*)
on any book bought on our website
www.poolbeg.com

Select the book(s) you wish to buy
and click to checkout

Then click on the 'Add a Coupon' button
(located under 'Checkout') and enter
this coupon code

 USMWR15173

POOLBEG (Not valid with any other offer!) POOLBEG

WHY NOT JOIN OUR MAILING LIST
@ www.poolbeg.com and get some
fantastic offers on Poolbeg books
*See website for details